THE LAND: MONSTERS

DR. ALERON KONG

The Land: Monsters

A work of Tamori Publications

Copyright © 2020 by Aleron Kong

CONTENTS

DEDICATION

This book is dedicated to my fans.
Creating these worlds has been one of the most amazing experiences of my
life. I'd always wanted to be a writer, to make worlds of wonder. I knew it
would feel amazing. What I never expected was that it would connect me
with truly wonderful people around the world.
Thank you for walking this path with me. There is so much more to come!

SUMMARIES OF EARLIER BOOKS

Doing something new this time! I've made a summary of the earlier books, short and sweet!

I don't disrupt the flow for those who don't need a refresher, though. If you'd like to read the summaries, you can visit:

https://www.litrpg.com/book-summaries-for-book-8

Everyone else, I present, *The Land: Monsters*!

CHAPTER 1

DAY 150 – JUREN 1, 0 AOC

*R*ichter cursed. He was in a lair! Not only that, he'd finally found out where the high-level monsters were hiding. The ichorpede skittered toward him faster now, clacking its pincers together in anticipation. It was only fifty yards away. The chaos seed ran to the left and grabbed the only weapon available, a gnawed leg bone. He had no idea what kind of creature had left it behind, but it was as big as a Louisville Slugger. Part of him realized that this bone was only here because the ichorpedes had been able to bring down such a large beast. A bigger part of him told that part to shut the fuck up. It was game time.

As the giant insect closed the distance, Richter began to prepare. *Minor Chitin Carapace* thickened his skin and increased his natural armor by +4. *Weak Haste* boosted his speed and *Weak Mirror Image* made two copies of him. He summoned a saproling and spider, evolving them both with Chaos magic into stronger versions. With the ichorpede only ten yards away, he dismissed his night vision, then cast *Grease* and *Weak Flame* in quick succession. The entire circle of brown-gravy sludge lit up, enveloping the giant insect in fire.

It reared back with a hiss of rage, its head towering five feet above him. Richter was raising his makeshift bone club to strike when he

I

heard a voice that made his mouth drop open in shock. Floating out of the darkness came a small winged creature only a single foot in height. His body was ash grey and black bat wings flapped behind him. The expression on his face was both bored and annoyed. When Xuetrix spoke again, his tone was a perfect match.

"I said, stop playing with those bugs, human. You owe me a Favor, and I'm here to collect."

The moment of distraction cost Richter dearly. The ichorpede, though damaged by the flames, dove through them. It shot toward the chaos seed's figure, its powerful pincers snapping shut on his unarmored body. To its surprise, the figure it had attacked shattered into countless shards of light a moment before disappearing. It was not Richter, merely one of his mirror images. Wasting no time, the real Richter spun and slammed his bone club down onto the head of the ichorpede with all of his strength.

The hardened bone slammed into its armored shell and forced its head to the ground. For a single instant Richter cheered in his heart, but then he was reminded why powerful weapons were a necessity when fighting high level monsters. Though the force of his strike forced its head down and away, it caused no actual damage. Before he could take a second swing with his impromptu bone club, the monster of the depths struck again, and this time, its aim was true.

Richter was knocked off his feet. He landed heavily, the rough rock digging into his bare back. The force of the massive insect's charge propelled him along the ground. Skin and blood were left behind in a gooey pink smear. For the second time in as many minutes, Richter was reminded of the horror of battling without armor or arms. The tattered remains of his clothes offered no real protection. This was not a movie where the action star never really got hurt. This was real life, and it was real agony flaring within him as he struggled for just one more minute of breath.

The ichorpede's serrated mandibles sped toward his face. There was not a doubt in Richter's mind that it could rip half his face off if they managed to snap shut. As he fell, his hands shot up and just managed to grab the pincers. The sharp spikes on the inside of the mandibles tore into his hands. Red-hot blood flowed in small rivers onto his face and chest. The scent drove the ichorpede wild, and it surged forward with a high-pitched keening noise.

As bad as the tearing pain in his hands was, this was not the worst agony. The monster's acidic spit flowed faster as it grew lustful and blood-drunk. The scant drops of Richter it had tasted were enough to make its terrible hunger soar. The green-tinted acid from its mouth immediately started eating into Richter's hands. A large drop fell from its mouth onto his chest with a sizzle, and he could smell his own flesh cooking. His muscles dissolved, cell by cell, sinew by sinew.

Richter screamed in agony as the skin and muscle of his chest began to melt and run. His Strength attribute was just enough to keep the insect from stealing his life. The lich's Curse of Eternal Servitude had been weakened when Singh suffered the final death, but it could still damn Richter's soul if he died within the next seven days. The scream of pain issuing from his mouth began to be mingled with rage. After everything he had gone through, he would not let his story end like this!

The ichorpede kept forcing its way forward, trying to bite Richter's head free of his body. Each time it pushed, its mandibles would inch closer before the chaos seed was able to force them back. They continued to skid across the rocky ground, leaving more of the young lord's tissue and blood behind. Richter managed to get his left knee up and brace it against the monster. It kept space between them, but in response, the ichorpede plunged some of its countless legs down into his right side. Five of its spike-like appendages sank into his chest, abdomen and leg.

His health dropped by more than twenty points from its first attack. It dropped by fifteen more as the legs sank in to the first joint of the insect's dagger-like extremities. If he hadn't cast *Minor Chitin Carapace,* increasing the natural armor of his skin from 0 to +4, the damage would have been worse. The high-level monster's poignard legs were even stronger though.

Richter howled.

If he had been wearing his wood sprite armor, he might have

been able to ignore the attack long enough to counterattack. Without it, his body was being savaged, and his spell-thickened skin was scant defense. Less than ten seconds into the battle, and he was already afflicted with a *Bleeding* debuff. As the sharp ends of the ichorpede's legs were still in his body, Richter's debuff had no time limit. The chaos seed's life literally oozed away as he fought the level thirty-one insect, struggling to just survive another minute. More drops of acidic spit fell onto his chest and neck, inflicting more damage and sapping his will to fight.

Though Richter did not know it, most men and women would have already succumbed. The pain of feeling one's own flesh liquify, after all, could easily drive one mad. His own Secondary Attribute Resilience was several times higher than most peoples of The Land. Resilience was a person's ability to withstand the worst of circumstances. The average person had a base value of +1. His own was +3.6, more than three times greater. It was in part due to his various life experiences, but mostly due to the boon he had received for eating the First Fruit of the Quickening. While others would have panicked, Richter's own mind became oddly still now that his life was balanced on a razor's edge.

The first thing he thought about was Xuetrix. Casting about, he saw that the imp had faded back into the darkness of the cavern. Richter cursed in his own mind, but was not surprised. How much could you trust a demon? Next, he turned his attention to his two summoned creatures. The spider and saproling had evolved into a mesmer spider and thorn element respectively. Both of these evolutions were magic-based, meaning they couldn't stand up to too much close combat.

Even if they could, they were on the far side of the fire. That was where they needed to be though. More ichorpedes were spilling into the cavern. Several were coming through a large doorway at the far end of the underground gallery. Others were coming through holes in the stone, crawling on the walls in defiance of gravity. He needed his summoned creatures to delay the others, if even for a few moments.

Those mental calculations took place in an instant. Richter was no stranger to battle at this point. He had lived and died and killed and saved more than he could easily count. He was without any true weapons or armor, but he was not without resources. He had his items: eight rings, a bracelet and his necklace. All of them power talismans. Baring his teeth to keep from screaming, he accessed his Ring of Shadow Shift. Looking up at the monstrous face of the ichorpede, he thought, fuck you!

Your Ring of Shadow Shift cannot transport 2 beings!

"No!" he grunted. "Fuck me!" Richter's mind raced. Whether it was because the massive insect's segmented legs were piercing his body, or just because he was in contact with an enemy, his ring wouldn't work. He strained to keep the ichorpede's pincers from savaging his face. It grew closer with every surge of its body. Even as he fought a losing battle, its acidic spittle fell onto his torso and face. His health literally dribbled away. As he struggled, he was reminded of his first life-and-death struggle in The Land with a wolf in the Forest of Nadria.

During his first days in The Land, he'd taken a quest from the Hearth Mother to kill diseased wolves. He had been attacked and borne to the ground. Only a bracer against the wolf's throat had kept it from biting his face off, just like the ichorpede was trying to do now. He'd killed the wolf, but had died minutes later when the other members of the pack tore him apart. It had been one of the more traumatic and horrible experiences of his life. The fear had nearly crippled his soul, broken his mind. He'd only been a level two noob, nearly helpless.

Despite the corollaries between his position now and then, he was not the same person. He had burned settlements, enacted revenge on those who had dared harm him and used the bones of his Mortal Enemy to adorn the central building of his village. He was not weak. He was not prey. He wasn't even just a predator. He was Richter. He was a monster!

With a strained shout, he pushed against the monstrous centipede's head and gained a scant inch of relief. At the same time, he shuffled through the notifications he had gained during the destruction of the Mausoleum. Some shocked and amazed him, others confused him, but he still minimized them all to the side to be viewed later. They were not what he needed and could not help him in that instant. That was, until he heard the sweetest sound any man or woman could ever hear. A snarling grin appeared on his face and he let the prompt wash over him.

TRING! TRING! TRING! TRING! TRING!
*You have reached level **40, 41, 42, 43,** and **44**! Through hard work you have moved forward along your path. You are awarded the following points to distribute:*

	Per Level	Total
Stat Points	As a Chaos Seed, you gain **6 Stat Points** to distribute to characteristics instead of the usual 4	30
Talent Points	As a Chaos Seed, you receive **15 Talent Points** instead of the usual 10. You receive an additional **15 Talent Points** from your Profession and Specialty for having a 100% affinity in Enchanting	190
Chaos Points	You receive **8 Chaos Points** due to your Blessing by the Lords of Chaos	41
Skill % Points	**+25%** to the skill of your choice	+125%

There was a new line at the bottom of his leveling sheet that he didn't understand.

Know This! You have reached a Threshold! The points from reaching level 45 will be locked until an Evolution branch is determined.

Further leveling blocked until an Evolution branch is determined.

Richter had no idea what that meant, but that didn't matter to him in the slightest. He had Character Points to burn. A deep and malignant chuckle rumbled in the depths of his chest while he poured points into Strength.

Six points arrested the forward movement of the ichorpede. Ten let him push it back. Pain flared in his body as his muscles and their attachments to his bones and flesh were enlarged and augmented.

Suffering had never been so sweet, and the insanity in his laughter grew stronger. Fifteen let him force its pincers wider and he was able to wrestle himself into a sitting position. Agony cut through his body as it underwent changes to accommodate his increased Attribute.

His musculature bulged and his bones strained. His dark skin stretched and then split. The magic of his augmentation healed his skin to accommodate, but then it split again, leaving jagged red tears across his body. If his Constitution were not already so high, the changes might have ripped and torn his body into a grotesque parody. A hunchback of the underworld, strong, but imbalanced. Thankfully, he had already invested heavily in Con, allowing his body to handle the changes.

The ichorpede hissed in surprised fury and redoubled its efforts. Richter was slowly pushed back toward the rocky ground as it brought more of its several-ton body to bear. His Strength was now twelve points higher than the thirty-foot long centipede, but it outweighed him by a great amount. Between that and his precarious position on the ground, he was not able to gain the upper hand. As he waged this struggle for life and soul, more insects flooded the cave system. His summoned creatures went to work.

Facing the largest concentration of monstrous centipedes, the mesmer spider released its magic. It stood three feet tall on its sharp, sleek legs. It had only one eye, which crossed its arachnid face like a prismatic band. The bejeweled organ lit with an inner fire, and a conical beam of light shot forth. The five ichorpedes caught in the beam were entranced and froze in place. The spider scuttled forward and tried to bite them with its poison fangs but was unable to penetrate their armor.

The thorn elemental joined the fray as well. Casting *Entangle*, roots broke up through cracks in the stony ground. Though much less effective than if it were cast in a forest, the evolved creature's magic was not weak. Inch-wide green vines ensnared the bodies of two ichorpedes that were within the ten-yard AoE. The insects hissed and snapped at the plant tendrils, breaking them with ease. More came, however, and the thorn elemental followed up its first spell with another. Yellow particles filled the air as it cast *Sleep Pollen*. The spores were inhaled by the ichorpedes, stilling their actions to a certain extent. Unfortunately, the high-level monsters were not easily quelled and only one fell asleep.

Using its last offensive ability, the elemental shot a poison thorn at one of the bound ichorpedes. It struck a lucky shot, threading between armored plates. The poisonous dart sunk into flesh. The giant insect hissed as its HP started to fall, but its health barely diminished. With half its mana gone and all of its skills on cooldown, the thorn elemental moved to engage with another ichorpede rushing toward its master. It would buy Richter all the time it could with its three-foot-tall body.

Richter did not have time to pay attention to the valiant efforts of his summoned creatures. With some regret in his "frugal" heart, he invested his last fifteen points into Strength. He had not wanted to invest them all in this one stat, but if he was miserly, his life might end right here, right now. This was not a time to worry about the future. With the points allocated, an honest-to-god bellow ripped itself from his throat. It was deeper than any yell he ever remembered issuing before. Power flooded his body. His physique underwent massive physical changes to accommodate his overall Strength nearly doubling in under a minute. His shoulders broadened, his arms and abs became a topographic map, and his legs bulged through the ruins of his clothing.

Suddenly, the straining battle he had been waging seemed silly. His hands had been wrapped around the ichorpede's mandibles, fighting desperately to keep it from biting through his face. It had been all he could do to hold it back. Now though, it felt like he was fighting against a child. With a wild grin, he tightened his grip and yanked his arms wide!

The left pincer was forced wide and back. Richter felt something crack in its mouth. That was nothing compared to what happened on the right. The chaos seed ripped the mandible completely free from its head. The two-foot curved bone dripped acid from the pointed end and gushed grey blood on the other. The ichorpede squealed, a surprisingly high-pitched sound that Richter had not heard it make before. Then again, he'd never made the bug his bitch before, so the sound was perfectly understandable. His left hand was cut as it reared back in agony. He barely noticed.

While it whipped its head back and forth in terrible pain, the chaos seed rolled clear. Tumbling backwards, he pushed up in a handstand while he did, easily launching himself up and onto his feet. The ichorpede had reared up ten feet off the ground. Gushes of grey ichor sprayed side to side from the hole Richter had left in its face. For the moment at least it was ignoring him, wrapped in its own personal hell. The chaos seed did not miss the opportunity.

With one hand, he wove a quick spellform cast of *Minor Slow Heal*. With his Life Mastery, Richter's spell was 50% stronger than it would have been otherwise. His Intelligence was also high, and Limitless maximized the bonus his attributes gave his spellpower. The extra 36.5% boost to his magic meant that over the next minute he would heal about one hundred and sixty points of health. The golden glow suffused his body, bringing relief from pain and a fifty-six point drop in his mana.

That done, Richter grabbed his bone club and took stock. His health was improving. He'd lost over three hundred HP during his scrape with the ichorpede. The monster's sharp legs had wrecked the left side of his body when it had pierced him. If his skin hadn't been thickened due to his *Minor Chitin Carapace* spell, the damage would have been far more extensive. It had only given his skin another four points of defense, but that had stopped the monster's legs from hitting any major organs. With eight hundred and twelve max Health Points, he'd been able to endure the pummeling. Within the next minute, he'd restore half of what he had lost. Richter would give a lot for a health potion, but that was just one more thing he would have to go without. His stamina had dipped as well during the struggle, but it was still three-quarters full.

His mana was another story. Preparing for the battle, he'd cast a good deal of buffs. Coupled with summoning two creatures and evolving them, he'd spent nearly seven hundred mana. His mana pool was respectable at seven hundred and seventy-four, but he'd still suffered a large headache from depleting his MPs so fast. Richter had long since become accustomed to such minor annoyances. What he could not ignore was the fact that he needed mana to power his spells.

The saving grace was that he had invested a large amount of points into Wisdom. A value of forty-five, coupled with his Ring of Flowing Thought, let him regenerate thirty-two mana a minute. Compared to his initial regen rate of six MP per minute, it was blazingly fast. Unfortunately, it just wasn't good enough to let him keep slinging spells nonstop. It would take more than twenty minutes to completely refill his tank. He didn't have twenty seconds before he would be in battle again.

The two minutes he'd been struggling with the ichorpede had given him sixty mana, but he'd used that to cast his healing spell. Currently, he only had eighty-six points of magic to spend. That was enough to cast two rank one *weak* spells or maybe one rank two *minor* spell. That would not be enough. He'd stored a spell in his Ring of Spell Storage that he might be able to use as a trump card, but it could only store *novice* magic, level nine or below. He needed time!

A cracking noise drew his gaze and he saw that his thorn elemental was being ripped apart. Two ichorpedes had clamped onto it and were pulling it in two directions. Its health dropped quickly. The mesmer spider was surrounded and was only seconds from being destroyed. It did not have nearly the same defense as the evolved saproling. Worse, the ichorpede had oriented on him again, backlit by the flames. It threw the length of its body toward him. Cursing, Richter dove at and under it. A moment before it made contact, he fell into the monster's own silhouette. He was in the shadow realm.

The first thing he did was frantically look about. This was the second time he'd broken his promise. The shadow realm was a place of intense danger where even low-level monsters could steal his life. Not only that, but it was filled with disease that could be resistant to his magic. He'd promised himself that he wouldn't reenter the realm unless he was at his full strength. There just hadn't been a choice though. Thankfully, his luck held. There weren't any monsters right next to him, though that didn't mean there weren't any close by. For the moment, he was safe.

The body of the ichorpede fell through him, having no effect except Richter feeling a faint resistance as they passed through each other. Richter paid it no mind. Until his time in the Shadow Realm elapsed, it shouldn't be able to hurt him. He glanced at the new icon in his vision. It was the silhouette of a man with the number "5" next to it. That was the time he had before he was ejected from this dark space. Time moved differently in the shadow realm. The last time he'd been inside it had been in the Barrow of the Chaos Serpent. When he had tamed the mauler, he'd had about five seconds of shadow time for every real world second. Hisako had told him it was variable, however, and the further removed he was from sunlight the longer the conversion would last. Keeping an eye on the timer, he started running.

Richter ran past the injured ichorpede and was about to run through the grease fire, but he felt heat even in the shadow realm. The fact that the fire could affect the shadow realm just reminded him of how much he didn't know about the magic he was using. He could just hear the Hearth Mother's lecturing tone. It wasn't that she wasn't right, but he had limited options at this point.

The chaos seed detoured around the grease fire and kept running through the cavern. A screech of pain made him look back. Three ichorpedes were attacking and eating the one he had injured. Everything else in the dungeon looked like it was moving through honey. He saw the wooden body of the thorn elemental snapping and saw a slow spray of fluid come from the mesmer spider as two of its legs were bitten off by an ichorpede. Its abdomen was also a melted mess as it suffered from the monsters' acidic spit.

The summoned creatures had not lasted long, but they had bought him time. Initially, Richter's goal had been to run out of the stone doorway, but as he watched, another five ichorpedes spilled through. He couldn't take the chance of his time in the shadow realm running out when he was in the middle of enemies. Looking around, there were small holes pockmarking the walls, but half of them had ichorpedes crawling through. He was already not a huge fan of enclosed spaces, but being trapped in one with acid-spitting monsters took his aversion to a whole new level. There was only one exit that didn't have ichorpedes streaming through it. A large and incredibly ominous hole angling down into the ground.

The further he ran from the fire, the more gloom occluded his vision. Especially in the dim Shadow Realm, it grew increasingly hard to see. Thankfully, while most magic was suppressed in this realm, Light and Dark magic worked fine. As he sprinted to the hole, he cast *Night Vision*. Black energy coalesced around his fingers during the one-second cast time. The spell only cost five MP. In the midst of a battle, every point of mana could count, but it was more than worth the price.

Richter's view became an overlay of green and black. Even the green was muted by the color suppression of the Shadow Realm. The dark hole became much easier to see into, and the chaos seed discovered why no ichorpedes were streaming out of that particular exit. The expletives that flooded the still air around him would have made an orcish sailor proud. All he could hear in his mind was Solo saying, "This is no cave."

The entire passage was lined with teeth.

CHAPTER 2

DAY 150 – JUREN 1, 0 AOC

ichter's *Analyze* skill triggered.

Name: Ichorpede Queen	Disposition: Ravenous Hate	Level: 45
When ichorpede nests grow to a certain size, the strongest among them converts into a queen. Much larger and more powerful, the queen pays for this boost in power with the loss of most of her mobility. She relies on the nest to feed her, unless prey is foolish enough to enter the radius of her tentacles. Queens can drastically and quickly increase the size of nests if given enough food.		
STATS		
Health: 3781	Mana: 517	Stamina: 2006
ATTRIBUTES		
Strength: 58	Agility: 12	Dexterity: 51
Constitution: 378	Endurance: 200	Intelligence: 50
Wisdom: 22	Luck: 21	Charisma: 4
SPECIAL ATTACKS		
Tentacle Lash – Can perform powerful and acidic whip-like attack		
Birth – Can quickly spawn new ichorpedes if given enough meat		

The entire tunnel he'd been sprinting for was actually the mouth of the lair's queen! His feet skidded on the loose debris littering the floor. Looking down, he cursed himself. If he'd paid a little more attention, he'd have seen that the slope leading to the queen was lined with shattered bones, rotting meat, scales and stray tufts of fur. He might as well have been standing in a medical waste trash chute. The darkness of the Shadow Realm made it a bit harder to see, but he knew he couldn't afford any mistakes. Not down here.

As soon as he was able to stop, he started running back in the other direction. He was greeted by the entire lair of giant insects crawling over and around each other. Many of the ichorpedes were still milling around the spot where he had disappeared. Their pincers clacked and gnashed in frustration. Others were crawling around randomly. The spot that was clear was by the fire.

Looking at the ichorpedes' avoidant behavior, he realized they had a deep-seated fear of the flames. There was no way the grease fire could do their giant bodies any real harm. It was dying down as the grease was consumed. Even at its height, it hadn't been able to destroy the first one he'd fought. Still, their fear wasn't too surprising. The creatures down here lived in perpetual darkness. He'd have to remember that in the future. Those thoughts swirled anecdotally in the back of his mind. None of that was as important as the icon in the corner of Richter's vision with a "1" next to it.

"Damn!" he shouted in panic. His head darted around before throwing his body toward a curve in the wall. Thankfully, the fire hadn't died down too much. The flames still illuminated the cavern. That meant there were areas of shadow and areas of light. If his time in the Shadow Realm elapsed while he wasn't in a shadow he would get the mother of all debuffs, *Shadow Shock*. It would majorly damage his health and also decrease his ability to concentrate by 75%. Stuck in a lair, it would mean certain death. With no time to spare, he passed through the shadow of a rocky outcropping. As he phased back into existence, he used *Stealth* and hunched down.

The world switched back to normal colors. Richter kept his attention on the ichorpedes. There were about thirty or forty in the cavern now, crawling on the ground, walls and ceiling with equal alacrity. Thankfully, none of them seemed to be able to see him yet. The chaos seed breathed a small sigh of relief. That was when the queen's tentacle gouged a deep furrow through the muscles in his back.

*Richter has been struck with **Tentacle Lash** for 204 damage. 13 points of acidic damage per second for the next 11 seconds.*

"Aaaaahhhhh!" he screamed. Instinct told him to roll forward. That saved his life. Three more tentacles whipped through the space where he had been hiding. Where he thought he'd been hiding, anyway. Richter spat an incantation even as tears welled unbidden in his eyes. The initial pain from the lash was horrible, but it was growing worse. He could *feel* the acid eating through his flesh. Luckily, he still had his Secondary Attribute Resilience to rely on. It was the kind of attribute that you rarely had to use, but was absolutely crucial when you needed it. When his body was pushed to its limits and death was only seconds away, he could push through pain and anguish to fight for just one more breath of life. Focusing his agony, he shouted, "*Igni!*"

Flames shot from his hand, bathing the questing tentacles. They scorched the outside of the fleshy tendrils. The damage was actually minor as each was coated in slimy acid, but the shock of the fiery pain was something the queen had never encountered before. She drew back in shock and caution, a high-pitched cry filling the air. A few seconds later, the boss monster retaliated. Forty tentacles shot out from the hole, quivering in furious rage, but Richter had already run out of her range.

As he moved he tried to reenter the Shadow Realm, but a red prompt greeted him.

*Cooldown on the **Ring of Shadow Shift** has not elapsed. 53:17 remaining.*

Shit! Richter had never tried to use the ring back-to-back because of the risk from shadow monsters. He was only now figuring out that that the cooldown was almost an hour. The ring was *superb* class, only one rank down from *rare,* but it clearly still had limitations. Pushing himself to run faster, he also cast *Weak Slow Heal.*

His mana dropped by another twenty points, leaving him with one hundred and three MP. It was worth it just to help alleviate the agony in his back. It didn't neutralize the acid, but the healing magic was now combating the damage. It itched something awful, but anything was better than that melting feeling. Thankfully, the five seconds of real world time he had spent in the Shadow Realm had been almost a full minute in that dark place. That had let Richter regen about thirty MP and stamina.

The time in the Shadow Realm had also let him gain almost all of the healing from *Minor Slow Heal.* Of course, he'd just lost those same HPs from the queen's lash attack. He was alive though, and he was going to stay that way. The healing-over-time effect of *Minor Slow Heal* lasted a minute, the same as the spell's cooldown. That was important, because right now he had barely half his health, less than a fifth of his mana and half his stamina.

Gritting his teeth, he cast *Minor Slow Heal* while running, thanking the banished gods that his high mental fortitude let him cast spells while under so much stress. Most new casters couldn't cast while moving, let alone in the middle of a melee battle. His mana dropped down into the forties and a wave of nausea hit him. The sudden stomach pain doubled him over slightly. With all his other injuries, the effect of his mana depleting was aggravated.

Richter had to chew back some vomit. His vision blurred from the mana headache, but he could still see the ichorpedes were all surging toward his position. He didn't have time to be human. They were hemming him in on three sides. It made him wonder how dumb they actually were. The only path they were leaving him was the way back to the queen. The chaos seed's head darted around frantically as he came up with a desperate plan.

He had to bite his lip to keep another scream from coming out when he twisted his body to the left. The raw edges of flesh in his back rubbed together like an exposed nerve, but he was able to fling his bone club over the ichorpedes toward the stone doorway that led out of the lair. He didn't waste time to see exactly where it landed. If his aim was off, he wouldn't be able to go back for it anyway. He only had seconds to act. When you got down to it, his idea wasn't brilliant so much as obvious. With the ichorpedes rushing at him from every direction, there was only one way he could go. Up.

Richter jumped, giving it his all. The *Spring Steps* enchantment on his shoes had been destroyed when his skeeling armor had triggered the *Shell* effect. The white armor had saved his life, but it had also destroyed itself and the rest of his clothes, leaving only rags behind. At that particular moment, he would have given anything for the +20% jump boost the shoes had provided, but he might as well wish to be back home. Fact was, he didn't have most of the items that had kept him alive again and again. Fact was, he wasn't home, he was stuck underground, alone and surrounded. All he could do was jump.

Pain rippled through his battered body when his muscles contracted. The edges of his vision blurred, but he made it into the air. To his pleasant surprise though, he still cleared nearly eight feet. As soon as he reached the apex, he used *Cloud Running*. This rare skill was a gift from eating the First Fruit of the Quickening and had saved his life more than once. He jumped again, pushing off the air like it was a stepping stone. This time, he launched himself to the side, his trajectory shooting him toward the wall. Once again, he was propelled further than he'd expected. As he sailed through the air, he realized the reason for his huge ups. His Strength was massive now!

It took one more jump to reach the wall. That meant the third jump drained his stamina by nine times as much as the first. All told, the three jumps had cost him one hundred and four stamina. He only had two hundred and sixty-seven points left when he grabbed an outcropping of stone. The ichorpedes squealed beneath him and rushed toward the wall.

Part of him wished he'd been able to hold onto his bone club in case he needed to fight them off, but that was just another empty wish. It would have been impossible to make the jumps he needed to, carrying the extra weight and without his hands free. Not only did the damn thing weigh at least twenty pounds, but there was no way he could have grabbed the wall with his hands full. The ichorpede pincer he'd ripped free was still stuck through what remained of his pants so he wasn't weaponless, but it was only about a foot long. He really didn't want to get close enough to the gargantuan bugs to use it. Holding onto the stone, he looked out over the lair of deadly monsters.

The queen released a hissing cry, like a boiler only a few degrees away from exploding. The ichorpedes must have understood because they picked up speed. Richter was given no quarter. They climbed the walls easily, sharp legs digging into the rock. Several spit gobs of acid toward him, each the size of baseballs. They all missed, sizzling against the rock. If they'd struck, it would have been him melting instead of the stone. The chaos seed didn't give them another chance.

With pain, fear and anger in his heart, Richter tensed his legs and shot out into space once again. Anyone watching would think he was throwing himself into the sea of ichorpedes blanketing the cavern floor. One last act of defiance so that he could die on his own terms. It wasn't like that was not in keeping with his personality. He had literally jumped into an abyss to kill an enemy just a few hours ago, fully thinking he would die. This time though, that wasn't the plan.

Reaching the apex of his jump, he pushed off the air and jumped again. This time, it carried him back to the wall. Each time he jumped off the air, it increased the stamina drain by a factor of three. By leapfrogging from the wall and back though, he was able to keep the expenditure down. It also let him climb just a bit faster than the bugs. His Stamina dropped by about thirty each time, but thankfully, his new muscle-bound form had no issue grabbing handholds when he came back to the wall. Ninety-one Stamina Points later, Richter was forty feet higher. The ichorpedes were continuing to climb, but he'd gained himself a few seconds of respite.

Richter took a deep breath. The ammonia smell was thick in the air, and the queen's irritating screeching still rang in his ears. It was all or nothing time. He jumped into the air once more. This time it wasn't to gain elevation. It was to reach a long stalactite hanging several yards away.

His luck didn't hold this time. One of the climbing ichorpedes spat acid onto the back of his calf. The Life energy was still coursing through him, but the pain was horrific. He couldn't hold a scream back. His own pained voice joined the clamor in the lair. A tear leaked out of his eye, but he still skated through the air. He only had a few seconds of glide time before gravity reasserted itself. So he focused on his goal, screaming the whole time.

A damage notification appeared.

Richter struck with Acidic Spit! 8 points of acidic damage per second for the next 7 seconds.

In this life and death moment, it took everything he had to keep going. Richter felt the flesh of his calf literally cook and slough off to run down his foot. The dual healing and destruction taking place made him yell as he flew through the air, but the magic preserved the muscles. Without the magic, he would have fallen. Though his skill let him run through the air, he still needed to be able to run to make it work.

Richter glided through the air for more than three seconds before gravity started to kick in. Pushing off the air with his good leg, he continued to skate toward the hanging spike of stone. The third push cost him one hundred and three points of stamina and took him down to seventy-three. Less than a quarter of his green bar remained filled. He did not have enough to jump off of the air a fourth time. His heart beat wildly in his chest as he reached out for the stalactite.

Richter's fingers extended and he grabbed the tip of the hanging stone. His fingers slipped off the surface, but his other hand swung up and grasped as well. He fastened iron fingers onto a rough knob of stone. As quickly as he could, the chaos seed reached up again with his first hand. With a desperate scrabble, he grabbed hold. His body dangled above the cavern as his feet swayed freely. A strained groan passed the battered man's lips as he pulled himself up. More precious points of Stamina faded away. Richter had never really placed a huge emphasis on his Endurance attribute. He now saw the error of his ways.

More gobs of acidic spit flew at the chaos seed from the sides and below. The ichorpedes trying to splash him from the ground did not have the range. The attacks coming from those on the walls were blocked by the stalactite. In a desperate bid for life, all Richter could do was hold on to the stone pillar to gain a brief respite. The ichorpedes continued to climb the walls, but it would take them valuable seconds to crawl onto the ceiling and then down the rocky outcropping he was clinging to.

Hanging on to the stalactite cost stamina, but with a Constitution of sixty-two, his SPs regenerated faster than they drained. Richter's heart thumped wildly in his chest. Each throb felt like it forced panic into his mind. He forced himself to breathe slower and wait for his moment.

Richter cast *Minor Slow Heal* again, ragged breaths coming easier as the Life magic did its work. Fifteen seconds, thirty, then forty-five. Gasps became harsh breathing became a measured flow of air. The ichorpedes reached the ceiling and began crawling across it in a sinuous pattern. Without pause, but definitely slower, they flowed toward the connection between the stalactite and the cavern roof. More than one lost its grip in haste and fell to the ground below. Richter took some pleasure in seeing fights break out among the enemy, insect blood flying through the air.

A minute passed, then another thirty seconds. Then, he was out of time. The ichorpedes had reached the base of the stalactite and had begun to crawl down it. It didn't matter. His desperate plan had worked. He had a chance.

There were dozens, maybe hundreds, of ichorpedes in the giant cavern. The number of them had always been daunting. What he was seeing now was worse. The entire nest was now clustered together beneath him, a disgusting, undulating sea. The only plus side was that there weren't any more coming through the walls. Most important, the large stone doorway was clear. That meant his plan was working.

When faced with an entire nest of monsters that wanted to eat him bite by bite, all he had been able to come up with was luring them to one spot. Admittedly, he hadn't realized just how horrifying it would be to look down and see a living carpet of dull carapaces, hungry pincers and sharp legs. In fact, now that he was looking at it, he was fairly certain he had some bad dreams and necessary therapy in his future. He was hanging above a sea of hungry monsters, and if he fell, he might not even live long enough to scream.

Richter couldn't think about that though. He just had to hope he could make it. The minute and a half of time he'd bought himself had restored thirty points of his stamina and many of his wounds had closed. His back still wept blood and felt like a line of fire, but his calf had healed. It was now or never.

With his feet braced against the stone, he shot off like a released spring. The ichorpede closest to him on the stalactite jumped forward to bite his body. It missed by inches. The jerking motion made the accursed insect lose its purchase. Its heavy body crashed down to the cavern floor. It landed hard atop its brethren. In moments, a dozen of the monsters had turned on each other, cutting, rending and creating a wonderful, bloody mess. Richter paid it no attention.

The chaos seed did not engage his Cloud Running skill for more than two seconds, letting his body pick up speed from the fall. Only twenty feet above the ground, he triggered it. By his will and skill, he denied gravity and coasted toward the door at high speed. Repeating the process once more cost him thirty-eight stamina, but he finally touched down and sprinted for all he was worth. The only thing that slowed him by a fraction was picking up the overlarge bone he'd thrown toward the doorway. It wasn't Black Ice, but it and the ripped-off pincer were the only weapons he had. The queen hissed in anger and the ichorpedes were already rushing toward him, but the way out of the lair was finally clear!

Richter passed through the doorway. Battery acid pumped in his veins as his stamina came ever closer to bottoming out. The chaos seed did not give up. Whether it was his *Resilience* Attribute or just being a stubborn sonofabitch, he did not give up!

Instead, he cast two spells in quick succession. Green light surrounded the fingers of his left hand as he cast *Grease* again. A brown-gravy slick covered the ground immediately before and after the doorway. A jump and coast took him over and past the AoE. As he sped away from the lair, he threw one hand back and breathed, *"Igni."* The grease caught fire and a blaze was born.

The ichorpedes' instinctive fear of flame stopped their pursuit for a few precious seconds. The queen began screeching orders immediately and the ichorpedes' fear and allegiance to her forced them through the paltry fire. They boiled out of the lair, slavering for their foe's blood. Seven seconds, that was all the time his signature move had bought him, but it was enough. His bare feet beat a quick tattoo on the ground, leaving behind a trail of bloody footprints and a horrendous cacophony as he was swallowed by the dark.

CHAPTER 3

CHAPTER 3 – DAY 150 – JUREN 1, 0 AOC

*R*ichter ran, crawled and jumped through the bowels of The Land. He quickly got sick of his newly enlarged shoulders. They weren't exactly an asset when he was squeezing through tight tunnels. Shouts of "Fuck these big-ass shoulders" and "Did I really need all these muscles?" echoed through the deep, dark corridors of the world. His new Strength had let him escape the lair, but if he got stuck in a small tunnel, that'd also be why he was eaten ass-first by the horde of bugs chasing after him!

Thankfully, his speed was faster than the ichorpedes', even when *Weak Haste* faded away. His stamina was another matter. The chaos seed had a good head start, but his battered body could not handle a sprint for long without a break. The green bar in the corner of his vision fell faster than he liked.

Too soon, his stamina dropped down to about 10%. At that point, even though everything in him was shouting to just keep running, he forced himself to slow. He didn't stop, but his speed was reduced to a painful hobble. That pace let him keep moving forward as his stamina bar slowly, oh-so-slowly, started to refill. Despite the danger he was in and the panic he was fighting back, Richter forced himself to follow the pattern. He couldn't risk his green bar bottoming out. A stamina of zero didn't just mean weariness and exhaustion, it carried the possibility of passing out. Every time he slowed down though, he heard the monsters getting closer.

To make matters worse, he reeked of blood. The monsters were obviously not dependent on light to get around, not living in the bowels of the planet. His scent must have been like catnip to the ichorpedes. At the very least, it felt like he'd been running for miles and they still hadn't given up the chase.

As soon as his mana had regenerated enough, he cast more healing spells. That closed his wounds, but his injuries had left streaks of dark red on his body and clothes. With no water to wash off the blood, his scent trail was as obvious as a well-worn path. All Richter could do was fight a running battle. When the passageways opened up, he was able to widen his lead. When they narrowed and he had to crawl, he'd almost been caught several times. No matter how far he ran though, or how many branching paths he'd chosen, the monsters still hungered for his flesh.

His greatest fear was running into a dead end or another monster that was too strong for him to just rush past. It was an ever-present knot in the pit of his stomach as, time after time, he would turn a corner and see a blank wall of stone in front of him. Richter's heart would drop in his chest. Each time though, he found a way to wriggle forward and stay ahead of the monsters trying to eat him. Relief would flood him, but the continuous adrenaline surges and stress were taxing even his superhuman heart. More than once the path he found was so small that skin and blood were left behind. Still, he was able to fight forward one more step. The entire time, he thought of the curse and his hatred for the lich that had cast it.

*You are CURSED! The lich Singh has cursed you with the **Curse of Eternal Servitude!** If you die before this is removed, you shall not be resurrected. Your soul shall not pass on. You will serve the lich until he himself suffers the final death and, even then, you will be bound to this plane. You will wander as a mindless shade, hiding in the darkest corners of The Land, never to know peace or succor. You shall be damned!*

Richter had come to accept that living to a ripe old age was not going to be in the cards for him. He had died several times since coming to The Land. Each time, he had wondered if he would come back again. Despite not knowing if he would, he had not shirked his duty, or failed to step forward when it was time for battle. Even when he had learned the truth, that chaos seeds had an unknown but finite number of lives, he hadn't felt afraid of death. He'd felt like he'd been freed. Without consequence, life had no meaning. You had to try and strive. The Land seemed to have been built on that premise, danger and reward always being closely linked.

The curse was different, and it did fill him with fear. It wasn't death that Richter dreaded, though he didn't welcome it. Singh's magic would turn him into a mindless undead thing, however, and that was a fate worse than death. He would be robbed of his memories, his soul, everything he was. The corrupted version of him would exist only to cause harm and pain. It was the antithesis of who and what he was!

Despite the fact that Singh was dead, hatred bloomed anew in the chaos seed's heart. That burning fire fueled his passage through the darkness as much as his desire to not be eaten alive. Again.

He would not let the lich win. He would survive. It was a promise he made to himself. Richter would return to his village. And just to round it out, he would kill every goddamn one of those fucking bugs that were chasing him!

Obviously, insect vengeance would have to come later. Mostly because if he turned to fight them now, they would literally eat the asshole out of him. Rage had not robbed him of reason. That was why Richter kept running and scrabbling through passages large and small. He had no idea if he was moving up or down, he just knew he needed to keep going. He might have traveled a mile or a dozen.

The cloying blackness of the tunnel did not impede him thanks to recurrent castings of *Dark Vision*, but the mountains of rock above him coupled with the thick darkness combined to create an oppressive feeling. Aside from the occasional screeching of the ichorpedes chasing him, all he heard was the harsh *huff* of his own breath. The spell also only let him see in the dark up to twenty-five yards. Everything past that was an impenetrable wall of black.

Nightvision would have given a much better sight range, but it required at least some ambient light. This far down, there were passages that had never felt the touch of photons. There was also the point that casting his own light spells could bring more monsters down upon him. The brief flashes of light from his spells were bad enough. He couldn't cast *Simple Light* and have a bobbing white sphere showcasing that there was fresh meat for every monster in the depths.

His Light spells were also too weak to provide a long-term solution. *Far Light* only provided as much illumination as a candle. Casting it again and again would be an even worse trail than the scent of blood on his body. As deadly as the ichorpedes were, he had no doubt that worse threats hid in the pits of the world. Richter kept going, darkvision leading the way. He prayed the whole time he rushed forward that there wouldn't be monsters waiting with open jaws just beyond the range of his sight.

The only blessing of his prolonged flight was that his stat bars all refilled over time. His health was the easiest to restore thanks to his Mastery in Life magic. His stamina always stayed low, but his Constitution was a massive seventy-four. The attribute let his stat recover at more than seven times the rate of a normal human. It was enough to keep him alive and going, albeit in terrible pain the entire time. His mana refilled even faster. While his stamina kept him in the race, his magic let him counterattack.

Fireballs, grease fires, lightning bolts and even summoned creatures were thrown at his pursuers. He also had to turn and fight hand-to-hand sometimes. With his new strength, the bone club was able to crack the ichorpedes' carapace armor. With more always coming behind him though, he was never able to make a kill. Despite everything he threw at them, no matter how far he ran, the monsters didn't stop. All he was able to do was buy himself time. While his breath came in ragged gasps, he convinced himself that was enough. To Richter, time was life.

The pursuit continued until he was crawling through a particularly tight tunnel, cursing his recently broadened shoulders for the umpteenth time. That was when he felt a gust of wind on his outstretched hand. Reaching forward blindly, he felt no more stone, only empty space. He'd found a hole into a larger chamber! The chaos seed wiggled forward until his head poked through into the cavern and looked around. He couldn't see anything. The tunnel he'd been crawling through hadn't just ended in a new chamber, it had ended in a cliff face! No matter which way he looked he couldn't see anywhere else to go. Panic filled his heart. There was no more tunnel to crawl through and he could still hear the ichorpedes!

Like a horrible promise, he heard an insect screech from further back in the tunnel. It reminded him that no matter what was in front of him, his choices were to move forward or fight. The latter was sure death, so he realized he needed to find a solution. He had to find it now.

Dismissing his dark vision, his hand wove into the spellform *Night Vision*. He lost even the little bit of sight he'd had, but then he started casting *Far Light*. Balls of light shot from his hand one after another. They flew one hundred yards before reaching the end of their range and winking out of sight. Again and again, he cast the spell, up, down, side to side and at multiple angles.

Richter heaved a sigh of relief when one of his balls stuck to a surface. He slung a few more in that direction and realized that what he'd found was another cliff face running parallel to the one he was hanging out of. It was about fifty feet away. So far, he didn't see another passage though. Another screech sounded behind him and he started casting again at a frantic pace.

More balls of light flew across the expanse, and he prayed he'd find another tunnel. He'd have to leave the one he was in one way or another, and climbing a cliff face of unknown height was not exactly a good life plan. Not with the potential of crawling, and perhaps flying, monsters coming out of the dark at any moment, called by the only light within miles. Five, ten, fifteen balls of light and still nothing. Then he saw it! His *Far Light* spell pierced the entrance of a large tunnel. It was set into the opposing rock wall, fifty feet up and twenty feet to the side.

The sounds of battle echoed behind him. The ichorpedes had found the evolved saproling he'd left behind. He heard furious screeching, but also the sounds of branches snapping. He knew from experience that his summoned creature would not last long against the high-level monsters. Richter wriggled forward, more and more of his body exiting the tunnel. Gravity asserted itself and tried to pull him into the abyss. Based on recent events, he decided that he'd had enough of plummeting to his death. The chaos seed started climbing.

A minute later, an ichorpede's head popped out of the tunnel. Its antennae quested around. It soon caught the scent of his blood trail again. With a screech, it climbed out of the tunnel after him. Its dozens of sharp legs found easy purchase on the stone. It climbed much faster than Richter could manage and quickly closed the gap.

The chaos seed's jaw clenched. He'd wanted to get a bit higher up, but there was no more time. With a shouted, "Yah!" he flung himself out into space. The giant centipede surged forward. It was too late. The chaos seed was already gliding toward the tunnel. Three seconds passed before he jumped off the air again. His stamina fell by twenty-four points, but he gained another seven feet of height. After that, it was just rinse and repeat.

The next jump cost him eighty-two points and the one after that two hundred and fifty-four. Richter couldn't have managed another jump as the stamina cost increased by around 200% each time. That didn't matter though. Just as his glide time was running out, his foot found the lip of the new passage. He leaned forward and his momentum carried him into the new tunnel. His landing was more like an ungraceful crash, and only 10% of his stamina bar remained, but he'd done it!

Richter's breath came out in pained wheezes, and his side ached like he'd just sprinted uphill. He still found the energy to look back across the chasm. Ichorpedes swarmed angrily across the cliff face he'd just left. There was no way for them to reach him though. Climbing on the ninety-degree slope, they couldn't even effectively spit acid at him. A few tried, but the gobs of burning saliva fell well short.

With a malicious grin on his weary face, Richter thought, let me show you how it's done. Sweat poured off his face and body, and his muscles screamed at him to just lay down, but he had a promise to keep. Raising both arms, his hands moved in concert, chiral images of one another. A red glow surrounded his fingers as a wisp of flame appeared between his hands. Over three seconds the magic grew larger, boosted by his *initiate* rank in Fire magic, his *Dragonkin II* Mark, his high Intelligence and his dual cast technique. The spell grew in power to be three times its base potency. Richter harnessed the fundamental powers of the Universe, each spoken syllable sounding like the crackling of burning wood and hissing licks of flame.

"Creshadaari Palun Ignis!"

Richter's mana dropped by three hundred points as he cast *Weak Fireball*. The large investment of magic made his head throb. It was worth it. There was nothing "weak" about his spell. The tennis ball-sized flame expanded to the size of a large beach ball as it flew across space. Not only did his dual casting increase the damage, but his *initiate* rank in the skill increased his spell's range by 20%. The roaring spell struck the ichorpede he had targeted and detonated!

It was the explosive effect he was after. Even boosted by his stats and other bonuses, the first rank *weak* spell would not have been enough to kill one of the powerful monsters. Knocking them off the cliff wall they clung to, however... well, that was more than possible. The chaos seed's grin was ear-to-ear as the ichorpede he had struck was flattened against the rock wall and stunned. It lost its footing and plummeted to its death. The fact that Richter didn't get the notification of gaining experience for nearly a minute showed how deep the chasm really was.

He might have felt bad about killing that one, but he made sure that first fucker had plenty of company. The flames from his fireball rippled out twelve meters in every direction, a wall of orange-yellow death. Five more insects fell to their deaths, hissing as they were claimed by the blackness. Joy bloomed in Richter's heart, but it wasn't enough to quiet the monster inside of him. Both hands raised, he started to rapid-fire spells.

Weak Lightning Bolt stunned an ichorpede for a moment and its legs lost their grip. By the time it came back to itself, it could only screech and writhe until it disappeared into the gloom below. Seven deaths. *Weak Magic Missile* shot three balls of colored light into the face of another. Dazzled by the pain and light, it bit at another insect. In retaliation, the monster struck back. Moments later, they both fell to oblivion.

Nine deaths.

The remaining insects scurried away, trying to escape the man they had considered prey. Richter smiled to see their panic, and thought he just might be able to smell their fear. His eyes locked onto one more. No, he thought softly, you cannot go.

Richter summoned his magic to cast a new spell. Four seconds passed while he channeled the arcane energies until a beam of pure sunlight shot from his left hand. He stood in the tunnel, looking down at his enemy, and a bolt of death fell from his hands like the petty vengeance of a vexed god. The passage of energy made the scent of burning ozone fill Richter's nostrils.

That was not what his target noticed. It just felt its eyes pop under the intense heat and light of the chaos seed's spell. It was struck with a *Blind* debuff, and it screeched in pain and panic. The monster ran down the cliff face until it reached an overhang. Like a lemming, it continued on. The monster realized its mistake too late, and its momentum carried it out into space.

With extreme satisfaction, Richter fell to his butt. Extending his favorite middle finger, and looking out into the black, he said, "Ten."

Richter dropped onto his back, and his rib cage heaved like a stallion after a race. Almost absently, he filled his Ring of Spell Storage. It had become a habit to keep the magic ring locked and loaded. It could only hold *novice*-level spells for a day before the magical charge expired, but all that was required to use the stored power was an exertion of will. The ability to instacast a spell had saved his life more than once. Battles and pain had taught him lessons that love and time never could.

As Richter collected himself and fought off the too-tempting desire to pass out, he heard the slow flap of wings. He might have rolled over and prepared to fight again, but right after, he heard Xuetrix speak with fascinated glee, "You have some anger issues, don't you?"

Without verbally responding or turning around, Richter rotated his shoulder until he could present the imp with the bird.

CHAPTER 4

DAY 151 – JUREN 2, 0 AOC

"*W*here the fuck have you been?" Richter spat at imp. The quiet heat in his voice could melt iron. "I could have used some help!"

"There are rules, human. I am a Messenger. I cannot directly intervene in the affairs of mortals."

"What does that even mean? What is a Messenger?"

Xuetrix answered in a language that Richter could not understand. It was something he was getting used to with the demon. The first time his Gift of Tongues ability was stymied had been with the imp as well. His ability was extremely powerful and let him understand *almost* any language. The so called "higher" and "lower" languages of more- and less-evolved beings were where it failed him. The imp responding in a language he knew Richter couldn't understand was the equivalent of the demon saying he didn't deserve to know, and then adding a healthy dollop of "eat me" on top.

Six or seven months ago, Richter had been new to The Land. Even though he'd been a top-notch gamer, and had known the VRMMORPG that had been based on The Land, none of that had translated into success in his new world. Put plainly, he'd been a noob. The imp had taken advantage of that and tricked him into a

Favor. Now Richter owed him a magical debt. That knowledge had been bothering him like a popcorn kernel between his teeth for the past few months. He could forget about it for long periods of time, but it would drive him nuts at odd moments. Now, after months of irritating worry, the demon was finally here to collect.

Richter's jaw clenched. He couldn't change the past, but he'd be damned if he made the same mistake again. He wasn't a noob anymore. He was Lord Mist, the Master of a Place of Power and a man who had reaped thousands of lives. More than that, he had learned one of the most important lessons The Land had to teach. Power was all that mattered. Xuetrix had tried to mock and bait him by speaking in a language he couldn't understand. That was a show of power. These days, Richter had power of his own. He glared at the imp and raised a hand. A magical glow appeared.

The small demon's eyes widened in astonishment. He had never imagined that Richter would actually attack him. The chaos seed chanted a short spell. The imp cast a protective spell while the chaos seed chanted. A reddish-black sphere of energy sprang into existence around his body. Xuetrix's lips twisted into a snarl as he prepared to defend himself. Richter finished his incantation and a harmless sphere of white light shot from his fingers and attached itself to the tunnel wall.

The demon stared at Richter in anger and irritation at having been tricked. The chaos seed smiled back maliciously, "Nervous much?" then continued to cast more illumination magic.

The tunnel quickly lit up, showing that it led straight back into the rock with no turns or hidden curves. Xuetrix dismissed his shield, a glare on his face. The chaos seed pretended not to notice and just kept looking around. Once he was sure there were no more monsters waiting to rush him, he still didn't give the imp any attention. Instead, he sat down and leaned his back against the tunnel wall. The imp had come to collect on a Favor, and Richter couldn't do anything about that. Before he dealt with the flying bastard though, he needed to go through the giant list of prompts he'd earned from destroying Singh's Mausoleum.

He'd waited long enough.

The battle at Singh's Mausoleum had involved thousands of enemies. The allied forces of the Hearth Tree and Mist Village had won the day, but the cost had been high. The fight had claimed the lives of too many of his people. As always, the deaths of comrades weighed heavily on him, but this time, some were so heavy they threatened to crush him.

In a way, he was glad that he'd been in a life and death struggle since raiding the necropolis. It meant he'd been able to avoid his survivor's guilt for a short time. Now though, the image of Caulder dying in such a horrific fashion flashed through his mind. One moment, he'd been right next to him, the same steady and gruff sergeant that was the backbone of the Mist Village's army. The next, he'd been twisted into a gross parody of himself, an undead thing perverted by Singh's magic. Now that he had a moment to breathe, all of it came crashing back. Richter felt a tight knot in his chest that he knew wouldn't quickly unravel.

For a few minutes he just closed his eyes, breathed and reflected. Xuetrix started talking, but the chaos seed just held up one hand. A magical glow surrounded his fingers again, but this time it was the red of Fire magic. The message was clear. If Richter cast another spell, this time, it wouldn't be "harmless." The imp decided to keep his peace. The entire time, he didn't open his eyes. After not hearing anything else, he put his hand down and tried to sort through what he was feeling.

First, Richter thought of the men and women that had bravely laid down their lives to protect their fellow villagers. He spoke each of their names in his mind. One after another, he paid them homage, and promised to remember them. Once he was done, his heart felt lighter. The truth was, he'd been through too many battles and had lost comrades before. The chaos seed did not let despair drag him down. Instead of focusing on their deaths, he reminded himself of their lives.

Richter had made sure to spend as much time with his villagers as possible. There were very few he didn't have at least one memory with. That was why his mind unerringly turned to Caulder. From their first meeting at Leaf's Crossing, to their time in the Whistling Hen and the sergeant moving to the Mist Village, Caulder had been a solid force in Richter's tempestuous life. He'd been funny, but also tough as nails.

Richter went through memory after memory, and settled on one with the man's mortal enemy, Shinecatcher. Remembering the shouting matches between Caulder and the kindir brought a faint smile to the chaos seed's lips. In that pleasant memory, with that final remembrance, he found the strength to do what was needed. He found the courage to let the deaths go. He would never forget, but he would allow himself to remember Caulder, and all the others, fondly. My friend, he thought, I wish you well.

The chaos seed opened his eyes and brought up his long-awaited prompts.

CHAPTER 5

DAY 151 – JUREN 2, 0 AOC

*T*he first notifications were the skills he'd leveled up.

*Congratulations! You have reached skill level 20 in **Archery**. +40% bonus to aim and +40% bonus to damage when using a bow.*

*Congratulations! You have reached skill level 20 in **Enhanced Imbue Arrow**. +100% magical damage. +200% speed of mana flow.*

*Congratulations! You have reached subskill level 9 in **Focus**. Max zoom increased to 190%.*

The gains to his archery-related skills were modest, only one skill level each. That wasn't surprising. He'd fought most of the battle with either his melee or magical skills. Modest or not, the skill level ups were enough to buy him some much-appreciated XP.

*You have received 5,000 (base 4,000 x 1.25) bonus experience for reaching level 20 in the skill: **Archery**.*

You have received 2,500 (base 2,000 x 1.25) bonus experience for reaching level 20 in the skill: **Enhanced Imbue Arrow.**

The experience gained would have been enough to catapult someone from level one to three, but to Richter it was a mere fraction of a percent of what he needed to reach his next level. Every little bit helped though, as shown by the 30 Attribute Points he'd been able to invest into Strength. Richter was distracted for a moment by his new physique. His muscles were gigantic. They almost looked swollen, and he felt as bulky as a bull gorilla. He even had muscles on top of his shoulders now. Who needed muscles on their shoulders? What were they even for?

A gurgle in his stomach stopped that line of thought. Banished gods, he was ravenous! His rapid growth had given him a powerful hunger. Dealing with that would have to wait, however. There were more skill prompts waiting to be read. The next windows dealt with his close combat skills, and the increases there were much more dramatic.

Congratulations! You have reached skill level 13 in **Dual Wield.** *Base accuracy penalty in primary hand reduced to -12% and in off hand by -37%. Dual attack speed increased by +13%.*

Congratulations! You have reached skill levels 5, 6, 7 and 8 in **Swordsmanship.** *+16% Damage and +16% Attack Speed when using a sword.*

Richter thought about the loss of Black Ice and felt an extreme sense of regret. The Named weapon was one of the strongest implements of war he had come across. Only Ranock Din, the ancestral hammer of dwarven kings, was more powerful. Sadly, his demon soul blade had been lost when he'd fallen into the abyss. Because it was soul bound, he had the potential to find it on his Traveler's Map. If he'd been in his village, he'd have done exactly that. The map wasn't a GPS though. It needed a reference and orientation. Lost as he was underground, he had no way to find the powerful weapon.

Point in fact, the current map around his location only showed his journey from the moment he'd woken up in the shell. Everything else was just black. He could still pull up an image of his village, but there was no way to tell how far he was from there. The blade was lost, most likely buried under a mountain's worth of rock. His only hope to see it again was if he died and was lucky enough to be reborn with his soul bound items.

Thinking of Black Ice made him think of his other missing items, arms and armor. Any one of them could have drastically increased his chances of survival. Hell, he'd dance a jig just for a single potion. All he had were his rings, bracelet and necklace. It was only in that moment that Richter realized just how much he'd come to rely on the advanced gear his village provided. Without that pipeline, if he wanted to survive the coming days he'd have to rely on his own wits and capabilities. Thankfully, the fight with Singh had indeed earned him some valuable skill levels.

*Congratulations! You have reached skill levels 18, 19, 20, 21 and 22 in **Light Armor**. +44% to defense of all Light Armor.*

*You have received 5,000 (base 4,000 x 1.25) bonus experience for reaching level 20 in the skill: **Light Armor**.*

The massive boost to his Light Armor skill basically meant he'd gotten his butt kicked during the battle. That was how armor skills went up. You had to be hit with heavy and sharp things. If he had any armor to speak of, it might have been valuable news. Sadly, he was almost as naked as the day he was born. If he wanted to survive any attacks in the days to come, he'd have to work on his dodge techniques. The fact that his *Grace in Combat* skill had only progressed a third as much as *Light Armor* underscored the fact that he'd basically been a punching bag during the last battle.

*Congratulations! You have reached subskill levels 18 and 19 in **Grace in Combat**. Dodge increased by +29% while wearing all Light Armor.*

Richter thought about the last prompt and his battle with the ichorpedes. He realized that fight had been the first time in a long time that he'd fought without armor. Thinking about it now, it occurred to him that even though he hadn't been wearing his gear, he'd actually felt "heavier" than when he was wearing his kit. It just went to show you that though skills were powerful, some of them were completely dependent on certain conditions being met. Case in point: without his light armor, he lost the bonus from *Grace in Combat*. That meant it was a lot harder for him to dodge attacks. It was just one more reminder of how much more vulnerable he was without his items. For a moment he thought about all the times Bruce Wayne had still been a badass even without his suit and utility belt. At least the comics had made it seem that way.

Richter was calling bullshit.

Sighing heavily, he kept going. The advancements to his magic skills were next.

Congratulations! You have reached skill level 20 in **Blood Magic***. New spells are now available.*

His prolonged mastery over the mauler had increased his skill level in the Deeper Magic of Blood. It was only by one level, but it was something. That was especially true as it took significantly longer to progress in Deeper Magic than in the Basic Elements. It was also potentially dangerous. There were spells he couldn't use because his skill level in *Blood Magic* was too low, but he'd never forgotten that there were powerful forces monitoring its use. He didn't know what a blood coven was, but he was pretty sure he didn't want one to find him.

Even better and more importantly, his *Beast Bonding* skill had improved.

Congratulations! You have reached skill levels 26, 27 and 28 in **Beast Bonding***. +28% effectiveness to Tame. +28% attack and defense of bonded creatures.*

Three levels might not seem like a game changer, but there was more to this skill than the prompt told. His probability of successfully using *Tame* was based on his skill level in *Beast Bonding* compared to the personal level of the monster he was trying to control. His chances of controlling higher level monsters had just increased and, if he did conquer their will, they'd be stronger for it afterward. *Tame* was a demanding and exacting spell, but it just might be the very thing that kept him alive down here.

None of his other magical skills had increased. Even though Richter had called on powerful magics in his fight with Singh, most of that had come from using high level items. He supposed you could say that where steel had failed him, gold had saved him. Those items had been incredibly powerful, but it was basically like fighting a monster by throwing sports cars at it. Of course, he'd happily burn more gold right now if it would get him a useful item. Then again, if frogs had wings, they wouldn't bump their asses when they jumped.

The next prompt showed an unexpected increase. Richter was somewhat surprised to see that his *Traps* skill had improved by a level.

*Congratulations! You have reached skill level 27 in **Traps**. All traps +54% more effective. +54% less likely to be found.*

This had to be because of the massive trap floor on the roof of the Mausoleum. The entire thing had been like a jigsaw puzzle of death. Hundreds, if not thousands, of snares were built into the roof. He hadn't been able to disarm any of them, but even identifying traps helped his skill. That had been enough to give him another few precious percentage points of progression in the skill.

The next advance was an even bigger surprise.

*Congratulations! You have reached skill levels 10, 11, ..., and 15 in **Diplomacy**. +15% to negotiating power. +15% more likely that representatives from other settlements will take both threats and offers more seriously.*

Congratulations! You have advanced from Novice to Initiate in: **Diplomacy.**
*Your strength as a leader is not only based on strength of arms, but also
strength of voice. The diplomatic actions you take now have farther-
reaching consequences.*

Diplomacy Initiate Bonus: +20% **Diplomatic Points** *generated from meaningful actions between settlements. This is cumulative with successive
ranks.*

Of everything he had done at the Mausoleum, one of the most
important events was his negotiation with the vampire brothers,
Mikaal and Lucasz. The perk from his Symbiosis Boon, Deadly
Charisma, had greased the wheels, but it had still taken serious fore-
thought and convincing to get the *master* magicians to betray their
lich lord. His high Charisma and Fame had almost definitely played a
serious role as well. That negotiation had been key to defeating
Singh. The more he thought about it, the more he understood why
his *Diplomacy* skill had advanced so far so fast.

It had also earned him more experience.

*You have received 2,500 (base 2,000 x 1.25) bonus experience for reaching
level 10 in the skill:* **Diplomacy.**

The last skill he'd advanced was no surprise. He gained nine skill
levels in *War Leader* and even more in its subskills.

Congratulations! You have reached skill levels 18, 19, ..., and 26 in **War
Leader.** *Sphere of Influence +26% larger. +26% attack and defense for all
allies within your Sphere of Influence.*

Congratulations! You have reached subskill levels 15, 16, ..., and 26 in
Beacon. *+260 to the Fighting Spirit of war party.*

Congratulations! You have reached subskill levels 10, 11, ..., 14 in **Inspiring**

Leadership. +14% to chance of war party members earning Field Advancements. +14% to the power of Field Advancements of any party members under your command or the command of your subordinates.

Richter had led the allied armies to victory. That had earned him so many skill levels. Thinking about that reminded him of the casualties. Too many had been lost. His chest tightened again, but he pushed past the feeling. Trapped beneath the ground with a demon breathing down his neck wasn't the time to backpedal. The point was, despite the high costs, they had prevailed. Not only had the lich been defeated, ending centuries of evil, but the Mausoleum had been destroyed as well. A bulwark of the undead had been eradicated. All that together had advanced not only *War Leader,* but two of its three subskills.

Beacon must have improved when he was at the forefront of the battle. He was literally a beacon to his troops, increasing their Fighting Spirit. The higher the FS, the more damage they caused. His presence had increased the hurt his entire army could bring. *Inspiring Leadership* advanced when he accomplished something truly amazing in a battle. Destroying a high-level Core building had certainly qualified.

He got two more notifications telling him about the seventy-five hundred XP he'd gained for reaching skill level twenty in *War Leader* and its subskills. What was more important was that reaching skill level twenty-five had advanced him to an entirely new rank!

Congratulations! You have advanced from Initiate to Apprentice in: **War Leader.**

Rank	Initiate	Apprentice
Title	Battle Sergeant	Battle Captain
Max Party Size	10	50
Subordinate Officers	2 Strike Leaders	2 Battle Sergeants 4 Strike Leaders
Sphere of Influence	100 yards	250 yards
Fighting Spirit Bonus	+200	+500

New Badges are available for purchase. New skilled positions are available.

All of that was basically just an advance of what had come before, but there were three additional bonuses to being a Battle Captain that changed everything.

*All combat-related skills will increase **25% faster** for members of your party. Cumulative with successive ranks.*

Not many things could help skills level faster. The Potion of Clarity increased the experience they gained by 25%. That affected personal levels though, not skills. The vials of sparkling solution could sell for about three gold per dose. While higher levels and more Attribute Points were always a good thing, you needed skills to succeed in The Land. With this perk, he could train an elite army in a much shorter period of time. The second bonus was even better.

*You may now issue a Captain's **Clarion Call**. When used, this special ability will increase the Damage and Attack Speed of every ally inside your Sphere of Influence by 250% for 5 minutes.*

Richter had to read it twice because he didn't believe it at first. He'd just found a berserk power! In a key moment, he could massively increase the damage of every ally within two hundred and fifty yards. That could be hundreds of soldiers who could wreak havoc on an enemy all at once. It wasn't just enough to turn the tide of a battle. *Clarion Call* would be enough to end it.

While the first two were great, the third really changed the game.

*You shall now be awarded bonus XP based on **5%** of the total XP gained from the members of your war party. This is cumulative with successive ranks.*

Richter had wondered about something for a while. War leaders were amazing in battle. They could increase the power of an entire army. That very fact made them vulnerable, however. If the enemy were able to take them out, the entire opposing force would weaken. It was all very well and good for brave kings in old stories to always ride at the front of their armies, but in reality, that was a great way to lose leaders quickly. Richter had learned that lesson himself too many times. He was not invulnerable and too many good men and women had died saving him in the past.

While he would never shrink from battle, he had also matured enough to realize that he was a precious resource to his troops. He couldn't always be in the thick of it. Sometimes he would have to lead from behind. Militaries had learned this fact on Earth millennia before his own birth. The question then was: if he wasn't involved in battles directly, how was he supposed to keep his own level from stagnating? While Richter had multiple options to gain XP thanks to his *Legendary* Limitless ability, most others would not. The perk from transitioning from a Battle Sergeant to a Battle Captain was the answer.

Now he could focus on leading his people, and still gain 5% of all the XP they gained in battle. While 5% might not seem like much, he could now field fifty soldiers under his command. When he added in the two Battle Sergeants and four Strike Leaders, that number increased to ninety. With a full contingent, it was like having another four or five people funneling their experience to him in every battle. The XP he could gain in even a single battle was potentially massive!

Richter couldn't wait to experience true power leveling. He would have to though. For now, he wasn't leading but two things, Jack and Shit. Sitting in a black tunnel, miles under the earth, it was clear that Jack had left town. At least until he got bored. Quelling his excitement, he turned his attention to his next prompts. He'd upgraded some of his War Leader promotions!

*Congratulations! Your war party dug out an entrenched enemy and slaughtered every member of the enemy force. For destroying an enemy that was 50 times your number, your Promotion **Sapper I** has advanced to **Sapper IV**. +20% to attack against an entrenched enemy.*

*Congratulations! Your war party destroyed an enemy in an underground battle. For destroying an enemy that was 50 times your number, your Promotion **Subterranean I** has advanced to **Subterranean IV**. +20% to defense when fighting underground.*

It certainly hadn't been easy to advance the two promotions to the fourth rank, but the rewards were amazing! Raiding entrenched encampments would improve the attack of his people by 20%. *Subterranean IV* might even be better. If the promotion had increased this far during the raid against the lich, it might have saved lives. Both could turn the tide of war in the future. Even better, these were not the only promotions that were upgraded.

Richter had hoped that there would be an increase to *Overwhelming Odds*. The promotion increased the fighting spirit of his warband, increasing the damage they caused in every scenario. But then he'd only gained the promotion after being attacked. Technically, his allied forces had invaded the Mausoleum, so it hadn't been affected. There had apparently been enemy war parties, however, because *Battle Lord* advanced.

*Congratulations! Your war party destroyed enemy war parties. For destroying 10 opposing War Parties, your Promotion **Battle Lord I** has advanced to **Battle Lord III**. Champions in your War Party enjoy +5 to all Base Characteristics when battling against an enemy war party.*

The original bonus was +1. That was good, but the extra five points meant another fifty points of health, mana and stamina. A higher Constitution and Wisdom also meant an increased stamina and mana regen. It would allow the Champions he led to deal more damage and last longer in battle. It did not affect him personally, unfortunately, but the promotion would definitely be helpful later.

He'd also gained a specific and, he had to imagine, rare promotion.

Congratulations! Your war party destroyed a level 4 Core building. For destroying such a powerful building, your War Party has gained a Core Token that can be used at the discretion of the War Leader. The number of levels the building possessed determines the max bonus from the Token.

For destroying a level 1 Core building: *Free Promotion of any non-Core settlement building which your settlement already possesses. This promotion can exceed the level cap imposed by the settlement's central building (ie Townhall)*

For destroying a level 2 Core building: *Increase the bonuses of any non-Core settlement building by 25%.*

For destroying a level 3 Core building: *Free creation of any building that your settlement possesses the blueprint to create. The level of this building will be your settlement's central building +2*

For destroying a level 4 Core building: *Free Promotion of any Core settlement building which your settlement already possesses. This promotion can exceed the level cap imposed by the settlement's central building (ie Townhall)*

This token can be summoned at any time by the War Leader. Once conjured, however, it must be used within 1 day. Only one of the above Token bonuses can be used.

CHAPTER 6

DAY 151 – JUREN 2, 0 AOC

*R*ichter couldn't believe what he had just read. It turned out that if a War Party destroyed a Core building, they would get a huge bonus to their own Settlement. He could see how this particular piece of information would be mostly unknown. The Land was a place of untold secrets. He had to imagine this was one of the biggest.

Destroying a Core building was insanely hard. They had a durability about a hundred times stronger than a normal building. Their defense was sky-high as well. They actively regenerated any damage that they suffered. Destroying even a level one Core building would take a team of roided-out giants armed with mithril hammers. The only reason the Mausoleum had been destroyed was because an Exile, one of the all-powerful beings imprisoned by The Land itself, had exerted his power. Even then, those beams of devastation had barely been enough. When you looked at all of that, he couldn't imagine how many people had ever destroyed a Core building. He also couldn't imagine too many people that would want to do so. A Magic Core could turn a simple village into a powerful force.

The chaos seed read all of the bonuses again but, truth be told, his eyes only had room for the fourth option. He could upgrade one of his Core buildings! Since coming to The Land he'd overcome many dangers and gained some truly awesome advantages. Even with those, his village was still outmatched in many ways compared to the forces that wanted to destroy it.

Of all the advantages he'd gained, the Core buildings were perhaps the most valuable. Even though they were only at level one, the Forge of Heavens and the Dragon's Cauldron had helped his small village beat armies. He couldn't even imagine what could happen if they were upgraded to level two. Richter smiled for a few seconds before he realized one pivotal point.

To use the token, he had to get home first. To be more specific, he had to survive down here for at least a week. He needed that long for Singh's curse to disappear. If he didn't make it seven days, he wouldn't just be reborn as himself. He didn't even know if he had another life to spare, but if the curse took hold, it wouldn't matter.

He wouldn't be himself anymore. Singh's dirty eldritch magic would steal his mind. All that would be left would be a malevolent undead thing. Looking around the cold, dark tunnel, doing his best not to make eye contact with the irritated imp, he realized that surviving a week wasn't something he could just assume would happen. It certainly didn't help that a nest of giant bugs had almost eaten him not twenty minutes ago.

With that splash of cold reality, his joy shriveled like a raisin in the sun. He turned his attention back to his next prompt. The numbers he saw shocked him out of his melancholy. It was a rundown of the War Points he'd gained. Apparently, the system credited him with every death that had come from the destruction of the Mausoleum. It couldn't even list the individual kills, just categories. According to this, he was responsible for tens of thousands of deaths!

*For slaying 5,816 **Skeletons**, you have been awarded 11,632 War Points.*

*For slaying 4,755 **Zombies**, you have been awarded 9,510 War Points.*

*For slaying 162 **Professional Skeletons**, you have been awarded 1,620 War Points. (War Points multiplied by 5 for slaying a Professional)*

…

…

…

The list kept unspooling. Skeletons, zombies, draugh, and other creatures he didn't even recognize the names of. They weren't just common enemies either. Thousands of Professionals and Specialists had been slain as well. Singh had amassed a truly massive army. Even keeping the eldritch lord's evil magic out of the equation, the legions of undead would have been enough to turn his village into dust. And not just his village; they could have swept through the entire Forest of Nadria. The lich's threat of invasion hadn't just been smoke. Richter wasn't sure exactly what had happened when the undead army had spilled through the portal into his Dungeon, but he was so very thankful his people had ultimately beaten back the horde. If even 1% had made it out of the Dungeon, every man, woman and child in the Mist Village would have suffered a horrible death.

Richter's eyes continued to take in the list of dead. For a moment he thought he'd just gained about a million War Points. With that, he could become the most powerful ruler in the history of The Land. Of course, The Land had to crap on his ice cream and call it sprinkles. There was a cap to the number of points he could earn in a single battle.

*Know This! As a **Battle Captain** serving beneath a **Battle Leader**, you are only entitled to keep 75% of the total War Points earned. Total War Points Gained (Adjusted): **117,933***

*Congratulations! You have destroyed enemy **War Parties**. The highest War Leader's rank was **Apprentice**. For killing a War Leader of the third rank, all War Points gained are tripled.*

*Total War Points Gained (Adjusted): **353,799***

That all would have been fine if not for this one last irritating line of text.

*Know This! At your **initiate** rank in War Leader, War Points gained in a given engagement are capped at 2,500. Total War Points Gained (Adjusted):*
2,500
Total War Points: 3,612

Richter had gained less than 1% of the total War Points he could have gotten. That was so annoying! It also wasn't wholly unexpected. The Land always had checks and balances built in to its paths to power. If it didn't, the entire planet would most likely have been ruled by some almighty dictators by the time he even arrived. No point complaining about it now either way. It wouldn't change anything.

Richter had the option to trade in his points for new War Badges, but decided to hold off for the moment. There was no time limit on when he had to spend his War Points. Seeing as how he didn't have anyone to follow him right now, it could wait. Sadly, his Army of One subskill let him use a small percentage of any War Party Promotions he obtained, but not any benefits from the badges War Points could buy. There were more notifications to read.

There were substantial dividends from having killed such a massive number of undead. The next series of prompts would have bothered him once. Now, he merely accepted them as his due. They were gone, he wasn't. No use wringing his hands about it.

SLAYER COUNT		
ENEMY	*SLAIN*	*TITLE*
Goblins	1, 134	Goblin Slayer V
Bugbears	42	Bugbear Slayer I
Undead	348	Undead Slayer III
Living Dead	59	Living Dead Slayer I

It was quite a butcher's bill. His slayer count only included those he'd personally slain, not deaths resulting from the Mausoleum's destruction, but it was still a large amount. Richter had originally founded his village to preserve life, and he supposed that would include the living dead like vampires as long as they didn't cause a ruckus, but the numbers did not lie. He may have helped hundreds to live, but he had slain thousands. He searched his feelings, but found that it was indeed true. The deaths of so many sapient living dead just didn't bother him. He didn't really need to worry about ill feelings from killing the skeletons and zombies. Those guys were dicks. Fuck those guys.

The next prompt showed that there were benefits to the slaughter.

Congratulations! By slaying **250** undead, you have gained and advanced a new Title: **Undead Slayer III**.

+**15%** attack and defense bonus when fighting undead.

Kill a total of **500** undead to reach next level.

Your spirit has been colored by the deaths of so many undead. Undead will attack you more ferociously

Congratulations! By slaying **50** living dead, you have gained a new Title: **Living Dead I**

+3% attack and defense bonus when fighting living dead.

Kill a total of 100 living dead to reach next level.

The living dead will be made slightly uneasy in your presence

The prompts showed that as time passed, he was only getting deadlier. Richter spared a glance at Xuetrix, who was flapping his wings in irritation. The imp had warned him months ago to not let people know about his potential. That they might kill him just so he wouldn't get stronger, like strangling a baby in its crib. The chaos seed's eyes turned cold. If the demon tried anything, he'd soon regret letting Richter grow in power.

That particular story would unfold in a few minutes one way or another. For now, he turned his gaze inward again. He'd completed a Quest!

> Congratulations! You have completed the Quest: **Sakeru I**
>
> Three of Elora's four missing children were returned. The fourth, the Life pixie, has died. You did not slay the pixie, but neither did you decide to save her. This is within the bounds of your quest, if only barely, as Elora charged you with slaying her children if they were too corrupted to be reclaimed. It is your choice to tell the whole truth to Elora when you see her next or to keep your peace.
>
> **Reward for ending the threat of her fourth *sakeru* child:** 3,750 (base 3,000 x 1.25) Experience Points. +1,000 Relationship Points with every celestial pixie of the Quickening.
>
> **Reward:** You have removed the threat of abyssal energy corrupting the lands around your settlement
>
> **Bonus Reward:** See Elora to claim this Reward and unlock the next link in this quest chain

A scene replayed in Richter's head. A golden blur flying toward the Singh. He didn't know why she'd attacked the lich. He only knew that the pixie child had saved his life and the lives of everyone in the village. He doubted the tiny winged child had even known what she was doing. *Sakeru* pixies were almost feral. What he did know was what had happened when she'd bonded with Singh. She had distracted the undead lord for a crucial second. He also knew what he had done. Without even hesitating, he'd decapitated Singh and let the undead's head fall into the abyss with her attached. Once upon a time he wouldn't have done that, but he wasn't that bright-eyed child anymore. He was a leader and a Master of a Place of Power. Sometimes sacrifices had to be made.

The chaos seed nodded to himself. Elora was a powerful ally, and she deserved the truth about how her child had died. If... when, he firmly corrected himself, he made it back to the village, he would let her know. After that, he'd let the chips fall where they may. He didn't regret his decision, only the loss of her young life. A man had to face his mistakes head-on. Any other option poisoned the heart and led to weakness. He could weather a great deal, but not weakness.

Richter dismissed that prompt and finally saw the one he had been waiting for.

CHAPTER 7

DAY 151 – JUREN 2, 0 AOC

Congratulations! You have completed the Quest: **Unlock your Power III**

Against all odds, you have defeated the eldritch lich Singh. This undead user of foul magic has been a cancer eating away at the roots of the Forest of Nadria for centuries, if not millennia. An even greater threat than his corrupted magic was the hidden truth that the lich had been a worshiper of an Exile. These beings of nearly ultimate power seek the destruction of The Land itself. For destroying a cult of the Exile, you have gained Bonus Rewards!

You have also fulfilled the **Optional** conditions of the Quest, greatly increasing the quality of the rewards:

    1) Deliver the Final Death to the Lich

    2) Destroy the Source of the Lich's power (the monument to the Exile Rakshasha)

Know This! You have fulfilled a **Secret** condition of the Quest and so are entitled to an additional reward:

Secret Condition: Destroy the Mausoleum and at least half of the undead Army

Rewards:

    3) 187,500 Experience Points (base 50,000 x 200% x 1.25)

    4) Unlocking 1-2 of the Powers of your Place of Power

Bonus Rewards:

    5) 12,000 Fame Points. Total Fame Points: **43,582**

    6) 250,000 Experience Points (base 200,000 x 1.25)

*R*ichter was starting to see why he'd been able to power level so much. The quest had given him over four hundred thousand XP! That was enough to push him up several levels even without adding the experience from his high body count. The XP was great, but the Fame Points were equally impressive. Experience could be earned every day just by killing monsters after all, but Fame was extremely hard to come by.

When he'd played the land as a game, having a higher Fame could open up new quests and opportunities. He'd actually doubted the usefulness of it in the real world until he'd spoken with Randolphus. According to the Spy, the effect of Fame was easiest to see in large cities. It affected how others treated you.

Seeing as how Richter spent most of his time in what the people of Yves considered to be a monster-filled wilderness, the unseen hand of Fame was less obvious. The Spy had pointed out the fact that the willingness of several waves of colonists to move their families into such a dangerous area had most likely been due to him and his Fame. The same with his ability to co-opt the Troll mercenaries in the hidden goblin valley, or to convince the famously xenophobic sprites to consider him not only an ally, but family. Even the ease he had had in motivating his hundreds of subjects to bend the knee and call him their lord was most likely influenced by the nebulous stat. There was no way to actually prove any of that, of course, but Richter had definitely gotten more good breaks than even his high Luck could account for, so he didn't discount his chamberlain's words.

He was even more excited about the boost to Loyalty and Morale. Loyalty and Morale were both village dynamics and improving them could increase Productivity, Fighting Spirit and even Population Growth. They were both useful, but Loyalty was much harder to increase. The fact that both got a boost of five hundred points would be an incredible boon to his settlement's growth!

Richter tried to see the overall rank of the village dynamics but got a warning prompt.

You are not inside the boundaries of your Settlement. You cannot access your village's interface!

He had been pretty sure that would be the case, but he'd wanted to try anyway. The same way he'd tried using his *Dungeon Transport* spell a few times while forcing his way through some tight tunnels. It was Settlement magic and so would only work within the ten-mile domain of his Place of Power. The same went for *Summon Mist Worker*. He'd have loved to have been able to summon one of the faceless constructs to carry things for him. Hell, to carry him! It was a no-go though. It was an absolutely true statement that he was missing his Bag of Holding. Having to schlep things around by hand was seriously annoying. The only bright side to being away from his domain was that Futen could continue to pay the upkeep for the villager's defensive enchantment, *Confusing Mist,* even while Richter was gone.

Experience was great. Fame was great. Loyalty and Morale were great. While all of those bonuses were strong, there was only one that really changed the game though! After long months, he had finally unlocked a new Power! The next prompt showed him his options.

> Choosing a Mastery will give you a **+50%** increase to the spell power of that branch of magic. You will also have **+50%** resistance to spells of that Power.
>
> Unique to being a Master of a Place of Power, however, is your access to each Power's specialized ability. You have already chosen:
>
> *Mastery of Life Ability:* "**Bounty of Life**" +30% growth for the physical manifestation of your Place of Power
>
> *Mastery of Air Ability:* "**Fast Learner**" All skill levels are obtained 30% faster.
>
> You may choose from the remaining two magic ley lines that comprise your Place of Power to unlock your 3rd Power:
>
> *Mastery of Dark Ability:* "Hidden Treasures" +30% yield from treasure
>
> *Mastery of Water Ability:* "Tranquil Soul" -30% mana cost for spells

All of this was as Richter had expected it to be, but what came next on the prompt really made him stop and think.

> Know This! The difficulty of the third quest to unlock your power was extreme. That,
>
> coupled with your thorough completion of the quest, has given you a special opportunity.
>
> You may now unlock both of your remaining Masteries!
>
> If you choose to only unlock one, you will also be awarded 1,000 Settlement Points.
>
> You shall be given the opportunity to unlock your 4th Mastery when hidden conditions are
>
> met, if you choose this second option.
>
> What is your choice?

Thoughts swirled through Richter's mind. He couldn't believe what he was reading. There were obvious benefits to obtaining Masteries. It increased someone's spell power and spell resistance to a level that was equivalent to that of a *master* mage. Anyone else would have to reach skill level one hundred in a branch of magic, a feat that was literally impossible for most no matter how hard they tried.

Better than becoming a *master* ranked mage though, there were bonuses to unlocking a Place of Power. That was the difference between a *master* of a branch of magic and someone who was a Master of a Place of Power.

The Mastery bonuses he'd gained so far had changed everything. *Bounty of Life* had not only increased the Mist Village's crop yields, letting him feed his people, but also the birth rate of both his villagers and the animals they kept. Herbs grew faster as well, allowing Tabia to make the potions that kept his soldiers alive.

Fast Learner had affected him profoundly on a personal level. Coupled with his Limitless ability, he'd been able to skyrocket through skill ranks. His skills let him cast stronger spells, enchant more powerful weapons, and be more ferocious in battle. While abilities could be more powerful, skills were the lifeblood of The Land.

He had picked those two Mastery abilities first because of his settlement and his Limitless ability. The other two were also attractive though. If he'd had the Water Mastery bonus, *Tranquil Soul*, in his fight with the ichorpedes, it would have allowed him to sling spells for another several minutes. More healing, more attack spells, hell, he could even cast double shields. It would greatly increase his fighting potential.

The Dark Mastery perk, *Hidden Treasures*, was powerful as well. What made it even more attractive was the Barrow of the Chaos Serpent. He had his own personal Dungeon, something kingdoms would go to war over. Abrams and Whedon help him if a hostile power ever found out about it. In the meantime, The Dungeon could generate coins like it was his own personal mint. *Hidden Treasures* would greatly help the village's economy. They were self-sufficient for now, but if the Mist Village wasn't proactive about rejoining the rest of the world, it wouldn't be ready when the world came knocking.

Even more important than the money, the Dungeon could generate precious resources that Richter just wouldn't have access to otherwise. The chance that a bar of elementum -- or even a chaotic shard -- could drop was enough to make him grind the Dungeon nonstop. The Dark Mastery would increase his yield by 30%. It was basically increasing the specialized resource production of his village by nearly a third.

He'd originally thought that *Hidden Treasures* was a perk that would only really help himself. With his Dungeon though, it could mean stronger weapons and armor for his people, rare herbs to make wondrous potions, and other bonuses that could save the men and women he'd sworn to protect. Coupled with his new Mark of Blood and Chaos, he would drastically increase the precious loot he could gain.

Just as was always true, however, power came with a price. He hadn't known this when he'd awakened his first two Masteries, but each one he claimed had a measurable effect on his entire domain. The ambient mana surrounding his Place of Power would increase. That both attracted stronger monsters and allowed them to reach higher levels. According to Randy, the Dungeon refined that mana and absorbed it to a certain extent, but the increase with each Mastery was exponential. His first awakened Power had led to relatively weak creatures occupying his woods like bears, wolves and the like. They had been mostly level ten and below.

The second Power he'd unlocked had brought lairs. Instead of solitary spiders, he'd had to kill a massive nest of arachnids, ranging in size from an ox to a Humvee. And instead of a black bear, he'd fought a bear that could harden its fangs and claws to the density of tempered steel. The monsters' levels had also risen to hover between level fifteen and twenty-five. He grimaced, thinking about how difficult it had been to kill the creatures. The dreemar, flying predators that could stun you with their banshee-like shrieks, had devastated one of his patrols.

It might not sound like there was a large gap between levels ten and twenty, but monsters did not level like sapient races. Each level increased their attributes in a predefined way. While a monster's Luck might only increase by a point every five levels, a mountain troll's strength might increase by three points per level. Richter had personally illustrated just how important strength was in the past hour. Rather than being eaten by the ichorpede, he'd been able to rip parts of its body off with his bare hands.

It also wasn't just an increase in attributes that made monsters more dangerous as they leveled up. That same mountain troll might have had its health regen rise from ten points per minute to thirty points. Its claws might harden enough that it could leave furrows in stone rather than just wood. It might even get smarter or gain new abilities. Increasing the number of unlocked Powers from two to four wouldn't amplify the danger his people faced from monsters by 100%; it could very well be closer to five times as dangerous. Maybe even ten times. That wasn't something he could ignore just to get stronger.

There was also the point that by unlocking only one Power, he would also get Settlement Points. Of all the various points he'd accumulated thus far, they were the most rare. Richter didn't understand the magic behind it at all, but it let him change the very geography of his village. He could flatten a hill, instantly construct a building or even add new resources to his land. This was only the second way he'd found to gain Settlement Points. The other was capturing another Master's Hearth Crystal, a nearly impossible task. Hisako had said there was a third way he might earn them in the future, but he had no idea how. All she had said was that he needed to obtain his initial Masteries.

Which raised yet another factor to consider. His battle with Nien, the Soul Eater, had taught him that unlocking all of the facets of his Place of Power was only the first step on his path to Mastery. There were higher levels to unlock after the first four. There might be more bonus abilities after he reached level two. There might also be new settlement options.

There was also the selfish argument that turned into a questionably selfless one, as all selfish arguments were wont to do. These two Masteries would help him survive for the next week. If he could outlast the curse, there was a chance he might make it back to the village even if he died first. Without being arrogant, he knew for a fact that if he didn't make it back, the entire village would suffer. He was not only Lord Mist, he was a Specialist Enchanter. The weapons and armor he made were powerful. He was also an experienced war leader and was the linchpin in the Mist Village's alliance with the wood sprites. If he rolled the dice by unlocking only one Mastery, he might die and be damned for all eternity. That would not be the best.

Finally, there was the practical argument to unlocking all his Masteries. Richter looked around at the tunnel he was in. It was lit only by balls of *Far Light* that burned with the intensity of a candle. It was about as dismal and pitiful a scene as there could be, trapped and lost far underground. He had escaped the ichorpede lair, true, but he could have died twenty times over in his desperate flight through the dark. The truth was, there was a very real chance that he wouldn't last a week. That Singh's curse would take hold and everything that he was would just cease to be.

Even if he didn't get back though, he had an Heir. If he could no longer be Master of his Place of Power, Sion would assume the mantle.

Though the battle with the lich lord had been insanely dangerous, there was a true war looming on the horizon. Bugbears, dark elves, goblins and worse were massing in the Forest of Nadria. So far, they hadn't been able to overcome the enchantments of his village, but Richter had learned that nothing was absolute. Sometime, somehow, they would find a way through the *Confusing Mists*. The kindir had already shown that a simple salve could penetrate the village's defenses. Richter just thanked his lucky stars that he'd secured the loyalty of Verget Kunig before they shared that secret with his enemies.

All that had done was buy them time though. Sooner or later, enemies would be coming to his doorstep. Factoring that in, increasing the power of the monsters around his village could be both a curse and a blessing. His people would have to fight the monsters back, but they also had home court advantage. Any enemies coming to attack wouldn't be so lucky. The monsters could serve as a "natural" barrier.

And if he did die, Sion was his Heir. At least the sprite would have more Masteries at his disposal. Hisako would guide her son and, between the two of them, they might be able to beat back the hordes that were coming. Thinking about thousands of enemy troops attacking his people brought a heaviness to Richter's heart. The chaos seed let out a sigh. There were so many factors to consider.

Someone else might have been overwhelmed, frozen into immobility. Richter had learned long ago, however, that a common thread could often be found in seemingly different arguments. For all the facets he'd just come up with to consider, it came down to a basic question.

Should he protect his people at the cost of limiting both their exposure to danger and their potential for growth, like a father would a child? Or should he let them enter a new phase of their lives, even though it would bring danger and pain? If he fully awakened his Place of Power, it would bring them horror, but it could also unlock their potential.

Like so many times in the past, it came down to a choice between fear or hope. To Richter, that was no choice at all. Focusing on the prompt, he made his decision. At long last, the Master of the Mist Village fully claimed his power. After millennia of somnolence, the Great Seal was awoken once again.

CHAPTER 8

DAY 151 – JUREN 2, 0 AOC

ack in the Mist Village...

Sion, Hisako, Randolphus and several others sat at a wooden table. The room branched off from the Great Seal. Dawn had broken over the forest a few hours before and the village was waking. Many of the villagers were in a jubilant mood. Once again, their modest village had triumphed over their enemies. There was a measurable boost to their Morale and Loyalty, but they were also happy that the casualties had not been as extensive as the battle for the Bloodstone.

There had been many wounded, but bringing them back through the portal had let Sumiko and her healers save lives. The families of those that had fallen grieved, but the overall mood of the village was one of relief and joy. That was not a sentiment shared by the men and women sitting around the table. One and all, they wondered if the victory had come at too high a price.

"We are fairly certain that he still lives," Hisako stated, looking around the table. "The fool made Sion his Heir before deciding to sacrifice himself. That means my son should know if he dies. At least, if he dies the final death."

Despite her words, the Hearth Mother could not help but look at her son and feel relief. If Richter had not tricked his Companion into using the Bracelet of Home's Heart, then her son could have been trapped and lost in the dark of the earth. Her irritation was just a thin cover for the heartache that was warring with the relief in her heart. Even though he was a gyoti, she had great affection for Richter.

Sion was not nearly as composed. He stared off into the distance. Once again, he had lived at the expense of a brother paying the price. He absently stroked Alma's dusky scales as he replayed the moment Richter had been swallowed by the dark. In his mind, he saw it over and over again, trapped in a private hell.

The dragonling lay in a basket of piled cloth. She still hadn't regained consciousness. Whatever Singh had done to her mind had been severe. As he couldn't do anything to reverse the damage, he just kept stroking her scales, hoping she got some comfort from it. All the while, he made a solemn vow that he would save the dragonling even though he had failed her master.

Quiet reigned around the table after Hisako stopped speaking. Each of their minds were occupied with thoughts of Lord Mist. A being who had come from nowhere only half a year before, but who had changed the world. Each of them held memories of the strange man, all of them contradictions in terms. Richter was both savior and devil, warm and callous, murderer and just lord. They may have varied in their affections for Richter, but they all wanted him back for their own reasons. Still, this council had not been called to commiserate. It had been called to decide on what to do next.

Seeing that Sion was not in a place to lead the meeting, Randolphus and Hisako stepped up. They spoke about the death toll, the damage to the Dungeon, the food stores, and the threat of the bugbears' alliance. A threat they could no longer ignore. They had just started to discuss troop allocations in their various territories when a ripple of Power radiated out from the first floor of the Catacombs.

It spread throughout the entire ten-mile radius of the village's domain. It looked like an inch-thin wall of water, but it had no actual substance. Everyone in the village was both shocked and frightened.

The creatures within the village's domain stopped whatever they were doing and turned toward the Great Seal, even if they were miles away. For a moment, every beast and monster quivered in fright, fearing at an instinctual level the power that had just been released.

Around the table, the village council looked at each other in concern and confusion. All except Hisako and Randolphus, who knew full well what it meant. They made eye contact, then rushed to the Great Seal. Before they made it down the hall, shouts of alarm echoed all around them.

As they rushed to the seal, three sounds reverberated throughout the Mist Village. The first was the *whoosh* of gale-force winds. The next was the sound of birds chirping, wolves howling and lions roaring all at once. The bellow of every creature in existence, calling out in a cacophony that was somehow in key and in concert. The third sound was the loud gush of rushing waters, like an ocean being emptied into a moon-sized vase. After that, there was a complete absence of sound, which seemed all the more profound in contrast.

Through this all, the eyes of the village council were locked onto the Great Seal and the powers that had manifested above it.

Above the spiral of Air was a miniature hurricane. It towered twelve feet into the air. Lightning crackled across the swirling storm clouds.

On top of the Life spiral was a ten-foot arched doorway made of pure, glowing gold. On the other side was a tree sculpted of the same bright metal, perfect in every way.

The blue tiles of Water had disappeared. In their place was a whirlpool, diving deep into the floor. Looking down, it could be seen to descend at least a dozen feet into the ground. White froth appeared and disappeared as the vortex spun dangerously.

The final spiral of Dark magic was a horrifying hole of nothing. No light escaped that perfect blackness. Everyone that looked at it felt as if they were being pulled in.

It was the same transformation that had appeared during Alma's summoning, the only time that Richter had drawn deeply on the raw energy of his Place of Power. This time, however, there was a fundamental difference. The Powers had manifested before, but each power had been mindless. Now, they were filled with awareness and purpose.

Golden birds nested in the metal Life tree. Fish jumped in the waters of the maelstrom, and eagles made of pure lightning surfed the winds of the hurricane. In the black void of Dark, tentacled things writhed beneath the ebon surface. No one could get closer than twenty yards to the seal. The power each awakened ley line exuded created a physical pressure. Only Hisako would have had the power to go closer. Thankfully, she had the wisdom not to try.

Each of the four manifestations surged in power. Each brought its own sound. Once all four were done raging, they sank or ascended back to the level of the floor. Seconds later, all anyone could see was activated tile again. Still, this was not the end. The four distinct spirals unraveled then intertwined with one another. This process continued until four new shapes were made, each a combination of two spirals: wind and darkness, darkness and water, water and life, life and wind.

The previously sorrowful expression on Hisako's face faded. With absolute certainty, she exclaimed, "He is alive! What's more, he has fully awakened his Place of Power!" Her heart cheered. Smiles bloomed on the faces of everyone present at her words.

Even Sion was able to break out of his melancholic mood. The newly changed Great Seal was finally coming to rest. The intense manifestations had faded away, and each of the new dual symbols glowed with a pulsing light. A cascade of prompts appeared in the sprite's vision, showing the new spells and powers available to the Mist Village. As Heir, he was able to read the interface, even though he could not cast them himself. A smile crossed his face. Get back soon, you bastard, because I'm going to kick your ass.

Of all the responses to the ascension of the village's Powers, the most profound took place in another room entirely. Alma's comatose form had been left lying on a pile of soft cloth. The soldier watching her had almost fallen in shock at what he saw.

The moment the four new symbols of the Great Seal had locked into place, Alma's eyes snapped open. Flashes of gold, blue, yellow and black energy shot through her eyes and electricity coursed through her body. She jumped from the basket, unfurling her wings at the same time. As she soared toward the Great Seal, the jubilant shouts of the others died down.

Every eye was locked on the glowing dragonling and her growing body. Her lengthening wings spread out and she soared to the center of the Great Seal. All four symbols pulsed and ribbons of energy flowed into Alma's draconic form. Beams of the same hue shot from her mouth and eyes. The lines between her scales were lit up as well. In front of their very eyes, she grew and became something... more.

With a deeper roar than she had ever managed before, she threw back her draconian head and screamed, "Master!"

CHAPTER 9

DAY 151 – JUREN 2, 0 AOC

*R*ichter did not know about any of the changes happening in the village. If he'd known about Alma, he definitely wouldn't have been able to keep reading the prompts so calmly. Even not knowing, his heart started beating faster as he read his next prompts. He now knew how Hisako obtained her most powerful spells! His attention was captured by the cascade of notifications that had appeared.

Congratulations! You have unlocked all four Powers of your Place of Power! For unlocking the potential of your Great Seal, you shall be given four new spells. Each of these spells is unique to your Place of Power, and may only be cast once per year.

Pure Waters				
Imbue a flask of liquid with the powers of Life and Water. This spell will make one dose of a powerful healing potion. It will remove all debuffs, curses, and injuries. Also restores all lost Health, Mana and Stamina. After summoning, this potion will disappear after one day. If not imbibed before then, the magic will be lost. It will be ineffective against Tier 3 and higher ailments.				
Cost	Duration	Range	Cast Time	Cooldown
1000 mana	Instant	Touch	5 minutes	1 year

It was a Restore All spell. He couldn't believe it. In a game that might not have been too impressive, but in real life Richter knew perfectly well how expensive and how valuable such potions could be. To make a single batch of a basic healing potion that could restore a few hundred points of health would normally take a Professional Alchemist several days. Even then, there was a high rate of failure, roughly 50% depending on the specifics of the formula. And that was in a best-case scenario, independent of human error. If the alchemist failed to perfectly measure ingredients, or lost their concentration at any point in the days-long process, that 50% chance could seriously slip. If that was the case, the Alchemist would have to start again. They might even lose all the valuable materials they had been working with. Alchemy was a difficult and demanding trade.

To be given a potion that could heal nearly any wound instantly was a powerful tool. It was a shame that he could only cast the spell once a year. He couldn't even stock up on the potions. The magic would only last one day, once cast. The cast time was also huge compared to other spells. Not nearly as large as the mana cost though. He would have to use the village's mana pool to manage it. Just another check and balance. Still, he was happy to have the option.

The next spell was a combination of Life and Air magic. If the last spell had made his jaw drop, this one took his breath away.

Breath of Life				
Breathe into the mouth of a being that has died in the last hour. The wind from your body will carry the power of Air and Life. At a cost of one year of your own life, you may rekindle the life of a dead being. They will be reborn in a weakened state.				
Cost	Duration	Range	Cast Time	Cooldown
1000 mana	Instant	1 foot	30 seconds	1 year
1 year of life				

The second spell was even more impressive than the first! Resurrection was possible in The Land, but only with the power of a master of Life magic. It was also one of the only spells he knew about that required a spell component, a root from the Hearth Tree itself.

Richter's Mastery allowed him to mimic the strengths of a *master* mage, at least in the four Basic Elements that comprised his Place of Power, but he couldn't cast spells of their level. He was limited by his own skill level. That meant spells of level twenty-two and above were beyond his capabilities to cast.

The fact that Hisako and Sumiko were true Life *masters* had saved many lives. According to the powerful sprite women, resurrection magic required a skill level of one hundred or higher. It also required a powerful talisman of Life energy that was consumed during the casting. *Breath of Life* would let him save one life, and he could cast it at his current skill level. Again, the spell cost was huge. The extra component being a year of his own life was also not something he was excited about. Still, he would happily make that trade to save Sion, Terrod or Cau...

He caught himself before his mind could complete that thought. It took several seconds to control his thudding heart, but he finally calmed down. Even though his thoughts had slipped, the truth was he could have saved Caulder if he'd had this spell only one day before. Looking at it that way, a single year was a small price to pay. He just wished he could have paid it yesterday.

Richter shook off his melancholy once again. Dwelling on things that couldn't be changed was emotional masturbation. It might scratch the itch at first, but you just ended up raw. Instead, he focused on the third spell.

Dark Wave				
The Power of Dark and Water combine in a powerful attack. 7 waves of pressurized water from the depths of the ocean shoot forth in a cone from your hand. Will cause 125-400 Damage per wave. Chance to cause *Blind*, *Freeze* and/or *Bleeding* status				
Cost	Duration	Range	Cast Time	Cooldown
1000 mana	7 seconds	40 yards	10 seconds	1 year

The chaos seed blew out an astonished breath. It was a killer! Seven waves of pure power. With this, he could destroy an army with a literal wave of his hand. He thought about the times when the spell could have come in handy. Destroying a particular lair of dickipedes came to mind. It certainly would have felt good to wipe them out. There was a time when he might have balked at the sheer damage this spell would deliver. When he would have been bothered by causing such wanton destruction to other living beings. All he felt now was excitement.

The spell wasn't all-powerful, of course. The cost and cast time were both high. Like his other unique spells, he could only use it once a year. Basically, it was a silver bullet and there were no quick reloads. In the times to come, he resolved to put it to good use. Richter read the details of the final spell.

Gloom Portal				
This spell binds the translocation of Air with the sucking eternity of Dark to assault a single point of space. *Gloom Portal* creates a microscopic black hole. The singularity does not last long, but it is sufficient to pull an enemy through this pinprick in space. Damage 1000-2500. There is a possibility that the enemy may be completely consumed.				
Cost	Duration	Range	Cast Time	Cooldown
1000 mana	25 seconds	50 yards	9 seconds	1 year

All four of the spells were massively powerful. One was a resurrect, another a complete heal, the third an AoE damager and the fourth an assassination spell. They weren't the same as Hisako's unique spells, but she'd told him each Place of Power had its own particular character. He'd seen her make a wall that could stop an entire army. Her magic had also been able to bind the most powerful creature he'd seen since coming to The Land. Richter realized that he'd seriously underestimated the power of Mastery. As long as a Master was willing to pay the price, they were a walking nuclear weapon.

Richter scanned the rest of the village upgrade prompts, hoping for an increase of the village's mana pool or maybe a new defensive Settlement spell. Sadly, neither of those had popped up. All he could think was that for either one to happen he'd have to actually upgrade his Settlement. That would require him conquering the first three floors of the Catacombs. Seeing as how one of them was populated with over a hundred thousand kobolds living in a warren of deadly traps... he had no idea how he was going to pull that off. An irritated and high-pitched voice interrupted his thoughts.

"Human! I am tired of waiting. I am here to collect my Favor!"

"I'm not done yet, you flying rat," Richter snapped back. "If you wanted more attention, maybe you shouldn't have left me for dead in a *fucking monster lair*!" He was shouting at the end with his fist clenched.

A red light glowed behind the imp's eye, evidence of the demon's ire. When he looked at the disrespectful human, however, he saw something that he hadn't expected. A literal light was swirling in Richter's eyes as well. Each pupil had the faintest speck of energy in its depths. The flash of color was there and gone so fast that it could have been taken for a trick of the light. It would have been missed by almost anyone else, but the demon was old, far older than Richter could possibly conceive. He knew what he had seen.

The threatening words Xuetrix had been about to spit out dried on his forked tongue. How, in the name of the Sacred Demons, had this paltry human started to form a Power Core? He'd only been in The Land for a few months! Xuetrix still didn't actually think that Richter posed any real danger, but he didn't understand what was happening. That made him uneasy.

The imp didn't let any of that show on his face of course, so he just harrumphed and said, "Hurry up, then. Unless you want to break your contract with me and suffer the consequences."

Richter continued to glare at him, completely unaware of the demon's thoughts. Nonetheless, Xuetrix's mention of the Favor reigned in the chaos seed's anger. He'd done a lot of questionable things since coming to The Land. He could admit that he'd earned his title of gyoti at least a couple times in the past. The one thing he hadn't done, that he hadn't even heard of anyone doing, was break an Oath, Vow or Favor. The penalties started at losing reputation with almost every sapient being and ramped up from there. It wasn't something he was willing to risk willie nillie. Before he made that kind of decision, he wanted all the information he could get. At the very least, that meant understanding the perks he'd gotten from the battle.

The next prompt banished at least some of his anger.

*Congratulations! Your familiar has reached levels **44, 45, 46** and **47**!*

His baby was growing up! Richter was surprised that Alma had gained so much experience. He wondered if she'd used *Brain Drain* on a high-level monster when he wasn't looking. Playing back his combat log though, he saw that almost all of the experience points came from destroying the statue of the Exile. It said that she had destroyed the "Personification of the Enemy," the Statue of Liberty-sized monument that had stood behind the Mausoleum.

Her level ups meant she had gained 4.2 new Ability Points. The remainder was due to her eating the celestial fruit of the Quickening. Every point would make her that much more deadly, increasing her psychic abilities. None of that was as impressive as the next single line of text though.

Your familiar has evolved.

That was it. There wasn't any other information. It was like a cruel joke, giving so little information about a loved one. Richter frantically tried to access the icon of his soul familiar, but was punished with a red prompt of warning.

You are too far from your familiar to access her current information.

He could have screamed in frustration. His Alma, his love, the other part of his soul had *evolved* and he wasn't able to know anything about it? Richter really, really wanted to hurt something. He'd been trying to keep his frustration and anger to a low simmer, but he was reaching his breaking point. The tunnel he was in now was big enough that he didn't feel trapped, but his claustrophobia was still alive and well, gnawing at the walls of his psyche. The only thing working for him was not thinking about it. When his anger flared though, his mind wandered and the fear could come creeping in.

Richter slammed his mind shut, using every technique he'd learned from Alma. He fortified his mind's defenses and felt the panic and nervous feeling ebb. They weren't completely gone, but he could pretend they weren't there. To focus his mind somewhere else, he read the last notification from the lich battle.

It was his leveling sheet. He'd gained five whole levels from the battle. His ability points had been distributed, but he still had Talent Points, Chaos Points and skill percentage points to allocate. The skill points went into Enchanting, his highest-level skill. Putting them in a lower level skill would have been a waste. Even with his Limitless and Fast Learner abilities, it could take more than a week to advance a single percentage point once they advanced high enough. He was also starting to find out that just practicing a skill wasn't by itself enough to earn him any progression at higher levels. You had to push yourself and try new things. That wasn't as easy as it sounded. For a skill like Smithing, for instance, Krom needed to not only make higher quality arms and armor, he might need to work with higher level Schematics or use higher level metals. Neither of those things were cheap or easily accessible even if you had the coin. 125% of skills progression advanced him an entire skill level and saved probably a year's worth of hard work.

*Congratulations! You have reached skill level 50 in **Enchanting**. All enchantments are now +50% more effective, and you have an increased chance of enchantments taking hold.*

It was his first skill to reach level fifty! He wouldn't advance in rank and become an *adept* until he reached level seventy, but it was definitely a milestone. He also earned himself some more sweet experience.

*You have received 10,000 bonus experience for reaching level 50 in the skill: **Enchanting***

Richter looked at the prompt with slightly mixed feelings. It was the first time in a long time that he didn't get the 25% XP bonus from drinking a Potion of Clarity. It was a reminder of just how alone and underequipped he was. The ten thousand was still helpful though. It should make a sizeable dent in however much XP he needed to level up again. That thought made him realize he hadn't actually checked what his next experience threshold was since the battle. If the overall pattern continued, he should need about two hundred thousand points. The chaos seed looked at the experience bar and received yet another shock. It seemed like everything had changed!

2,893,011/3,845,000 XP to Level 46

He needed nearly a million experience to level up again! It had only taken him a thousand points to level up the first time. That was 0.1% of what he needed now. Richter checked quickly. Even going from level forty-four to forty-five had only taken two hundred and five thousand points. The level before that had only needed one hundred and ninety-five. Why the hell had the overall amount quintupled? How was anyone even supposed to earn that?

Alma's *Brain Drain* had power leveled him a great deal in the past. It gave a percentage of a slain creature's total accumulated XP. This meant that if she kept absorbing low level monsters, the XP gained would be only a drop in the ever-deepening bucket of what they both needed. Of course, the problem with higher level creatures was that they were dangerous. *Brain Drain* would still let him level faster than anyone else he'd heard of, but higher-level monsters weren't only harder to find, she took a huge risk every time she used the ability. It rendered her helpless. Richter just didn't think he could rely on her to reach these new experience milestones. He was sure he didn't want her risking her life against high level monsters.

So how the hell was he supposed to get a million XP? Did everyone that reached level forty-five go through this? Was this another of The Land's goddamned checks and balances? How the hell was this balanced? Richter tried to keep his nostrils from flaring, but they definitely got bigger. What the hell!

He had wondered why Randolphus was only forty-seven despite being over one hundred years old. This huge leap in required experience would definitely explain it. While that was interesting and all though, it didn't fix the problem that the points he'd just gained might be the last ones he got for a while.

Richter took some deeps breaths and forced himself to be calm. This was a problem. It was a serious problem. He needed the points that came from leveling and not just the Attribute Points. This million-point barrier seemed liked it basically promised him that he was stuck at his current level. That everything he had was all he was going to get. This was a serious problem, but... he exhaled slowly, every problem could be overcome. It was time to work the problem.

He had met people with levels higher than forty-five. If they could advance, then he could too. Now, the most common way to gain levels was to battle. If you fought creatures that were lower level than you though, the XP you gained was heavily penalized. If there was too great a gap, you would get no XP at all. You could also gain experience from increasing your skills. But most people in The Land only had a few skills they developed. Definitely less than ten in most cases, and it would be rare for more than one to reach *apprentice* rank. There was no way the couple-thousand XP they got through that method could cross this million-point canyon. It certainly wouldn't cover it twice to get to the level after that, or three times to reach the level after that. So how the hell did people keep progressing?

Richter racked his mind, not coming up with anything. That was until he remembered the prompt he'd auto-minimized right before assigning his Strength points. It was understandable that he'd forgotten about it, seeing as how he'd had a giant bug trying to eat his face. Because he'd dismissed it, it had gone to the bottom of the stack. He'd gained more alerts since being in the tunnel system, so he hadn't read it yet. It was the work of a moment though to retrieve it now.

Know This! You have reached a Threshold! The points from reaching level 45 will be locked until an Evolution branch is determined.

Further leveling blocked until an Evolution branch is determined.

There had been more to the message, but as he'd been fighting for his life, he hadn't had a chance to read it. Now that he did, his shock went from "whoa" to "god damn!"

Know This! Every creature is born with a finite potential. This is mirrored by the Threshold, a severe plateau of their leveling speed. This occurs because lower-tiered beings are constrained by the small amount of energy they can contain. After this point, while leveling is not impossible, it is substantially more difficult. Your race, human, has a Threshold of forty-five, one of the lowest among mortal sapient races.

That answered a couple questions. The XP jump was because of this thing called the "Threshold." It was indeed one of The Land's checks and balances, keeping certain races from climbing past certain levels. It also meant humans hit that point faster. Seemed like a fair helping of BS so far as he could see. Humans already got less Attribute Points per level compared to other races. Now they couldn't even level as high? Where the hell was his balance? Why was it all checks? And what did the prompt mean by "lower-tiered?"

The next prompt both answered his last question and showed that "threshold" was not the same thing as "stopping point." Not even close.

Your situation is different than most mortals, however. While most believe the Threshold the end of their journey, the truth is far more complex. It should be understood that every level adds power to an individual. The tangible effects of adding Attribute Points and other bonuses are only side effects of that growing power. Each level adds to your cohesive being. You are not merely a collection of body, mind and soul. You are also intent, consciousness and many other aspects. Increasing your level allows these various elements to coalesce into a Power Core. This powerful yet intangible focus provides the opportunity to ascend past your Threshold to a higher tier of existence.

Know This! Few ever reach their Threshold. Of those who do, even less form a Core strong enough to ascend past this hidden goal, but you have done so. Your potential will not be limited! Instead, it now has the possibility of being unlocked. For the few who actualize their Core, even fewer can use it for its true purpose: Ascendance!

At this point, Richter blinked and then reread everything carefully. It was rare for a notification to give this much information. It was basically hidden Lore. Once he was sure he'd internalized the information he had gotten so far, he moved on.

To evolve, one must not only form a Core, but also possess the Potential to achieve a higher form. Potential can be created by pursuing any number of paths, but most beings lack a true avenue upon reaching their Threshold. Learn this truth of The Land and all reality: it is the application of Power, not Power itself, which matters. Pity those who increased their level without consideration for their Potential!

In a greater surprise than Richter had experienced yet, he heard a voice speak the final words of the prompt. It was androgynous, but filled with intent. Someone, something, was speaking *to* him through the notification.

You are most fortunate, Richter from Earth, as your ability Limitless seems to have been prophetic. While many reaching their Threshold lack even one path of Potential, you have earned yourself many. Now you must choose whether to evolve or continue on as you are. Be warned, the consequences of failing your Ascension can be dire.
Watch well, human, and choose your path.

CHAPTER 10

DAY 151 – JUREN 2, 0 AOC

*T*he prompt darkened in front of Richter's vision, going from translucent to pitch black in an instant. That darkness spread out to every corner of his vision. Before he could even curse or panic, he was falling. He could feel the adrenaline inject into his heart, like a spike of electricity. His heart rate leaped to two hundred beats a minute, and he flailed his arms and legs. A second later though, he realized something strange.

Even though he heard air whistling in his ears, he felt like he was being pulled upward, rather than falling downward. As neither he nor anyone else he'd ever heard of had experienced anything like this, he was understandably confused. What it really felt like was that he was falling *up*. Then he realized something even more strange; he didn't have a body. For a second, he wondered how he'd possibly been flailing around without arms and legs, but that just seemed to be another mystery.

Richter tried to move again, hoping he was just blind and had lost his ability to sense his body. It occurred to him that you were really screwed when being senseless was the better option, but he knew that wasn't the case. Somehow, the only thing he seemed to consist of right now was his consciousness. Of course, that raised other questions.

Like how could his "ears" hear the wind whistling past? Or how did he "feel" like he was falling? A part of him wondered at the metaphysics of what was happening. A larger part of him was screaming at that first part, "We're falling! We're falling! Bitch! Is you crazy? We're *falling*!" Even after countless battles, this feeling of being nothing and something at the same time was threatening his sanity. He felt panic bloom, and it was only through his strong will that he kept it at bay.

There is nothing I can do, he thought to himself. That was the truth. He couldn't even shout in frustration. Long ago, he'd learned that there were times in life that you had no control. This was one of those times. While it was easy to panic, from another point of view it was the one time in life that you didn't need to feel fear. Whatever would come, would come. Instead of panicking, he tried to pay attention to what he could hear. For a long moment, there was only blackness, the sound of whistling wind and the perception of movement. That might change though. If it did, he'd be ready.

Time passed and the darkness remained. Since he seemed to have no control, he just let the force propel him ever upward. It was hard to gauge time. He didn't even feel bored. He could have been falling for seconds or hours or longer. At some point, however, he passed through a palpable layer of darkness. It felt like slowly moving through a waterfall of paint. Like a thin skin of tangible nothing. The sensation of movement stopped right after, and he felt firm ground under his feet. That was when he realized his body was back.

With snapping sounds, torches lit up in a circle around him. They were only ten feet away, and he stood in the center of the firelight. Looking down, he saw that he was wearing a simple black tunic with gold thread piping tracing along its edges. It was a far sight nicer than the ruined rags he'd been wearing only a few minutes before. What was more interesting was that his body looked completely different. Actually, not exactly different, but forgotten. This was the physique he'd had when he'd first come to The Land. Not the muscled hulk he'd become, but a man with brown skin, a slight build and average height.

Shaking his head at the inanity of his personal appearance, he looked around. Unfortunately, he couldn't see anything past the light of the flickering torches. Richter was about to leave the cordon of fire-light when he heard footsteps. They rang like hobnailed boots on stone. The steps got closer. Richter readied himself for whatever might come.

He even tried to access his status page to make sure he still had his high attributes despite his current physical appearance. A moment later, his brow wrinkled in confusion. It wouldn't come up. Hearing those steps get closer, his features smoothed in controlled panic. The stride had a certain cadence that he'd heard before. A particular gait that come to trigger a Pavlovian fear response, because it always preceded hours of agonizing pain. It had been in a strange, timeless dimension. He'd fallen into darkness then too.

Suddenly, he had a horrible suspicion about just who was walking toward the firelight. Seconds later, an ebony-skinned giant wearing a pitch-black suit straight off the Versace rack walked into the light. Richter fell back into an involuntary defensive stance. His lips pulled back in a snarl. Horrible thoughts shot through his head while he looked upon the face of the face of this old torturer.

An irritated grimace crossed Nexus's face, "I swear to god! You are one dick pimple away from hillbilly heaven! What could you *possibly* want?"

CHAPTER 11

DAY 151 – JUREN 2, 0 AOC

*R*ichter stared at the Auditor, the creature that was in charge of Trials in the Mist Village. The giant was responsible for some of his greatest suffering. The chaos seed wasn't sure what to do. He'd thought about Nexus more than a dozen times and had played out seeing him again a dozen more. Pretty much every time he thought about their next meeting, he fantasized about beating the ever-luvin' shit out of the black-and-gold giant. Every time though, he'd let that go. He'd learned his lesson the last time. Even with his higher level and boosted attributes, he wouldn't stand a chance. There were some people you just did not fuck with, at least not on their own turf. For now, Nexus was one of those guys.

Richter was also strong enough to admit his faults. At least, given enough time he was. Nexus had tortured him, but the truth was, if Richter had said the right words last time, his Trial wouldn't have been nearly so traumatic. There was a ritual to becoming a Professional. You basically had to pronounce what your Profession should be, like "I am Alchemist," or "I am Enchanter." Then you would be tested by the Auditor. As simple as that was, Richter hadn't done that. He hadn't known that he had to, but he also hadn't taken the time ask before his Trial. Being ignorant was never a defense that mattered.

To compound his bad decisions, he'd attacked the Auditor. Yup. He'd been sucked into another dimension and had decided to attack the demigod that ran it. He felt very comfortable saying that Nexus was a sadistic asshole, but he'd been the one that had attacked a sadist. That was what had led to the weeks and months of torture.

If Richter was a more zen person, he might have let the experience go completely. Truth was, zen was not his modus operandi. If he'd had a chance of taking Nexus down, he might have taken it. He wasn't a total idiot though, and he'd learned more lessons than that a lack of knowledge could make life insanely painful. He'd learned to pick his battles. He'd learned to wait.

That wasn't to say that he was calm. The agony of his long imprisonment had imprinted itself on Richter so deeply that he couldn't stop his heart from racing upon seeing the black-and-gold giant. Nexus's form could change based on his whim. The giant was currently about twelve feet tall. The more salient point was that he was looking at the chaos seed with an extremely irritated expression. As much as Richter wanted to hurt the bastard, he swallowed his pride and said, "I am Enchanter."

Nexus looked at him. Richter looked back. Nexus kept looking at him. Richter kept looking back. Nexus cocked his head forward, widened his eyes, and stared at him. Richter started feeling like he might have made a mistake... again. He was preparing to defend himself when the Auditor threw both hands in the air and complained, "Argh! I *know* you're an Enchanter, numb-nuts. I'm completely aware. Those are the words for your Trial! *You* are here..."

Nexus stopped talking and really stared at Richter, as if he were searching for some hidden meaning. When he spoke again it was with surprise in his voice, which quickly turned back into derision. "... for the Rite of Ascension. Something that I absolutely cannot believe you are qualified to undertake."

"If I weren't qualified, why would I be here?" Richter shot back.

Nexus shook his head like Richter had just tripped getting off the short bus. "You must have reached your Threshold. Everyone that does is brought to see their Auditor. Most are wise enough to immediately leave if they have not thoroughly prepared. You don't belong here."

"You're telling me I shouldn't try to ascend?"

"No," Nexus told him, and for once, the giant sounded earnest. He gently placed a hand on Richter's shoulder. "I'm telling you," he squeezed ever so slightly, "that you're the worst. No one likes you," he breathed deeply through his nose, "and you stink."

Nexus kept massaging the now-seething chaos seed's shoulder, "So are you here about your ascension or not?"

"You're damn right I am," Richter growled.

"Great," Nexus replied with a self-satisfied smile. "That's one," he said holding up his middle finger.

Richter's heart dropped at seeing the Auditor's smug face. He felt like he'd just fallen for something here. If there was one lesson he'd learned, it was that words had power. He'd just agreed to something and Nexus seemed pleased about it. That meant there was something Richter didn't know.

"What aren't you telling me? What happens to me if I don't pass this Rite of Ascension?" he snapped, grabbing Nexus's arm.

Somehow, the darkness surrounding them grew even blacker. The air grew heavy and Nexus's body seemed to swell. His voice became more formal. The speech pattern was older, more imperious. "Do not put your hands upon me, mortal! You are no one to demand anything from me! I curse the day you and your ridiculous villagers came into my domain!"

Richter dropped his hand and took a step back. The vehemence in Nexus's voice was thick and visceral. The giant was seriously pissed! For the first time, Richter wondered if all this animosity might not be entirely about him. Even though he'd fought Nexus, he'd never actually hurt the Auditor. In fact, the whole time he'd been tortured, Nexus had kept a pretty pleasant demeanor. If Richter wasn't the cause though, what could possibly have made the Auditor so furious?

Not knowing how to respond, Richter just stared back at him. Nexus's expression grew even uglier. If he was angry before, now he was furious. Like, a second shy of making tummy pancakes when the doorbell rang kind of furious. The enraged Auditor screamed into Richter's face, "I swear to god, shit break, I will *beat* that doofy look off your face! If you came here to waste my time, I'll do to you what I'm going to do to that mus-"

Whatever Nexus had been about to say was interrupted by the loudest crack of thunder Richter had ever heard. It sounded like two mountains being slammed together and then shaken like dice in an unbelievably massive hand. Richter winced at the cacophony, but he also noticed that Nexus did something completely unexpected. The giant flinched. There was no mistaking the fear that was on the Auditor's face when he looked up. Whatever had caused the thunder was something he was afraid to anger. What the hell could scare a being with near-infinite power in his own dimension?

Richter still had no idea what was going on, but it appeared as if someone was making sure Nexus couldn't just abuse him this time. Looked like that old adage must be true: everyone had a boss. Ironically, the Auditor seemed to be under review. The chaos seed's mind tried to conjure up what Nexus could have done. He'd tortured Richter for months and that hadn't raised any alarm bells. What could possibly have happened to put the giant on a short leash?

Richter just shook his head. There was so much going on that he didn't understand. All he could do was keep his guard up and hope it did some good. The Auditor looked back at him, even angrier now that Richter had seen him flinch. Right after though, it seemed like the wind went out of his sails. With a heavy sigh, Nexus started speaking again. The aristocratic imperiousness was gone. This time, his words were intoned with an air of ritual. Somehow, he still managed to say them like an absolute dick.

"Worthy traveler. Your path to power has led you to a moment of Ascendance. Your journey has been fraught with danger," the Auditor rolled his eyes expressively, completely belaying the content of his words, "but you have prevailed."

It looked like he was chewing nails, but he also added, "And it is my pleasure to answer your earlier question, as you are entitled to know. There are indeed consequences if you fail your Rite of Ascension. You will be immediately removed from my dimension. You will also lose points from every one of your attributes. The higher-ranked the path you choose, the greater the loss of points you will suffer. Finally, if you fail your ascension, you may not attempt it again until you reach a new level, and subsequent Rites of Ascension will be more difficult. So, knowing this," Nexus gritted his teeth so hard Richter thought they might crack, but he still forced the words out, "*noble traveler*, do you still wish to proceed along your path of Ascension?"

Richter had no idea who or what was making Nexus play ball, but he was grateful. Just like he'd expected, this Rite of Ascension hid serious consequences. Even when Richter died, he was able to gain back his Attribute Points when he leveled up again. To lose points, not just from one but from all nine of his Primary Attributes, was not a small thing. Nexus had also just told him that the loss would increase with certain choices. If he lost one point in each of the nine, that was something he could deal with. If he lost five or ten from each... that would be like wasting a third of his progression since coming to The Land, and he would never be able to make up the lost ground. He wouldn't be crippled, but his dream of growing strong enough to protect his people would be extinguished.

Nexus waited for his response. Richter ground his teeth. These damned checks and balances. Now he had to make a choice. Did he stay where he was, stuck at this damn Threshold? Or did he risk losing his Attribute Points? A choice that, trapped down here in the deeps, could lead to his death and Singh's curse taking hold. The giant stared at him, daring him to say yes.

It was a large decision, but he wasn't one to waste time, especially when there was something difficult to be done. The simple fact was, if he wasn't moving forward, then he was moving back. "I want to proceed," Richter told him defiantly.

"As such it is my honor and duty to lead you to your evolved avatars. Come with me, dick cheese." There was another crack of thunder. Nexus coughed and corrected that last bit, "I mean, if you please."

Nexus immediately started walking away, though he made sure to look back and throw up two fingers. That's two, he mouthed.

They quickly left the ring of burning torches, but more fires sprung to life on either side as they walked. Nexus didn't slow or turn to make sure Richter was following behind. There was no conversation. That suited both men. The torches winked out of existence behind them, never more than ten lit at a time. All the chaos seed could see beyond them was blackness. Even his Traveler's Map didn't work in this place. If the light or Nexus disappeared, he would have no frame of reference. The only impression he had was that they were slowly moving higher.

The two of them walked for what felt like hours. Richter wasn't worried about the passage of time though. It didn't flow normally in this dimension. No matter how long he was here, he might leave Xuetrix waiting for a minute or a year. There was nothing he could do about it either way. Richter was a passenger for the moment. He had to go where this path led him.

They finally stopped. With a wave of Nexus's hand, the torches around them were extinguished, and they were plunged into darkness. Richter's fingers twitched to form the spellform *Darkvision* instinctively, but he stilled the impulse. His frantic run from the ichorpede's lair had ingrained the reaction. Dark could mean that a monster was inches away, that you could fall into a crevasse, that a shelf of stone could slow you down long enough to be eaten. Dark meant death. He didn't want to risk anything that could be considered threatening by the Auditor though. After waiting for a few seconds, his eyes adjusted and he realized that the blackness wasn't as deep as he'd believed. Without the light of the fire to blind him, he could see much more clearly.

The light he was seeing by had no real source, but it was enough for him to make out what was around him, if just barely. From out of the gloom, he could distinguish dimly illuminated figures. They were arranged in concentric circles around him and Nexus, even extending back in the direction they had just come from. The details of the statues were almost imperceptible. They looked to be faceless humanoids made of black sand. As far as he could see they were featureless and identical.

Congratulations! Your road has been long and fraught with peril, but you have persevered and increased your power. Your Core of Power will light your way.

The chaos seed turned to Nexus, "What happens next?"

The giant didn't face him when he responded, he just intoned his answer with a hint of resignation, perhaps even pity. The lack of annoyance in the being's voice worried Richter more than any of his animosity had, "Do you want to turn back and stay as you are or ascend and become more?"

Richter's guard was immediately up, "What happens if I try to ascend?"

"Do you want to turn back and stay as you are or ascend and become more?" Nexus repeated, still not deigning to look at him.

The chaos seed's anger surged, but he didn't let himself lash out. He wouldn't make that mistake again. He also wasn't foolish enough to think that if he asked again he would get a different answer. There was no crack of thunder this time; it seemed Nexus wasn't required to answer any more questions. Richter had all the information he was going to get. There was no point turning back now.

"Let's do this."

Nexus's response was simple, but heavy with magic, "Thrice heard and witnessed."

CHAPTER 12

DAY 151 – JUREN 2, 0 AOC

*E*ven though Richter had known that was coming, his breath got a bit more shallow at hearing the words. A lair full of monsters he could face. The power of Three... he wasn't about to take that lightly. Even though he couldn't feel them, he knew invisible strands of magic had just bound him to his choice.

Nexus continued to intone, "Now you will be tested. Let go of what holds you back."

Before Richter could question that quizzical response, he felt a pulling from inside of him. The sensation turned into a ripping. He tried to take control of himself, but lost the battle moments later. Strands of black-and-gold energy pulled from his body and a scream was torn from his throat. The energy began to coalesce in the air, a riotous mix of colors. A second tether shot out from the battleground of light and reentered Richter's body, completing the circuit. Through it all, a cascade of suffering swept through him. The agony was horrific.

It was not a boast that he was no stranger to pain at this point. He had been eaten, stabbed, burned, struck with lightning and castrated. This was different. It was... his mind scrambled to even find words that could describe it. In the face of such unrelenting torment, his reason failed him. It felt like the lining was being ripped free of his stomach walls. Like the calcium of his bones was being siphoned away. It felt like his very molecules were being divided with no care toward the tender flesh they comprised. His mind nearly fractured. Richter did everything he could to try and stop whatever was happening to him, but it was to no avail. The torment only worsened.

The giant finally turned to face him. Richter was in so much pain he couldn't even feel shame at weeping in front of his former, and now current, torturer. His gaze centered on Nexus's face, expecting to see a smug expression. Instead, the Auditor's face was impassive, the definition of stoic. Suddenly Richter knew that whatever was happening, it wasn't because of the giant. He'd thought Nexus had somehow tricked him into being tortured again. Now he understood that this was all occurring because of his own choice, because he'd chosen to ascend to a higher tier. On a deep level, Richter knew that this was his final test to becoming something more.

The pain increased and he felt more being pulled out of him. Through the suffering he realized that he was becoming less. With a horrible suspicion, he pulled up his status sheet. Every one of his attributes was falling. His level, attributes, skills, health, mana and stamina were all rolling back. His very essence was being pulled out of him and collected as a sphere of roiling black-and-gold liquid. To Richter, it looked like the two colors were fighting for dominance. That battle made the sphere nearly lose cohesion again and again. Then more energy would pour into it from his own body. It would regain its structure by feeding on his very essence. Then the process would begin again. Through it all, the pain grew worse.

Time passed and his voice grew raw from screaming. He was forced to fall to one knee, then both. The one thing he managed to do though, was keep his head up. Tears flowed from his eyes like crystal rivers, but he kept his eyes trained on the sphere. Sometime in the midst of all that agony, he knew he was looking at his Power Core. A strangled gasp tore from his throat as more power was pulled out of him. The sphere lost cohesion again, and that was when it finally clicked.

At a base level, he suddenly knew that he had to preserve the structural integrity of the sphere, that every time it lost cohesion, he risked failing the Rite of Ascension. He'd thought that the black and gold were two opposing sides of his nature, that one had to win and the other had to fall. In a flash of insight, he understood that both aspects were part of who he was. It wasn't that they couldn't coexist, it was that he was forcing them into conflict. It was he that was keeping the fundamental parts of his nature from being whole. He couldn't force himself to be something he was not. He couldn't force either part of himself away. He'd learned long ago that you did not gain power over yourself by denying what you were. You had to accept and hold close the various parts of yourself, the gorgeous and the ugly alike. Then, and only then, could you choose how much to indulge your various impulses. By pretending part of you didn't exist, you had no control at all. That was why, though it was hard, the chaos seed stopped struggling against what his path would pull out of him and put back in.

Instead, Richter stopped running from the suffering. He began to accept it. Slowly but surely, he did what he could to embrace the pain. It would have been wonderful if that had magically made it lessen or go away. Sadly, that wasn't how life worked. It didn't get better because you learned a lesson about its nature. Sometimes if you were lucky, however, understanding why you had pain could bring a kind of peace.

While his nerves were fried and his senses were flayed, a random thought appeared in his mind. In a perverse way, his torture at the hands of Nexus months ago might have actually prepared him for the hell he was currently enduring. It had taught him a lesson that only prolonged suffering could convey. That pain was not defeated by fighting against it. Agony was not conquered by trying to overcome it.

No, pain could not be beaten into submission. It was not an enemy to push away. It was a piece of you to be cherished. Even his castration at the hands of Sonirae could not have taught him that. Only by surviving and living with anguish long enough for it to adopt a cruel normality could you come to understand it. For to truly understand something was to love it. His mind was filled with swaths of scarlet suffering, and he now knew that trying to deny that was holding him back. There was only one choice. He had to let go.

He stopped struggling and rode the river of pain. He held it close like a lover. Not tight, to master it, but soft, to welcome it. Slowly, his mind began to accept a truth that his heart calmly repeated again and again. This torture wasn't happening to him. It was him. He was agony, as much as he was joy, anger and chaos. The pain he was feeling was the pain of life, which would both take and give. His suffering was a searing knife, cutting away everything but his core self. Over time, minutes or hours, he would never know, Richter calmed and began to understand. By accepting his pain, he gained power over it. Even though every part of him felt scraped raw and rubbed with salt, he slowly stood back up on his own two feet.

The flows of energy coming from and entering into his body grew calm. The surface of the sphere stabilized and the two colors, gold and black, flowed together in harmony, no longer in opposition. The power continued to stream out of him, into the Core, before returning on tendrils of gold and black. His status page cycled down until it was the same as his first moment in The Land. The entire time, the pain had continued until he'd finally recognized it. He was feeling every sensation he'd experienced since coming to The Land, but in reverse. Not only the physical sensation, but also how this magical world had impacted his mind, soul and very essence. That was what his core was. It was everything. Suddenly, the pain was gone, and he was as he had been when he was first born into The Land.

Name: Richter	Level: 1, 0%	Age: 24
Race: Chaos Seed (Human)	Alignment: Neutral	Languages: Sapient Mortals
Reputation: Level 1 "Who are you again?"		
STATS		
Health: 100	Mana: 100	Stamina: 100
ATTRIBUTES		
Strength: 10	Agility: 10	Dexterity: 10
Constitution: 10	Endurance: 10	Intelligence: 10
Wisdom: 10	Charisma: 10	Luck: 10
RESISTANCES	**SKILLS**	**MARKS**
None	None	None
ABILITIES		
Limitless: 100% affinity in any and every skill		
Gift of Tongues: Ability to comprehend almost any sapient languages		

Nexus had stood by the entire time. His gaze had been more focused on the Core of energy floating in the air than the man it had come from. While Richter had been on a journey of self-discovery, the Auditor had seen this scene play out countless times. Most creatures never reached this point. They could not achieve the simple yet profoundly difficult goal of accepting both who and what they were. That was the minimum of what was required to ascend. After all, how could you move beyond the bounds of your current self if you could not even understand it?

To his great surprise, Richter had not only been able to do so, but had done it with a binary soul. The number of beings he had seen achieve that on their first try could be counted on one hand. That was why he examined the man's Power Core so intently. Nexus's gold-flecked black eyes seemed to be able to discern truths in the ball of liquid light that most could not see. When Richter finally stood, a master of himself and his pain, Nexus turned his attention back to the chaos seed. The two men locked eyes, and Nexus gave a rare nod of respect.

Now stabilized, Richter's Power Core rose higher into the air. As it did, the darkness receded and figures began to be illuminated. At the same time, a prompt appeared in Richter's vision. It was accompanied by a voice that sounded almost robotic. He had never heard anything like it before. It bothered him. The lack of emotion coupled with the strength of the voice made him feel like he was being spoken to by a being infinitely more powerful than himself.

Test Completed. Integration of Self and Nature has been achieved at... **98%.** *Evolutionary options up to rank 8, Legendary, are now unlocked.*

Richter stared at the sphere above him, both shining with light and reflecting nothing, and he was astonished by its beauty. Is this what I am without the strain of what I could be? Is that enough? He had no answers, but he continued to gaze up in wonder. When a voice filled his ears, it took his addled mind a few seconds to realize that it was Nexus who had spoken. Thankfully, the Auditor repeated himself.

"Choose your ascendance."

CHAPTER 13

DAY 151 – JUREN 2, 0 AOC

*R*ichter looked at the giant with a calm that was earned only after great suffering. Nexus began to cast a spell. The ebony man moved both arms in a flowing pattern that became more and more intricate. Magical light of various shades sparked on his fingertips. Some of the shades were familiar to Richter; others were new. Even if he had recognized them all, however, the chaos seed would still have been astonished by their beauty.

He knew the flashes were ambient magic. Light would build on someone's hands and arms when they cast a spell. The color of the light would give you a clue as to what type of magic the person was harnessing. For Richter, and most every other spellcaster he'd encountered, the light was always just one hue as they cast a spell.

What was so astonishing was the wide array of ambient magic surrounding Nexus's fingers. Unless Richter was wrong, Nexus was using more than a dozen schools of magic at once to cast the spell he was weaving. Moreover, he did it with the deftness of a virtuoso. The appearance of different lights at once showed that he wasn't only shifting between different schools, he was using multiple types simultaneously. It made plain just how massive the gap was between the

Auditor and himself. For the first time in a great while, the chaos seed was humbled.

Nexus did not notice Richter's uncharacteristic humility. The chaos seed was most definitely correct; the Auditor stood several tiers above him in regard to raw power, but even the giant was being pushed to his limits. This complicated spellform sorely taxed both Nexus's magic and mental energy.

There was a reason Nexus had been chosen as an Auditor, however. Difficult or not, the magic never faltered and the complex spellform took shape. As he continued his mystical work, incantations spilled from his lips and a wind built around both of them. It grew stronger and more powerful as time went on. At this moment, if god had stood in his way, then god would have been cut. In the eye of the gathering storm, the two figures, lord and Auditor, remained safe. The storm connected to Richter's Power Core and the winds turned gold and black in hue.

The casting continued for minutes and the storm continued to expand. As it did, it washed over countless figures wearing Richter's face. The whirling winds wore down each and they collapsed into black sand. All except a precious few, which were not destroyed by the wind but instead were polished like finished marble. Rather than the shapeless forms they had once been, each now had Richter's face. The rest of their bodies had various differences, but they were all clearly him.

Through it all, Nexus continued to chant, his movements becoming even more frantic and the words of Power growing louder until he was shouting them into the void. The light and wind extended outward until the eighth ring of figures was revealed. Suddenly, he looked at Richter, his gaze fierce and exhausted at the same time. He spread his arms wide apart before slamming his hands together with a sharp *crack!*

His fingers snapped together so close to Richter's face that the chaos seed felt the sound on his cheeks. A vibratory sensation passed through his body and, with no other warning, the swirling winds around them stopped. Silence reigned. The chaos seed felt the vibration rebounding through his body, mind and soul. Nothing was hidden; his every secret was exposed. It did not feel like a violation so much as an impartial evaluation. The energy rippling through him was as old as the turning of the Universe. It knew all, and knew him.

Seven seconds later, the sensation intensified within his chest. It passed up his throat and out of his mouth. Richter shouted a Word of Power he could not know and would never remember, a tone and frequency that was all of what he had been, but not all of what he would become. The reverberations of that Word rippled across the statues that were still standing. Power flowed into them, and though they did not move, he could feel life had been breathed into them. Each opened their eyes and revealed one orb of shining gold and another of fathomless black.

Every one of the figures was unclothed. They stood still as statues in their original positions. Except for not moving, they were incredibly lifelike, even if some were bizarre. Now that the storm had disappeared, he could see them easily.

The closest was only three yards away. The furthest was more than ten times that distance, in the eighth ring of figures. The light from his Core extended only another foot beyond that. The sky above him was a featureless black and he was standing upon a pit of black sand. The granules were as fine as powder, but hard-packed enough to be firm.

Richter turned his head to see the first figure but, unexpectedly, Nexus spoke again. His tone was heavy with warning, "Stay in the light."

The chaos seed stared out into the darkness. Before the storm had ended, he was sure he'd seen more shapeless figures beyond the eighth ring. If that was true, then the figures in the dark should even be above *legendary* rank. He understood the necessity of Nexus's warning. Who wouldn't be tempted by such a path to power?

Richter resolved to follow the warning though. A long time ago, he'd been told that if an asshole took the time to give you advice, then that was advice you should take seriously. He was allowed to examine everything in the light, but nothing more. Staring out into the darkness now, he was sure he saw something move. He also couldn't shake the feeling that all the statues in the light were staring at him, and that something was looking at him from the darkness as well. Staying in the light was one piece of advice he fully intended to follow.

Richter was about to take a step forward to examine the figure closest to him, when a series of prompts appeared.

Know This! Every figure before you represents a path to ascension from a Tier 1 being to a Tier 2. Each figure is only possible due to your actions having imprinted a Potential on your Power Core.

Know This! The further you travel from your Power Core, the higher-ranked the Path of Ascension will be. Beware the folly of choosing a path that offers power at too high a price. Higher-ranked evolutions will have greater consequences if you fail to ascend. While you may choose any of these paths, success is not assured. Even the greatest of beings may be buffeted by the winds of chance.

It looked like the pain he'd gone through had only qualified him to make a choice about how to ascend. The tranquility Richter had been feeling started to fade. After all that, *I still might not ascend?* Always a fucking catch, he thought bitterly. There was one more prompt, and it seemed to describe who he was currently.

Know This! You are more than what can be seen and felt. At your current Tier, you have only just begun to understand the many facets of your complete self. Understand where you have come from so that you may know how far you might go.

Your current state of existence is:	
Tier 1 Human	
You are currently a Tier 1 Human, also known as a Mortal Human. Your race is one of the most recent stages of evolution in The Land. Humans possess Refined souls. These are not inherently more powerful than the souls of beasts or monsters, but often possess greater potential and resilience. Humans are one of the shortest-lived yet most prolific breeders in the Land. With the correct combination of Attributes, they have a maximum life expectancy of 150 years. Humans have a broader affinity for skills than other races. No special bonuses to race. Humans receive four free Attribute Points per level.	
Facets of your current incarnation	
Body	Tier 1 Human
Mind	Tier 1 Human
Soul	Tier 1 Human
Special	Chaos Seed

As powerful as Richter had become, it looked like he hadn't moved past the potential of any other human at this point. He was the same as any other mortal human. The fact that he had one hundred and fifty years of life expectancy with the right "combination" of Attribute Points let him know he wasn't immortal, but it was still longer than he'd expected to live so it wasn't that bad.

The "refined" descriptor of his soul helped him understand something that he'd wondered about for a long time. Namely, why he wasn't able to soul trap the spirits of humans, goblins and other sapient races. What "refined" meant he had no idea. The best people to ask, Sumiko and Hisako, were both Life *masters*. The two found the idea of trapping sapient souls to be so abhorrent that they'd almost attacked him the one time he'd asked about it.

The prompt gave him even more information. As he focused on each term, descriptions would appear.

> *Body* – The corporeal form of a creature
>
> *Mind* – The psionic potential and intellect of a creature
>
> *Soul* – The strength and character of a creature's spirit

Each of the first three descriptors also stated that his form was consistent with other mortal humans. The next line was apparently a catchall for anything that did not normally appear in a Tier 1 incarnation. This was apparently where he differed from other mortal humans.

> *Special* – Miscellaneous factors affecting a given incarnation

None of that was too surprising or even that insightful. Even his own status page listed him as human with "chaos seed" in parentheses. He hadn't known about the tiers before now, but it wasn't too different from the concepts of leveling.

The last descriptor was what he found to be particularly fascinating. Focusing on the word "aura," it gave him a basic definition.

> *Aura* – A field that surrounds the incarnation. This can be seen or unseen, felt or undetectable, passive or active.

Discovering that he had an aura was a bit of a surprise. Even more so that auras weren't just something hot, weird chicks made you hear about before they gave it up. Still, that wasn't what captured Richter's attention. It was the description of his aura that finally gave him some clue about his Chaos Seed nature. It confirmed something that he'd long suspected, but hadn't been able to substantiate.

Chaotic Gradient – An aura that is unique to creatures of Chaos. Simply by existing, they can affect events around them, twisting the strands of fate. This aura can be a curse or a blessing, depending on the Luck and power of the owner. The only thing that can be definitively stated about this aura is that it will trigger powerful events in the life of the one who possesses it.

Pity those who are caught in the web of such a being. A byproduct of this gradient will be that other chaotic creatures and energies will be drawn to whoever possesses this aura. The strength of this attraction is proportional to the grade of an individual's aura, with stronger auras attracting weaker.

This Aura has 7 grades: *Paltry, Lesser, Weak, Moderate, Strong, Greater* and *Grand*

Paltry – Potentially affects your life path and immediate surroundings

Lesser – Occasionally affects your immediate surroundings

Weak – Regularly affects your immediate surroundings and those you have prolonged contact with

Moderate – Affects your nearby surroundings. The strings of fate will twist to bring change to your life and the lives of others. All auras of this rank or higher exhibit a constant effect.

Reading about the aura, a great many things started to make sense. He had only been in The Land for half a year, and yet he had already accomplished so much. He'd had to fight tooth-and-nail just to survive, but the dangers that had come his way had also let him become powerful. He'd waged wars, revived an ancient race and brought wonders to his village that hadn't been seen in millennia. The fact that he had this aura finally explained why he always seemed to be at the epicenter of events. The Hearth Mother had suspected something very similar for a while. Knowing that he was literally attracting and warping the threads of fate, not just for himself but instead for entire civilizations, was mind-boggling.

There was also an implication to this that he didn't like. He realized that without his aura he probably wouldn't have been able to accomplish nearly as much as he had, but it also meant he was a threat to those around him. The prompt said as much. "Pity those who are caught in the web of such a being." His aura wasn't even the strongest grade, yet it could affect entire civilizations. The implications and responsibilities of that were intense. How many deaths was he responsible for that he didn't even know about?

Richter immediately stopped that line of thought. There was no point in guessing. He could just as well ask himself how many lives he'd saved simply by breathing. Maybe one of the people he'd personally killed would have had a son that grew up to be the next Jack the Ripper. Maybe they would have grown up to be the next Ghandi. There was no way to know. Which meant it was a waste of energy worrying about it.

Hell, even the Doctor hadn't understood time completely. If that was true, then it was definitely beyond his ability to do so. Richter focused on what he knew. That was all any man could do, and far better than most managed. Carrying guilt over things he could not control was a fool's choice. No one made it through life unscathed. No one made it through life with causing at least some destruction. No matter what unintended consequences he created, he was a damn sight better than the bastards that actively worked to make the world worse every day.

Whatever his sins, he wasn't one of them, so beating himself up was kind of self-indulgent BS. So far, he'd done a lot more good than harm. After thinking about that, he shrugged. To be fair, that was probably a matter of perspective. The goblins, bugbears and undead he'd slaughtered would probably disagree. On the other hand, fuck those guys.

It wasn't the unknown that bothered him about his aura. It was the fact that he and other chaos seeds would be attracting each other. That was a recipe for a straight up Highlander "there can be only one" situation. Not only that, but because he had the next-to-strongest ranked aura, he'd be pulling in virtually every other chaos seed out there. The reason he'd only encountered one was probably because the Mist village was a South-Parky mountain town in the middle of nowhere, but now he knew it was only a matter of time before he met more. That thought made his blood run cold.

His life had been insane and filled with blood and gore ever since coming to The Land. One of the craziest people was that bastard Heman though. The man had abilities that made him an insane threat. For all he knew, the next chaos seed he met could be stronger. Richter gritted his teeth and clenched his jaw thinking about Heman. That guy had been such an asshole.

All he could do was get stronger as fast as he could. He'd already resolved to do that because the worst of The Land seemed to be gunning for him and his village. Now it looked like he'd have to deal with the worst of Earth too. Gah! This shouldn't be how this worked. This shouldn't be how any of this worked! Richter sighed heavily. He just had to hope the next chaos seed he pulled into his orbit wasn't such a raging douche nozzle.

He turned his attention back to the statues in front of him.

*Know This! Ascending to a Tier 2 existence allows a being to harness and utilize the power of a **Bloodline**. Most ascended beings cannot utilize this power but, for the fortunate few, this offers a path to much greater power.* Richter focused on the bold word and a further explanation appeared.

Bloodline *– The power and legacy inherent in the blood of a creature, most often left over from a powerful progenitor*

What was that supposed to mean? Would he have the power of a chimp? Or did it mean he was unlocking some power hidden inside himself? Maybe something that had been present the whole time, but sleeping? It raised interesting possibilities. Not only for himself, but for his villagers. Just what hidden power might be sleeping in his sprite best friend for instance? Or inside of a chamberlain who was half-elemental? The diversity of his village had been difficult to navigate several times since the settlement was founded, but now that very same variety guaranteed a better chance of his people manifesting useful powers... With this new bit of Lore, Richter's heart thumped in excitement. He had to get back!

First things first though. There were more windows waiting to be read.

Know This! Choosing a path of ascendance does not guarantee success. Each path available to you is based on your nature, experiences and Potential. Some Paths of Ascendance will be better suited for you than others. Choose wisely!

SOME OF THE excitement Richter had been feeling faded. He'd thought that ascending a tier would make him a superhero. He'd been banking on it being his ticket to climbing out of the depths. This didn't look like enough to ensure his survival. His mind, body and soul would advance to Tier 2, but he had no idea what that meant.

The only real change in becoming a Tier 2 human looked to be the attribute bonus. That was definitely a substantial boost. If all nine of his stats got +5, it would be like gaining seven levels all at once. That wasn't even taking the 10% boost to his highest stat into account. From what Richter saw though, the real difference between being a Tier 1 and Tier 2 being was that ascending allowed you to use a bloodline, whatever that meant.

Even though he didn't know the significance, he was absolutely certain that it mattered. If it was only available to Tier 2 and above, then what would happen when he ran into a Tier 2 enemy that did have a bloodline? For the first time, Richter felt like his natural gifts might be inadequate. His stats were stronger than regular humans' because he gained 50% more points per level. Yet attributes weren't everything.

He had no idea what bloodlines could do. Which meant he had no idea what powers an enemy might have that he couldn't match. What if it let them spit acid or gave them diamond-hard skin? If he was going to ascend, he needed a Bloodline. It was obvious now that the stronger he got, the more challenge he invited. Without all the perks ascension could offer, he might be better off staying at a lower tier.

Richter was going to examine his other options, but first he examined the Tier 2 human's physical appearance in greater detail. The figure looked just like him. Try as he might, he couldn't really see any differences in this Tier 2 human.

The physical appearance of the avatar didn't hold his attention long, so he turned his attention back to the chart. While he was still a bit disappointed by the absence of a bloodline, the evolution did increase his stats significantly. Attributes weren't everything, but they were up there!

There were even nuances to each category that he used to not understand. Something Richter hadn't known for several months after coming to The Land was that while attributes could give godlike powers, a lack of them could cause serious issues. There was a difference between Intelligence, which gave you mana and increased your spell power, and intellect, which was how smart you were. The two were related, however.

Increasing your Intelligence would increase your intellect in some small, barely detectable way, according to Hisako. What wasn't hard to deduce was the impact of having attributes that were too low. Every race had a minimum value they had to meet in each of the nine or they would suffer a potentially debilitating debuff.

With low Intelligence, the person would be, simply put, a dummy. Low Strength would make them a weakling that anyone could slap around, and low Charisma would make you fugly and unlikeable. Low Luck was a bit harder to define, just like the benefits of high Luck, but you'd find things were always turning against you. You'd trip on every rock, get stung by every bee, and that hot chick you'd been scoping at the bar? She was a nun that somehow still had the clap.

The bare minimum for attributes varied from race to race. For an adult human, it was tens across the board. For sprites, the Strength requirement was only eight, but Dexterity had a demand of twelve. Every race seemed to have their own perfect balance. Now it seemed like he had learned another secret effect. The prompt hinted that there was a "correct" distribution of points to maximize a human's lifespan. Did that mean there were other distributions that were detrimental, or gave other boons? It was something to research in the future.

What he did know was that +5 to all his stats would let him lift another hundred pounds. It would give another fifty points to health, mana and stamina, and provide many other bonuses to his other attributes. Perhaps more powerful than the +5 was the modifier to his highest attribute.

For Richter, that meant a 10% boost to his Intelligence. Coupled with the bonus from consuming the First Fruit of the Quickening, that was a permanent +20% increase to this attribute! Every attribute did many different things, but every point in Intelligence made his Basic Element spells 2% stronger and gave another ten points of mana.

The 10% boost to Intelligence wouldn't matter much if his numbers were low, but in his case the modifier would be like being awarded an additional one to two levels-worth of free points. Intelligence was his highest attribute, so it would translate into more than a hundred mana points and a healthy boost to his spell power.

The extra points would also be a powerful boon even at level forty-five. Not enough to solve his current problem, admittedly, but certainly nothing to scoff at. When you factored in that humans gained four points per level, they would have gotten only one hundred and eighty free attribute points by the time they were eligible to ascend to the next tier. +5 to all attributes was forty-five points. That meant just for ascending their overall Attribute Points would increase by 25%! Just ascending would make a warrior hit harder, and a mage able to cast more spells.

Also, the basic description of a Tier 2 Human showed that a human's innate bonus to learning a wide range of skills would be increased. Humans got less Attribute Points per level than most other races, but they also had a broader affinity for skills as a balance, if you could call it that. Choosing this path of ascendance seemed to lean into that.

A 25% boost to skill leveling was a serious boon. Coupled with his *Fast Learner* ability, which gave a 30% increase to his skill leveling and his Limitless ability, it would be enough to skyrocket him even when his skills reached higher ranks and leveling became more difficult. In fact, the boost to affinity might even get him free skill levels immediately. After eating the First Fruit of the Quickening, his affinity in Enchanting had gone above 100%. That had automatically earned him a free skill level, and had saved him weeks to months of effort.

Richter nodded to himself. Even this *common*-ranked ascended form would greatly increase anyone's power. When he had first come to The Land, his nine primary attributes were all set at +10, giving him 90 points total. Even without the bonus to his highest stat, the +5 that evolving into a Tier 2 human was forty-five points. That was half his level one starting amount.

The first evolution could definitely be helpful. As great as it sounded though, it was only *common* ranked, so he turned his attention to the next figure. Walking forward, the sphere of light remained hovering in the air behind him.

The next figure was about seven yards further than the first one. He looked at Nexus as he walked over, still not trusting the powerful being. To his surprise, the Auditor was not even paying attention to him anymore. He was holding something that looked for all the world like an iphone, and his thumb was swiping right.

Shaking his head at the weird demigod, he examined the next figure. It looked like the last, but the top of its head was slightly larger.

> **You have found an *Unusual*-ranked evolution:**
>
> **Tier 2 Human Telepath**
>
> This path of evolution transforms you into a human being with psionic capabilities. Mind reading, mental communication and mind control are all possible with this form.
>
> No appreciable changes in body type besides a slight increase in skull and brain size.
>
> Maximum life expectancy is increased to 250 years.
>
> Mental defenses are substantially increased by adding +1 to the Secondary Attribute: **Mental Aegis**. Your base MA is currently **1.16**.
>
> The racial tendency of humans to have a broad affinity for many skills is strengthened. Skills are learned 10% faster and affinities are randomly increased by up to 15%. As with all evolutions, many factors will be affected by your ascension.
>
> As an *unusual* ascended form, there are **4 ranks** of this evolution.
>
> You will begin at Rank 1.
>
> Advancing ranks will unlock greater power, and > 50% of ranks must be unlocked before Ascendance to a new form is possible.
>
> **Ascension Likelihood:** 77%
>
> **Penalty for Failure:** -3 points to each Primary Attribute, -3% chance at next Ascension attempt

This evolution was clearly superior to the first one. The attribute bonus was the same, but he was twice as likely to earn a bloodline with each level he reached. The only downside was that the boost to skill acquisition and affinities were a bit weaker. That was a small price to pay for a boost to his mental capabilities. He knew full well the power of psionic abilities. Those that lacked mental resistances were easy prey to those who could make psi attacks. Alma had shown that many times when her *Psi Blast* cut through magical shields like they weren't there. Mental capabilities fell under the province of Thought, which was a Deeper Magic, an order of magnitude stronger than magics of the Basic Elements like Life, Dark or Fire.

This particular evolution had been made possible by his training and his bond with Alma. If not for her, his Mental resistance wouldn't have been nearly high enough to qualify. This Path of Ascendance would increase his mental defenses even further, nearly doubling them. When you factored in that his Psi Bond ability increased his base Thought defense by 60%, it meant he would actually gain +1.6 rather than just +1.0 to Mental Aegis. His current mental defenses were already much stronger than the average person. Despite that, they weren't high enough. Even with his psychic fortifications, he'd nearly had his mind shattered by the lich lord. In the wake of that battle, a stronger mental defense was a very attractive choice.

It could also be ranked up four times rather than the *common* evolution that could only advance twice. He didn't know what perks that would manifest, and he didn't know how to advance its rank, but he'd figure it out. Also, he had to imagine that being able to advance more ranks would translate into more power down the road.

The ranks of these Paths of Ascendance looked to follow the normal pattern of The Land. *Common, Uncommon, Unusual, Scarce, Rare, Epic, Mythic,* and *Legendary.* There were more ranks beyond that like *Relic* and *Artifact,* but they seemed to not completely fit within the normal ranking progression. From the first two prompts, he was deducing that the number of possible advancements in an evolution was the rank of the ascended form plus one. The next form he examined would confirm that.

CHAPTER 14

DAY 151 – JUREN 2, 0 AOC

*H*e turned his head to the next figure. So far telepath was the clear winner, but he wouldn't make a decision until he had all the information. Also, it said he only had a 77% chance to succeed if he went down that path. Richter had a high Luck, but this decision could determine if he made it back to the village or was damned for all eternity. A 23% failure rate wasn't a good look. The increased cost of failure made it even worse. He didn't relish the possibility of losing twenty-seven Attribute Points.

The next figure was five feet beyond the psychic. This one looked markedly different than the first two. The entire avatar was hazy like it was occluded by a thick grey mist.

> You have found a *Rare*-ranked evolution:
>
> **Tier 2 Mist Lord**
>
> This Path of Ascendance transforms you into a creature of pure elemental power. Due to your Mastery of a Place of Power, you can infuse your essence with these energies permanently. Your form will be partially insubstantial, providing -50% damage to physical attacks.
>
> Spells dealing with the ley lines of your Place of Power will be increased in strength by 50% and cost 50% less. Such power does not come without cost, however.
>
> Choosing this form will require you to stay within your domain. Without the specific combination of ambient magic your Place of Power provides, your form will quickly degrade. Conversely, further Mastery of your Place of Power can drastically increase your strength. As with all evolutions, many other factors will be affected by your ascension.
>
> The racial tendency of humans toward skill will be lost.
>
> As a *rare* class ascended form, there are **6 ranks** of this evolution. You will begin at Rank 1. Advancing ranks will unlock greater power, but > 50% of ranks must be unlocked before Ascendance to a new form is possible.
>
> **Ascension Likelihood:** 83%
>
> **Penalty for Failure:** -5 points to each Primary Attribute, -5% chance at next Ascension attempt

Prerequisites: Level 45 Human. Master of a fully unlocked Place of Power containing Air, Life, Water and Dark

Evolution Rank: Rare

	Changes if Tier 2 Mist Lord evolution is chosen		
		Tier 1	**Tier 2**
Body		Tier 1 Human	Tier 2 Elemental
			-50% Physical Damage
Mind		Tier 1 Human	Tier 2 Elemental
Soul		Tier 1 Human	Tier 2 Elemental
Special		Chaos Seed	Chaos Seed
Aura		Chaotic Gradient (*Greater* rank)	Chaotic Gradient (*Greater* rank)
Bloodline		N/A	No Cohesive Bloodline
Attribute Bonus		N/A	+5 to all Primary Attributes
			+15% to highest Primary Attribute

The Mist Lord evolution was *rare* for a reason. Richter was somewhat shocked at the perks. Including the boost he already got from his Place of Power, his spell power would be doubled! His spells would also only cost half as much.

Basically, the evolution was the wet dream of wizards. It not only increased his magic strength dramatically, it also gave a 50% reduction to physical damage. There was also the fact that it was a scalable evolution, growing as he unlocked more of his Place of Power. It was the perfect answer to the many enemies that were turning their gaze toward the Mist Village.

If only there wasn't that pesky catch. All that power came at a horrible price. He wouldn't be able to leave his domain. That was not a small amount of space. It was a ten-mile radius extending out from the Great Seal north, south, east and west. That meant three hundred square miles. Still, Richter could never allow himself to be so constricted. Even though he had devoted himself to the village, he still personally wanted to explore his new world. Sometimes he felt that the wonders and dangers of The Land were calling out to him. He wouldn't let go of his freedom, not even for more power.

There was also the matter of the increased number of ranks this evolution possessed. What had at first seemed like a perk was now looking like a potential problem. He still had no idea what it took to advance a rank. If it was easy, then no problem. But in the past Richter had also gotten quests that were still beyond his ability to complete. If he couldn't progress in ranks, then his next ascension would be in jeopardy. This Threshold threatened to slow his progression to a crawl. The next one might drop him in quicksand. He had to be able to ascend, not just this time, but next time as well. The ranks weren't enough to dissuade him, but he was paying closer attention to them.

He was used to the axiom that danger and power went hand-in-hand in The Land. it looked like he might have discovered another fundamental truth through his Rite of Ascension. Choosing a higher path of power would lead to greater achievements, but would also require greater sacrifices. Put another way, choosing a more powerful form now might keep him from an even stronger evolution in the future.

Power and danger went hand-in-hand. He'd learned this long ago, and had survived many external dangers. The choice he was facing now was a different type of danger, the lure of temptation. This was a danger from within. Richter examined the form of the mist lord for a few more seconds and realized something. The simple truths of The Land actually hid deep wisdom and warnings.

He was going to move on to the next figure, but he decided to give the Mist Lord one more look. Not at its stats, but at the physical representation. There was no denying that it looked insanely cool. The body was defined by semi translucent mist. The edges were hazy. As he looked at it some parts of him went hazy and others were as solid as he was now. The Mist Lord would obviously have a serious boost to Concealment as well. With a sigh, he moved on to the next figure. Cool or not, it wasn't for him.

This next figure was seventeen yards away from the center. If the Mist Lord was cool, this one was seriously badass! Richter looked at a face that was his own, but covered in black scales. His mouth was elongated into a faint snout, and talons tipped his fingers. The figure's musculature was smaller than his current real-world form, but looked like it was carved from marble. A tail, six inches thick, fell to the ground behind him.

None of that was as impressive as the wings extending out from his back. Both were scaled on the outside, but were covered in a soft velvety skin on the inside. Unfurled, they reached six feet to either side. The bones that filled the wings shone a soft gold through the blackness of the membranes. Everything about the figure radiated violence and power.

Shaking his head in wonder, Richter pulled up information about the awe-inspiring figure.

WHEN HE HAD FIRST RECEIVED his Mark of Dragonkin, it had strengthened his Fire magic, in addition to increasing his Constitution and Strength. When the Mark was upgraded, those bonuses had increased. That had been great enough, but he never thought that it might actually allow him to become a dragon!

Richter had no idea what to think about first. He could actually transform into a dragon! Well, not a dragon, a draike, but still, it was a fucking dragon! The power he felt when he melded with Alma was astounding, but it only lasted for a few minutes. If he chose this Path of Ascension, he could have that power, or greater, all the time.

He walked around the figure and his breath was taken away by the raw power it exuded. He thought it might be his imagination at first, but the draconian body did actually have a palpable presence surrounding it. It wasn't exactly stifling, but he felt the danger the body possessed.

Looking at the draike's stats, it was no wonder it radiated menace. The physical changes alone were a marvel. If he chose this Path of Ascendance, he'd never be without weapons and armor again. Even now, without most of his items, he would still have a fighting chance. Also, the boost to his attributes was insane! His Strength was already above sixty. Between the stat boost and the modifier, he'd have almost a hundred points in that one attribute. He could literally lift a ton!

The draike wasn't merely physically superior to humans. It seemed like it would be a human's natural predator. Its attribute modifier was almost as powerful as the angel Hisako had summoned, albeit only to one attribute rather than all of them. Richter had no illusions that he could go toe-to-toe with a heavenly creature. The angel had been strong enough to slaughter almost an entire company of bugbears in minutes.

The bonus to Strength might be even more powerful than the Attribute Points would indicate. He'd suspected for a long time that Attribute Points might not be equal for all races. For a human, every point of Strength let him lift ten kilos. Dwarves seemed to be able to do more with the same amount of points. Sprites, on the other hand, did less. At one point he'd thought it might be a height or size modifier issue, but dwarves weren't much taller than the woodland race.

Conversely, the sprites' Agility and Dexterity let them climb trees insanely fast and run along tree branches. Richter's own Agi and Dex were higher than many of the sprites he knew, but he still couldn't match their grace. The point was, reading the draike's racial description, the incarnation might enjoy those very same hidden bonuses. Also, there were the wings. Wings were for flying. Richter could one day be able to fly. He might freaking fly!

Richter calmed himself down. The draike was amazing, but before he decided anything, he needed to get all the information he could. It certainly hadn't escaped his notice that the chances of him successfully completely this evolution was less than 50%. If there weren't so many amazing benefits, he wouldn't have wasted any time on it at all. This was the first evolution that came with a guaranteed bloodline. According to the prompt, a draike's bloodline was an integral part of the evolution. Even more so than the strengthened body and buffed up stats. The chaos seed focused on it and more information appeared.

*Know This! There are many bloodlines, but only the strong, lucky or cursed are blessed with such power. The **Unyielding Dragon Flame Bloodline** can start a fire inside the cells of your body, greatly increasing your physical prowess, perception and will for a short time. Increasing the rank of this bloodline adds capabilities to a draike's mind, body and soul.*

*Higher ranks also add a Fire element to your attacks. This Bloodline arose during the 5th evolution of The Land, after the 4th Cataclysm. As such, it is part of a grouping of Bloodlines known as **Primal**. It is also a **rare** bloodline of that period. As such, it has 5 ranks per tier. It begins with **35 Bloodline Points** to expend before it is exhausted. A bloodline can be exerted with more or less force and will consume Bloodline Points in accordance with this exertion.*

A smile crossed Richter's lips. It was afterburners. This bloodline worked like afterburners! He had absolutely zero idea how long thirty-five Bloodline Points would last, but even if it was only a few seconds, it might make all the difference in a battle. The bloodline could also be upgraded. He had no idea how, but it was possible. The draike evolution was looking better and better. How powerful would he be if he had the body of a dragon?

There were a lot of strong arguments toward choosing this form, but he wouldn't. It wasn't even the fact that he wouldn't look human anymore. Taking on a Messeji form with Alma had shown Richter just how much power he could have. With all the enemies he had, he needed all the power he could get. More than that, he had come to crave great strength.

No, what stopped Richter was that in his time leading the Mist Village, he'd become a lord in truth as well as name. He was not just a gamer that had been pulled into a new world. He was someone who knew the importance and the gravity of leading a diverse population. Despite what others might think, he knew on a fundamental level just how much stronger his tribe was for counting so many different peoples among its population.

The strength of the dwarves, the grace of the elves, the honor of the sprites, the wonder of the pixies, the passion of the humans; they all combined to make the Mist Village something powerful and unique. It brought its own issues as well, but the reward was more than worth the price. While the draike form was very tempting, he could not become something that his people would hate or fear. The power of one person would always be finite. The strength of people working together was limitless.

With regret, he moved past the dragon evolution and walked to the final form awaiting his inspection. The light only illuminated another three yards past the draike. At the very edge of the darkness waited a statue that looked much like the first. Richter thought he could see another statue past that, out in the dark, but he couldn't be sure. The gloom was not simple darkness. Looking at it, Richter had the impression of movement, like it was shifting and flowing, a midnight ocean. He kept staring, and had the distinct feeling that something was staring back at him. Something that did not mean him well.

Richter remembered Nexus' simple warning, "Stay in the light." Assholes and advice, he reminded himself. He abandoned his curiosity and examined the final figure.

CHAPTER 15

DAY 151 – JUREN 2, 0 AOC

*A*t first, he was confused. It looked exactly like the *common* ranked, Tier 2 Human. Just a simple human. He walked around it, careful not to stray into the darkness, but couldn't find a single difference. For this last possible evolution, he had expected something grand, especially after seeing the draike. As impressive as the physical stature was, however, there just didn't seem to be anything overly special about it.

Then he looked into its eyes.

Pools of silver spun in the center of each pupil. The portals to Chaos linked to the seed within him, and Richter suddenly felt compelled to choose this form without even reading the prompt it provided. He could feel endless possibilities pulling him in. Before he knew it, he'd taken a step forward, drawn by the siren song of those swirling grey eyes. Only with a supreme act of will did he stop himself.

Richter focused, and that kernel of power at his center, his chaos seed, responded. Other beings found looking at pure chaos to be terrifying, but to him it had always seemed beautiful. He had never forgotten the raw danger and power within that realm, however.

Using the seed of Chaos that was uniquely his, he was able to firm his will against the pull of this strongest evolution.

The chaos seed closed his eyes for several long seconds and steadied himself. When he was done, he could still feel the compulsion, but it was weaker. Richter was in control of himself once more. Opening his eyes, he looked the figure over again. It was just as emotionless and remained in the same position, but he noticed something he hadn't before. Not in its eyes, but near its feet. He could see small swirls of nearly imperceptible dust moving around the figure's toes.

Frowning in thought, Richter reached down and grabbed a bit of fine sand from the ground and threw it into the air. Most of it gently floated back down, but some seemed to be pulled toward the figure, moving as if caught in invisible eddies. None of the black sand touched the avatar, but it was clear that it was affecting its environment, just by existing.

Richter looked at the form's stats, and saw the amazing orange gleam of a *legendary* evolution.

You have found a *Legendary*-ranked evolution:

RICHTER WHISTLED SOFTLY. This evolution was truly powerful. It didn't have the raw combat strength of the draike evolution, but it was commanding in its own right. He still didn't understand the intrinsic difference between tiers, but he had to imagine that two was better than one. He also got a 20% boost to his Luck stat!

Richter's Luck was artificially boosted right now. It was clocking in at forty-nine, thanks to the +20 Luck he'd gotten from making the kindir of Verget Kunig his vassals. That large boost would only last for a week, but afterward, he would still get a +4 bonus and his Luck would be thirty-three. If he chose the chaos lord evolution, his Luck would boost back up all the way to sixty-one!

Now, it was true that Luck was an unknown entity for the most part. It was hard to determine what it did or when it would manifest.

Because of that though, Richter had seen that most people ignored the Attribute. It was a hard sell getting someone to invest a precious point into Luck when that same point could give more health, or power an extra spell. There were nine primary attributes, and most races only received three free points to distribute each level. Humans got four to distribute, but less overall points per level. Those were the main reasons that even higher-level enemies might have just ten to fifteen points in the attribute, even though their other categories could be sky high.

More important than his stats, he would also get a new bloodline. It probably wouldn't be as good as the *rare* Unyielding Dragon Flame bloodline of his draike evolution, but then again, his Luck was pretty insane. It might even be better. The biggest differences were the *special* and *aura* categories though. His chaos seed would evolve!

It had always been in the back of his mind; if he was a "seed," what could he grow into? He didn't fully know what it would mean to be a chaos lord, but how could he turn his back on something that felt like his destiny?

There was also the point that his aura would advance to the highest rank. *Chaotic gradient* was why he'd been able to gather so much power in a short time. He wasn't a fool, and he knew that his strength came at the cost of risking his life. If it wasn't for his ability to be reborn, his story would have ended in the first few days in The Land. And death was not the only danger. He'd been tortured in mind, body and soul. When he thought about the dark aberration, and what could have happened, his heart still raced. Richter was honestly shocked at times that he had been able to keep it together through everything he had endured. Now he knew that was, at least in part, because of his aura.

No, there was no denying it; the chaotic gradient offered great power, but had brought danger and suffering in equal measure. As he thought about it, Richter realized that his aura was completely consistent with The Land and the Labyrinth. "Danger and reward are close bedfellows." He'd heard it again and again. It had just never occurred to him that his very nature would fit the saying so completely.

Yes, his aura was dangerous, but didn't death stalk everyone? Besides, he was more than a bit dangerous himself. Richter smiled a devilish smile. His enemies had definitely learned that starting shit with him was hazardous to their health. Usually right before they died. Even though he was stuck far underground, in the deep dark of the earth, there was not a doubt in his mind that anything that wanted to come at him would regret it.

To him, his aura wasn't something to be feared. It was a loving promise for what he truly craved: power. Power was what he needed. Remembering that, any reservations he might have had about strengthening his aura faded away. If he could advance it from *greater* to *grand*, that was something he needed to do.

Lastly, there was the increase to his Chaos powers. The Sea of Chaos gave Richter access to some of the strongest items he'd ever seen. Currently he was able to buy *epic*-ranked items from the fourth stratum. *Epic* items were enough for nobles to declare war.

Becoming a Chaos Lord would give him access to the fifth. He couldn't even imagine how powerful the offerings would be for that stratum. Also, *Akaton Evolution* made his summoned creatures far stronger already. Just what would he be able to accomplish when the spell was 25% stronger?

Richter walked back to the center of the light and looked at all five potential evolutions again. The *common*-ranked, Tier 2 Human was obviously not in the running. The Tier 2 Human Telepath wasn't too bad. The idea of having true telepathy was alluring. He would definitely choose it over the Mist Lord, despite the fact that the psychic evolution was only *unusual* rank instead of *rare* like the elemental evolution. The original prompt had been right, that some paths would suit him more than others. The powers of the Mist Lord were great, but he didn't like the idea of being trapped within the confines of his domain.

His eyes looked longingly at the draike evolution for just a moment. The power in it called to him. He could envision his talons ripping out the throats of bugbears and his scales deflecting arrows. There was also that awesome bloodline, *Unyielding Dragon Fire*. Despite all of those things, there was zero doubt in Richter's mind what the right answer was. The Universe itself seemed to agree, as there was a more than 99% chance of success. The answer was clear.

The Land would welcome a chaos lord.

CHAPTER 16

DAY 151 – JUREN 2, 0 AOC

*B*efore Richter made his choice, he had three questions to ask Nexus.

"Nexus," he called. There was no response. Sighing heavily, Richter walked directly in front of him with only a foot of space between them. Looking up he repeated, louder this time, "Nexus."

This time the Auditor responded. That response was one index finger held up in the universal "just a sec" motion. He didn't even look up from the phone. He just. Kept. Swiping.

Anyone who thought the phrase, "his vision went red," was just poetic license had never actually been furious before. It is a real thing. The medical explanation is that anger triggers the sympathetic nervous system, causing an increase in heart rate and blood flow. That, coupled with selective constriction or dilation of certain vessels, will make the vessels in the eye grow larger, giving a red appearance to the eyes. This same phenomenon can tint a person's vision. Of course, the last thing on Richter's mind was physiology. To him, it just felt like an anger demon was trying to claw its way out of his throat and lay waste to the asshole Auditor in front of him.

With the muscles in his neck tight as steel cables, he forced the demon back into its cage. With his eyes closed, he mumbled, "Do not attack the demigod. Do not attack the demigod. Do *not* attack the demigod!" After about a minute, he could see straight again. With a tight neck, and pure evil in his heart, Richter waited while Nexus swiped through some sort of cosmic Tinder. What made it worse was that the chaos seed had to listen to the giant's muttering.

"Not hot." Swipe. "Not hot." Swipe. "Kinda hot?" Pause. "Nah." Swipe. "Not that hot... then again her mouth *is* open... is there a bikini pic? Come ooooon... Jackpot!" Right swipe!

Ten minutes. Richter had to stand there for ten minutes. That might have been ten seconds or ten years in the real world, but to him, it was an eternity. At long last, Nexus put the phone away. With a tone that implied Richter was the one that was wasting time, the giant asked, "What?"

Plastering a fake smile on his face, Richter asked his question through anger-thinned lips, "Can you tell me if I have to make a decision right now, or can I come back later?"

Nexus rolled his eyes, "Of course you have to make a choice now. Look at your body. You've reverted back to a level one noob. Unless your Core is reinserted, you won't regain your progression. You'll probably die. I don't know for certain because no one has been dumb enough to ask me that before." Richter started to huff in irritated disappointment, but then a gleam appeared in Nexus's eye.

"I would be happy to just mark your Rite of Ascension as a failure, if you'd like." Nexus's smile could have made a marathon runner diabetic. "If you request it, I am obligated to restore you back to your previous state, with all penalties in place, of course."

"Penalties? I didn't choose a path."

Nexus looked at his fingernails, checking for dirt, "In that case, it is within my discretion to choose which path you failed."

"No, no," Richter quickly responded, waving his hands wildly. There was no doubt in the world that Nexus would give him the highest penalty.

"You're sure?" Nexus asked with a smile still on his face. "You'd only need to wait until your next ascension opportunity. It shouldn't take you that long."

"No," the chaos seed replied again. This time with a bit of heat.

"Come on," Nexus wheedled. "You've got that flying rat to help you get XP."

Richter's hot anger dropped to subzero in an instant. He took a step toward Nexus, closing the space between them. Even though his level one body only came up to the bottom of the giant's chest, he tilted his head up to look in the Auditor's eyes. His voice was deadly serious.

"Watch what you say about Alma. I know that I can't take you out like I am now. Probably couldn't even if I had all my power back, but I won't have you saying a single word against her. From the sound of that thunder before, you're under review by whatever you call a boss. Insult my familiar one more time, and I *will* call for a Judgement against you."

Nexus eyes widened in shock. Richter nodded at him quickly with a look that could only mean one thing: "Oh yeah, motherfucker. I gotchu!"

After Richter's harrowing Trial to become an Enchanter, he'd been thoroughly embarrassed when he found out his own ignorance was the reason he'd had to endure so much pain. Though he'd known it would get him a tongue-lashing, the chaos seed had humbled himself and told Hisako about it. After she tore him a new one, she told him about the beings called Auditors.

Each section of The Land had at least one Auditor, and they handled Trials and other issues for the creatures that lived there. They were secretive and there was much that wasn't known about them, but she had confirmed they could regulate time. It was an absolutely necessary ability for them. Otherwise, there was no way one being could meet the needs of thousands of people. As impressive as that was, there were limits to their power. One of those was that they were bound to follow certain rules.

According to the Hearth Mother, if an Auditor broke those rules, you weren't helpless. You could invoke an ancient magic to have their actions reviewed. The process wasn't complicated. In fact, all it took was for someone to speak the phrase, "I call for a Judgement." That would bring the attention of whatever beings were superior to the Auditor. If they found in your favor, then not only would the Auditor be bound against harming you, but you would also be provided restitution for the Auditor's poor behavior.

The downside to calling for a Judgement was that, according to Hisako, the Auditor's superiors almost never sided against their agents. Also, while you would gain benefits if they ruled in your favor, the consequences of losing a Judgement were, in a word, horrifying.

Loss of levels was the lightest punishment Hisako had mentioned. She'd also spoken of death, loss of limbs, being returned to the mortal world as an idiot or gaining a permanent debuff. She'd given one example of a woman who had failed a Judgement, and when she came back to The Land, she'd had an effective Charisma of zero. She hadn't actually suffered the loss of any Attribute Points, but every time she opened her mouth, a wet, cheesy substance would fall out. To Richter, it had sounded like a curse of smegma mouth. It was enough to make the chaos seed promise himself to never call for a Judgement.

So why was he willing now? There were a few reasons. One, the thunder that had made Nexus fix his attitude earlier. Richter couldn't be sure, of course, but he was guessing, and banking on, those being the Auditor's superiors. If they were already watching and warning him, then the giant must already be on thin ice. If the chaos seed called for a Judgement, he had to think that would play in his favor.

The second reason was that, like it or not, Richter knew he had to reset his relationship with Nexus. The guy was a total asshole, but he was also the Auditor for his domain. They would probably never be besties, but at the very least they could treat each other with respect. That would never happen if the giant continued to think of him as a punk.

Nexus had to understand that there would be consequences if he treated Richter badly. It was a weird truth that one of the best ways for two guys to bury the hatchet was to beat the crap out of each other and then share a beer. Richter knew he couldn't actually beat

Nexus up, but a genuine threat might serve the same purpose. He'd figure the beer part out after.

The third reason was the most important. Simply put, he was lying his ass off. There was no way in hell he was going to call for a Judgement. Not for something like Nexus insulting Alma. He loved his dragonling to death, but he wasn't going to risk eternal dick-cheese breath over it. He wasn't crazy!

Of course, Nexus did not need to know about any of those reasons, let alone the last one. So, as Richter looked up into the giant's surprised eyes, he did his best to communicate one simple message, "That's right, muthafucka. I'm cray-Z!"

A quick mix of emotions washed over Nexus's face. Richter recognized anger, that was easy enough, but he thought he might have also seen consideration and, quite possibly, fear as well. It all passed in a second and he couldn't be sure. In the end, Nexus didn't apologize, but he didn't push the point either. Richter took it as a win. The giant just asked in a resigned voice, "What are your other questions?"

Richter nodded and took a step back, removing himself from the powerful being's space. Inwardly, he heaved a huge sigh of relief. Before posing his second question, he tried to capitalize on the emotional moment he'd just made, "Look, I know you don't like me. I also know you're pretty clear on how I feel about you. What you need to understand is that I have more than just myself to think about. I have over a thousand people relying on me. I can't afford to keep this petty drama going between us. That's why I want to tell you..." Richter gritted his teeth. What he was about to say next was going to hurt.

"I'm sorry," he grated out.

If Nexus had been taken aback by the threat of a Judgement, he was absolutely floored by Richter's apology. It had never occurred to him that this pompous lord, this never-quite-reached itch on his jock, this... dick pustule that seem to come back pop after pop, would *ever* actually apologize for attacking and disrespecting him. The unexpected nature of the apology moved Nexus and, in spite of himself, he began to think of the dark-skinned human in a different light. The

Auditor regarded Richter for long minutes before finally responding...

By laughing in his face.

"You fucking pussy!" he shouted. "Ha ha ha!"

Nexus slapped his thighs and roared with laughter. He laughed so hard that even his immortal sides hurt. Tears flowed down his face. After a minute, he stopped for a second, looking up at Richter's face. The chaos seed's nostrils had never before expanded to the size they now reached; the man was literally shaking with anger. That just made Nexus laugh even harder. He started howling in glee, and even his powerful body couldn't take it. The pressure was so high that he farted, startling himself, which just made him lose it even more. After another minute he fell to one knee, panting, "I can't. I can't! Your fucking face! Ha ha haaaa!"

The peals of laughter were only interrupted by strained wheezes as he tried to get his breathing under control. There would be a sharp intake of air followed by an audible exhale that sounded like a whoopie cushion. Every time Nexus almost got himself back under control, he would look back up at Richter's enraged expression and the cycle would start all over again. Long minutes passed, and the whole time, the chaos seed got to see what it looked like when a twelve-foot-tall giant was laughing in your gods-damned face!

Finally, after long, loooong minutes, Nexus stood up and wiped the tears from his face. Despite his words and the roughly half an hour of disrespect, he felt neither derision nor anger toward Richter. For the first time since the chaos seed had been dumb enough to attack him, weeks or months ago depending on your understanding of the space-time continuum, he wasn't actively rooting for the man to fail. With a contented sigh, Nexus made a fake frowny face at him. "Heeeey, pucker-face. Stop being such a pucker-face. Come on, come on. Really. For real, I want to help. What questions do you have?"

Richter kept glaring at him. The angry sweats were strong. He'd gotten so mad that his body had made a swamp-like atmosphere round his nethers, just to have another attack option. He wanted nothing more than to tackle Nexus and slap him silly... but instead he heaved a heavy sigh. This certainly hadn't been how he'd intended to bury the hatchet with Nexus, but he'd have to take what he could get. Fact was, he had done something stupid when he'd threatened Nexus during his Trial. If this embarrassing laugh session was the tax he had to pay, he might as well man up and pay it. Of course, it was easier said than done. Thinking about burying an actual hatchet in Nexus's face one day helped a bit. Many, many wusahs later, he had himself under control and he told Nexus the situation with Xuetrix, and what his ramshackle plan was to deal with it.

During the past few months, Richter had had several conversations with Hisako. The information he'd gained hadn't been limited to Auditors. Another topic he'd discussed with the Hearth Mother was how Favors and Vows worked. He knew that there were vague, but severe, consequences if you didn't keep your word after committing to either of these geasa. Aside from that, Richter hadn't known much.

He'd had to be circumspect when having those conversations. Wood sprites weren't exactly known for their tolerant nature. They were more of a slaughter-on-sight kind of people, and that was just for anyone who mistakenly wandered into their territory. Toward anything they considered "evil," they were downright Old Testament.

Seeing as how the Hearth Mother could crush him with a wave of her hand, he'd not explicitly told her that he owed a Favor to a demon. Instead, he'd talked about how he'd let a thief go in Yves but not before extracting a Vow. The terms of that Vow were vague, just like what he owed Xuetrix. The man just had to help Richter sometime in the future. What the chaos seed had wanted to know was just how far these geasa could be pushed.

The answer hadn't been simple. It was downright complicated, in fact. At least, that was the case if you didn't want to do what the other person asked. If you did accede, the Favor or Vow simply disappeared once the objective was completed. It was a one-time deal. The process to resist was much more complicated.

The Hearth Mother had explained that magical accords were not as simple as just keeping your word. They were heavily dependent on the strength of the two parties to the contract. The example she'd used was of someone making a deal with a demon. That had made Richter look at her side-eyed, but she hadn't given any indication that she knew about Xuetrix. He chalked it up to the super ability every mother seemed to have of always knowing when men and boys had done something wrong, even if she didn't know exactly what. Still, she hadn't gone any further down that particular road and had just continued her explanation.

If two creatures of equal power entered into a magical contract, then the person who owed the debt couldn't be asked to do anything overly extraneous. What constituted extraneous would be up to the attitudes of both parties. Apparently, if the person who owed decided to refuse, then an actual contest of wills would take place and exert pressure on both of them. That pressure was a real thing that could affect the body, mind and soul.

If, for example, the person who owed the Favor was asked to help the other person clean their house, then that would most likely be considered an extremely reasonable request by both parties. As such, the person asking would have the weight of their "rightness" behind them. Conversely, the person who owed the Favor would also know that the request was reasonable, and so they would have no strong bulwark of faith to fall back on if they sought to deny the request. A person's belief that they "should" agree to a reasonable request would make it likely they would lose any battle of wills over it.

In this scenario, even if the strength of the two people was roughly the same, the person asking would have, in effect, a much stronger position. The high ground, in Jedi parlance.

If the difference in their power was, say, considered to normally vary by a value of +1, then under these circumstances the person asking the reasonable request might be considered to have a power of +5 instead. Similarly, the person owing the Favor would know that they should agree to what was a very reasonable request, and so their personal power might be modified down to +0.2 of its normal value. Comparing the two, +5 to 0.2, well, it would be no contest. In this case, the person asking the Favor would almost certainly win.

Hisako had gone on to explain that her scenario could be vastly different if one factor was changed, e.g. the person that owed the Favor was a killer-for-hire. In that case, asking such a person to help you clean your house might be seen as ridiculous by both parties. The positive modifier of the asker would probably be much less and the negative modifier to the killer would also be minimal. The assassin might even get a positive modifier to their strength. When the battle of wills began, the outcome could be very different. Oddly, asking an assassin to kill someone might be seen as completely reasonable by both parties, and that request might favor the person who was owed the Favor. It was all about context.

At that point in the explanation, Richter had developed a slight headache. He was still pleased to hear it though, given his own situation. The concept was a bit tricky, but so long as Xuetrix didn't ask anything crazy from him, then there shouldn't be a problem. If the demon did ask him to do something abhorrent, then he should get the high ground in a battle of wills. Also a good result.

That was, of course, when Hisako had dropped some bad news. Even if the two parties had about the same strength, and the request was neither unreasonable nor ridiculous, essentially when everything was equal, the person who owed the Favor would still be at a disadvantage. She said that the Universe took no sides, and delivered judgement fairly.

The fact that a person had previously agreed to a geas put that individual at an immediate disadvantage. Even if that person had been pressured into the contract, they would still be handicapped, though perhaps a bit less so, depending on the situation. Again, the perception of both parties came into play. In a battle of wills, what was "true" was always less important than what someone believed. The main point, she'd said, was that Vows were not to be made lightly, and that in The Land, words had Power.

It all reminded Richter of a lesson his mother had repeated to him over and over, usually when he was about to get spanked. He would protest his innocence with arguments that should have swayed the Supreme Court, or at the very least, convinced her that her heavy hand of justice should not fall. She would always listen, but her response never wavered: "strong never wrong." That basically meant that even if she was actually wrong, her belief was strong enough to win the argument. Another way to look at it was that since she was stronger, it really didn't matter what he said. As a child, it had seemed like the worst of injustices, but it was kind of hard to argue with her logic when he always ended up with a sore ass and eating snot. It wasn't until he got older that he understood the irony of that.

Even learning that he'd be at a disadvantage -- all things being equal -- hadn't been horrible news. Richter had agreed to the Favor after all, and he was prepared to pony up so long as the request wasn't too crazy. He had actually felt pretty good about everything after he had gotten more information. Tragically, what Hisako had told him next had made Richter's blood run cold.

If the person under magical contract refused a request, and then lost the battle of wills, one of three tragedies awaited them. The lightest and least stringent consequence was that the person who had broken their Vow or reneged on a Favor would be cursed. They might lose levels, have their sight or hearing taken away, or become paralyzed. The Universe would amplify the initial horrifying consequences of breaking a geas if the person failed the battle of wills. The long-term consequences of failure were enough to keep children up at night when they heard about them. Despite that, it was still the best-case scenario. The other two options were far, far worse.

The first scenario would only occur if the power difference between the two beings was minor. If, however, the difference in power between the two was great enough, then the loser might be magically compelled to complete the task whether they wanted to or not. Rather than the contract ending, the geas would take control of the person's body. If that happened, the person would do absolutely anything to accomplish the task they were given.

Richter had asked if she personally knew of anyone that had suffered such a fate. Her answer had been a very unladylike barking laugh. Hisako had told him she did not know of anyone stupid enough to willingly break a Vow. She had added that very few people were stupid enough to engage in such magical contracts, and that only the *dumbest* gyotis ever born would make a Vow to a being much stronger than they were.

Personally, Richter still felt her attitude at the end had been completely unnecessary.

The Hearth Mother had then told him that while she herself had never met such a fool, she had heard stories and read old accounts of beings that had been trapped within their bodies for years or decades, bound by a magical contract, forced to serve the being to whom they had owed a Favor. Such stories were told to children so that they would never be foolish enough to make a Vow lightly. Richter remembered that he'd hurried her along at that point.

The stories she'd told him had almost always ended in death. The happiest tales only involved the death of the person who had made the Vow. Most, however, involved the massacre of anyone who stood in their way. Family members, friends, children, it didn't matter. Anyone who tried to stop them would be slain without mercy.

Even if the person under contract was normally moral and upright, they would not hesitate to slaughter entire cities if it was the most expedient method to accomplish their goal. She told him that magical contracts had no time limit and took no pity. Through it all, the person was trapped in a living nightmare, forced to watch evil acts committed by their own hand without the power to stop themselves.

Hisako told him that she had heard of only one case where someone fulfilling their Vow had regained control of their body, mind and soul. It was a dwarf woman who had spent years living in filth and committing acts of savagery. The moment her task was completed, the woman had reportedly looked around in confusion before falling to her knees and wailing in anguish. She had clawed out her own eyes before biting through the flesh of her wrists. She had bled to death, screaming for forgiveness the entire time. A woman who had once been a princess in a far-off kingdom had died in a gutter, her soul stained with the deaths of thousands.

That was obviously horrible, but Richter still hadn't been scared.

He'd grown in power by that point. Even if his body was compelled to complete a task, he might be able to escape the geas if he died and respawned in the process. He couldn't be sure, of course, if that would free him of the contract, but there was a chance.

That was when Hisako had told him about the third and worst outcome of losing a battle of wills. "This," she'd intoned with a serious look in her eye, "is why you never make a deal with a demon."

With great solemnity, she had explained that the "power" calculated for a battle of wills was determined by many things. One's Attributes would come into play, as well as one's levels. Secondary Attributes, and the determination of those involved, were also important. There were many factors, but what made dealing with demons so dangerous in particular was that they were often considered to be a higher order of being, at least as compared to most denizens of The Land.

According to Hisako, there were few things that affected "power" in a battle of wills more than that. He remembered that she had specifically said that demons could be several "tiers" higher than the fools they tricked into owing them favors. Up until this point, he'd thought "tier" was just an expression, a description of some abstract concept. Now he knew a tier was a very real thing. It meant that demons had ascended.

Richter cursed himself for not having asked more questions back then. Even after learning the hard way that The Land had untold secrets, he'd still made an assumption. Not for the first time, he promised himself that he would do better. As disappointed as he was with his past self, Richter was also excited. Suddenly, just as Xuetrix showed up to collect his Favor, he had an opportunity to ascend to a higher tier. If he hadn't learned about his aura, he'd suspect he was being played. The timing was too perfect. But, as insane as it sounded, it might be that just by existing he was manipulating fate.

The point was, he could ascend. If he had to refuse Xuetrix's request, then hopefully his "power" might be the same as the demon's. That was very important, because the tragedy of failing a battle of wills had made his blood run cold.

While being magically compelled to do something sounded horrible, Hisako had told him of an even worse fate. If the difference in power between the demon and the person who owed it a favor was great enough, then not only would that person lose control of their body, but they would lose their soul as well. Even if they died, their spirit would be owned by the demon for all eternity.

As Richter heard all of this, he couldn't help but see the parallels to old myths on Earth. Possession, losing your soul to a demon, such stories were in almost every ancient culture of his home planet. Hisako had told him that she didn't know what happened to souls after a demon claimed them, but every folktale on Earth had said it was the worst fate a person could suffer. He had no desire to learn if the truth was even more horrifying than the myths.

As soon as he'd learned about tiers and Ascension, he'd started formulating a plan. The entire time he'd been looking at his potential incarnations, it had been percolating in the back of his mind. That was why he'd resolved to do two things that otherwise would have been unthinkable. The first had already happened. He'd apologized to Nexus. The outcome of that was worse than he'd expected, but at least the giant had seemed to buy that whole 'I'm doing this for my people' bull crap.

The second was about to happen. He needed to ask Nexus for a favor. Not a Favor favor, of course. He wasn't about to stick his berries in that bear trap again. Instead, he planned to appeal to the Auditor for help. When he'd snapped at Xuetrix, he'd been hoping there was something, anything, in his prompts that might help him stave off whatever request the imp was about to make of him. Never in his wildest dreams did he think he'd find something like the Rite of Ascension.

The fact that he could now ascend was the greatest proof he'd ever had that Luck wasn't just a dump stat. He had no idea what tier the demon was, but he knew that Xuetrix was an ascended being. The imp had told him as much during their first meeting. Now that he could evolve as well, at least he had a chance. He just needed to couple it with a bit of strategy. After that, it was tuck it and fuck it time.

Thankfully, laughing in Richter's face for an entire half hour had put the Auditor in a good mood. Nexus listened to the chaos seed's request with a smile on his face. Sadly, when Richter finished speaking, the giant didn't seem moved by the man's request for help. That is, until an idea seemed to occur to him and a calculating and malicious gleam appeared in his eye. The chaos seed was immediately on guard, but all that happened next was that Nexus said he would agree to Richter's request, if the chaos seed would agree to one of his own.

"What do you need?" the chaos seed asked with utter suspicion. He was already about to be screwed by making a deal with a higher-tier being. He wasn't about to enter into another magical contract with the twelve-foot-tall dickhead that had tortured him for months.

"Nothing really," Nexus said with a faint smile. "I have heard from another Auditor that there is a caravan of humans, elves, dwarves and other races that is preparing to flee the Kingdom of Yves. There is apparently a formidable, if rather short, woman who goes by the name "Mama" who is organizing this procession. She is planning to come to your village."

Richter's eyes widened. He had often wondered if he would get another wave of refugees from the human kingdom. So much had happened since he and a small flotilla had escaped from the kingdom's capital city of Law, months ago. Since then, another wave of migrants had infused some much-needed new blood into the village. They had found a better life, and many of them had quickly advanced their levels. As much as his settlement had to offer though, there was no denying that there was a relatively high mortality rate for the Mist Village's fighting men and women. He needed more people to grow the village and to fill out the ranks of its army.

The fact that Mama was leading the caravan was a double blessing. She was a fierce little lady, and with her particular skill set, there was no denying that she could help with the village's management. The woman ran an incredibly tight ship so far as he could recall. Adding her capabilities to Randolphus's own nearly supernatural management skills might even get the Mist Village some new bonuses.

He was sure she would also be bringing some highly skilled people and maybe even some Professionals with her. The problem was that, while this was all good news, Nexus seemed way too happy. Richter could not remove the sense of foreboding in his heart. Why would the Auditor be offering him this great information right before asking for a favor? The whole thing made his asshole itch.

"Yeah?" Richter responded uneasily.

"Yeah," Nexus repeated with a smile.

"And what does that have to do with my favor?" Richter asked.

"Well," Nexus said in a clipped voice with a silent 'now that you mention it' hanging in the air, "after helping so many of your villagers through their trials, I started to take an interest in some of them. I'm sure you can understand that it's highly irregular to have such a large number of Professionals pass their Trials in one place all at once."

Nexus stopped speaking until Richter nodded in agreement. The chaos seed's eyes remained narrowed though, Richter not trusting the giant for a second.

"Well," the Auditor continued with a magnanimous voice, "Elora, Isabella, Sumiko, the mustached one," Richter thought he heard a little stress enter the giant's voice during the last words, but the Auditor kept a smile plastered on his face, "they are all very fascinating. I found myself curious as to where they came from, so in order to get more information I reached out to Auditors in nearby regions. That is how I discovered that there is a caravan of nonhumans coming from Law. The Auditor for that region told me."

Nexus paused again, but this time Richter didn't grace him with a nod. The chaos seed felt the other shoe about to drop. He didn't know what it was, but he was pretty sure it would be narrow, sharp, and fit squarely between his cheeks.

Not getting a response, the Auditor continued. "In the course of my research, I found out about a very interesting young wood elf. She's a Librarian, and she could probably help the research of your village progress much faster. My request is simple. I would like you to give your permission to let her join the caravan."

Richter blinked, waiting for more, but Nexus just looked back him, calm as a Hindu cow.

"That's it?" the chaos seed asked, voice thick with disbelief.

"That's it," Nexus responded simply.

"What's wrong with her? Does she have a disease? Is she an assassin coming to kill me? Is she possessed by a demon, or something like that?"

Nexus nodded with a smarmy, 'I don't blame your baseless suspicion' look on his face.

"I am sure that you distrust my intentions, but I promise you, by the powers I represent, this woman poses no threat to your village." A faint rumble of thunder punctuated his statement. Not with a warning overtone like last time, but as if to witness and verify Nexus' words. Richter still would have had doubts but, to his surprise, a prompt appeared.

The Powers which preside over Nexus have witnessed his promise and verify its veracity. If his words turn false, he shall suffer a hundredfold.

Richter blinked in shock. It looked like the sadistic black giant really meant what he was saying. Based on the consequences the prompt hinted at, it wasn't something Nexus would have said lightly. He still didn't trust the Auditor, but he no longer doubted he was being told the truth.

"Why do you need my permission for her to come?" Richter asked. "I thought there was already a caravan on the way."

"Yes," Nexus acceded, "but currently, she is not planning to be in the caravan. If you give your permission, however, I can ask my fellow Auditor to arrange it so that she does accompany them. Nothing negative will be done to her or anyone else. She will just be... nudged toward deciding to come."

This all stank to high heaven, but all Richter could think to ask was, "Why do you even need to have my permission?"

"Ah yes. Now we come to the rub. As you so clearly demonstrated when we spoke about a Judgement," Richter tensed, but there didn't seem to be any anger in Nexus's voice when he referenced the threat. He didn't even pause his speech, "I must adhere to certain rules. I cannot directly affect the material realm without invitation, let alone the area overseen by another Auditor. If you allow it, however, my counterpart has agreed to use her influence to encourage the wood elf to join Mama's caravan."

"Agreed?" Richter interrupted. "Agreed when?"

"Just a moment ago." At Richter's doubting frown, Nexus wiggled his fingers in a mystical manner, "I am able to bend the rules of time and space while in my own dimension. Woooooo."

Richter rolled his eyes... hard, but motioned for the black-and-gold giant to continue.

"As I was saying, she will make sure the Librarian joins the caravan. That is all I ask in return for doing you this favor. I want to add a single highly useful Professional to the next influx of refugees coming to your village." Seeing that Richter was going to ask yet another question, Nexus sweetened the pot.

"Additionally, I will work with my fellow Auditor to remove several pitfalls that might have caused some loss of life while they travel to your domain. I will even nudge one of your people to the right location so they can see the caravan as it approaches the mist. I believe you know the dangers they would face traveling through the Forest of Nadria, especially now that you have fully awakened your Place of Power. Dangers that would be compounded if they were forced to wait outside the mists of your domain until they were randomly noticed by your people... or by a bugbear patrol."

Richter gritted his teeth. The bastard was painting him into a corner. He was absolutely right. The forest was dangerous all the time, not even including the fact that the monsters would now be getting stronger. The need to check for refugees was actually something he'd discussed with Terrod and Randolphus several times. Obviously, they wouldn't be able to get through the *Confusing Mists* spell. The only answer they had come up with was to send patrols periodically to the edge of his domain and check if there were any boats waiting in the main river leading to the Kingdom of Yves. Each patrol could only travel the ten miles of wild forest once a week at most. A week waiting in the forest was as good as a death sentence for at least some of the refugees.

If Nexus could streamline the process and help deliver the people safely, that was an amazing offer. The only problem was that Richter was sure there was an angle he wasn't seeing. What was the hidden consequence of welcoming this woman into his village? The chaos seed was sorely tempted, but he just couldn't move past his heavy suspicions. Before he could take the time to come up with another question, Nexus sealed the deal.

"I further promise you, by the powers I represent, that I intend neither you nor your village as a whole any ill intent by my request. I also promise that this will settle any formal debts between us." Another short roll of thunder confirmed his veracity and a prompt appeared.

The Powers which preside over Nexus have witnessed his promise and verify its veracity. If his words turn false, he shall suffer a hundredfold.

Richter really felt uneasy about the whole thing, but he just couldn't find fault in what Nexus was asking. And the truth was, he needed Nexus's help. There was also no denying that the Auditor had sweetened the pot to candy level. The idea of not having any formal debts was insanely attractive. He hadn't even known that he had formal debts, but he sure as hell didn't want to keep them if he had them. Also, it wasn't such a bad idea to get a clean slate with Nexus, even if the giant did still irritate the hell out of him. Finally, the Auditor had even sworn that his request wouldn't be a danger to Richter or the village. Something about the giant's wording tickled the back of his mind, but try as he might he just couldn't find any fault with it.

With regret bordering on foreboding, he reached out and shook Nexus's hand. He verbally agreed that the Librarian could come to the village with Mama, and that he'd give her the same chance as any other refugee. Richter did not feel any better when Nexus started grinning like the Cheshire cat after the deal was struck. They entered a magical contract, then the Auditor asked Richter what Path of Ascension he would choose. The chaos seed declared his new form and the golden light of his Core descended onto the avatar of his choice. The energy began to fuse into the body with a flare. The light grew so bright that all Richter could see was white.

And, blinded once again, Richter started falling.

The last thought he had was how strange Nexus's request was. Why did he want that Librarian in the Mist Village so badly? And who the hell named their daughter Tamitu, anyway?

CHAPTER 17

DAY 151 – JUREN 2, 0 AOC

*R*ichter blinked.

Looking around, it seemed like everything was the same as before he'd left. Xuetrix was still hovering nearby with a foul expression on his little demon face. His body had all its points back. The unpleasant sensations that had been absent in Nexus's dimension came flooding back: hunger, thirst and exhaustion. A check of his status page showed no change either. It looked like Nexus had kept the first part of his promise. Richter had been returned, unchanged, to the material plane a bare moment after he'd left for his Ascension. The imp looked none the wiser.

That belief was shaken a moment later when Xuetrix cocked his head in suspicion. Richter held his breath, but the demon only kept glaring. The chaos seed decided not to waste time. The clock was ticking. There were a few more prompts to be seen, but he kept them minimized. It was time to deal with his demon.

"Xuetrix," he called out, standing up once again. "I'm tired of your stench. What do you want?"

"What do I want?" the imp basically screeched. "You dare to speak to me with such disrespect? Do you remember how my pet bug made you its bitch? That was nothing, not even the barest inkling of my power. I can snuff out your soul, human!"

Richter kept his face impassive, even though his heart started beating faster. When he spoke, it was with a bored tone, "But then who would carry out your little task? I have other things to do than banter with someone who manipulated me on my first day in this world. You broached the subject of my Favor. Now I am asking you again. What do you want, you silly parakeet?"

The anger on the imp's face grew even greater. He opened up his mouth to deliver a scathing rejoinder or a spell that would burn Richter alive. The chaos seed never found out. All of a sudden, the anger left Xuetrix's face and a calculating look replaced it. Then the imp began to laugh. He pointed one finger at Richter while he chortled, before moving it back and forth like a metronome.

"For shame, young human. You have been speaking to someone about the nature of Favors. Did you think I would not know this simple Lore? That if the Power of Three could bind you to me, that it could also set you free?" The imp laughed in derision at the aggrieved look on Richter's face.

While the imp mocked him, the dark-skinned man laughed on the inside. The sad look on his face should have earned him the *Acting* skill as far as he was concerned. Hisako had indeed told him of a way to dissolve a geas if the other person were foolish enough to allow it. Neither a Favor nor a Vow had a time limit, but once the person who held the contract broached the matter, there was a small chance to negate it.

If the promisor asked the promisee to speak the terms of the contract three times, and they failed to do so, then the Favor could fade away. As Xuetrix had said, while the Power of Three could bind a contract, it could also tear it asunder. The Hearth Mother had told him that nearly everyone knew of this fact, so no one would be foolish enough to fall for such a trick.

Richter had not actually thought it would work against a demon. He did think that Xuetrix's own arrogance could be used against him though. The chaos seed needed the imp to formally state his demand

and do it quickly. The demon was not foolish enough to fall for such a simple gamble, but he was cocky enough to think that Richter was too stupid to realize that. What happened next was exactly what the chaos seed had intended. One more piece of his plan fell into place.

Xuetrix was still laughing at him when he spoke again. His wings beat lazily and he flew in a slow circle around Richter, forcing the chaos seed to turn to keep him in view. "Seeing as how you are so eager to conclude our business, I will answer your question. You owe me a Favor, and I plan to collect." He paused again, savoring the fake panic on Richter's face before finishing his statement. "I need you to kill someone. Agree and ask no questions, or face the consequences, mortal!"

A Favor has been claimed!

You have been asked to kill another being. No other information has been provided and none can be requested until you agree. Once accepted, failure to accomplish your set goal will cause a punishment three times greater than refusal.

Will you agree to this? Yes or No?

He read the prompt carefully, then looked up at Xuetrix. The imp was smiling lasciviously. If Richter had not understood the nature of magical contracts, he might have thought the Favor was strange, but it was actually quite ingenious.

Richter was a killer. There was no denying that. He even had several Slayer Titles to his name. No one could ever think that asking him to kill would be an unreasonable request. The fact that he could not ask questions was definitely a bit off, but it still didn't make the request irrational. On the contrary, Xuetrix was taking the very approach that Hisako had warned him about.

Oftentimes, a demon's true goal was not the request itself. It was to enslave the soul of any who were foolish enough to owe them a Favor. To accomplish that, they would ask for something that the other person would refuse. The request would not be so outlandish that the magical contract might be broken. If Xuetrix was asking him to kill a murderer or the leader of a den of thieves, he might actually agree. The problem was that Richter would never agree to kill a random innocent or, even worse, to kill someone he loved and cared about.

He couldn't even stall. The geas did not allow him to just agree now and decide to renege later. Agreeing in bad faith would probably trigger dire consequences. Hisako had been clear about that. Refusing a Vow would have a cost, but attempting to lie would bring ten times as much pain. The better choice was what he was about to do. Refusing to perform the Favor would mean a battle of wills, but at least the penalty wouldn't be magnified. Over time, he might recover. If that penalty was increased, however, it would cripple him.

Looking at the imp's evil grin, Richter had no doubt that Xuetrix knew exactly what was going through his head. The imp wanted to trap him. The chaos seed still had no idea who had sent the demon to help him when he first came to The Land, but it looked like that "helpful" phase had passed. The imp was practically salivating. Laugh it up, Richter thought, I've got plans of my own.

Staring defiantly into Xuetrix's eyes, he selected "No" on the prompt.

Immediately, a shared notification appeared in both of their gazes. Xuetrix's sneering smile turned into a predatory grin. Richter stared back and thought, bring it!

CHAPTER 18

DAY 151 – JUREN 2, 0 AOC

A *Favor has been **DENIED!***

*A Battle of Wills will now begin between **Richter, a Tier 1 Human**, and **Xuetrix, a Tier 2 Ashdark Imp**. Xuetrix has reached ascended rank 6 out of 6. Judgement shall now be passed upon the two combatants.*

The news was both good and bad insofar as Richter was concerned. It was good that Xuetrix was only one tier above him. When Nexus came through with his part of the plan, that would even out. What wasn't so great were the ranks Xuetrix had reached. There were six, which meant the demon's ascended form was a *rare* incarnation. Not only that, the demon had managed to maximize the power of his incarnation. He didn't know what that would mean for the upcoming contest, but it couldn't be good.

Another prompt appeared, followed by a slight pause.

Base Power of Richter is determined by the following factors:

The next prompts showed the calculations for Richter's base power.

Body	Tier 1 Human	+1
Mind	Tier 1 Human	+1
Soul	Tier 1 Human	+1
Special	Chaos Seed	+2.5
Aura	Chaotic Gradient (Greater)	0.0
Total		5.5

Richter had no frame of reference, but seeing that he only amounted to a +1 as a tier 1 human in his body, mind and soul didn't make him feel great. What was interesting was that his Chaos Seed increased his power almost as much as everything else combined. He was confused by the double zero next to his aura, but then he realized it made a kind of sense. *Chaotic Gradient* wasn't there to help or hurt him. All it did was make things more likely to happen. Its effects were just as random as the name implied.

Unfortunately, there was no information regarding what Xuetrix's power was. There was also no time to worry about it. As soon as he finished absorbing his own information another series of notifications appeared, and he had to focus on them.

The base Power of both combatants has been determined. The specifics of both the Favor and the situation have been calculated. The following Modifiers will be made to each contestant's Power:

The next lines dealt with the specific Favor Xuetrix had requested. Richter was initially pleased by the description, but the lines after that felt like nails being driven into his coffin.

*The Request has been deemed: **General in Description, Stringent in Conditions** and **Reasonable.***

*The following Request Modifiers are applied to Xuetrix's Power: **-10%, -15%,** and **0%.***

A Tier difference of 1 to 2 increases Xuetrix's Power by +25%

Xuetrix advancing his Tier 2 form to rank 6 of 6 further increases his Power by +25%

As Richter read the modifier breakdown, he cursed softly. It appeared the Universe did agree that the request was unreasonable. Unfortunately, the tier difference between them was enough to neutralize any benefit Richter would have received. The fact that the Universe had decided that asking Richter to murder someone was *reasonable* had also not escaped his attention. It also didn't bother him overly much. He was what he was.

The bigger problem was that Richter had been right. The fact that the ashdark imp had maxed out the ranks of his incarnation was a problem. Starting at rank 1, each of the five progressions had increased Xuetrix's power by another 5%. The rank modifier was even stronger than the tier difference. The demon was getting the same information and was more than happy with it. He stared at Richter with a leering grin. The chaos seed just firmed his jaw and stared back. The battle was going to begin soon. The time for regrets had passed.

Of course, the next line didn't help his mood too much either.

A level difference of 34 has been detected.

Xuetrix's Power to be modified by +17%

Richter was shocked to see just how many levels the demon had on him. Especially after the battle had catapulted him up to level forty-five. It was just one more thing he'd have to overcome. What did strike him was how much less important levels were than tiers. Xuetrix having ascended had given the imp a 25% bonus, but levels only offered a 0.5% modifier each. If nothing else, it underlined the power of tiers versus levels.

The next several lines showed the final modifiers. The first one hurt deeply.

The fact that Richter agreed to the Favor decreases Richter's Power by -50%

It was made only slightly better by the next one.

The fact that Xuetrix tricked Richter into the Favor increases Richter's Power by +25%

Xuetrix's face was filled with glee. Of course, he already knew that a Favor he had tricked someone into would not be as strong as one willingly entered into, but the overall modifier was still heavily in his favor. The demon was confident he could win even if it was an even playing field. This was not false confidence. Being an ascended being had greatly increased the power of his mind, body and soul. Even the base power of a Tier 1 demon would be enough to defeat the average human. He was not so foolish as to consider Richter 'average,' but then again, he was not an average imp. "You will serve me for eternity!" the imp hissed with glee.

Right after that, which came as a surprise to both of them, a final modifier prompt appeared. It was especially shocking to Xuetrix. The demon had claimed many souls and won many battles of will. He had never seen this happen before.

Special modifier for Chaos Seed Nature triggers a random modifier change heavily affected by the main Primary Attribute of a Chaos Seed. 1-5% for every 10 points of Luck. Richter's Power increased by +11%

Richter cheered slightly, but in the end, it made very little difference to the bottom line.

Total Modifier: -14% Richter, +42% Xuetrix

That was all of it. There was no complaining and there was no time for appeal.

The Battle of Wills will begin in 7, ...

As horrible as the modifier was, especially knowing that Xuetrix's base power was probably higher than his, Richter smiled.

For some reason, that irritated the imp to no end. "Why are you smiling, mortal? You cannot win."

The chaos seed laughed in his face, savoring the fact that it was finally his turn to do so. "I'm laughing because I know something you don't know. I, am not, left-handed!"

Then he thought, "Now, Nexus!"

4, 3...

Richter blinked in panic. He tried again, "Come on, man. Ascend me now!" His mental tone had a jokey-panic to it. He'd needed Xuetrix to start the Battle of Wills before he advanced his tier. If the imp had known it was going to be a more fair playing ground, he might have changed his request at the last minute, and the chaos seed needed the modifier. Of course, he hadn't intended for Xuetrix to be nearly two whole tiers above him in power, but the modifier should improve as soon as Nexus came through on the second part of his promise.

That was entirely dependent on the Auditor not screwing him over.

2, 1... Battle Commencing.

Time ran out. The last thoughts Richter had as golden strands of force surrounded both him and Xuetrix was, "Inconceivable!" He'd been betrayed. Again!

CHAPTER 19

DAY 151 – JUREN 2, 0 AOC

*W*hile Richter's grin died, a prompt appeared.

As the injured party, Xuetrix the Ash Imp is given priority in determining initiative.

Initiative, Richter questioned in his mind. Like who could go first?

Xuetrix wasted no time answering the silent question.

The demon clenched both fists and shouted, "You goin' pay me what you owe me!" He then sent an attack of pure will at Richter. The power of his resolve was magnified by 42% and the rings of golden force surrounding the chaos seed squeezed tighter.

"Aaaargghh!" Richter screamed. There was a flashing light in the corner of his vision, and for the first time he noticed that his health, mana and stamina bars had been replaced with a single golden bar called "power." Even as agony lanced through his very essence, he accessed information about it.

Power – The sum of all that you are. Power is both attack and defense, health and the energy to attack. In a Battle of Wills, Power will fuel your attacks, but it will also determine your ability to survive the attacks of your opponent. Choose your strategy well.

Richter could see his own gold bar starting to decrease. To make matters worse, the end of his power bar was bright red. The number 14% was emblazoned on that section. It didn't take a large mental leap to get that it indicated the disadvantage he had started at. That was bad enough, but he could also see Xuetrix's power. What he saw made his stomach drop.

The demon's power was represented by a gold bar as well. Way more important than the color though was the fact that it was about three times longer than Richter's. Before the chaos seed could even recover from the attack, Xuetrix pointed at the two bars. His smug nod clearly communicated that he thought Richter didn't measure up.

Richter couldn't even be bothered to respond. That was because his eyes were glued to the long green extension at the end of Xuetrix's power bar. His had the number 42% on it, representing the demon's own modifier. All told, the imp had about five times more power than he did. All of this washed over Richter along with waves of pain from Xuetrix's first attack.

The golden rings that surrounded him were not only compressing his body, they were damaging his mind and soul. Pain flashed through him, and his very thoughts became more sluggish. His desire to resist was attacked, and after only the imp's first salvo he felt himself consider bowing to the demon's will.

The chaos seed was no stranger to pain and doubt though. His strength was not a weak shell covering a craven person. Again and again, he had faced his internal doubts and come through the crucible. Despite the pain in his body, he made himself stand tall, and he banished the doubt from his soul. Even though the golden bands were still squeezing him, he forced his mind to think about Alma, Sion and all the people that relied on him. The pain did not vanish, but the first threat passed.

He took stock. He might be standing tall, but that single attack had decreased his total power by nearly 10%. Richter didn't waste time worrying about it though. He just looked back at Xuetrix with anger in his heart and spat, "You are just a parasite who betrayed my trust and the trust of whoever hired you. Let me go!"

His denunciation of the imp carried his will and fury. Richter instinctually knew that he could have used his energy to relieve the pressure on himself. He also felt this would be a trap. Hisako had told him that combatants would take turns in a battle of wills. Each round would give them seventy-seven seconds to attack, but would first give them seven seconds to heal. Either action would drain their power.

The contest wasn't only about power, but also about a person's will to endure. If he wasted some of his power just to lessen his pain, he'd be in an even worse position overall. He wasn't going to win this by playing defense. Also, it just wasn't his style. He poured all of his anger into the attack and his power dropped by 5%.

Richter followed his instincts, and used his very will as a weapon. A feeling of extreme satisfaction spread through him when he saw the golden bands squeeze tighter on Xuetrix. The demon's face twisted in pain and his wings quivered in distress. The imp's first attack had used up about half of the demon's green modifier. The chaos seed's attack decreased it further. More of the green power drained away and Richter's heart soared as he saw it decreasing bit by bit.

This was only the first time he had engaged in such a battle, however. How could his first strike, weakened by his modifier, do true damage to the imp? How could he expect to lay low a demon trained in subterfuge and the corruption of souls with only one strike? Too soon, Xuetrix stood tall again and smiled maliciously at Richter.

"Is that really all you have? You are weak. You are nothing, and you have failed your people again and again. How many of them have died under your command, your lordship?" Without Richter even noticing, the demon's voice became melodic, enchanting. The cadence worked its way into his mind and spirit, eroding both like an insidious acid.

Whereas the demon's first attack had been as strong and brutal as a hammer, the second was a silent dagger sliding into Richter's ribs, searching for his heart. The battle of wills was nuanced in ways that the chaos seed had never expected, and the imp was accomplished in the art of corruption. This attack was focused on weakening the soul. The imp's power bar smoothly emptied as the demon poured more energy into the assault. As powerful as the attack was, it was only the green modifier that was emptied. The length of Xuetrix's base power bar remained untouched.

The golden bands began to tighten around Richter again. It was slower this time, and the physical pain was almost like an afterthought compared to the lashing his spirit was taking.

"No, no, no," Richter breathed softly in denial of the demon's words. Xuetrix kept speaking, showing the true power of words, each accusation eating away at his enemy. Killer, betrayer, weak, powerless, these and worse spilled from the demon's lips. Richter's face quickly shifted from sadness to doubt to despair. The rebuttals he initially declared quickly became a question, "No?"

Without realizing, he fell to one knee, staring at the imp's smile which seemed to grow wider by the second. If felt like Xuetrix's Cheshire-cat grin would swallow him whole. Accusations and insults flowed even faster from the demon's lips. Seeing his attack was so effective, Xuetrix used some of his base power in hopes of wearing Richter down. He struggled to respond, but this attack was not as easy to resist. It was not a frontal assault; it focused on his weak spots and weakened them even more. Xuetrix's plan was to have his prey crumble under the weight of his own insecurities. There was a reason the imp was smiling. The plan was working.

Richter was lost in a hell of his own mind. His power continued to fall. He would have already succumbed if not for the trials he'd survived and the blessing of the Quickening. The demon committed a great deal of his power to this attack, eating into his base power. Despite everything he had invested Xuetrix had plenty to spare, and Richter was in a sorry state. The chaos seed's power had dropped below 15% and was continuing to fall. Xuetrix's evil black heart thudded in excitement and he practically drooled over the thought of possessing a soul as strong as the chaos seed's! He would have more than enough power left to permanently bind it into his service!

The imp's plan would have worked if not for one thing: the bonus Richter had received from eating the First Fruit of the Quickening, the boost to the chaos seed's Secondary Attribute, Resilience. In every life many trials arose, and many people would be overcome. Some could find buried strength within themselves. In The Land, this was not a poetic description. It was an Attribute, Resilience.

Resilience: In every life trials arise, and many fail their tests. This Attribute is a measure of your ability to withstand the worst of conditions before succumbing to death. You may cling to the mortal coil with spectral fingers, holding on to life for a scant few additional moments than should be allowed by gods and demons. You will be able to withstand the blows of fate, with your head held high, bleeding and bruised and pale.

As Richter's consciousness was suppressed and forced deeper into the depths of his own soul, a pair of eyes looked up out of the dark. They glared in equal parts anger and defiance. The eyes were his own, and they communicated a simple message: "No!" Unlike the soft denials that Richter had been muttering before, this voice was loud as thunder and strong as folded steel. "This far. No further!"

The bands of force that had been restricting the chaos seed loosened their grip and he locked eyes with the demon once again. To both of their surprise, Richter's Resilience attribute refilled his power to nearly 50%. Xuetrix's salacious smile slipped, and what was left in its place was a sneer of malevolence.

Despite Richter having triggered his Resilience attribute, this was not the first time the imp had corrupted and claimed a soul. It was also not the first time he had seen this happen. Xuetrix probably knew more about the attribute than the chaos seed did. Even though the imp was surprised at the strength of the human's Resilience, he also knew that such reserves were finite and could only be relied upon once. That was why, in the last seconds he had left to attack, he poured even more of his power into the assault. More of the demon's power disappeared as he tried to overcome Richter's resurgence.

The demon was destined to be disappointed.

The last seconds of Xuetrix's round elapsed, and Richter was still standing. He shook off the doubts and fears that Xuetrix had been able to infest his mind and soul with. With brutal efficiency he faced those uncertainties with a firm sense of self. The pain remained, but that was nothing new.

Glaring at the imp, he spat, "I am Richter. I am not perfect, but fuck you, I'm trying!" Even though the demon had given it his all, the chaos seed was still weathering the emotional and mental attacks faster than the imp could muster them. Even after Xuetrix's last-ditch effort, the chaos seed's power stabilized at 38%. The demon was left panting and glaring death at his foe. Richter had won a moral victory that round.

Sadly, power did not care about morality. The battle was not done. Richter had proven stronger than the demon had thought, but Xuetrix still had nearly five times as much power as his opponent. If only he hadn't been stupid enough to trust Nexus, but he had. This time, the Auditor would cost him everything. There was nowhere to hide in this contest, and his only gambit had failed. The two stared at each other, buried beneath the earth and locked together in enmity.

Richter glared at the demon with a furious gaze, but in his heart, he knew it was all for naught. Xuetrix's attacks were too strong. The difference in their power was too great. The reality was, he just didn't have much power left. Once it was gone, even if he was willing to endure more agony than he already felt, it would be over. His only hope would be that Xuetrix's power wouldn't be enough to completely enslave him.

Squaring his shoulders, he prepared to give it his all. If this was going to be his end, he would make it count. All he could do was go all out and hope for the best. But as he prepared to attack, he realized that wasn't exactly true. There was one other thing he could do.

A lifetime of gaming had taught him an impressive repertoire of insults and curse words. As he stared at Xuetrix, he unleashed them all on Nexus in a truly inspired barrage. He had no idea if the Auditor could hear his venomous tirade but, just in case, he decided to vent his frustration. His winged enemy stared at him like he was crazy, but Richter didn't care. If this was the end, then that dickhead was going to know!

Every vile and horrible thing he could conceive of spilled from his lips and echoed off the walls of the tunnel. He really dug deep, wanting the duplicitous giant to feel his ire. He thought up dreadful things until his time ran out, then added one more for good measure.

"And that's why you're just a load that your uncle should have swallowed! Okay, now go fu-"

Before he could finish the thought, he finally heard Nexus respond inside his head, "What's with the potty mouth? I thought we were starting to get along?" The Auditor's voice was mocking inside of his head.

Where the hell have you been? Richter thought back. Despite himself, a quick look of relief crossed his face. As short lived as it was, Xuetrix still caught it. It was something the demon didn't understand, which meant it was something he absolutely didn't trust. What could possibly have brought hope to this man who was about to lose his very soul?

In a split-second decision, which showed the experience of the demon, he decided to do something drastic. The battle of wills normally required each combatant to take turns attacking. Knowing how little power Richter had left, the demon was content to fight off the man's last attack then finish the battle during the next round. Resilience or no, he was sure that he'd sweep aside Richter's remaining defenses. He would then use his remaining power to bind his enemy's soul.

What not even Hisako had known, however, was that it was possible to make two attacks in a row. The downside was that it would require Xuetrix to use a precious Token he'd gained from a previous battle of wills. It was a resource the demon would not use lightly, as it would burn through a great deal of the power he had left.

Nevertheless, after seeing that flash of hope on Richter's face, his instincts were screaming at him to finish the battle, and finish it now.

Richter saw the demon's resolve firming and did the only thing he could think of to buy time. He got into "Crane Kick" position, also known as the "Arms up Captain Morgan" and made the karate sound "waaaaaah!" In true Cobra Kai style, Xuetrix pulled back, utterly confused, buying Richter a few precious seconds.

"Where the hell have you been?" he mentally shouted again. There was still fury in his tone, but his precarious situation banked the flames substantially.

"Just abiding by the terms of our deal," the Auditor thought to him smugly. Then, in Richter's own voice, he repeated what Richter had asked of him verbatim. "Trigger my ascendance when I call, okay?" Then in his voice again, Nexus finished, "You didn't call 'okay' until just a moment ago. Never forget, in The Land, your words have power."

Richter felt like his brain was melting out of his ears. He was standing in Danny Laruso attack pose, about to lose his soul, and this bastard was playing games? He'd literally never hated anyone as much as he hated Nexus in that moment. It was like... Gary-Kevin-level hate. He dug deep and unleashed an even worse stream of obscenities at the giant. The entire time, he was holding the crane-kick position and Xuetrix was definitely realizing it was just a stupid delaying tactic. Just as the demon was about to attack again, Nexus interrupted the stream of mental diarrhea Richter was firing at him.

"Whoa, whoa, whoa. You suck your daddy off with that mouth? Just ascend and be happy." A stream of energy flowed into Richter's mind, body and soul, finishing the process that had been nearly completed in Nexus's personal realm. As the profound changes washed over him, the Auditor sent a final message, "Good luck. I hate you."

In the moment before Xuetrix was about to use his Token, everything changed. Millions of former Earthlings were sent a notification that filled them with anger, terror, jealousy and hope.

*In this Age of Chaos, the First **Chaos Lord** has been born! Rejoice and Lament oh creatures of the infinite!*

If Richter had known that message had gone out to every single chaos seed in The Land, he would have vomited out another masterpiece of profanity, but he barely spared the prompt a moment's notice. Even Nexus's underhanded adherence to Richter's exact words was pushed to the back of his mind to be dealt with at a later date. His attention was solely focused upon the notifications that both he and Xuetrix were sharing. To his delight and the demon's chagrin, they showed new modifiers and the consequences of his ascension.

Roiling grey fire flared in the demon's eyes. That was not hyperbole; actual power flared inside of the imp. Richter just stared back with a shit-eating grin. His power bar lengthened and refilled to reflect his new tier and *legendary* ascended form. An invisible and intangible wind began to swirl around the chaos lord. His mind and body remained the same, but his soul became more powerful and complex by an order of magnitude. The blood flowing through his body changed, and Richter felt like his veins were pumping battery acid. There was pain, but what was pain compared to pure, unadulterated power?

"Now," he asked with an insane grin, "where were we?"

CHAPTER 20

DAY 151 – JUREN 2, 0 AOC

The two foes read the notifications brought on by Richter's ascension.

*Know This! Richter, **Tier 1 Human**, has ascended to become a **Tier 2 Chaos Lord**. As such, the Battle of Wills is suspended for 77 seconds while his base power is tabulated and modifiers are recalculated.*

Xuetrix started cursing in his native tongue. To Richter's great surprise, he could finally understand what the demon was saying. He didn't have time to more than peripherally listen. His gambit had worked, but he had barely a minute left to absorb the information on his new form and come up with a plan.

The next prompt was only for him.

The following changes will be used to calculate your base Power

	Tier 1 Human	Tier 2 Chaos Lord
Body	+1	+2.5
Mind	+1	+2.5
Soul	+1	+2.5
Special	+2.5	+5.0
Aura	+0.0	+0.0
Bloodline	+0.0	+4.1

Base Power improved from +5.5 to +16.6

Richter's grin was only matched by Xuetrix's grimace. The demon was looking at his own status windows, and didn't like what he was seeing. The human, however, was celebrating the fact that his base power had more than tripled! He'd also gained a bloodline! The next prompt showed the modifiers.

Modifiers are now adjusted accordingly:

Most of the factors hadn't been altered. Richter still had a -25% modifier because he had agreed to do Xuetrix a Favor. Xuetrix still had a boost to his power because of maxing out the ranks of his Tier 2 form and having more levels than Richter. Richter advancing his tier had made a major change though.

Both combatants possessing a Tier 2 form has removed the +25% modifier from Xuetrix.

Not only had Xuetrix lost his tier advantage, but Richter had gained positive modifiers!

Special modifier for Chaos Lord Nature triggers a random modifier heavily affected by the main Primary Attribute of Chaotic creatures. +1-10% for every 10 points of Luck.

Previous Modifier increased from +11% to +36%

Richter was confused for a second, but then he remembered the attribute boon from evolving into a chaos lord. He'd gained +10 to his Luck. According to the prompt, chaos lords could utilize Luck even more than a chaos seed. All together it meant that he now had a +36% extra modifier to the attribute!

All the changes cumulated in the next prompt.

Total Modifier: +36% Richter, +17% Xuetrix

His power adjustment was even stronger than Xuetrix's! While the demon understandably hated the change, the chaos lord couldn't wait until the seventy-seven-second timer elapsed. Even with the small amount of energy he had left, he had a chance now. He had a chance. That was when the something happened that made Richter take back every mean thing he'd ever said about the Universe.

He got some of this power back!

Know This! A Determination has been made. While full restoration of power is unacceptable, there must be some allowance made for one of the parties involved in this Battle of Wills not having possession of his ascended status at the beginning.

It has been decided that half of the power removed from his original negative modifier will be replaced: +0.385
It has also been decided that half of the difference between Richter's Tier 1 and Tier 2 base power will be awarded to him: +5.55

As this was no fault of the other party, the same amount of power will be restored to Xuetrix.

The Battle of Wills shall resume in 58, 57, 56, ...

Xuetrix stared at him with pure hatred on his demonic face.

Richter didn't care because his gold bar started refilling at a prodigious rate. It was true that Xuetrix's power bar refilled as well, but the ratio between them decreased appreciably. Xuetrix's power bar was still larger, about half again as big as Richter's, but these were the best odds Richter had had all night. Now that his modifier was a bit bigger, the chaos lord was ready for a fight. After all, it was what he did!

There was still time left before the battle resumed though, so he familiarized himself with his newly ascended form. A host of new prompts had flooded his consciousness along with his ascension. They were accompanied by a sound like a crescendo of horns followed by drums.

Bwaaa-bwa-bwa-bwaaaah-dom-DOM!
*Congratulations! You have ascended to the Tier 2 form: **Chaos Lord!***

Advancing your level now offers improved points!

	Tier 1 Human	Tier 2 Chaos Lord
Stat Points	As a Chaos Seed, you gain **6 Stat Points** to distribute to characteristics instead of the usual 4	As a Chaos Lord, you gain **15 Stat Points** to distribute
Talent Points	As a Chaos Seed, you receive **15 Talent Points** instead of the usual 10. You receive an additional **15 Talent Points** from your Profession and Specialty for having a 100% affinity in Enchanting	As a Chaos Lord you receive **30 Talent Points** You receive an additional **15 Talent Points** from your Profession and Specialty for having a 100% affinity in Enchanting
Chaos Points	You receive **8 Chaos Points** due to your Blessing by the Lords of Chaos	You receive **100 Chaos Points** due to your Blessing by the Lords of Chaos
Skill % Points	**+25%** to the skill of your choice	**+75%** to the skill of your choice

Richter quickly thought about the increases. On the surface, his tier ascendance was an amazing boon. What counterbalanced it was the increased experience it would take to level. It was practically five times as much.

In contrast, he gained two-and-a-half times as many Attribute Points, three times as many Skill Percentage Points, and only fifty percent more Talent Points. It was easy to see that even though each level would give him more points, his overall progression would slow considerably. To advance another ten levels would require more than fifty times as much XP, but would only provide the equivalent of half as many Attribute Points. It seemed that The Land conspired to limit the raw power of high leveled individuals.

This was especially true for his Profession and Specialty. Both were fueled by Talent Points, and those would drop off considerably. There were quests which also gave TPs, but it looked like he would have to be very deliberate with how he invested those points in the future. Thankfully, his point conversion Talent gave him options that other ascended beings would lack. Unfortunately, it was an extreme option that came with serious downsides. Richter didn't regret how he'd spent his points so far, but he now knew there was a bottleneck coming. He would have to get more Profession quests in the future.

Even though he didn't like the effective reduction in points, he considered himself fortunate. It occurred to him that some people must fail to ascend when they reached a Threshold. If he hadn't gained his new incarnation, then even though the XP barrier had massively grown, the points he would gain upon leveling would have remained the same. After a few levels, anyone that had completed the Rite of Ascension would have a substantial advantage over those who didn't.

The one area he would see a major increase was in the Chaos Points he would now receive. Having ushered in the Age of Chaos, he already gained twice as many CPs as any other kidnapped earthling. He was now gaining one hundred CPs per level rather than eight. That meant the base number of points had increased from four to fifty. Even though he needed five times as much XP to level, he was being awarded more than twelve times as many Chaos Points. He couldn't wait to see what the Sea of Chaos now offered, especially since he could choose from the 5th stratum as a Chaos Lord!

There was more information about his newly ascended form.

*Congratulations! You are the first Chaos Seed to evolve into the **Legendary** form of a **Chaos Lord!** You have earned a Choice! This is your 2nd Choice. As such, you will be awarded one extra option and 7 more seconds to decide. Never forget, Choice is the essence of Chaos.*

Richter had been half-expecting this. When he'd touched the Chaos Shard, he'd both ushered in the Age of Chaos and earned himself one of several bonuses. He'd only been given seven seconds to decide which option to take and, in retrospect, he wasn't sure he'd chosen the best one. Having fourteen seconds this time would be great. He quickly checked how much time was left before the battle began. Forty-eight seconds. More than enough time. He gave the options his full attention.

1) +1 Vassal Slot per 3 Chaos Lord Ranks

2) Double bonuses to chaotic vassals

3) Double benefits to you from chaotic vassals

4) +1 to available levels on Liege Page

You have fourteen seconds to decide, starting now. 14, ...

Suddenly the extra time didn't seem like enough. What did any of this any mean? That old, "I don't know enough" anger reared its ugly head and expletives fell from his lips. He had no idea what these options meant! All he could do was quickly shuffle through some of the other prompts waiting for him to read.

Time continued to tick away.

13, 12, 11, …

Richter quickly looked and minimized the windows one after another. He could have just absorbed the information from each, but honestly, it wouldn't have helped. While the act was nearly instantaneous, it still took time for his mind to process and file the info. If he got a massive data dump, the time needed to sort through it all would eat the seconds he had left to make his decision. All he could do was open, scan and close the windows as quickly as possible.

A noise triggered when he opened one of the prompt windows.

TRING!

Immediately, he had a pavlovian response to the leveling-up sound, his hindbrain already registering that it was going to get a treat. It wasn't something he could control, and his sorting paused for a moment before his conscious mind could reassert itself. As pleasant of a surprise as it was, it cost him precious seconds.

8, 7, …

"Shit!"

Richter closed the window. He couldn't even afford the time needed for self-recrimination as he pulled up the next prompt. His eyes scanned the top line, and he realized with relief that it was what he was looking for. He envisioned "pulling" the window toward him until it grew large enough to fill his entire field of vision. The notification disappeared and the knowledge washed over him. More precious time passed by, never to be reclaimed.

5, 4, …

Very few seconds were left, but Richter had found the knowledge he needed!

*As a Chaos Lord, you may now tie other Chaotic beings to your service. Each will consume a **Vassal Slot**. The exact details of this bond are unique to each lord and vassal, but are immediately dissolved if either takes direct, deadly action against the other.*

This bond serves the same function as a Vow or Favor, but is several times more powerful. You may convince other beings to serve you in this capacity, but they cannot be directly forced to do so. Remember, Choice is the essence of Chaos!

There is much that can be gained on both sides of this magical contract. Upgrades can be purchased on your Vassal page.

Richter had no idea what that was, but he kept reading.

*Your **Legendary** incarnation of Chaos Lord has 9 ranks.*
You are currently at Rank 1, Weak. Spend 500 Chaos Points to advance to Rank 2, Low. Each Vassal you obtain will decrease this cost by 100 CPs per point of Chaotic alignment.

At Rank 1:

*You have 1 **Vassal Slots***
Each Vassal will generate Chaos Points for you at the rate of 1 CP per Chaotic alignment of the Vassal per week
All Chaos Spells and Abilities increased by 25%
You can access Level 1 of your Vassal Page
Icon for Chaotic Liege page now available on your interface.

Richter's eyes unfocused in a practiced way, bring his interface into view. Indeed, there was a new icon in the corner of his vision. It was a crown composed of the ever-changing grey energy of Chaos. Curiosity pawed at him. He would love to open it and learn more. So far, all he really understood was that if he gained a chaotic vassal, that person would earn him a steady supply of Chaos Points! That was amazing, but there was still so much he didn't understand.

Basically, it looked like this evolution let him bind other chaos seeds to his service. That might have been a strange thought once, but he'd been a lord in truth for months now. His vassals would be an ongoing source of Chaos Points. It didn't sound like too many, only one or two points a week, but then again, purchases from the first stratum of the Sea of Chaos cost less than ten CPs. They were far less powerful than purchases from the higher stratums, but they were still valuable. Even an extra point a week meant he could make a purchase every two to three months.

Chaos Points were not easy to come by. The fact that his new evolution offered so many for each level was great, but the costs of purchases from the Sea of Chaos rose dramatically with each stratum. If the first stratum cost five to ten points, the third cost fifteen to thirty. Costs for the fourth were in the fifties to sixties. If the pattern held true, a hundred points might be used up with just one purchase from the fifth stratum.

The point was, even as a Chaos Lord leveling would not be enough to give him as many Chaos Points as he wanted. Unfortunately, there were only two other ways to get them. The first was to find a concentration of chaos, either a chaotic shard or particle, which were not exactly just lying around. He'd only found one chaos shard and he'd had to fight a damn war to win it. The other way was to kill chaos seeds. In his heart of hearts, he knew he would take that option in the future. He wouldn't just slaughter someone because they were from Earth, but he also knew his people. There were plenty who would try to kill him just for the power he offered. In those cases, he would respond in kind. The power that Chaos Points offered was too great a lure.

On top of that, there was an almost sexual thrill of pleasure when you harvested Chaos Points from someone else. The one other human from Earth he'd met had been addicted to it. Of course, Richter was pretty sure Heman had been a sadistic sumbitch even back on Earth, but he was also sure the man would not be the last evil chaos seed he'd meet. Again, Richter knew the nature of humanity too well.

The Point was, having another source of Chaos Points would be excellent. That made him want to choose the option that doubled the gains he got from vassals. On the other hand, he had to take the long view. As the years went by, he would need allies that could grow with him. Doubling the bonuses to his vassals would both make them stronger and make others more likely to pledge themselves to him.

The other two options could also be helpful. One let him have more vassals and the other let him access higher levels of his Liege Page. Accessing higher stratums of the Sea of Chaos was extremely valuable. It was mostly likely the same case here. As the final seconds ticked down on his Choice, he gritted his teeth. There just wasn't enough info to go on. Still, time and tide and all that. With a single second left, he chose.

Congratulations! You have chosen the bonus: **Double benefits to you from chaotic vassals.**

Base bonus for obtaining a Chaotic Vassal is increased from +1 to +2 Chaos Points per number of Chaotic alignment per week

If he'd had more time, he might have made a different choice, but this was the only option that gave him a definitive bonus if he ever managed to obtain a chaotic vassal. The countdown timer of the choice window manifested a final line before disappearing.

This is your 2nd Choice. For making a Choice in the allotted time you are awarded: **7 Chaos Points.**

Total Chaos Points: **648**

Richter's eyes bulged out of his head. How the hell had he just gotten so many CPs? When he'd leveled up just now, he only had forty-one. The chaos lord's gaze flashed to Xuetrix, still bound within the golden rings. The demon stared at him in silent fury, wordlessly promising to savage him mind, body and soul. Richter didn't waste any energy responding. That particular situation would unfold soon enough, one way or another. He still had about half a minute before the battle restarted. He'd use that time to go through the rest of his ascension prompts, and hopefully find one more edge to use against the demon.

33, 32, ...

He pulled up his minimized level prompt.

Leveling block has been removed now that your Rite of Ascension is complete!

TRING!

You have reached level 45! Through hard work you have moved forward along your path. You are awarded the following points to distribute:

	Per Level	Total
Stat Points	As a Chaos Lord, you gain **15 Stat Points** to distribute to characteristics instead of the usual 4	15
Talent Points	As a Chaos Seed, you receive **30 Talent Points** instead of the usual 10. You receive an additional **15 Talent Points** from your Profession and Specialty for having a 100% affinity in Enchanting	235
Chaos Points	You receive **100 Chaos Points** due to your Blessing by the Lords of Chaos	648
Skill % Points	+75% to the skill of your choice	+75%

Goddamn! The extra points from being tier 2 added up quick! He now had another fifteen Attribute Points to distribute. As great as that was, time was running out and it didn't seem like his primary attributes came into play during the battle of wills. He left it alone for now. Same for his Talent Points, though he'd be checking out his Enchanting tab as soon as he could. He would love to use some of these Chaos Points, but again, there wasn't time for that.

He still didn't know where they had all come from. By his count, he there was a five hundred point windfall that had come from out of nowhere. Similarly, his Skill Points were something to be excited about, but could also wait. It might be enough to buy him another skill level in Enchanting.

None of the points could help him with the battle of wills. There was one more line that did though. Now that Richter had claimed his level, the difference between him and Xuetrix had reduced.

Level difference between the two combatants has been adjusted from 34 to 33.

Xuetrix's Power modifier will be reduced from +17% to +16.5%

It wasn't much, but Richter would take it.

27, 26, 25, ...

He pulled up the notifications about his ascended form again and focused on the pages dealing with his ascendance, hoping for something, anything, that would help him beat Xuetrix like the winged rat he was.

Greetings, Chaos Lord! You have ascended. Your body, mind and soul have now progressed to the state of being of a Tier 2 Human. There are no special benefits to this, but Tier 1 attacks are now 20% less effective against you. Your own actions will be 20% more effective against Tier 1 opponents.

Richter didn't quite get that, but he kept reading.

As a Chaos Lord, you have been awarded a Quest that is Unique to your Evolution!

You have been offered a Quest: **Chaotic Flux**

As a *Legendary* evolution, your body, mind and soul will remain in flux for the next 25 days. If you nourish any of these three facets of your existence within that time, you may be awarded a unique bonus that could greatly augment your power.

Absorb 100 points of relevant energy to fulfill this quest.

Success Conditions: Absorb 100 Points of energy, Tier 2 or greater

Rewards: In addition to the benefits from augmenting your body, mind or soul, you will be offered another boon that is customized to you. This will greatly benefit you!

Penalty for failure of Quest: None

This Quest cannot be refused!

Richter wasn't exactly sure how to "nourish" his mind, body or soul. Actually, he had no earthly idea. And what the hell was "relevant" energy? The quest was about as vague as vague could be, something that really ratcheted up his annoyance meter. At least there wasn't a penalty for failure. Also, if only people that managed to get a *legendary* evolution got these kinds of quests, then the rewards literally had to be better than *epic*.

He'd have to figure out what the quest meant later. It was just one more item to add to the list of things he didn't understand. A list that was regrettably as long as his johnson... which was long... unregrettably.

Absorbing the info about his level up had burned a couple seconds, but hadn't provided anything to help him win. To his delight, the next prompt dealt with his bloodline. He immediately pulled the prompts to him, educating himself about his new capabilities. The first line almost made him freeze in apprehension.

*In addition to the changes to mind, body and soul, you have been randomly awarded a Bloodline! You now possess the Epic Vile Bloodline: **Petrifying Ghost Harvest***

The name did not bode well.

*This Bloodline arose during the 4th evolution of The Land after the 3rd Cataclysm. As such, it is part of a grouping of Bloodlines known as **Vile.***

Know This! There are many bloodlines in The Land. The capabilities and powers of bloodlines are as varied as grains of sand.

*As an Epic Bloodline, **Petrifying Ghost Harvest** possesses 6 ranks. Increasing the rank of the bloodline will increase its powers.*

Richter had hoped there would be some explanation on how to strengthen the bloodline, but unfortunately there wasn't. If he survived this contest with his soul intact, he'd have time to figure it out later. Still, the next lines explained the perks of his new blood-line, which would definitely come in handy.

Know this! Bloodlines consume Bloodline Points (BPs) to unleash their power. In some cases, additional BPs may be spent to increase the effect or the duration. At rank 1, your Bloodline has the following powers:

Harden: Increase your defense by +1 for 1 minute. Further BP expenditure can increase effect and/or duration proportionally. Cost: 1 BP

Ghost: Increase your Concealment by +1 for 1 minute. Further BP expenditure can increase effect and/or duration proportionally. Cost: 1 BP

*Harvest: This is the special ability of the **Petrifying Ghost Harvest** Bloodline. You may use your bloodline on the dead remains of other creatures to isolate and claim the best components of their bodies. This can be used multiple times on the same set of remains, but each use will degrade the remains as a whole. Degraded, aged and/or altered remains have a significantly lower success rate of Harvest and will net a lesser yield.*

All three powers could come in handy. *Harden* was obviously beneficial in a fight. Extra defense was the difference between a small cut and a deadly wound. The base effect only lasted a minute, but there didn't seem to be a cooldown. He could spend more BPs to extend the duration or increase the effect.

Ghost was also great. Richter's *Stealth* skill was at level fourteen, taking him to the second rank. Being able to hide was heavily dependent on a Secondary Attribute called Concealment. Each skill level increased his base Concealment by 2%. That was helpful, but not nearly as beneficial as advancing a rank in the skill. After becoming an *initiate* in *Stealth*, each skill rank increased his base Concealment value by +5.

As a Secondary Attribute, Concealment couldn't be increased by simple leveling like Intelligence or Charisma. Even a hundredth of a point in a Secondary Attribute could make a big difference. Richter's current Concealment value was +7 while stealthed. It was much better than the average human's base value of +1, good enough to turn him effectively invisible.

The enemy of Concealment was the Secondary Attribute Perception. If two enemies were playing hide and seek, whoever had a higher value would beat the other, outside factors notwithstanding. While Richter's +7 Concealment was much better than nothing, it would be useless if he were up against a perceptive enemy or monster. The fact that he could boost his Concealment now opened up a lot of possibilities. Whether he was trying to avoid a fight or to assassinate an enemy, his bloodline made him much more powerful.

As cool as the first two were though, it appeared that *Harvest* was the real prize, at least from what he had understood so far. It sounded like something Hisako had mentioned during one of their talks. Richter had been asking about skills. Just like with *Stealth*, ranking up in a skill frequently provided a much better bonus than just improving its level. He'd wanted to know what to expect if he came across highly skilled opponents in battle.

Rather than answer his question about combat skills, she had cautioned him to not disregard the power of noncombat skills. One of the most valued by the wood sprites was *Zootomy*. It was one of the few skills Richter had heard about but not yet achieved.

While hunting, he'd cut apart plenty of beasts and monsters. Once, he'd even stood chest-deep inside the body of a slain mortal enemy, a rock giant. That apparently hadn't been enough to earn him the *Zootomy* skill. Simply performing an action was not enough to learn a skill. Skill acquisition required three things: an affinity for the skill, a specific action to be performed or criteria to be met, and luck.

Herb Lore, for instance, had required more than just picking a flower. He'd had to connect to the life force of the plant, first. He'd needed to understand its nature and then gather it in a manner that was consistent with its function. This had sounded dumb to Richter until he'd actually connected with the energy of a patch of dark cave moss, much to Sion's surprise.

Similarly, *Zootomy* had criteria that needed to be met before one could acquire it. Specifically, you had to have an advanced under-standing of the anatomy of the creature that was being dissected. Just cutting a creature apart wasn't enough. That was why the hack job Richter had performed on the rock giant hadn't counted.

The point, Hisako had told him, was that *Zootomy* experts were able to use a passive magic that increased both the quantity of meat that an animal would yield and the potency of harvested organs for crafting and potions, and which could even extend the length of time that collected animal parts would resist degradation. In sprite society, even lower-ranked individuals with the skill were highly valued.

Once the skill's practitioners reached the fifth rank of *adept*, the skill underwent a formative change. *Adepts* were able to magically conjure the best pieces of a carcass without even cutting into it. Becoming a *master* let them get rare drops from a beast's remains that could be turned into some of the most powerful items imaginable. These were crafting components that could not be gained in any other way, at least not to the Hearth Mother's extensive knowledge. A *master* of *Zootomy* was viewed as a strategic resource by kingdoms and empires alike.

The item that had just saved Sion's life, the Bracelet of Home's Heart, had been created using a rare drop from a wyvern: the last drop of blood the dying monster's heart had pumped, collected by a *master* of *Zootomy*. From what he was seeing, *Harvest* gave him the special ability of a *master*-ranked skill!

The next prompt told him how many BPs he had to work with.

*Epic Bloodlines have a base **30 Bloodline Points** to expend before they are exhausted. A Bloodline's age can greatly increase its potential power. **Vile Bloodlines** arose after the 4th Cataclysm, and so are 75-150% more powerful than newly awakened Bloodlines.*

*Petrifying Ghost Harvest is one of the strongest bloodlines of the Vile era. It sees a 139% bonus compared to other Epic Bloodlines; accordingly, you will begin with **72 Bloodline Points**.*

With a start, Richter realized there was a new status bar in the upper left corner of his vision. Since coming to The Land, there had only been three. The top bar was red, for health; the middle was green, for stamina; and the bottom was blue, for mana. Now a shorter bar had appeared beneath the first three; it was a malevolent purple-green in color. He knew without being told that this was his bloodline pool.

It was easy for Richter to understand why having a bloodline was a game-changer. Used properly, a... Blooded creature could overcome even a battle Professional.

A Mage could dominate several opponents at once. A Warrior's skills could kill an enemy before they had time to react. Both were powerful, but they had easily identified limitations. If a Mage exhausted their spell repertoire, they were helpless until their cooldowns elapsed, even if they had a full mana pool. Warriors could keep fighting, but their special moves were similarly useless until their cooldowns finished.

From what Richter could see, bloodlines didn't seem to have these limitations. Their use was limited only by the number of Bloodline Points. He could keep spamming it until his pool ran dry. A Mage's spell or a Warrior's *Thrust* were both finite abilities. Outside of a small margin, they wouldn't get stronger. A bloodline user, on the other hand, could expend all their points at once. That could make for a stronger effect than any Professional could match. If he maxed *Harden*, for instance, his skin would gain 72 points of defense. It would only last for a minute, but while it did, he would have a defense stronger than any armor he'd seen. In battle, a minute was a lifetime. Richter didn't like the whole "vile" appellation, but there was nothing he could do about that. What mattered was that the bloodline would give him a better chance to survive.

It was also clear that there were wide variations between the powers bestowed by bloodlines. The *Unyielding Dragon Flame* bloodline of the draike evolution would have made him significantly stronger and faster. *Petrifying Ghost Harvest* increased his defense and could make it possible for him to evade detection. As pleased as he was with his own new powers though, he immediately thought of how dangerous other enemies with bloodlines could be in a fight.

There was so much he didn't understand. The significance of Cataclysms and the relationship of bloodlines to them was still unclear. Hisako had told him that The Land had suffered several Cataclysms, each named for an era of inconceivable destruction. Not only would kingdoms fall and empires collapse, but entire continents might sink into the oceans. The death toll was beyond imagining.

During each Cataclysm, The Land had been taken to the brink of destruction, but had somehow survived. Despite the horrors of each Cataclysm, they were also times that mana concentrations would spike in The Land. The abundance of magic would suffuse the bodies, minds and souls of survivors, granting them amazing powers.

Oftentimes these abilities would be passed down to a creature's descendants. These inheritable powers were called bloodlines. Hisako had said that they proved the balance of all things. Each Cataclysm would, by its very nature, provide the powers and weapons needed to defeat and survive the calamity. She'd also told him that older bloodlines rarely appeared anymore, as they were diluted through the generations. Even when they did, the power a bloodline carried would be too much for a person to bear. They would be consumed by it. Richter now understood why only Tier 2 creatures, those who had ascended to a higher state of being, would possess one.

Hisako's countenance had been grave as she recounted the disasters that had threatened all life in The Land. Richter had had trouble envisioning destruction and loss on the scale she had described. The closest analogy he could come up with was a nuclear war, but from what he had heard, that was still inadequate. Even during the third world war, the thought of destroying the world had scared the various superpowers enough that they had stuck to conventional weaponry. Afterwards, they had even destroyed their nuclear stockpiles and their caches of other world-ending agents. He couldn't really wrap his head around the fact that The Land had suffered seven such catastrophes.

Cataclysms were a field of Lore that he had found fascinating but hadn't had the time to learn much about. For the umpteenth time, Richter promised himself that he would read more books from Hisako's library. It was just that there was always more to do, more enemies to fight and more crises to survive. Richter wracked his brain as he tried to recall any other helpful information. All he was able to bring to the fore was that one of the Cataclysms Hisako had mentioned had had something to do with undead attacking every civilization of The Land. With a sinking feeling, he realized it was the third Cataclysm that she had been describing, the one that had created his bloodline.

With that realization, his mind made a troubling and horrifying connection. If bloodlines really were due to people in the distant past being exposed to high concentrations of certain types of mana, then his was probably no different. The fact that it was called "vile" and that fact that his bloodline had the word "ghost" in the name just clinched his suspicion. His bloodline had evolved due to high concentrations of Death magic. Richter didn't have the deep-seated hatred for necromancy that his Life mage allies did, but it still made him uncomfortable. The fact that such a bloodline was now an intrinsic part of him was something he liked even less. What the consequences of this would be in the future he didn't know, but he did know one thing: Hisako was going to be pissed.

14, 13, 12, ...

Xuetrix was flexing his hands as he stared at Richter, his sharp talons glinting in the light of the golden rings. He gave Richter a glare that that chaos lord assumed was supposed to be intimidating. The imp's opponent paid him no mind. That was because the notification Richter was reading finally gave him two answers: where the other Chaos Points had come from, and how he could improve his chances to take the cocky flier down. He'd gotten another bonus!

Congratulations! You have been awarded +500 Chaos Points for becoming the first Chaos Lord!

*Know This! You have fulfilled the conditions to advance the rank of your Tier 2 form, **Chaos Lord**. Do you wish to advance from **Rank 1** to **Rank 2** for **500 Chaos Points**? Yes or No?*

The "money prudent" part of him hated the idea of spending so many precious Chaos Points. Especially right after he'd earned them, but then he thought, easy come, easy go. An expression his uncle had warned him long ago did not apply to unprotected sex, but did seem to work right now. He needed every advantage he could get against Xuetrix. There wasn't much time left, so Richter didn't hesitate more than a second. He chose "Yes."

*Congratulations! You have advanced your Tier 2 form, Chaos Lord, from the 1st of 9 ranks, **Weak**, to the 2nd rank, **Low**.*

Vassal Slots: 2 (Previous 1)

Chaos Point Generation (CP/Chaotic alignment/week): +3 (Previous +1)

Chaotic Spells and Abilities Bonus: +30% (Previous +25%)

To progress to Rank 3: Pay 1,000 Chaos Points. Chaotic Vassals can be claimed to decrease this cost at a rate of 100 Chaos Points per point of Chaotic alignment.

The bonuses weren't huge, but he'd only progressed to the second of nine ranks. The hefty cost to progress again wasn't great news either. It occurred to him that he probably could have reduced the cost of ranking up if he'd waited until he found chaotic vassals, but that would probably have been a long wait for a train don't come. Besides, he hadn't gotten excited about rank progression because he thought it would help him beat Xuetrix directly, it was because of the message that popped up next, something he'd been hoping to see.

Know this! Calculations for the Battle of Wills have been reconsidered and adjusted accordingly.

Richter advancing his Tier 1 form from rank 1 to rank 2 of 9 has increased his Power by +5%

Total Modifier: +41% Richter, +17% Xuetrix

It wasn't much, but it widened the gap between the two of them even more.

4, 3, 2, ...

The timer counted down to zero, and Richter met Xuetrix's anger with a smug southern grin, "Now! Who, is, the master?"

CHAPTER 21

DAY 151 – JUREN 2, 0 AOC

The countdown reached zero and both combatants bared their teeth as the pain washed over them anew. During the hiatus, the assault on their minds, bodies and souls had stopped. With the battle of wills resumed, it came roaring back all at once. Even the demon needed time to process the horrible violation of it all.

This round will begin with Xuetrix possessing the initiative.

The demon continued to glare furiously at Richter, but couldn't keep his eyes from flashing to their bars of power. The imp's was full, but that was only because his modifier had decreased so dramatically. Richter's, on the other hand, was just shy of full. The problem was that the human's gold bar was more than three times as large as it had been before. Xuetrix still had more power, but only a fraction more, rather than five times as much.

The imp launched an attack and Richter's howls filled the tunnel. For seventy-seven seconds, Xuetrix poured his power into blows that wrecked the chaos lord's mind, body and soul. All of the green of his bar emptied and some of the gold as well. Richter's power was consumed as he was assaulted on all sides.

When the demon's turn was done, Richter felt like he was holding a live wire. He'd never been more awake and had never wished more for unconsciousness. The chaos lord spit on the ground and counter-attacked. It was the demon's turn to wail. Richter exacted vengeance, knowing that in seventy-seven short seconds it would be his turn to suffer once more. He didn't worry about that. He just cherished the precious moments of pain he was able to deliver to Xuetrix.

Back and forth they went. Their larger power bars let them deliver a level of suffering to each other that no Tier 1 being could have endured. Each time, Xuetrix was sure that Richter would succumb. At the very least, he was convinced the human would waste energy to relieve the suffering. Each round, the demon was surprised. Richter may have writhed and screamed, but when Xuetrix's turn was done, the chaos lord bypassed his healing phase and just attacked again. It was maddening! No mortal should have been able to endure that level of castigation. He found himself wondering just what could have happened to the human to make him accustomed to not only physical agony, but attacks on the mind and soul as well.

At the start of the seventh round, Xuetrix had only about 8% of his power left. Richter had only five. The chaos lord's fists were clenched so hard his ragged nails had broken the skin on his palms in eight places. Sweat drenched him and a foul odor wafted off his unwashed body. His mental defenses lay in ruins and his psychic avatar was being squeezed by the merciless golden rings of the battle. His soul was so battered, he was hearing voices whisper to him about his failures, inadequacies and weaknesses. He was a man pushed to the very limits of his soul and the edge of sanity.

Still, if anyone had been fool enough to ask him how he felt, Richter's answer would have been simple.

"You should see the other guy."

Trapped within his own golden bands, Xuetrix no longer flapped his wings. He'd landed during the fourth round and hadn't been able to muster the will to rise into the air again. Drool fell out of the demon's open, retching mouth. His arms hung limp to his sides. The fury had left his eyes. In its place was pain, shame and disbelief. It had never occurred to the demon that Richter would be able to push it this far. Even when he won, the imp wouldn't have the energy to claim the human's soul. He hadn't been in such a position for millennia. Even with his power reduced to only the second tier, the ignominy of being forced into such a state by a mere human was heinous.

Richter had just finished his latest attack and now it was Xuetrix's turn. With the time he had, he spoke in a raspy voice, "You have surprised me, human, but it is over. Give in. If you will admit defeat, I will forswear any vengeance, claim on your soul, or penalties. You only need to submit."

The chaos lord looked at the imp with contempt. He would have spit, but his mouth was too dry from screaming. He had to work his tongue around his mouth several times before he managed to say, "One day." He had to work up more saliva to finish his statement. Xuetrix looked at him expectantly. A few seconds later, Richter finished with, "I'm going to fuck your mother." He had one last thing to add. "In her messy, messy butthole."

Several times during the battle, Xuetrix had stared at Richter with hot fury. For the very first time, the demon's anger froze cold. He was nearly as strained as the human. He was not immune to the battle of wills. No being was. His soul was beset by doubts and his mind was being ravaged by demons of his own. The pain coursing through his body made it hard to even stay conscious. All of that faded in the face of the absolute cold of his ruthless ire.

When Xuetrix spoke this time, his voice had changed. It sounded gothic and possessed the grandeur and majesty of a lord of the deeps. The shadows of the tunnel gathered like worshippers before their god. In the dark, Richter felt like he could see a larger horned demon standing behind the imp.

"Do not mistake to whom you are speaking, frail human. I have drunk the blood of gods. Your feeble mind cannot begin to under-stand the majesty of my existence. You would dare to speak of my lineage? My family ruled an entire plane of hell while your ancestors were but single cells clumsily grappling in a fetid pool. You do not even deserve to hear my true name!

"I tell you now to bow before me or die! If I so choose, not one minute shall pass after this battle of wills before I steal the breath from your lungs. Not one minute! Do not attempt false bravado. I smell the curse of death upon you. Did you think you could hide it? The stench of it is like a bloated corpse in the sun. I will damn you to that accursed half-life! What do you say now, human? Will you kneel or will this be where your story ends?"

By the time Xuetrix had finished speaking the shadows were so thick, Richter could barely make out the imp's body. All he could see were red flames dancing in the demon's eyes, and the palpable presence that wanted to break out of the creature's small body. Nearly anyone else would have bowed under that horrible pressure. Xuetrix had not even used his power to attack. It was sheer force of personality, but from a being who could kill with a glance. In the depths of The Land, in that dark and dismal tunnel, Richter knew in his heart that everything the demon had said was true, especially that Xuetrix could destroy him utterly. He did not know what that presence was coming off the imp, but he knew it was far beyond his own ascended state of existence. Tier 3? Tier 4 or 5? He did not know. He only knew it could kill him as easily as snuffing out a candle.

Despite all of that, Richter did not hesitate in his response. Looking at both Xuetrix and the *thing* struggling to get out of the demon, he spoke simply and without fear.

"You can die every day."

That was it. When any sane man would have blinked, with the devil himself staring at him with hunger, Richter stood with his head high. They locked eyes, an unstoppable force and an immovable man. He understood that these were his last minutes, but he'd made a choice. In accordance with his true nature, he chose. It wasn't a lack of fear that motivated him, but instead, an acceptance of what he was. It was better to go out now than be bound to the demon's will. Richter heaved a heavy sigh, but the once-turbulent waters of his soul calmed. The storm of thought cleared from his mind and his body relaxed, muscles unclenching. He was still being assaulted, but in this key moment he found the true power and freedom of Chaos. He found peace in his choice.

It was time.

Richter prepared for Xuetrix's attack, but all of a sudden, the demon's intimidating aura vanished. The shadows scattered and became lifeless once again. The very real red light in Xuetrix's eyes faded, and a smirk plastered itself onto the demon's face. The imp spoke a single word, "Halt."

Upon request of the Favor holder, the Battle of Wills shall be halted for 77 seconds. This cannot be done twice.

Like someone had flipped a switch, the assault on Richter ceased. The pain disappeared, his head cleared and his mind firmed. He almost swooned in relief. It was true that he had come to accept his fate, but the pain of Xuetrix's assaults was still there. To have it just vanish was more shocking than diving into a pool in the middle of a hot day.

"Well," the demon acknowledged with a laugh, "you are a pain in the ass. I don't see any reason to keep continuing this, however. I've decided to make you a deal."

"A deal," Richter asked, his voice still raw, but now also thick with disbelief.

"Yeah," Xuetrix replied with another chortle. "We demons like deals. I will release you from your Favor, right now, if you accept a quest from me instead. Where it will lead you is the very location you're looking for, a pathway home. If you finish the quest, you'll get some good experience and I'll get you home. If you lose, well," Xuetrix cocked his head up as if he was considering the matter, "let's say I get all the experience you've gathered so far. You'll go back to level one, your skills will reset, but you won't have any permanent injuries or debuffs. Either way, you'll be closer to finding a way back to the surface. Now what d'ya say?"

Richter glared at him, obviously expecting a trick, but a prompt appeared.

You have been offered a Quest: **Deal with the Devil I**

Xuetrix desires a wand of magical power. It is known as the Wand of Rotush, and it is held by the ogre lord, Nureuk. You will be given a magical beacon that interacts with your Traveler's Map which will show you the general location of the underground city of Omru. Once there, you must make your way to the stronghold and acquire the wand from Nureuk's treasury.

If you accept this Quest, Xuetrix will release you from your Favor.

Success Conditions: Steal the Wand of Rotush

Rewards: Instant transport back to the Mist Village

Penalty for failure of Quest: Loss of all of your accumulated XP

Penalty for refusal of Quest: Immediate resumption of the Battle of Wills

Do you accept? Yes or No

Before Richter could respond, Xuetrix held up one taloned finger, "Wait!" Then the demon snapped his fingers and summoned, of all things, a small piece of parchment and a quill. After scribbling for a second, he gestured for Richter to respond.

The chaos lord had no idea what had just happened, but he did ask a question, "Why do you want this wand? What does it do?"

Xuetrix grinned ear to ear. He slowly turned the piece of paper so Richter could see what he'd written. It contained three lines of text. The first two were basically paraphrases of the questions Richter had just asked.

"What can the wand do?"

"Why do I want it?"

The third line was why Xuetrix was grinning like a maniac.

"Will you _ever_ stop being so basic?"

The letter was so mocking and Xuetrix's expression so ridiculing that Richter almost refused the deal right then and there. Before he could snap at the demon, however, Xuetrix pointed at their respective power bars. They were both depleted, but the demon had more energy left than Richter. If the battle resumed, there was little doubt the chaos lord would lose.

"Is it worth it?" Xuetrix asked.

Richter wished he could have said something else, but he knew the answer to the question. It wasn't. Xuetrix's deal, while not fair, was far better than him suffering the unknown consequences of losing the battle of wills. It would be a serious setback losing all of his levels, Talents and powers, but he knew he could recover from that, given enough time. The unknown penalties for not only refusing a Favor, but also losing the contest, might cripple him forever.

He could ask Xuetrix for more information, but the demon had already told him no in a particularly embarrassing way. More questions wouldn't get answers, just more insults. Also, the timer on the hiatus was still counting down.

22, 21, 20, ...

The last thing he wanted was to tie himself to Xuetrix yet again, but he had little choice. He'd fought the devil to a standstill. He'd have to be pleased with that victory, pyrrhic or not. He clicked "Yes" on the quest prompt. The window disappeared along with the golden rings surrounding them both. They were both plunged into darkness. A quick spell fixed that. On Richter's minimap, a red dot appeared in the faraway darkness. There weren't any other details on the map besides what the chaos lord assumed was the location Xuetrix wanted him to get to.

Richter looked at the demon uneasily as the imp rose back into the air. "The red dot is this city of Omru, I'm guessing?"

"You guess right," was the flippant response. From his tone, Xuetrix could care less about the quest or the fact that he'd just tried and failed to steal Richter's soul.

Richter's eyes widened in disbelief. Was this bastard really just about to leave? After all that? He was! He was actually flying away. *Lazily* flying away!

"Hey, asshole. You didn't give me a map. Just this blinking red dot surrounded by nothing. This isn't Zelda, you know!"

"I held up my end of the deal. Anything else is on you, human. I have more important things to do and much more important people to see. Much more important... So much more. It's really unbelievable, how much..."

"I get it!" Richter snapped. "If you want this wand though, you could at least give me more information. How am I supposed to sneak into an ogre stronghold? I'm human, if you hadn't noticed."

"Let's not discuss your shortcomings," Xuetrix suggested, waving one hand. "Good luck, human."

"Yeah," Richter smiled with bared teeth, "You too."

Xuetrix's grin didn't have a drop less animosity. His fingers wove into a spell form, and a reddish-black portal snapped into existence. A moment before he disappeared, he got in the last word, "Try not to be such a hungry, thirsty bitch, huh?"

CHAPTER 22

DAY 151 – JUREN 2, 0 AOC

*X*uetrix poofed out of existence, leaving behind two things: the rotten-egg stink of brimstone and that last, relatively weak insult. Why did he call Richter a hungry, thirsty bitch? Hungry bitch wasn't even a thing. The chaos lord was honestly kind of disappointed in the demon. As last words went, it was pretty sad.

That was until red warning prompts flashed in his vision.

*You are **Dehydrated**! Any lost health cannot be restored.*
*You are **Ravenous**! Stamina regeneration decreased by 25%. Emotional control decreased by 25%.*

*You are **Exhausted**! Concentration decreased by 50%.*

*Know This! Your evolution has placed a great strain on your body. For the next **28 days**, its metabolic needs will be greatly accelerated, requiring several times the normal amount of food and water.*

"I hate him so much," Richter breathed out. All of a sudden, it felt like he'd just gone through hell week. An almost physical weight settled onto his shoulders. He didn't think he'd ever been this exhausted before. To cap it off, he was starving! Cotton mouth was also an inadequate description. It was more like... rusty-brillo mouth. It was all he could do to stick out one hand and brace against the side of the tunnel. He blew out several labored breaths just trying to center himself. If an enemy or monster had found him in that moment, it could have delivered the coup de grâce with barely any effort.

He had no idea how the demon had known these debuffs were coming, but it made him fucking *furious* that Xuetrix had managed such an appropriate insult! That goddamn flying rat! If he ever got his hands around the demon's little neck he would... Richter's mental training asserted itself and overrode his spiraling emotions. He took several deep breaths while he mastered his anger. Not by denying it, that never worked. The way you control your emotions is to accept that they are part of you, bring them close, then decide that they will not define you. It takes a bit more time than mere repression, but it works far better.

Several minutes later, he got himself under control. He even let out a self-deprecating chuckle, "Decreased emotional control. Right." Even his *Self-Awareness* skill was no match for hangry.

He'd never been the most even-keeled guy even in the best of times. Now that he was hungry, in pain and suffering under the loss of emotional control debuff, he was a powder keg. It wasn't that he thought there was anything wrong with anger, it just wasn't helpful right now. Right now, he had to work the problem. Namely, deal with these debuffs, survive the week, and finish this new quest. The debuffs would obviously have to be dealt with first.

Almost like that thought had summoned the demon, Xuetrix popped back into existence holding a clear glass full of water. The glass was even frosted! The demon raised it to his mouth and Richter couldn't help but stare. Richter's mouth opened and closed several times involuntarily, as if he were drinking the water. He stared at the crystal-cold water in desperate need. He was pretty sure his soul cried as he watched the truly demonic creature bring the water ever closer to his grey-black mouth. A faint croon came out of the chaos lord's mouth.

Before Xuetrix actually took a drink though, he turned his head toward Richter as if he'd forgotten the human was there, "Oh, did you want some?"

Richter nodded before he could help himself, his fluid-starved body betraying him. His mind shouted, 'Don't do it! It's a trap!' Xuetrix had already seen his response, though.

"Yeah, I thought you would," the demon spoke with supreme satisfaction, smiling a needle-filled grin. Then he brought the glass up to his lips and drank the precious water, one loud and wet gulp at a time. A cry of rage came from Richter's parched throat as he lunged at the imp. Xuetrix just lazily flew to the side while he continued to drink, easily evading his attacker's clumsy attempt at retribution. One small taloned finger was held up, asking the chaos seed for "just a sec" while he kept drinking.

The demon didn't actually finish the water. Instead, when it was half empty, he turned the glass upside down. If Richter had any fluid in his body, he would have wept upon seeing the water fall to the ground. The liquid was immediately absorbed by a thin layer of rock dust.

Xuetrix patted the bottom of the glass while it was still upraised, making sure to clear the last drop. Then he looked at Richter and spoke in a calming tone, "Whoa, whoa buddy. No need to be so angry. I didn't forget about cha!"

The chaos lord looked back at the imp with a bit of madness in his eyes. Xuetrix just smiled and flew a bit further away before putting the glass on the ground. Then, lifting his loin cloth, he revealed a surprising large grey dick that, good god, looked like it had thorns sticking out of it. With a sigh of supreme satisfaction, Xuetrix unloaded his bladder into the glass, filling it with orange, *glowing,* demon piss. That done, he flicked his prick, releasing the last few drops, one of which fell on the stone with an acidic *hiss,* and said, "All yours... bitch," and disappeared again.

What followed next was some truly epic swearing. Energy surged in his limbs as he stomped and swung his arms at thin air like a crazy person. He took a bit of care when he picked up the glass, but then threw it against the wall of the tunnel as hard as he could. It shattered and the hellish urine hissed like a sack full of spastic cats. Richter didn't calm down for about half an hour. His emotional lability was in full effect.

Once he gained control again, Richter made himself stand up straight. He needed to find a way to eat, drink and sleep. Weapons and armor, even a pair of shoes, wouldn't be a bad idea either. The soles of his feet were bloody and raw in places. The Land was a magical place, but in some ways, it was no different from Earth. He couldn't afford to ignore mundane concerns.

He needed to deal with his thirst first. He remembered dungeon diving with Sion once. The sprite had been trapped in a dream for days. When he had finally snapped out of it, his friend had been afflicted with not only the *Dehydrated* debuff, but also *Severely Dehydrated*. Once it progressed to that point, not only would his health not be able to be replenished, it would begin to drop at a fast rate. Plainly put, if his debuff evolved, his life would be in danger. He needed to find water.

Richter looked down the tunnel. The only source of light was the glowing ball of his spell. To his left was the drop-off that had claimed the ichorpedes. Too many steps in that direction and he'd suffer the same fate. On his right, the tunnel continued into the darkness. His little island of light seemed just as isolated as the dark walk in Nexus's realm.

He might only be a few miles underground, but then again, he might be several hundred. The Land was a planet the size of Jupiter, tens of thousands of miles thick. That was one hundred *trillion* square miles. There could be caverns inside The Land that were literally the size of the planet Earth, but would still just look like a bubble in a glass of soda. He needed to get home but had no idea which direction, or even a rough idea of how far away the Mist Village was. All he had was this tunnel and that damn flashing red dot.

Richter extinguished his *Simple Light* spell and cast *Darkvision*.

The spell only had a base range of twenty-five yards, but that was greatly extended now. Between his Dark Mastery and high Intelligence, the distance was more than doubled. He could have seen further with *Simple Light*, but the sphere of light was as good as ringing a monster dinner bell.

The chaos seed noticed the casting was significantly harder with his decrease in concentration, but the spells were low level. Even at half-mast, he was still up to the challenge. To his happy surprise, he saw that the spell cost less mana than before. When he'd cast *Simple Light* after the battle of wills, he'd been too distracted to notice. Now he couldn't help but smile.

As he walked, he got ready to finally review the rest of his prompts, but his stomach rumbled. It was then that something occurred to him. He had a tool at his disposal that he hadn't used yet! Thank you, Randy! Richter made a silent promise to sit through one of the man's lectures. He wouldn't even sigh heavily or try to leave early. At least, he amended, he'd do his very best. The half-undine Spy deserved it, and a fruit basket! Randolphus had taught Richter exactly the spell that he needed!

Richter stopped and started to dual cast *Weak Find Water*. The original spell only detected water within a hundred feet of his location. With skill level fourteen in Dual Casting, the spell was 156% stronger. When you factored in the bonus from his high Intelligence and his Water Mastery, the spell would be able to reach almost one hundred yards. He had to concentrate harder than normal, but his Psi Bond ability also greatly enhanced his mental focus. The spell wasn't too difficult. As long as he didn't need to chain cast spells in battle, his debuff shouldn't be a problem.

The blue glow from his hands faded a moment later, and an invisible, intangible pulse shot out from his body. It extended like a growing sphere in every direction, looking for water. And... found absolutely nothing. Richter sighed. That would have been too easy. He started walking again. As exhausted as he was, all he wanted to do was pass out, but he couldn't risk his debuffs getting worse. Currently, they were a potentially dangerous inconvenience. If he waited, they would be deadly.

While he made his way into the dark, he dealt with the last prompts from his battle at the Mausoleum. The first was a complete surprise, and made him miss his elementum short sword even more.

*Congratulations! You have progressed in a Combat Art! The sprite-based fighting style Sutinn Sumotri, "The Stinging Storm!" This fighting style incorporates 2 skills, **Short Blades** and **Dual Wielding**. It is possible to progress the weapon form through either skill, but the only way to truly master this form is to use both skills together.*

The following bonuses are possible for novices *of this form:*

DUAL WIELDING NOVICE
Requirements
Dual Wielding Skill Level 10
Agility 15, Dexterity 15
Bonus
+5% attack speed when dual wielding
1 Free Special Move

SHORT BLADE NOVICE
Requirements
Short Blades Skill Level 10
Agility 15, Dexterity 15
Bonus
+5% damage when using small blades
1 Free Special Move

TRUE NOVICE
Requirements
Dual Wielding Skill Level 10, *Short Blades* Skill Level 10
Agility 20, Dexterity 20
Bonus
+10% attack speed when dual wielding
+10% damage when using small blades
2 Free Special Moves

Through hard work and honing the techniques of Sutinn Sumotri, you have advanced to the rank of **True Novice** *in this weapon form.*

There are 5 Special Attacks for the Novice rank of this Weapon Form. As a True Novice, you may now choose 2!

QUICK STAB		
(Short Blade Attack)		
Increase Attack Speed by 50% for one attack. +5 Attack		
Cost: 20 Stamina	Cooldown: 10 seconds	Expertise: 0/250

SHARP BLADE		
(Short Blade Attack)		
Ignore 5 points of Defense.		
Cost: 25 Stamina	Cooldown: 10 seconds	Expertise: 0/250

WHIRLWIND		
(Dual Wielding Attack)		
A spinning attack striking enemies in all directions within 1 second. +50% damage.		
Cost: 30 Stamina	Cooldown: 2 minutes	Expertise: 0/250

WEAPON MAZE		
(Dual Wielding Attack)		
Weaving your 2 weapons in an intricate pattern will mesmerize (watching) opponents for up to 5 seconds.		
Cost: 25 Stamina	Cooldown: 3 minutes	Expertise: 0/250

STRIKE WHEEL		
(Dual Wielding Attack)		
Rotate your weapons in concert to perform 4 strikes to the same spot in 1 second.		
Each strike causes +50% damage.		
Cost: 30 Stamina	Cooldown: 2 minutes	Expertise: 0/250

Richter got more excited the more he read. All that hard work, all the time he'd spent on sword forms, all the damn sticks Yoshi had hit him with... So many sticks! At long last he had something to show for it!

His Enchanting Profession was powerful. It was one of the main reasons the Mist Village army could punch above its weight. After all, his fighters had almost all been shopkeepers, farmers and handymen only a few months before. Natheless, they'd been able to engage in pitched battle against battle-hardened goblins. The magic weapons and armor he enspelled were a force multiplier.

There was no denying the power of an Enchanter. As great as it was though, it was still a noncombat Profession. In a head-to-head fight, he'd been beaten on several occasions when he'd gone up against those trained in the combat arts. He'd only come out ahead because of his allies, advanced planning or, in the case of the Assassin Sonirae, because he was insane enough to detonate an acid bomb in his own hands.

Combat Professions just had too many active and passive bonuses. A Warrior could use Talent Points to purchase powerful attacks. *Power Blow, Double Strike, Thrust* or *Lunge* could let a Warrior take away half of an enemy's health with just one move, assuming the fighter didn't just one-shot his foe altogether. A Professed Warrior's Talents could make him an absolute terror on the battlefield.

Access to these kinds of attacks were one of the reasons that Richter had been so excited to buy a combat expertise book from the Sea of Chaos. He had cursed loud enough to make angels blush when he'd found out he hadn't met the minimum requirements to use the techniques it held. Now, it seemed that his months of training and, ahem, torture at the hands of Yoshi had paid off!

The battle of the Mausoleum must have finally advanced his combat style enough for him to qualify as a *novice*. It might not sound like much, but Yoshi had told him that there were plenty of Professional Warriors who never even reached this rank. Practicing the various sword styles had definitely made him deadlier, *novice* or not.

What he hadn't known was that it would let him get special attack techniques. He now had access to some of the same perks as a Warrior, without even needing a combat Profession! It even looked like they could upgrade the more he used them. There was a lot he didn't know about Professions, but he'd never heard of a Warrior's attacks getting stronger. Not for the first time, Richter learned that there was always more than one path to a destination.

Now which two attack moves should he choose? He liked the idea of the first two. *Quick Stab* and *Sharp Blade* would make him more deadly with a short sword, but he had to be practical. He needed to make choices that would help him survive down here in the dark. If he died before the curse was lifted, what would be the point of any of this?

While he'd love either of the first two choices, he didn't have his blades right now. Sadly, the ichorpede pincer didn't register as a dagger, so he couldn't use it to trigger these techniques. Down here in the bowels of The Land, there was no reason to think he'd find one anytime soon.

The last three, on the other hand, didn't require a specific weapon, or even a formal weapon at all. They only required that he dual wield. He already had the large bone. He very well might find something else to serve as an impromptu club down here. What mattered was surviving for the next week until the curse wore off. Also, if (when, he corrected himself) he got back to the village, he'd have access to his armory again. He would probably keep dual wielding, but he was increasingly using a normal-sized weapon in his main hand. That made the last three techniques the best options.

Honestly, *Weapon Maze* just sounded super cool. An AoE technique that could befuddle multiple enemies? He was definitely getting that one. Like, for real. That meant he just needed to decide between *Whirlwind* and *Strike Wheel*. The first was another AoE, letting him attack multiple enemies at once. The second let him attack one enemy multiple times.

He thought about the many battles he'd been through. Conversely, he'd fought relatively few duels. That was a point for *Whirlwind*. On the other hand, with the enchanted weapons he would wield again sometime soon, hitting someone four times in a second with *Strike Wheel* might be enough to fell even a high-level opponent all at once. Richter thought it through for a few more seconds, then made his choice.

Congratulations! You have learned the Combat Techniques: **Weapon Maze** *and* **Strike Wheel.** *Continued use of these techniques in battle will allow you to advance both to more refined states, including but not limited to: increased damage, decreased cooldown and additional effects.*

Having the combat techniques brought him a sense of comfort, even crawling around in the bowels of the earth. He kept walking and checking the last of his prompts from the Mausoleum.

Here was something he hadn't even considered. He knew a sizable portion of the lich's army had gone through the portal to his Dungeon, and he knew his people had defeated them. What he hadn't thought of was the effect it would have on the Dungeon itself. Their energies had been greedily consumed by the Barrow of the Chaos Serpent and put to good use.

Congratulations! Your Dungeon has reached Levels 4, 5, ... and 14. Your Harbinger has grown stronger and now has a minimum level of 34

Know This! Every 5 levels creates a new entrance to your Dungeon. This is normally randomly placed, but your Dungeon Keeper can assign the locations at his discretion.

Know This! Upon reaching level 10, your Dungeon may now serve as a portal into the Labyrinth. Do not tread these paths of power lightly!

Know This! Upon reaching level 10, your Dungeon has begun to create its own dimension. It is no longer completely bound to the location it occupies. As such, occupancy of the Dungeon is now unlimited.

For reaching level 14:

Dungeon Point Bonus: +14% Dungeon Points generated each day

Harbinger Bonus: Monsters and Traps +24% harder to detect

Item of Power Bonus: +24% Bonus to Monster Health

Your Dungeon has earned a total of **6 physical floors**.

Mean Level of Dungeon Monsters is now:

Floor 1: 8-17	*Floor 2: 12-20*	*Floor 3: 15-24*
Floor 4: 20-28	*Floor 5: 25-33*	*Floor 6: 30-38*

Dungeon Experience: 1,339,614/1,700,000 until level 15

Richter cheered internally to see how much stronger the Dungeon had gotten. When that bolt of pure destructive energy had flown through the portal, courtesy of the Exile Rakshasha, it had done more than just destroy every undead creature. It had also flooded the barrow with pure energy. While much of that power had been lost to destruction and entropy, some of it had been siphoned off and converted into Dungeon Points. Only the sheer magnitude and intense purity of the energy had allowed that to happen, something that would most likely never occur again. The Exile's power, coupled with the massive reaping of undead, had both catapulted the Dungeon in levels and helped fulfill some of its Motivations.

The Dungeon was also strong enough to allow passage into the Labyrinth now. He didn't know what making its own dimension meant, but, with an excited flutter in his heart, he thought it might be a TARDIS-style situation.

He would have to wait until he got back to find out. Besides, there was plenty more to be excited about now. The next prompt was accompanied by the sound of a hundred people celebrating in Richter's ears.

YAAAAAHHHHH!

*Richter of the Mist Village, you have achieved the impossible! In less than one week, you have advanced your settlement to **Level 4** of your Adventurer Specialization. For this amazing act, your settlement will gain a **Mythic** bonus.*

Congratulations! You have progressed the **Adventurer Specialization** of your settlement to **Level 4**. Having access to a Dungeon has inspired your people: "*Adventure is in our blood!*"

+250 Morale, +100 Loyalty for having access to a Dungeon
Specialization Level: 4

Dungeon Master Bonus:

+40% Attack and Defense while in a Dungeon or the Labyrinth
+40% Chance to find Nodes
+30% Trap Detection while in a Dungeon or the Labyrinth
+20% Movement and Attack Speed while in a Dungeon or the Labyrinth
+10% Attack and Defense for your Dungeon party while in a Dungeon or the Labyrinth

Settlement Bonus:

+40% Dungeon Points from any source
+40% Dungeon Loot Generation
+30% Dungeon Resource Growth
+20% Ambient Mana Seepage
+10% Ambient Mana Refinement
For each Treasure Chest rank, up to +5% occurrence

Leveling Conditions:

Generate 11,153/10,000 Dungeon Points
Add 481/7 new Beasts to the Dungeon Bestiary
Add 3/3 new Rooms
Consume 7,928/500 creatures
MYTHIC Bonus: The Barrow of the Chaos Serpent will receive the
Blessing: *Reliquaries of the Labyrinth*

Richter shook his head. He had no idea what the *mythic* bonus
meant, but Randy had basically creamed his shorts over the previous
epic-ranked bonus. When the Spy had seen that the Dungeon would
get a Master Node, he'd been rendered speechless. Sadly, there was
no information about what this blessing entailed. He would just have
to look forward to learning more when he made it back home. The
other bonuses were great too. All the individual bonuses he got as a
Dungeon master were cranked up. What's more, anyone he was
adventuring with in a Dungeon now got a boost to attack and defense
as well.

The bonuses to the Settlement were also cranked up. The
Dungeon was making more points, loot, and resources. It was also
seeping more mana into the surrounding lands. According to Randy,
that would make it more likely for valuable herbs, resources and rare
magical creatures to appear in the region. The mana refinement
vastly accelerated the overall process in a way that the chamberlain
had tried to explain, but Richter just hadn't followed. By which he

meant his mind had wandered off. He promised himself that he'd pay more attention in the future... again. One thing he did understand though was that the Dungeon would be making more treasure chests now.

Randy had told him that treasure chests were the holy grail of Adventurers. Most Dungeon loot came from the reliquaries, small objects that appeared when a monster was slain. It didn't happen every time, but it happened often enough that countless people risked their lives on a daily basis in pursuit of them.

There was also the possibility of finding hidden caches throughout a Dungeon, especially when lairs were cleared out. The treasure obtained from the first two options was nothing compared to the loot that came out of a chest though. Both in quality and quantity, the treasure from chests was of a substantially higher grade.

When Richter had asked how likely it was for a chest to appear, Randolphus hadn't known the answer. He'd only known that there were different chest ranks that followed the same order as items: *common, uncommon, unusual, scarce, rare, epic, mythic* and *legendary.* Randy had said there could very well be even higher-ranked chests, but in his one hundred years of life, the highest-ranked chest he'd ever personally seen was *rare.*

The highest-ranked chest that he'd ever heard of anyone finding in his lifetime was *epic.* The discovery of that one chest had sparked a war between three countries. Richter had been surprised by that, but the Spy had explained that while Dungeon loot was normally limited to the treasure the Dungeon could generate, treasure chests were filled by the Labyrinth itself. Put simply, the Labyrinth had no definable limits, and neither did the treasure it could create.

Even though Randy didn't know the incidence of chests appearing, that was only because he had never had access to a Dungeon Keeper before. Talking to Roswan had given more information. One of the primary powers of the mustached elf's Profession was to influence where a Dungeon invested its points. As soon as he'd heard about treasure chests, he'd had Roswan check what it would take to make chests appear more often. It would be a great boon to the village after all.

The conversation had ended there. Roswan had looked up the likelihood of the lowest-ranked chest appearing each day, and it was less than 1% for even a *common* chest. The Dungeon Keeper could allocate 10% of the Dungeon Points generated each day to any one thing without substantial penalties, but even using all ten, the needle had barely budged. Now it might be different, seeing as how the number of DPs/days had increased drastically, and the fact that there was now a one-in-twenty chance of a chest appearing each day was something worth getting excited about.

Richter was already in a slightly better mood after reading how the village's specialty had reached level four. He was absolutely shocked by how great the bonuses were, but he soon realized he ain't seen nothing yet!

YAAAAAHHHHH!

*Never in the history of the Tamorith continent has anyone accomplished such a historic achievement! In less than one week, you have advanced your settlement to **Level 5** of your Adventurer Specialization. For this amazing act, your settlement will gain a **Legendary** bonus.*

Congratulations! You have progressed the **Adventurer Specialization** of your settlement to **Level 5**. Your people are drawn to the call of Adventure and extremely grateful for having access to a Dungeon: *"Adventure? It's our way of life!"*

+500 Morale, +250 Loyalty for having access to a Dungeon
Specialization Level: 5

Dungeon Master Bonus:
+50% Attack and Defense while in a Dungeon or the Labyrinth
+50% Chance to find Nodes
+40% Trap Detection while in a Dungeon or the Labyrinth

+30% Movement and Attack Speed while in a Dungeon or the Labyrinth

+20% Attack and Defense for your Dungeon party while in a Dungeon or the Labyrinth

+10% Concealment and Perception while in a Dungeon or the Labyrinth

Settlement Bonus:
+50% Dungeon Points from any source
+50% Dungeon Loot Generation
+40% Dungeon Resource Growth
+30% Ambient Mana Seepage
+20% Ambient Mana Refinement
For each Treasure Chest rank, up to +10% occurrence
+5% Affinity for every member of your settlement in one of the Basic Elements

Leveling Conditions:
Generate 11,153/25,000 Dungeon Points
Add 481/15 new Beasts to the Dungeon Bestiary
Add 3/7 new Rooms
Consume 7,928/2,500 creatures

LEGENDARY Bonus: A God Node

Richter's excitement peaked again upon reading the level 5 effects. Once again, he'd been thrust into the jaws of danger, but he'd been proportionally rewarded. His life proved that power and danger were close bedfellows. The lich had been an existential threat to his village, to the entire Forest of Nadria. His allied army had almost lost, but it was also true that without the lich's forces swarming through the gate, the Dungeon would never have been able to consume enough energy to advance so quickly. Because it had, his entire village would benefit.

The chaos seed had no idea what a "God Node" was, but reaching level five of the village's specialty had increased all of the previous bonuses and those had already been substantial. He personally had gotten a boon to Concealment and Perception while he was adventuring in a Dungeon or the Labyrinth. The possibility of treasure chests appearing had also doubled. What made his breath catch though was the last line of the settlement bonus.

There was no other information, but it looked like the Dungeon's ability to increase and refine ambient mana around it might actually increase the affinity of his people for magic! That meant more Life mages to heal, more aeromancers to cast thunderbolts, and maybe even more necromancers to raise the bodies of slain enemies to fight on behalf of the Mist Village. He just couldn't believe it.

His enchantments were able to make common men and women the equivalent of real soldiers. He couldn't turn them into casters, however. A powerful magic user could be worth an entire platoon of soldiers. That power was reflected by the low likelihood of someone having an affinity for magic skills. There was almost zero chance of someone awakening a skill if their affinity for it was less than 50%. Usually, only one out of a thousand to ten thousand people met that requirement when it came to the Basic Elements. With this settlement-wide boost in magic affinities, the Mist Village could become a mecca for magicians. It truly was a bonus worthy of a *legendary* achievement.

Richter was already resolved to make it back to the village. With so many amazing developments waiting for him, he was more excited than ever. He'd have to wait to find out just what the *mythic* and *legendary* bonuses meant for his village, but they were just icing on the cake. He would make it back to his people. He would make it back to Sion. He would make it back to Alma! The chaos seed's resolve hardened to steel. It didn't matter who or what was standing in his way. He'd get to this damn red dot, finish Xuetrix's quest, and make it back to his people. And he would absolutely cut down any bastard dumb enough to stand in his way. He was Lord Mist. It was what he did.

CHAPTER 23

DAY 151 – JUREN 2, 0 AOC

*R*ichter cast *Weak Find Water* every hundred yards. The pulse would ripple out, but still found nothing. Walking through rough stone tunnels without shoes, the only sound his own breathing, was nerve-wracking. It also occurred to him that, short-lived as it was, every time he cast his spell the blue light of the casting broadcast his position. The only life he'd come across so far was a nest of carnivorous four-hundred-pound centipedes and a demon. He wasn't super excited to get to know any more of the local wildlife.

While he walked, he dealt with the very last prompt from the Mausoleum. He'd been saving the best for last.

Congratulations! You have slain your second Mortal Enemy. Most beings live their entire lives without ever gaining this level of enmity. Few that do survive the experience. You have slain not one, but two creatures whose powers outstrip your own. For this amazing feat, you have earned a Mark!

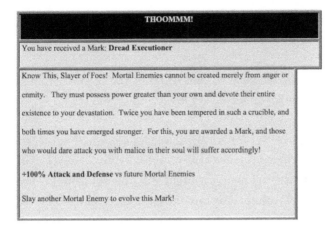

THOOMMM!

You have received a Mark: **Dread Executioner**

Know This, Slayer of Foes! Mortal Enemies cannot be created merely from anger or enmity. They must possess power greater than your own and devote their entire existence to your devastation. Twice you have been tempered in such a crucible, and both times you have emerged stronger. For this, you are awarded a Mark, and those who would dare attack you with malice in their soul will suffer accordingly!

+100% Attack and Defense vs future Mortal Enemies

Slay another Mortal Enemy to evolve this Mark!

His first Mortal Enemy had been the rock giant. The second was the mauler. If only they could see him now. Thanks to the two monsters going out like a bunch of punk ass bitches, he was stronger than ever. In fact, if he ever got another Mortal Enemy, he'd hit twice as hard. All thanks to those two knuckleheads. Richter chuckled to himself. Thanks again, dickheads!

He looked at the inside of his right forearm, and saw a midnight-black square appear. It had a grinning skull inside with the number "2" carved onto the skull. After a moment, it disappeared.

His new Mark was the very last Mausoleum prompt, but he still needed to assign his Attribute Points from unlocking level forty-five. He didn't want to waste time doing that until he dealt with his debuffs. As far as his Talent Points went, there was also no real point. As powerful as his Enchanter Profession could be, it had a serious weakness. It needed materials.

He could do nothing without captured souls and powdered crystal. He knew the spell to make more soul stones. He might even be lucky enough to find a solitary creature that he could kill and trap. Without the powdered crystal though, he was stuck. He was a driver without gas, a sniper without bullets, an old guy without Viagra. He was boned... so to speak.

With nothing else to do, and to distract himself from the gnawing in his belly and dryness of his throat, he examined the prompts he'd gotten since waking up in his skeeling shell. The first came from his fight and flight from the ichorpede lair.

Congratulations! You have reached skill level 3 in Unarmed Combat. +6% to unarmed combat damage. +0.3 to natural armor.

It looked like ripping off the ichorpede's pincer had earned him a skill level. *Unarmed Combat* was potentially an amazing skill because it also hardened his skin. Problem was, he could only level it if he didn't have any other weapons in hand. Even holding a dagger and punching and kicking at the same time wouldn't increase the skill. It was just kind of a hard sell to go into a life-and-death situation without weapons when his Profession was literally about making magic weapons.

He pinched his skin, seeing if it felt any different than he remembered, but it looked and felt the same. Shrugging, he moved on to the next prompts. More skill levels greeted him, thanks to his bone club.

Congratulations! You have reached skill levels 9 and 10 in Mace Wielding. +30% damage when using maces or clubs. Ignore up to 5% of an enemy's armor.

Congratulations! You have advanced from Novice to Initiate in: Mace Wielding. You have progressed down the martial path. Few truly understand the satisfaction of literally crushing the life from your enemies.

Mace Wielding Initiate Bonus: Maces and Clubs weigh 10% less in regard to wielder. This is cumulative with successive ranks.

You have received 2,000 bonus experience for reaching level 10 in the skill: Mace Wielding.

The experience was helpful, even if it was a drop in the bucket at this point. The boost to the skill was also helpful, especially seeing as how his only weapon was a club. He could also see the *initiate* bonus being useful. Stamina drain in battle increased with exertion, and it was obviously harder to swing something heavy than it was to swing something lighter. This perk would also increase his attack speed while keeping the mass and overall weight of the weapon the same when it hit his enemies.

As great as all of that was, it was nothing compared to the notification that awaited him next. As Richter read it, he couldn't help but fist pump twice, "Yeah!" At the same time, many miles away, a book flashed with grey light inside of the chaos lord's Bag of Holding.

Congratulations, Chaos Lord! You previously purchased knowledge from the Sea of Chaos that you were not qualified to access.

You now meet the qualifications:
*Strength 15: **Achieved***

*Mace Wielding skill level 10, Initiate Rank: **Achieved***
Do you wish to absorb the Novice *rank knowledge of the Expertise Book:* **Granite Breaker?** *Yes or No?*

So excited that he stopped walking, Richter mentally reached to click "Yes." He was only a split second from finishing the action before an errant thought stopped him cold. His excitement had nearly killed him.

It had never occurred to him that he would be able to access the expertise book remotely. He didn't know if it was because it was soul bonded to him in some way, or because he had bought it from the Sea of Chaos, or just because he'd leafed through the book and unconsciously retained the knowledge. Whatever the reason, this was an amazing opportunity. One that could greatly increase his chances of surviving.

That was because an expertise book was potentially far more valuable than a skill book. Advancing a skill would give you bonuses to a specific action. *Mace Wielding,* for instance, increased his damage using clubs. It also gave the possibility of ignoring a portion of an enemy's armor. That was great and all, but it only mattered if you actually managed to hit your opponent.

Just because your skill level increased didn't actually mean that you knew what you were doing. An easy example would be a super-muscular guy getting into a fight. He could probably hit harder than a smaller guy, but that didn't mean he actually knew how to box.

An expertise book, on the other hand, actually gave you the knowledge of how to perform a certain action. It bypassed the ten thousand hours that were usually needed to become good at some-thing and just poured it all into your mind. The split-second calcula-tions, foot positioning, even the breathing that a true mace fighter would employ in a battle, all of that would become like second nature to Richter. His attack power with clubs and maces would skyrocket.

The problem was, gaining knowledge didn't always happen in an instant. When he had used the *Unconventional Materials* skill book, his mind had been hijacked. For hours, his body had been comatose. He'd been stuck in one place, reliving the memories of an orc *master* tinker. That entire time, he'd stood stock still while his friends and Companions had protected him. They'd had to kill over a dozen monsters, any one of which might have eaten him alive.

That had only been a skill book. Who knew what would happen if he absorbed the knowledge of an expertise book? What would happen to him while he was defenseless in this dark tunnel? What if he was stuck in a fugue for hours or even days? Even if he wasn't attacked, what would happen to his debuffs then? They might liter-ally kill him.

Richter stared at the notification window, regret replacing his earlier excitement, and chose "No" on the prompt. It just wasn't worth the risk.

You have decided not to learn the novice *rank knowledge of the Expertise Book:* **Granite Breaker** *at this time. This knowledge will remain available to you unless the book is destroyed prior to use.*

He heaved a small sigh of relief. He'd been afraid that choosing "no" would mean the end of his chances. Now if he found a safe place to hole up, he could access the information later. Looking at the featureless grey rock all around him, he dual cast *Find Water* again, but to no avail. After refreshing *Dark Vision,* he continued his journey into the darkness and examined the last of the prompts that had come when he changed his tier.

The first was a final note about his bloodline. He'd wondered about how quickly he could replenish any points he used. The window explained how it worked.

Your Bloodline will replenish itself at a rate dependent on your Constitution. Every 10 points of Constitution will replenish your Bloodline Pool by one point each hour.

Richter blew out a slow breath. His bloodline definitely had power and potential, but he would have to be judicious in how he used it. Once it was exhausted, he'd have to wait nearly half a day for it to completely refill. Thankfully his Constitution was high, further bolstered by his Mark of Blood and Chaos, so he'd replenish 7.4 Blood Points/hour.

The next prompt was about his new aura. He'd never known that he even had an aura before. Hisako had strongly suspected he was somehow triggering events. Even Randolphus had hinted that too many things seemed to happen around Richter, but neither had mentioned an actual aura. Maybe because such things were rare, or at least they used to be.

Every chaos seed could have the same aura. They could all be manipulating the lives of everyone around them without even knowing it. The chaos lord shook his head. If every chaos seed really did have the Chaotic Gradient, then thousands, hundreds of thousands, or millions of people snatched from Earth were essentially the equivalent of a biblical plague, literally spreading chaos everywhere they went. The magnitude of it all came crashing down upon him. The devastation to people's lives must be incalculable.

*Your Chaotic Gradient aura has increased in rank from the **Greater** to **Grand**. Your aura transcends time. Your existence ripples through the past and future, changing the fates of all.*

Richter had barely absorbed the information before his vision blacked out. Seeing as how he had *Darkvision* activated, he was confused for a half second. The spell duration couldn't have already run out, could it? Then the pain came. Searing, bubbling, agonizing pain. It was the exact feeling a person would have if a slime had detached from the roof of the tunnel and landed on their face.

As the slime's acid began to slough off his eyebrows and skin, he was struck with an inane thought. Dissolving flesh sounded like rice krispies in milk. It was just an errant neuronal connection from a panicked brain, but it played on a loop. The slime was pushing its pudding-thick body into his eyes, nose, ears and mouth. Dread bordering on hysteria seized him in response to the sudden attack and mind-numbing pain. Most men would have fallen backwards and succumbed, the fight over before it began.

That was not going to be his fate. Months of battle had changed Richter. Despite the feeling of acid eating his face, he resisted the urge to scream. That saved his life. If the ooze had managed to get down his throat in that first second, his life would have ended. That was the slime's preferred method to kill. It would slide its malleable body through any convenient orifice, and then dissolve its victims from the inside out. The best part was that if another predator came to eat the body, the slime would get a second meal with little effort. As the new monster ate, the slime would wait for the right moment, surge down this new throat like jelly, and begin its feast anew.

Not opening his mouth only gained Richter a second, maybe two, before it forced its way past his clenched jaw. In that crucial time though, he used his bloodline for the first time. It was almost instinctual. He had to make the conscious choice, but then it felt almost like something that had been ingrained in him since birth. His new tier was saving his life. Richter found a strange power inside himself and spammed it with every point he had in his bloodline. A cold feeling grew in his veins. Not the cold of winter or ice, but a life-sucking numbness, almost as if he was already in the grave.

Richter couldn't see it, but all his major blood vessels were glowing purple-black. They traced under his dark skin, making him look like a fell creature. Then, less than a moment after he'd thought it, his skin grew harder than stone. Even his eyes could have deflected a blade strike with no issue.

With his body strengthened to this extent, he should have died. It should not have been possible for him to move, for his heart to beat, for his nerves to conduct information in flashes of electricity and bursts of chemicals. By his understanding of the human body, this being harder than stone was incompatible with human life. It defied everything that he'd learned before coming to The Land. The power of his bloodline went beyond biology.

In a second, his defense soared by seventy-two points, stronger than any armor in the Mist Village. Richter probably hadn't needed to use the full power of his bloodline. Half as much would have let him resist the slime's acid, something in his mind was screaming. As soon as his skin hardened, the pain had started to abate. That didn't stop the message that was on repeat in his head, 'It's eating me. It's eating me. It's eating me!'

A prompt appeared in his vision even as he raised his hand to his head.

*You have used the **Harden** power of your bloodline. **Defense** +72 for 60, 59, 58, ...*

The prompt was absorbed and processed by Richter's hindbrain, barely registering. What he was focused on was one of the few items he had left. A little ring that was one of his most versatile and well-used items. With his lips and eyes still screwed shut, he lifted it to his head and released the spell from his Ring of Spell Holding.

Waves of violent sonic energy released a bare inch from his own head. In any other circumstances, this would have been as deadly as smashing a hammer into his temple. The invisible rings of sonic force would rupture his eardrums, vibrate his retinas until they detached, and scramble the fluid in his ears until he couldn't stand straight. Now, the gritty and viscous body of the slime protected him from the worst of his own attack, and his bloodline defense negated the rest. He was truly as hard as stone now. The magic of Death filled him.

The monster was not so lucky. Sonic energy vibrated every molecule of the creature's body. The colloidal beast had no mouth to scream, but agony spread through its being in response to the point-blank attack. With his other hand, Richter sank his fingers into the slime's body and began to peel it off his face like playdoh off a newspaper. His pain ratcheted back up. Even though his defense was up in the stratosphere now, the acidic properties of the slime coupled with its firm grip made him feel like he was pulling his own face off.

The monster was also still fighting. Despite the pain it was in, the predator was no stranger to life-and-death battles. It did not want to let go, and a podocyte lashed fire across the chaos lord's face as it tried to hold on. Richter wished his bloodline could have deadened his pain receptors when it increased his defense, but he wasn't that lucky. He didn't stop pulling. He kept his spell ring trained on the slime, continuing the spell, and after a few seconds it finally lost enough control that he was able to wrench it free.

Richter threw his attacker into the wall of the tunnel. His mouth popped open and he gasped for air like a fish out of water. The chaos lord's high stats would let him hold his breath for several minutes if need be, but that didn't matter if he barely had any air to begin with. The slime's attack had been so fast that he'd been caught during an exhale. While he sucked in the sweet, sweet air, he didn't forget about his enemy. The battles he'd survived had trained him to compartmentalize and stay focused. His eyes remained glued on the slime despite the pain he was in. He couldn't afford to lose sight of it and be ambushed again.

Despite his efforts, Richter failed. As soon as the slime landed, it disappeared from his sight. It hadn't turned invisible, it just moved so fast he lost sight of it. A moment later, the worst happened. His *Darkvision* spell elapsed. His sight turned black in an instant. Primal terror gripped him. He scrambled backwards while he cast *Simple Light*, trying to keep space between himself and his unknown enemy. He fumbled the spell three times thanks to his hacking breaths and *Exhausted* debuff, but finally managed it.

In the corner of his vision, the counter for his increased defense counted down.

51, 50, 49...

Ten of sixty seconds already gone. If he had had the time, he would have cursed his panic. The bloodline had saved his life, but he probably hadn't needed to use all his points at once. Time was something he didn't have. His spell completed and a ball of white light floated from his hand to hover over his head. Looking about frantically, he finally caught sight of his nemesis.

It looked like a grey-black oil slick sliding along the stone. With one hand out to ward it off and other pressed against his skinned face, he tracked it with his eyes. It shifted this way and that, never staying still for more than a second, and covering a yard each time it moved. Then it started to move much faster. The faint light of his spell was barely enough to see it. Between its color and lightning speed, it almost vanished into the gloom each time it moved.

Richter's breath came fast and short while he kept his eyes glued to the monster. It slid up the side of the wall and began surging toward Richter again. It clung to the tunnel surface as easily as a spider; it moved creepily fast and eerily silently. It was clear that the blob planned to drop on him from above. The chaos lord kept stumbling backwards the whole time. His fingers wove into a dual cast incantation, *Weak Flame*. At the same time, he used *Analyze* on the beachball-sized monster.

Name: Nesting Stone Slime	Disposition: Hungry
Level: 37	Tier: 1

Nesting Stone Slimes are among the smallest examples of ooze-type monsters. However, any who underestimate these voracious monsters are fools. These creatures not only have the physical resistance ubiquitous to their kind, but the Earth magic that permeates their bodies gives them strong defense. Their stone nature also allows them to have a high Concealment when lying against rock.

STATS		
Health: 1,288/1472	Mana: 138/138	Stamina: 614/636

ATTRIBUTES		
Strength: 31	Agility: 45	Dexterity: 37
Constitution: 147	Endurance: 63	Intelligence: 13
Wisdom: 15	Charisma: 8	Luck: 17

SPECIAL ABILITY

Harden – Can force all of the stone particulates in its body to the surface, greatly increasing its defense for a short time

Nest – Can go into a state of near-hibernation, remaining perfectly motionless and even suppressing its life force to avoid detection

The information washed over Richter in an instant, filling him with knowledge of the stone slime. At the same time, he finished his incantation. A red glow surrounded both hands... and nothing else happened.

Spell casting failed!

Dammit! He hadn't failed a casting since he'd begun slinging spells! Now he'd miscast several times in a row. Fuck these debuffs! It was true that dual casting a spell greatly increased the chances it would miscast, but *Weak Flame* was only a level one spell, for god's sake! Richter didn't have any more time to complain because the slime threw itself at him again.

He dove to the side, narrowly dodging the monster. It simply struck the ground where he had been standing and shot at him again without pause. It was almost like it ignored the laws of momentum as it reached parts of itself toward him. The creature moved at the speed of a sprinter and could change direction at the drop of a dime. It propelled itself into the air in a leap toward Richter's face. The chaos seed had started another casting, one-handed this time. He had to abandon the spell when the slime forced him to dive aside again.

The fight was moving fast and he had split seconds to make his decisions and process information. The nesting stone slime was strong, but Richter was far from weak. His *Weak Flame* had been interrupted, but his frustration didn't slow him down. After reading the analysis of the monster, he realized that fire probably wasn't the best option anyway and made a quick decision to change tactics.

This time, Richter finished his incantation while the slime sailed through the air at him. When it was only three feet from his face, he opened his mouth, and once again, invisible rings of sound flew toward the monster. Every strength could be a weakness. For a creature with a high rock content in its body, sonic attacks were kryptonite. The spell had already worked once, so he had no reason to think it wouldn't work again.

As the Earth magic hit it, the slime started freaking out. Its body lost some cohesion and it shot podocyte tendrils in every direction. Its momentum still carried it forward, but it fell next to Richter, instead of on top of him. Richter kept his mouth turned toward it, even as the spillover sound made his already tender eardrums throb. The slime retreated immediately away from the anathema attack, and moved beyond the twenty-foot range of *Weak Sonic Wail*.

It needn't have bothered. The spell had only a three-second duration, and had a one-minute cooldown. If it had just stayed in place and weathered the attack, there would have been nothing Richter could have done to block it. He wasn't complaining though, and he wasn't going to waste the opportunity. As soon as the sonic attack ended, he began a defensive casting. It took two seconds. The slime could have stopped it by attacking, but whatever intelligence it had made it hesitate for a full second after the sound attack ended. By the time it was once again surging toward Richter, he'd completed his next spell.

Just in time, a soap bubble of green Earth magic sprang into being around him. The colorful light hurt his Darkvision-enhanced eyes, so

Richter dismissed the Dark magic. As soon as he'd done that, a solid thud echoed in the tunnel. The slime had landed on the outside of his protective shield. It sent protrusions of itself over the surface of the sphere, but there were no breaks it could fit through. Richter heaved a sigh of relief, then immediately winced in pain.

The stone slime had taken off more than twenty of his health in the first moment of battle. As he peeled it off afterwards, he'd lost another fifteen. Richter was happy he couldn't see his own face. Blood was flowing down his chest. He was sure his face was a ruined, bloody mess. Exhaling a heavy sigh, he prepared to cast *Weak Slow Heal* on himself. His *Dehydration* debuff kept his health from restoring, but the spell should at least fix the tissue damage he'd suffered. As long as the Earth shield held, he should have plenty of ti-

"Shit!"

His healing spell failed. Richter was about to curse his *Exhausted* debuff again, but another prompt appeared.

Life magic cannot be cast while your bloodline is active!

The defense from *Harden* had saved his life, but he'd already found a weakness in his new power. He knew that Vile bloodlines had something to do with Death magic. Now he learned that using his bloodline cut him off from his Life spells. It meant that while *Harden* could increase his defense, he couldn't use magic to heal himself. Now wasn't the time to worry about that though, so he just resolved to own the pain. He had problems. Looking at the slime, he amended his thought. Much bigger problems.

The slime had stopped searching for an entrance to his shield and had instead gathered itself in one spot. As Richter watched, the creature began to quiver violently. To his horror, it forced a tendril through the shield! He stared in shock. That shouldn't be possible. The only thing that could pass through a magic shield was... That was when he realized it wasn't overcoming the defensive magic, it was bypassing it.

Magic shields were powerful defenses for magi, but they had their weakness. Lower level shields, like his own *Weak Static Earth Shield,* would stop swords, arrows and magical attacks from other

Basic Elements, but it would not prevent other Earth energy from passing through it.

The body of the stone slime must qualify as Earth energy, at least in part. If it was fully resonant with the spell, it could have passed through the shield like it wasn't even there. Thankfully that wasn't the case. But completely in sync or not, it was clearly able to use its Earth nature to bypass his defense. Which meant that instead of having minutes to recover and strategize, he only had seconds before it would be on him again. Hence, his completely reasonable expression of shock and dismay.

"Shit!"

Richter racked his brain while a quarter of the beach ball-sized slime forced its body through his shield in a second. He came up with an idea, but it meant taking a serious risk. He went for broke. Reaching out to his bloodline, he dismissed the *Harden* effect, letting the power leave his body. After that, he furiously cast, praying his magic wouldn't fail him again. He gave the spell as much of his diminished concentration as he could. Just as the monster made its way all the way through the shield, he took a step back and finished his next casting. Relief flooded into him even as magic flowed out. He could use Life magic again!

Another shield sprang into existence, this time gold in color. A second bubble of magic now surrounded him. It arrived in the nick of time. A moment later, the stone slime had crossed completely through the Earth shield. The monster wasted no time before flinging its body at this second barrier. Richter was well aware that without the defense his bloodline offered, the next time the slime touched him would probably be the last.

The chaos lord started another incantation, resisting the urge to rush. Every second counted and he couldn't allow for a miscast. Golden light surrounded him again as healing magic flowed through his body. The pain in his face and shoulders faded as tissues reknit. Unlike every other time he'd healed himself, this time his red health bar did not refill. Cursed with the *Dehydrated* debuff, his health wouldn't refill until he found water. Of course, that would be a moot point if he didn't survive the next few minutes.

The slime was stretched over the surface of his Life shield, like oil over a golden ball. Seeing the monster pour itself over the gold film, only three feet away from his face, was macabre and disturbing. It was not nearly as disturbing as what it did next though. A thick tendril coalesced on the side of it, about the size of a cop's baton. The protrusion changed in color from the grey-black of the slime's main body, to the color of pure grey rock. Richter remembered the description that said it could focus the stone inside of its own body to one specific spot. Then it slammed the rock club down on his shield with a solid *thud!*

"Well that's not good."

The monster raised its tendril, then slammed it down with even more force. A small web of cracks appeared on the magical shield, making Richter curse. He knew that the Life shield wouldn't hold for long. Not only did it have less HP than his Earth shield, but it also had a lower defense. If the slime kept up its attack, there was nothing keeping it from getting through in seconds rather than the minutes Richter had hoped to buy himself. He needed a plan and he needed it now!

The chaos lord took stock. His health was down nearly 10%. The slime hadn't been in contact with him for long, but the fact that it had enveloped his head had apparently increased the damage it could wreak. His stamina was nearly full, and his mana pool was still around 70%. Unfortunately, the only spells he could cast through the shield were Life magic. The only offensive option was *Weak Life Bolt*. The damage it caused was so low he could spam it all day and not make a dent in the slime's health.

Richter's mind worked furiously. How the hell was he supposed to kill this thing? He didn't have any armor. Even his bone club was out of reach. He'd dropped it when the slime had first attacked. Now his club was on the other side of the tunnel, the slime between him and it. Even if he had the impromptu weapon, the monster had a high defense. His sonic spell had definitely hurt it, taking away about 10%

of its health each time, but it had a one-minute cooldown. He couldn't cast it continually. Even if he was able to rattle off the spell one more time, it would be on him right after that.

It continued to pound away at his shield, widening the cracks. Richter only had seconds left before it would break through. If it covered his face again, he was done! He blinked, fear gripping his heart, threatening to overwhelm him for a half-second before he pushed it down. With anger, he realized his *Ravenous* debuff was compromising his emotions again.

He used that anger to focus. He wasn't going out like this. He just needed some help. Richter's fingers contorted as green light surrounded them. His concentration debuff weighed on him, but he was no simple conjurer of cheap tricks. He was the Master of a Place of Power and soul bonded to a psi dragonling! His mind was trained and his will would not be denied.

Richter finished the last syllable of the spell and stepped back at the same time. His shoulders brushed the edge of the Life shield, banishing it. The slime fell several feet to the ground. At the same time, a rent in space appeared, bringing with it the scent of evergreens.

Before the slime had even hit the ground, a saproling had stepped through. In a perfect world, Richter would have dual cast the spell, raising the creature's level and combat power. He couldn't risk a spell misfire again though, or even worse, spell feedback. That would be a death sentence.

He also couldn't spend his MPs frivolously. At skill level 14, *Dual Casting* increased his spell's power by 156%, but it also increased his spell cost by 272%. His new Water Mastery would help with that, but it would still be a horrible drain on his magic reserves. He had to hope that the base power of the spell coupled with his *rare* Summoner's Ring would make it strong enough to hold the slime back for a few precious seconds.

Richter eyed his summoned creature even as he began his next spell. The saproling had taken the form of a four-foot-high badger made of living branches and leaves. Two dark stones nestled where its eyes would have been. He stared into the stones, making a weak psychic bond so that he could control it mentally. All of this took barely a second.

The slime quivered for just a moment. It was about to attack Richter again when the saproling hurled itself at the black monster. It was no match for the slime, but Richter wasn't done yet. Praying for a good result, he began to cast *Akaton Evolution*. The cast time was four long seconds. He had to hope that his level twelve summoned monster could hold back the level thirty-seven monster for at least that long.

His mind was clouded and his body ached, but if there was one type of magic he could use without fail, it was Chaos. The words of the spell, which had always flowed as easily as water, were now even more familiar. They caressed his lips like cool silk. His relationship with Chaos was a love affair that not even his debuffs could affect. The two spells dropped his mana again, this time by nearly two hundred points, leaving him with barely four hundred points. It didn't matter. It was time to go all in.

The slime was quickly dissolving the saproling. The creature was biting and clawing the ooze, doing some damage but not nearly enough to matter. The forest elemental was simply out leveled. Truth be told, even if they had been the same level, the slime was just a superior monster. It had a body that could harden like stone and eat like acid. How could a creature made of leaves and wicker resist it?

Of course, Richter had never expected his saproling to defeat the slime. Not as it currently was. Four seconds elapsed and the roiling grey energy surrounding his arms shot forward in a beam toward his summoned creature. Prompts appeared and were consumed by his mind as *Akaton Evolution* did its masterful work.

Know This! You have cast Chaos Magic for the first time since your ascendance to the Legendary *incarnation of a Chaos Lord. Your understanding of Chaos and its magics has increased. +30% effectiveness of Chaos magic!*

Your spell Akaton Evolution will now list the total number of possible evolu-

tions along with their rank and maximum tier, though you must success-fully discover the evolutions to gain full knowledge of them.

Know This! Higher-ranked evolutions are generally stronger than lower-ranked, but are less likely to appear.

Know This! Your increased power with Chaos Magic has unlocked a new evolution for your Saproling.

*Know This! Your spell Akaton Evolution has evolved your **Saproling** into an **Albino Arborast**, a rank 3, **Unusual** Evolution. This is 1 of 4 possible evolutions. The maximum evolved tier of your Saproling is **Tier 1**.*
Attack increased by +10. Defense increased by +8.
*Special ability: **Rage** – increases Strength, Constitution and Endurance dramatically for a short time. Mentation decreased during this state. When Rage has elapsed, the creature will be weakened for an extended period of time*

Richter watched as all color was leached from the saproling even as the slime continued to try and consume it. What had been a losing battle for his summoned creature changed in that moment. The saproling no longer looked like a badger composed of loose branches. The gaps in its body completely filled in. Its leafy exterior was replaced with sculpted muscle that stood out starkly under its white fur. Two large rabbit-like incisors filled its mouth, and it stood on two strong back legs. The knees inverted and its arms ended in gorilla fists. The slime continued to do damage, but its body was no longer large enough to easily envelop Richter's summoned creature.

The process of evolution was nearly instantaneous, yet there was one fleeting moment where the monster, pet and summoner took stock of their new normal. Richter shattered that stillness with vindictive glee and a single psychic command.

Rage

The already muscular Albino Arborast triggered its special ability. Its stats shot up considerably and its body changed once again.

Whereas before it had the physique of a martial artist, now its muscles nearly doubled in size. It let loose a shriek, and grabbed the slime trying to erode its chest with two impressively large white hands. The evolved pet completely disregarded its own pain as it plunged its hands into the thick gel of the slime's body. It lifted the viscid creature off the ground and then screamed at the monster with a furious anger. Blood and melted flesh streamed down the arborast's arms, marring its white fur, but in its fury it didn't notice. All it cared about was causing pain to the creature that had hurt it.

The slime was slammed down onto the rocky floor of the tunnel and the arborast began to pummel it. Thick fists rose and fell while it carried out an attack of caveman-level savagery. The grey-black blob fought back, forcing stone particles to the surface to increase its defense even as it lashed podocytes across the albino's skin. The arborast's flesh became a ruin of red in seconds. It might have succumbed, even its *Rage* state, but for one thing. The one fact that had always helped Richter himself prevail against impossible odds. It was not alone.

Golden light suffused the arborast as Richter cast *Minor Slow Heal,* followed by *Weak Haste.* His pet's bloodied white fists began to rise and fall faster. The chaos lord targeted the slime next, this time with Water magic. It only took a second to cast *Weak Slow.* All three spells were boosted by his Mastery in those elements. Coupled with Richter's insanely high Intelligence, the spells were game-changers.

The fight was over; the monster just didn't know it yet. What Richter had realized when he was watching the slime beating on his shield, the sound reverberating like the footsteps of doom, was that he could not defeat the slime as a man. He couldn't calculate, hold back, or try to weigh costs and benefits.

It was a monster. It would kill him or it would be killed. That oneness of purpose was a strength. If he wanted to survive, then he needed to do the same. It was time to go all in. When he'd broken his own shield to summon the saproling, he'd risked his life. If he had faltered or delayed for even an instant, his life would be over.

That was what it meant to live as a monster: life and death, separated only by a moment. There had been no surety of success, but that was fine. Assurances were hollow lies cherished by those who loved order. He was a creature of Chaos. He didn't need platitudes or false safety. All he needed was the impermanent perfection of the truth. And the truth right now was that he was fucking this mother-fucker up!

The slime's health dropped rapidly under the arborast's assault. Richter had no idea how smart the ooze monster was, but it seemed to be perceptive enough to recognize that the black man, rather than the white creature, was the real threat. It tried to break away from his albino pet, but the chaos lord simply cast *Weak Sonic Wail* again. The cone-shaped attack enveloped his summoned creature as well, but another healing spell fixed that damage. The bigger threat of using the sound spell indiscriminately was that attacking a summoned creature risked losing control over it, though here his mental training made that unlikely.

After that, the battle became predictable. Anyone that had ever seriously gamed knew a simple fact of combat. When two melees went at it, the one that had magical support, especially if they had a healer, would be the one standing at the end. Despite the still drastic difference in levels, Richter's wide array of spell buffs let him support the arborast as it continually pummeled the slime to death.

The beatdown took a while. While he waited, Richter considered using his Blood magic on the thing. Having a tamed slime that could sneak up on other creatures could be very useful. In the end, he decided against it for a number of reasons. First and foremost, in his current state of emotional volatility and decreased concentration, he'd almost certainly be overtaken by the unrestrained id of the Deeper magic.

Besides, Blood magic was not to be used lightly. It had a cost beyond mana, requiring health and sometimes stamina as well. Losing more HPs would not be a good idea, not with his debuffs preventing healing. Finally, the spell might not even work on slimes. They didn't exactly have blood after all. There was so much he didn't understand about Deeper Magic; it just wasn't worth the risk.

Instead, he just kept buffing his summoned creature while it did the heavy lifting. Minutes later, the battle was done.

The stone slime's body shriveled in death. It leaked fluid across the tunnel floor, no longer the size of a beach ball. It was now only softball-sized and might have been mistaken for a simple, lumpy rock if Richter had just been walking past it. The arborast continued to pound on it, but in its reduced form it seemed to have lost all of its fluidity. The albino's fists still made dents in the dead body, but had no more effect than a pizza man pounding dough. Richter briefly considered trying to pull his summoned creature away, but then thought about its enraged state and his decreased concentration. When he'd hit it with the sonic attack, it might very well have turned on him if it wasn't still fighting the slime. Safer to just dismiss it back to where it came from.

With an exertion of will, another rent in space appeared and the evolved creature passed through it back to its home. He wondered if it would turn back into a saproling, or if some weird quirk of magic would leave it in its newly evolved form even after it had returned to its original plane of existence. The chaos lord shrugged. He'd probably never know.

The effects of his battle adrenalin faded, leaving behind an involuntary tremor in his hands. Coupled with his existing debuffs and the depletion of his magic, Richter only had the energy to crack a half-manic smile before collapsing to the ground in a half-stumble, half-fall. He looked at the body of the monster he'd slain, and thought, "Ha! Blue screen, muthafucka!" before he lost his grip on the conscious world.

CHAPTER 24

DAY 151 – JUREN 2, 0 AOC

"*G*ah! Clown penis!"

Richter jerked upright in confusion. That feeling swiftly morphed into panic. He was blind again! He felt a nearly pants-wetting terror at the thought that another slime was on his head. But over the next few seconds it all came back, and he realized that it was just that the spell which let him see had elapsed. He cast *Darkvision* in a state of near-terror. His head darted up, down and all around, scanning for more monsters.

With a profound sense of relief, he realized he was still alone in the tunnel. He put one hand to his chest while he waited for his heart to stop thudding. The shriveled body of the slime still lay next to him, and a blinking light in the corner of his vision let him know that he had notifications waiting to be read. He allowed himself a few more calming breaths before he addressed the waiting information.

*You have slept! **Exhausted** debuff removed. Concentration returned to normal levels.*

Richter heaved a sigh of relief. The *Dehydrated* and *Ravenous* debuffs were still there, along with the gnawing pain and sandpaper throat that accompanied them, but at least he could think straight. That miscast spell had nearly ended him at the beginning of the fight. He couldn't allow for that kind of mistake again.

Thankfully the powernap hadn't been so long that the other two debuffs had worsened. If he became *Severely Dehydrated* and started to lose 10 HP/second, he'd be out of options. He had to find water and fast. Now that he could think more clearly, he also realized he couldn't just keep rushing through the darkness.

He was fortunate to still be alive. Either his Luck was kicking in or the nesting stone slime had been the apex predator of this particular little patch of nothing. If there had been even one other monster in the area, he'd be dead. He didn't forget for a second that the lich's curse was hanging over him like an axe. He *had* to survive until it disappeared in a week. That meant being smarter, and better, than he'd been so far. Before he took another step into the dark, he needed to maximize his chances.

That meant allocating his points and coming up with a game plan. He pulled up the one notification he'd earned in the fight with the slime.

Congratulations! You have reached skill level 5 in **Chaos Magic.** *New spells are now available.*

That was good news. Advancing his Chaos Magic was definitely slower than the progression of his Basic Elements, or even his Deeper Magic. He only knew one Chaos spell so far, but hopefully that would change soon.

He had fifteen Attribute Points to distribute. The question was where? The +20 to his Luck along with the tier 2 bonus had catapulted the stat. It was heavily augmented by the one-week bonus of having the kindir as vassals, but even at the end of that week he would still get +5. There was a strong argument to invest more points into the attribute in light of the 20% modifier. He would in the future, but for now it was high enough.

He looked down at his body. His muscles were huge now. Like

Terminator huge. Truth be told, he was having a little buyer's remorse. More Strength was definitely not what he needed.

Honestly, when he moved around now, he felt... stiff. All the muscle felt like he was out of balance in some way. It might just be that he was still adjusting to his new physique. It also might be because he'd never added thirty points all at once to what he considered a "physical" attribute before.

Str, Agi, Dex, Con and End all resulted in an immediate and noticeable change to his physical body when they were increased. Intelligence, Wisdom, and Luck didn't. Charisma definitely had a physical effect as well, but it seemed as much about how people perceived you as getting flawless skin or perky nipples... not that that was his thing.

The point was, even though he wasn't exactly slower after putting so much into Strength, he felt... off. He hadn't noticed at first, but after ascending to a higher tier his awareness of his own body had increased. It wasn't something he could put his finger on, but he knew he was right. It made him wonder if there was something he could do about that.

His eyes went to his Agility and Dexterity. They were his lowest stats. He'd ignored both for many levels, but now he reexamined their descriptions.

Agility – Determines movement speed. Each point increases walking speed by 0.1 mph. Determines dodge. Improves attack with melee weapons

Dexterity – Determines attack speed. Improves damage with ranged weapons. Improves Dodge. Improves Attack with ranged weapons

Those were just the surface descriptions. Each attribute had a lot more to it. Dexterity, for instance, could impact any number of skills. The stat directly increased the damage he could inflict with a bow. It helped some people more and others less, but his Limitless ability made sure he always got the maximum modifier. Every point increased his archery damage by 2%. Likewise, Agility didn't just let him move faster, it greatly improved his balance. Either could be helpful.

He also couldn't ignore the other options. A boosted Constitution would give him more health. That was always good. On the other hand, he still had two rings that increased it by +154 HP. Having almost a thousand health made him resilient, to say the least.

Increasing his Endurance would increase his stamina. He'd definitely ignored the attribute for far too long in the past. If there was one thing he'd learned since waking up underground, running out of stamina was deadly and dangerous. He needed to increase that as well.

Richter blew out his breath. He didn't have time to debate this in his head over and over. He needed to get moving again soon. His debuffs were a ticking time bomb, and he'd already lost hours while he was passed out. Richter thought about it a bit more, then made his choices.

Two points went into Endurance and three into Constitution. Then he poured five into both Agility and Dexterity. As soon as he did, he felt his muscles loosen. His center of balance grew more firm, and he felt lighter on his feet. There was no doubt about it. He felt more at ease in his body. He'd been hoping that that would be the case. Richter hadn't had much to go on, but on Earth, stretching was always supposed to balance weightlifting. That was why he'd thought putting points in Agility and Dexterity might solve the "off" feeling.

What Richter had intuitively picked up on was a little known fact about attributes. It wouldn't impact most people, but he'd caused an imbalance in his body when he'd upped his Strength so massively. His musculature and raw power had swelled, but his overall physical capabilities had become less efficient.

Though he didn't know it, Richter had stumbled upon one of the lesser known differences between the various races of The Land. While a giant or ogre could have their Strength be tens of times higher than their other "body" attributes, other races had a maximum ratio that, once exceeded, would have both immediate and long-term repercussions. The chaos lord's Luck was definitely in play as well, having kept him from turning himself into a cripple.

He'd felt, and looked like, a roided-out weightlifter. He might have been able to pick up a truck, but he couldn't scratch his own back. Now that his increased attributes had adjusted his body he felt much more at ease. Even his tendons loosened, giving him greater range of motion and better balance. He immediately felt more limber, and his form started to resemble a barbarian warrior more than a muscle-bound idiot.

He brought up his status sheet, limiting it to his basic info, attributes and stats.

Name: Richter	Age: 24	Level: 45, 3%
Race: Human (Chaos Lord)	Tier: 2	Languages: Sapient Mortals
Reputation: Lvl 5 "You are a man worth following."	Profession: Enchanter Specialty: Essence	Alignment: Chaotic (2) Neutral
STATS		
Health: 944	Mana: 828 *Regen/min: 36*	Stamina: 480 *Regen/min: 47.4*	Bloodline: 15/72 *Regen/hour: 7.4*
ATTRIBUTES		
Strength: 67 *(base: 65 w. Dragonkin + Goblinhold: 2)*	Agility: 42	Dexterity: 33
Constitution: 79 *(base: 69 + mark: 14%)*	Endurance: 48	Intelligence: 78 *(base: 71 + Quickening: 10%)*
Wisdom: 50	Charisma: 41 *(base: 35 + Honorable: 4 + Impassioned: 5%)*	Luck: 65 *(base: 34 + Vassal: 20 + Tier 2: 20%)*

Richter twisted at the waist and swung his arms. There was definitely a markedly improved ease of motion. His stamina and health had increased as well, making him feel, at least a bit, refreshed and revitalized. The health he was missing didn't refill, but his total swelled. All in all, he felt better. Not good, but definitely less like crap. He'd take it.

The next thing he did was look at his Chaos Points. More specifically, the new table he had gained with his new status as a chaos lord. At least, he tried to.

Chaos Lord upgrades are locked until at least 1 chaotic vassal is obtained!

So much for that, he thought, though it made his choice even easier. Instead of thinking about what upgrades he might purchase, he could just dive back into the Sea of Chaos. With his new Luck, he just had to get something good. He could now dive deeper than ever before due to his tier upgrade. Despite his battered and depleted body, Richter even managed a smile of anticipation. The gamer in him wasn't dead. It was time to get some loot!

*You have accessed the **Sea of Chaos**. The Sea contains everything that was, is, or could be. Choose wisely, for you may choose the Catalyst for your own death and salvation.*

*You may reach the first stratum at a cost of 1 **Chaos Point**.*

*You may reach the second stratum at a cost of 3 **Chaos Points**.*

*You may reach the third stratum at a cost of 5 **Chaos Points**.*

*You may reach the fourth stratum at a cost of 7 **Chaos Points**.*

*You may reach the fifth stratum at a cost of 9 **Chaos Points**.*

Which level do you wish to access?

There really wasn't a question. He eagerly chose the deepest stratum. The cost was nearly as many Chaos Points as he used to earn from leveling up, but now he had money to burn. Besides, despite the high cost, each stratum offered the potential for much greater rewards. The first stratum had provided second rank, or *uncommon,* items. The third stratum had provided *scarce,* fourth rank, items. He'd even purchased a sixth-ranked *epic* potion from the fourth stratum. If his luck held, the fifth might give him a *mythic* item. Possibly even something *legendary!*

His number of Chaos Points updated and new offerings were presented.

Total Chaos Points: **139**

Know This! No purchase is required. This window may be dismissed at any time, but it will last no longer than 7 minutes, and sometimes less. The purchase price of accessing this level cannot be retrieved. Each time a stratum of the Sea of Chaos is accessed, the offerings are randomized and may never come again.

THIS WAS the first time he'd accessed the Sea of Chaos since ascending. The first thing he noticed was that there were colors tinting the swirling grey energies of the stratum offerings. The first two were pinkish to show they were *epic*. The last was the yellow of a *mythic* offering, a full rank higher. His increased understanding of Chaos was already paying off. The descriptions of each offering were also much more expansive. Richter read over the options closely and was honestly a bit let down.

He'd finally reached the fifth stratum, and this was what he got? He'd been hoping for a weapon like Excalibur or a goddamn Gundam! What he got instead was a list of objects that looked like they helped various craftsmen. He needed things that would keep him alive right now!

The rarest was the sewing needle but, unless he was missing something, it was definitely cursed. It was probably owned by a demon that would steal a person's soul when they died. He'd had quite enough of that. Even if it wasn't demon-related, it sounded like there was a high price to pay for using it. That, coupled with the fact that a sewing needle wasn't of much use underground, surrounded by monsters, made it easy for Richter to rule it out.

The Ring of the Hardings sounded like something Krom would trade his fourth-through-sixth girlfriends for. The dwarf had explained once that each rank in Smithing allowed someone to make higher quality weapons and armor. A *novice* smith had a 99% chance of creating items in the four lowest quality ranks: *poor, average, above average* and *well-crafted.*

When Krom had initially explained it, he'd drawn a standard deviation curve. The middle two quality ranks both had a 34% chance of being created and the outer two had a chance of 13.5%. When Richter had heard that, he'd thought it was great news. That meant as a *journeyman*-ranked smith Krom should have had a 13.5% chance to make *exquisite* weapons. Even better, when reaching the *adept* rank, the dwarf would have the same likelihood to make a *masterwork*, right? Wrong. Wrong!

The problem with what the dwarf had taught him was that it was way too general. It was like teaching someone the concept of "round peg in a round hole" and expecting them to be good at sex. That only worked on 70, 80% of women, tops. For the rest, you needed some nuance.

Richter had been thoroughly annoyed with his smith when he found out that the deviation curve was only equally balanced for unranked smiths. Even *novices* did not have a 13.5% chance to make the highest quality for their rank, at least not at the lower-skill levels for their rank. A *novice*-ranked smith actually had a fair likelihood of making weapons of four different qualities: *trash, poor, average,* and *above average,* with a small chance to create something *well-crafted.*

When he'd expressed his irritation over the bad info to the mountain dwarf, Krom had just guffawed and said, "Real men only need ta count one cock, two tits and three sets of lips!" Then he'd proceeded to slap Richter on the back hard enough to make the mist lord stumble, and had chugged several ales in under a minute. It wasn't until the next morning that Krom was coherent enough to tell him that as a *journeyman*, the dwarf only had a roughly 1-3% chance of making the highest quality items for his rank, *exquisite.*

Once Richter had understood that, it really cleared up just how powerful one of the bonuses of the Forge of Heavens was. There was a 10% chance of a forged item being upgraded by one quality rank. It was how Krom had managed the near-miracle of creating a *masterwork* piece of armor even though he was only a *journeyman*. Richter winced as he remembered that that particular piece of armor was currently in tiny bits. He'd tell Krom it had saved his life, but the salt-and-pepper dwarf had an almost sexual connection with the items he created.

The convo would definitely be easier if Richter had a present like the Ring of Hardings to give his village Smith. If he was understanding the description correctly, the ring would increase the likelihood that smiths would create higher quality weapons and armor while they were forging. Coupled with the bonus from the Forge of Heavens, the quality of the Mist Village's armory could skyrocket. Which would be great, because higher quality weapons not only increased durability, they increased the damage they could inflict, and, most importantly for Richter, drastically increased the strength of the enchantments they could hold.

The problem was, while the ring would be priceless if he were back in the village, a forging ring was as useful as three nuts on a taco while he was trapped underground. Even if he did plan for the future, he might die down here. If and when he was reborn, there was no guarantee that any of these items would be soul bound to him.

If it wasn't, then this ring that he had spent an insane amount of Chaos Points to buy might be left underground, lost again for centuries. He had the capability to soul bind objects to him, but he still needed powdered crystal. His much-vaunted Enchanter Profession was completely impotent without it.

The Harding ring was a no, which only left the first option, the Monocle of the Master Craftsman Niclewis. If he didn't pick anything, he could just let the time elapse, but that meant he'd wasted nine Chaos Points. Nine CPs was enough to access and make a purchase from the first stratum, so it wasn't a small sacrifice.

He read the window again. The eyepiece was a boon to craftsmen, the same way the Harding ring helped smiths and the needle helped weavers. Richter wished he'd spent more time learning about the skill. He'd invested almost all of his time into forging and enchanting, with a bit of time left over for alchemy. On the upside, he'd been able to absorb a little-known skill book for the *Crafting* subskill, *Unconventional Materials*.

Crafting wasn't like *Forging*. When a smith made a weapon, he took an ingot of metal and pounded on it over and over. Krom had made endless jokes about how it made him every woman's soulmate. He had to know about how to heat it and cool it and bend it, but it all basically made sense. Crafting items wasn't like that. To make a simple magic ring that gave +5 to health, you had to follow a Template to the letter.

One line of magical script had to be written on the inside of the band, counterclockwise, and the second line had to be written clockwise on the outside. The band had to be pure copper, and a jewel of a certain cut, quality and type had to be affixed to the top. After that, it had to be enspelled by someone who knew the right Life enchantment. All of those steps had to be followed to the letter to make the simplest of magic rings.

Unlike *Forging*, where you needed better materials and more experience to make a higher quality sword, to make a stronger ring you might have to follow a completely different set of criteria and use a different combination of metal and gems. He might need to bathe his hands in the menstrual blood of a virgin for all he knew, though that would mean he could only craft for four to seven days a month, so hopefully not.

The point was, you had to had to have specific knowledge of Templates to craft magic items, not just metal, heat and skill. It was possible to make your own Templates, but just going by what was needed to make a low-effect health ring, the chances of that were abysmal. His *Unconventional Materials* subskill gave him an advantage, but he was still stumbling around in the dark.

That last thought was what decided it for him. Having actually stumbled around in the dark, and then having been nearly eaten by a slime, made a solid argument. A light to illuminate the dark made all the difference. It was true of physical light to combat the actual darkness he was in and it might be true for the metaphorical darkness of learning how to craft. The monocle could be his light. The slime didn't really fit into the metaphor, but he'd almost had his face melted off. Anyone that didn't like his analogies could suck it.

Richter did not want to dwell on his recent suffocation and face melting. Instead, he made a choice. A disc appeared in midair. Nothing could be seen inside it except a tumultuous grey nothingness. Most beings would be filled with anything from unease to horror at seeing the raw stuff of creation. To Richter, it was actually quite pleasant. He reached his hand through and closed his fingers around a smooth disc attached to a leather strap.

He pulled it out and the disc vanished. In his hands was a clear disc about two inches across. It was set in a rim of pure silver. Straps of a silvery type of hide extended out from either side showing how it could be secured to someone's head. Richter looked at it and a prompt appeared.

You have found:

You have found:	Durability: 653/653
Monocle of Niclewis	Item Class: Epic
	Quality: Masterwork
	Weight: 0.1 kg
	Traits: This is the monocle of the Master Craftsman Niclewis. Imbued with lost technology and forgotten alchemies, it allows the wearer to see and understand the latent energy of objects. Practice will increase the depth of this magical sight.
	Using the advanced sight of the monocle will drain your mana at a minimum rate of 1 MP/sec. Deeper inspection can increase this drain with no upper limit. It is advised that the wearer exercise caution. This practice can be toggled off and on at will.
	There are also 2 passive traits of the monocle:
	There is a specific increase in the success rate of creating items of higher quality. This bonus is dependent upon the wearer's skill level in Crafting.
	There is also a fixed +2% chance of successfully crafting items.

Total Chaos Points: 16

*Know This! When using the Monocle of Niclewis, as an **Apprentice** crafter you now enjoy a +10% chance of creating an **Exceptional** quality item and +3% chance of creating a **Superb** quality item.*

Looking at the item, there was no way it should have cost him this much. It was such a small and simple thing. Physically speaking, the only impressive thing about it was that the durability was crazy high. Even in a fight, there was a fair chance the monocle would make it through unscathed. Not only did the durability number in the hundreds, but it took a crazy amount of energy to make glass lose even one point. The leather strap he couldn't speak to, but it was the monocle itself that mattered.

As he read the item description, he realized that the monocle was worth every proverbial penny. He didn't understand the active effect, but he'd figure it out through experimentation. The 1 MP/sec meant his mana would drain at 60 per minute. It wasn't a small amount, but it was completely manageable for someone like himself. His high Intelligence and items gave him a mana pool higher than eight hundred. Coupled with his substantial Wisdom, he could use the monocle without rest for more than thirty minutes.

It wasn't the active effect that impressed him. The passive effects made the monocle worth thousands of gold in the right hands. Like Forging, each rank that someone reached in the Crafting skill conveyed a certain percentage for items to be produced at various qualities. The class of an item was determined by the materials used to create it, among other factors. Using the right Template, for instance, might determine whether a ring was *common* or *epic*.

The quality of an item, however, was only based on a crafter's skill rank, expertise and luck. And an increase in quality was nothing to scoff at. When Richter made higher quality rings, the health bonus they offered was increased. There were also other perks to increasing quality. Enalise, one of his villagers and a Professional Crafter, had told him that higher qualities could sometimes add extra properties to crafted items.

She had also told him that quality really became important when trying to use powerful Templates. Some items had a minimum quality level before they could be successfully created. When that meant *exquisite* or even *masterwork*, it was easy to see why highly ranked craftsmen were worth their weight in gold. Even *adept*-ranked crafters had a less than 1% chance to create a *masterwork*.

That was why the monocle was potentially so valuable. In the hands of a lower-ranked Crafter, the effect it could have wouldn't be that much. In the hands of someone more skilled, however, the chances to create a *masterwork* might increase by several hundred percent. In the hands of that same *adept* crafter, their chances of making a masterwork might double, triple or improve even further.

The second passive boost was also impressive. It increased the chances of successfully making an item in the first place. After all, the quality of an item only came into play if you succeeded. Again, the bonus didn't matter too much to someone like Richter. He was only an *apprentice* and he didn't have any advanced Templates. For a *master* Crafter tackling Templates of high difficulty though, a +2% fixed chance of success was something wars might be fought over.

He would still trade the monocle in a heartbeat for a weapon or a piece of armor, but there was no denying it was impressive. He dismissed the prompts about the monocle and decided to empty his bank of Chaos Points. He affixed the item to his head, and then spent two more CPs to access the second stratum of the Sea of Chaos.

Total Chaos Points: **14**

These are the current offerings of the second Stratum of the Sea of Chaos:

2nd STRATUM OFFERINGS		
Offering	Chaotic Cost	Traits
Vial of Chaotic Noxious Scent	11 points	Provides a vial containing a liquid of such disgusting stench that it will drive away most creatures. Those exposed may be dazed, driven to temporary madness, afflicted with intractable vomiting or swoon. The exact nature of the scent will not be known until manifested
Chaotic Lute	15 points	Provides a musical instrument that has a chance of triggering a random buff.
Chaotic Psi Scroll	14 points	Provides a scroll of the Deeper Magic of Thought. Properties of the scroll will only be known upon acquisition.

Know This! No purchase is required. This window may be dismissed at any time, but it will last no longer than 7 minutes, sometimes less. The purchase price of accessing this level cannot be retrieved. Each time a stratum of the Sea of Chaos is accessed, the offerings are randomized and may never come again.

Richter blew out a breath. He'd been hoping that his high Luck would have kicked in this time, but it didn't look like it. It was the nature of Luck. It might turn things in your favor in a random situation, or it might have no effect at all.

This time, the choice was easy. He couldn't even afford the lute, not that he'd buy it anyway. The Thought scroll could be powerful, but it might also be completely useless. That was the problem with the Sea of Chaos. Random powerful objects might fall in his lap or it could just be garbage. With these options, he chose to buy the potion.

A stank that could drive someone temporarily mad had to be truly horrible. He'd have to be careful not to spill it, but it could save his life if it drove a monster away. Who knew what else was hiding in these tunnels?

The disc of chaotic energy appeared. Reaching his hand through, he very gingerly grabbed a smooth vial.

You have found:

You have found:	Durability: 7/7
Vial of Chaotic Noxious Scent	**Item Class:** Unusual
	Weight: 0.3 kg
	Traits: Contains the fermented smegma of a sunbaked undead giant. Any creature coming in contact with this solution will exude the scent for no less than one week.
	Any who smell this foul concoction have a high chance of suffering the following debuffs: *Unlovable, Intractable Vomiting, Compensatory Explosive Diarrhea, Temporary Madness* and *Swoon.*

Richter had to fight the involuntary urge to gag. It even looked disgusting. The solution had the consistency of cottage cheese in some places, but bubbled in others. The color ranged from moldy green to a slightly glowing urine yellow. Richter's nostrils spasmed involuntarily. Just thinking about fermented smegma, gwalaaah! He looked very carefully at the tattered remains of his pants. There was barely any fabric left. The garment had already sacrificed so much of itself. After reading the prompt, Richter decided it was going to have to sacrifice some more. Even if he had to rock daisy dukes down here, he could *not* risk this vial breaking.

Richter placed his skull-crushing fingers on the fabric. With a quick tug, he tore a strip away. After he'd wrapped the vial, providing it as much cushion as possible, he looked down. Seeing what remained of his pants, he couldn't help but shake his head. He was now the proud owner of mid-thigh-high shorts so tight on his massive quads that they might as well be painted on. If his dick and balls were his secret place, then the secret was out!

The chaos lord carefully removed the remnants of his shirt. It had fallen into tatters already. Folding what was left in half, he grabbed four ragged corners to make an impromptu pouch.

He'd been spoiled by his Bag of Holding. Having to actually carry everything was a serious pain. That brought him to the next item on his agenda though. His Talent Points were waiting to be spent. He'd need to move soon, but not until he did everything he could to prepare. Richter's eyes shifted to another icon and he accessed his Profession page. He didn't think spending his Talent Points would be of much help, but he had to try.

Man! He'd never enjoyed being wrong so much!

CHAPTER 25

DAY 151 – JUREN 2, 0 AOC

A sound like three cymbals clashing together resonated inside his mind.

Kush-Kush-Kush!

Congratulations, Enchanter!

Know this! You have accessed your Profession page for the first time since ascending to a higher Tier. **Tier 2 Talents** *are now available!*

Know This! Most higher-Tier Talents require the purchase of a Talent of the lower Tier in order to be unlocked.
In addition to new Talents being accessible, you now understand the flow of soul stuff and the binding of magic to items at a much deeper level. Whereas before an enchantment's outcome was determined by absolute success or failure, now your enchantments may increase in power due to your **Enchantment Efficiency.**

It hadn't occurred to Richter that evolving to a higher tier would also increase his Profession. Would the same thing be true for his skills? His spells? And what was "Enchantment Efficiency?"

The background of the notification window showed the same starscape as before. On the left were the blue spheres of his Enchanter Profession and on the right were the red spheres of his Essence Specialty. There was now, however, a very noticeable difference. Hovering above both were another two sets of spheres.

Above and on the left, there was a larger blue sphere, darker than the ones beneath it. Words carved on its surface read, "Tier 2 Enchanter." Five spheres extended out from this central hub, connected by gold filaments. More filaments extended out from these spheres but the metallic threads were shrouded in fog. From experience, he knew that this fog wouldn't clear unless the preceding Talent was purchased.

On the right, there was only one red sphere. To his surprise, this new central sphere was, itself, shrouded in fog. A red prompt greeted him.

> The ascendant Talents of the Essence Enchanter are locked until an Enchanter reaches Tier 3! Be comforted in the knowledge that if you stay the path, Monster Enchantments may one day be yours!

The chaos lord blinked in shock. Monster enchantments? Monster enchantments! His Essence Enchanter Specialty let him make an enchantment out of any spell that he knew. Did the evolution of the Specialty mean that he could make an enchantment from any power a monster had? Just thinking back over the myriad and powerful capabilities of the monsters he'd slain made his mind go numb. Could he really one day steal the powers of any monster?

He felt like a fourteen-year-old kid who'd just been shown the Lexus he could one day drive. Gah! He *had* to advance his Profession to the next tier! It then occurred to him that would only happen if he increased his levels. Levels that required a minimum of a million XP now. His excitement died down, but just a bit. One day he would unlock the new powers of his Specialty. Lord Richter, Monster Enchanter!

With a grin on his face and a flutter in his heart, he turned his attention back to the blue spheres of his Profession. Reading the Talent descriptions rekindled all of his lost enthusiasm.

Congratulations! You have revealed 6 new Tier 2, Orbit 1 Talents!

The line explained that the central sphere had six Talents branching off it. The next showed how much coin he had to play with.

Total Talent Points: 190

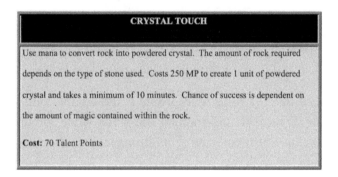

"Yeah!" Richter shouted as soon as he read the prompt. The shout just slipped out. He quickly looked both ways down the tunnel to make sure he hadn't attracted any unwanted attention, but after a minute of nothing, he turned his excited gaze back to the glowing blue window.

He just couldn't believe it. Let's hear it for being a Tier 2 badass! "Oh my god," he exclaimed again, softer this time. He'd been pumping himself up this whole time, promising himself that he'd make it back, but he'd still known there was a *pretty* good possibility some monster down here was going to eat him, then crap him out. Now though, ha ha ha, he might survive! Woooo! Let's hear it for faking it 'til you make it!

He wasn't even dissuaded by the fact that the process wouldn't work every time. You couldn't have it all. Thankfully, with his high Wisdom, the mana required wouldn't ever slow him down. His MP regen was up to 36/min. During the ten-minute process to make the crystal, he'd replenish his mana pool with over a hundred points to spare. It took all of his willpower to look at the other four Talents first and not just snatch up *Crystal Touch* immediately.

The next prompt also showed something incredible.

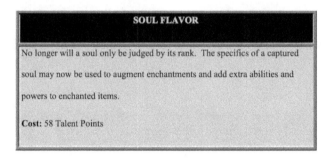

It looked like the souls he captured could augment his enchantments now. If he had soul-trapped the stone slime for instance, it might make his Earth enchantments stronger. This Talent was a definite must-buy as well.

The only downside so far was that these Tier 2 Talents cost ten times as much as Tier 1 Talents of the first orbit. His bank of 190 Talent Points didn't look like a whole lot anymore. That was especially true after looking at the next Talent.

ACTIVATED ENCHANTMENT

Enchantments which have a chance of discharging under certain conditions can now be forcibly activated. This uses 2.5x more charges than otherwise and has a 5-minute cooldown. During this cooldown period, the previous chances of triggering enchantments still apply.

Requires +2 extra measures of Powdered Crystal per item

Cost: 63 Talent Points

Banished Gods! This was awesome! The weapons he enchanted had magnificent effects. They could freeze an enemy solid, immolate a body, or shatter their armor so that it shot through their back like a shotgun. The only problem was, there was a fixed, and usually small, chance of that happening with each successful strike. His enchantments were strong, but relied too much on chance. It looked like *Activated Enchantment* took that uncertainty out of the equation! Even though there was a big cooldown, with this Talent a squad of his soldiers could freeze a group of enemies all at once. It would let his forces do massive damage at the very beginning of a battle. Maybe enough to win the fight before it had really even begun.

What was not awesome was the extra powdered crystal required to get this new effect. Crystal was not something that could just be used willy-nilly. It was an expensive resource that greatly increased the cost of making enchanted items. That is, he thought with a grin, unless you had your own crystal garden or could make your own powdered crystal from bare rock... which he did have and now could do, so fuck it!

With a smile on his face, he pulled up the next window.

SUPPLEMENTAL ENCHANTMENTS

Normally creatures are limited to the number of standard enchanted items they can wear. 1 necklace, 2 bracelets, 8 rings. Exceeding these numbers negates the additional items' magical effects. Purchasing this Talent will allow rings that you enchant to exceed a person's ring limit by 2

Requires +1 extra measure of Powdered Crystal per item

Cost: 75 Talent Points

Even though he was stuck in a dark hole right now, Richter literally heard a "cha-ching" sound in his head. He could just see top-notch adventurers, fighters and magi selling their mother for his enchantments now. He'd personally hemmed and hawed over what combination of rings he would wear plenty of times. Magic items just provided too huge a bonus not to want to wear as many as possible.

Nearly every strong enemy he'd overcome had possessed a full complement of eight rings. As he'd gotten more spoils of war, Richter had needed to decide between a ring that gave instant healing vs one that increased his overall health. Should he wear a ring that boosted his summoning powers or another that protected his mind from spells like *Charm* and *Sleep*?

Rings could be incredibly powerful, something that was definitely stressed by his current situation. Without his weapons and armor, his rings were the main items that were keeping him alive. Without his Ring of Spell Storage, he might not have been able to pull the slime off his face. Without his Summoner's Ring, his summoned creatures would have been far less powerful.

His rings were keeping him alive in the dark. The only problem was, the effects they offered were far too specialized. Choosing to gain one boost meant shutting yourself off from a thousand others. This Talent could fix that. *Supplemental Enchantments* increased the number of rings someone could wear by 25%!

The reason he was seeing dollar signs was because if a normal health ring would sell for one gold, then a ring that didn't take up a ring slot could probably sell for five! Richter gritted his teeth a bit at the high Talent Point cost, but he was pretty sure he'd purchase it anyway. It could even help him down here if he managed to get his hands on any materials. Another two Rings of Health might be the margin between life and death for him.

Richter held to his promise to not purchase a Talent until he knew everything though. The fifth option of the first orbit made his eyes open wide in shock.

SHARED ENCHANTMENT

Harness the power of another enchanter. The soul stuff a second enchanter can harness can be used in your enchantments with a 50% loss of Soul Points from your helper.

Cost: 68 Talent Points

Richter whistled softly. One of the other main barriers to making stronger enchantments was that he was limited to the amount of Soul Points he could use. Richter could only use a finite number of soul stones for each project. That meant if he was making a stronger enchantment, he had to use stronger captured souls. The problem was, stronger souls came from stronger monsters, the type that could use your balls for jujubes.

There were never enough *luminous* level souls to meet demand. They only came from boss and alpha monsters. His village couldn't even supply enough *common* souls for its needs. With the *Shared Enchantment* Talent, he could have the other village Enchanter access lower rank souls to augment his own work.

It would be like repurposing a Honda's parts to fix a Ferrari. Honda parts were much easier to come by; they also cost a good deal less. This Talent could really help the supply problems he faced in

practicing his Profession. *Shared Enchantments* didn't have any immediate benefits, but the long-term potential was staggering.

Richter was starting to see a pattern to these new higher-tier
Talents. They were meant to allow an Enchanter to move past the
limitations of the Profession. From making your own enchantment
components, the powdered crystal, to now allowing collaboration
with other Enchanters, these Talents were built to set you free and
help you reach new heights. It was easy to see how a Tier 1 Enchanter
could be easily eclipsed by someone that possessed Talents of even
this first orbit.

As great as all that was, it was the sixth Talent that was the holy
grail.

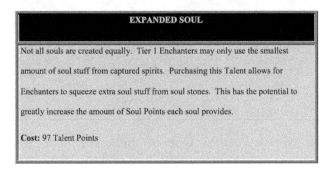

EXPANDED SOUL

Not all souls are created equally. Tier 1 Enchanters may only use the smallest
amount of soul stuff from captured spirits. Purchasing this Talent allows for
Enchanters to squeeze extra soul stuff from soul stones. This has the potential to
greatly increase the amount of Soul Points each soul provides.

Cost: 97 Talent Points

If there was one thing that slowed an Enchanter down, it was
souls. Richter's village had a crystal garden, so while that resource
was valuable, given enough time they would always have more. Souls,
on the other hand, could only be gathered from slain monsters. Souls
powered enchantments and allowed him to make weapons and items
of great power, but there were never enough.

That was because stronger enchantments required a greater
number of Soul Points. There had been plenty of times that he'd
wasted SPs because an enchantment required a certain amount of
soul stuff and he'd had to use a higher-ranked soul stone to make the
quota. If there were too many points invested, you didn't get them
back. They were just lost to the ether. If he didn't get any other Talent,
he had to grab this one.

Richter considered the six Talents of the first orbit. In addition to *Expanded Soul, Crystal Touch* was a definite must. *Soul Flavor* and *Activated Enchantment* were also potentially useful right now. The problem was, even if he wanted to get just those four, it would cost more points than he had.

There were one hundred and ninety Talent Points in his pool. It had seemed like a lot, but with the price of these new Talents, it was about to be wiped out. He still didn't even know what other Talents might be revealed by buying spheres on the first ring. They might be even more helpful than the first five. A Talent that hadn't yet been revealed could be what ensured his survival down here. He couldn't afford to spend all his points before he found out.

That was why he was about to do something in typical Richter fashion. Meaning it was equal parts awesome and stupid. It was something he'd half-promised himself he wouldn't do again. The time had come to buy some Talent Points.

While being an Enchanter was powerful, being an Essence Enchanter was a gateway to nearly limitless power. Essence was a rare Specialty of the Enchanter Profession that let him convert his spells into enchantments, providing a versatility to his craft that other enchanters could only dream about. The downside to his Specialty was that it was a Talent Point hog. Luckily, there was a fix for that: *Talent Point Conversion*.

He could burn his accumulated XP to buy himself more Talent Points. The downside was that he had to earn it all back. Until he did, his level was effectively frozen. Even worse, there was a penalty to any experience earned until he paid back the debt. Right now, he'd upgraded *Talent Point Conversion* to rank four. Every seven thousand XP gained him one TP. He'd also suffer a 100% penalty to any experience gained after the conversion. That meant he'd have to earn twice as much experience as he spent just to pay back the debt.

That was the decision he was facing right now, and why he was having to do some quick math. Richter checked his total experience.

2,893,452/3,845,000 XP to Level 46

Looking at all his total experience was a bit of a surprise. He'd gained nearly three million XP. It might be more than that actually, seeing as how he'd paid back XP debts before. In his months in The Land, he'd come to enjoy battle. He'd even come to enjoy killing. Seeing millions of experience worth of death though, that sobered him. He was lost in his thoughts for a short while before he forced himself to snap out of it.

Comparing his total to before killing the slime, it looked like the monster had earned him a few hundred XP. Despite the level discrepancy between him and it, the tough bastard had at least giving him a good bump. He did some mental math.

With his current numbers, if he burned all of his experience it would net him four hundred and thirteen TPs. The other option though, was to upgrade *Talent Point Conversion* again. He hadn't done it before because the cost was prohibitive. It would require one hundred and seventy-five points. Once it was done though, it would only cost him six thousand experience to gain a TP. That meant he'd be able to earn four hundred and eighty-two.

If he was just looking at the number of Talent Points he could get right now, then upgrading Talent Point Conversion would be foolish. Using the conversion now would give him a total of six hundred and three. He couldn't forget the penalty though. If the pattern held true, the 100% penalty would decrease to 50%. It would make it a lot easier to repay the debt. Even if he did upgrade the Talent, he'd still have almost five hundred TPs to use.

Richter thought about it for another few seconds before deciding to pull the trigger. He couldn't just bank everything on right now. He was a leader, a lord, and he had to plan for tomorrow. Besides, he needed a goddamn million experience to level up again. By the time he earned that much he might already be out of here or dead.

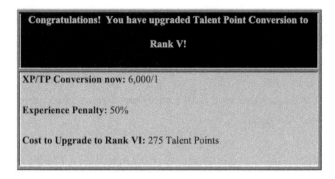

Congratulations! You have upgraded Talent Point Conversion to Rank V!

XP/TP Conversion now: 6,000/1

Experience Penalty: 50%

Cost to Upgrade to Rank VI: 275 Talent Points

Total Talent Points: **15**

Now that he was in, he went all the way.

You have used **Talent Point Conversion V.** By expending **2,892,000 experience,** you have now gained: **482 Talent Points**.

All experience earned will suffer a 50% penalty until this experience is repaid.

1,452/3,845,000 XP to Level 46

You have: **497 Talent Points** *remaining.*

The first Talent he bought was the one that made everything else possible.

You have Purchased: CRYSTAL TOUCH

You may now use mana to convert loose rock into powdered crystal. The amount of rock required depends on the type of stone used. Chance of success dependent on the amount of magic contained within the rock.

Cost: 250 MP

Duration: 10 minutes minimum

*No further upgrades for this Talent

*You have: **427 Talent Points** remaining*

He'd expected the fog to peel back after that, but instead, he saw a prompt he hadn't seen before.

*Checking if prerequisite Tier 1 Talent has been obtained: **Increased Enchantment Strength...***

Congratulations! You are qualified to reveal 3 new Tier 2, Orbit 2 Talents!

It looked like in order to access Talents past the Tier 2 first orbit, he needed to buy Talents of the first tier. That made sense to Richter. It ensured that a Professional couldn't just buy ascended Talents without creating a foundation first. Luckily, Richter had already bought almost all of the lower tier Talents.

The fog peeled away from the *Crystal Touch* sphere. Three golden filaments filled with light, and the Talents they led to were revealed.

CONDENSED CRYSTAL
Combine 20 measures of powdered crystal created by *Crystal Touch* to create 1 measure of Condensed Crystal. Condensed Crystal increases the strength of a successful enchantment by 100%. Also increases maximum rank of active enchantments by +1.
Duration: 25 minutes
Cost: 65 Talent Points

Jesus! The Talents of this tier just got better and better. He'd just found a way to double the strength of his enchantments! The only thing was the amount of powdered crystal it would take to make it. If each measure of the plain stuff took 10 minutes, it would take almost four hours to make a single unit of the better version. Still, this was exciting.

The only other substance he'd found that could augment his enchanting like this was the concentrated crystal from the crystal guardian. That had an even stronger effect, but the resource had come from an almost unique monster. Such a creature arose only from a centuries-old, well-established crystal garden. It was because of that scarcity that Richter had avoided using the powerful resource. Now though, all he needed was time to greatly increase the power of his Profession.

As great as the Talent was, it didn't help him right now. His hunger and thirst debuffs notwithstanding, he didn't have time to make twenty measures of powdered crystal. That was even assuming that the process worked each time. He still had no idea what his success rate would be. If he failed even half the time, that would increase the time required to make condensed crystal by up to seven hours. It just wasn't a feasible option right now.

The second revealed Talent, on the other hand, was an automatic "Yes, please!"

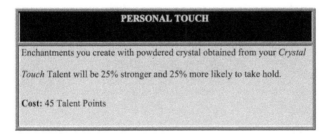

PERSONAL TOUCH

Enchantments you create with powdered crystal obtained from your *Crystal Touch* Talent will be 25% stronger and 25% more likely to take hold.

Cost: 45 Talent Points

The Talent was too good to pass up. There was an analogous purchase on the Tier 1 spheres called *Increase Enchantment Strength*. It cost less, but only provided a 5% bonus. To get a 25% total bonus, Richter would have to pay 75 TPs and he still wouldn't have the boost to his enchantment success rate. Looked like *Personal Touch* was a bit of a gimme after paying the high price of *Crystal Touch*. At only forty-five TPs, he scooped it up without hesitation.

You have: 382 Talent Points remaining

The sphere lit up and the information updated. He could

purchase the next rank of *Personal Touch*, which increased the enchantment boost to 50% and made enchantments 50% more likely to take hold. It cost ninety TPs though, and Richter wasn't sure it was worth a quarter of his remaining points. What captured his eye were the filaments that led off into the fog. The impenetrable gray peeled back and two new spheres were revealed.

Buying this second orbit Talent might have been a bit rash, but there was a secondary benefit. Richter wanted to know what a third orbit, Tier 2 Talent looked like, and how much they would cost. On the first tier, higher orbits always cost more. He wanted to know if the same thing held true here.

Just like with the second orbit, his Profession checked to make sure he had the requisite knowledge.

Checking if prerequisite Tier 1 Talent has been obtained: **Increased Item Enchantment...**

Congratulations! You have revealed 2 new Tier 2, Orbit 3 Talents!

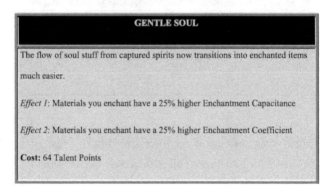

GENTLE SOUL
The flow of soul stuff from captured spirits now transitions into enchanted items much easier.
Effect 1: Materials you enchant have a 25% higher Enchantment Capacitance
Effect 2: Materials you enchant have a 25% higher Enchantment Coefficient
Cost: 64 Talent Points

Definitely not the sexiest one he'd seen so far, but Richter could see the benefit. When he'd started enchanting rings, he'd tried to substitute copper for wood. The wooden band had immediately exploded. The same thing could happen with enspelled weapons. He'd almost blown his face off once, trying to put too strong of an enchantment into a high steel mace. That catastrophe nearly put every village smith in the hospital.

Both of those near-calamities had happened because every material had a maximum amount of energy it could hold. That was called enchantment capacitance. The next effect dealt with another aspect of what the chaos lord thought of as the science of enchanting: enchantment coefficient.

Not only did a specific material have a max threshold of energy it could hold, its capacitance, it also had a resistance to being enchanted at all. Materials that were very resistant to enchantment, like iron, were said to have a low coefficient. Elementum, which almost drank in enchanted energy, had a high coefficient.

Gentle Enchanting seemed to be perfect for Enchanters that were tackling high level enchantments or were using subpar materials. He was humble enough to admit that the first category didn't fit him, but the second very well might. *Gentle Soul* could definitely come in handy, but it didn't hold a candle to the other revealed skill.

LATENT POWER
Tier 1 Enchanters rely solely upon the quality of items to determine the maximum enchantment potential. Purchasing this Talent allows a Tier 2 Enchanter to use the potential of the material itself as well.
Cost: 58 Talent Points

It was the counterpart to *Expanded Soul*. While that Talent let him squeeze more Enchantment Points from captured souls, *Latent Power* increased the number of EPs the item he was enchanting could contain. Both third orbit Talents could wait, however. Richter went back to the other must-buys in the first orbit.

The first cost as much as five other Tier 1 Talents put together, but he had to have it! Ninety-seven TPs later, it was his.

You have Purchased: EXPANDED SOUL

Not all souls are created equally. Tier 1 Enchanters are bound to the lowest value of captured souls. Purchasing this Talent allows for Enchanters to squeeze extra soul stuff from soul stones. This has the potential to greatly increase the amount of Soul Points each soul provides.

Captured souls will now provide a range of Soul Points.

You have Purchased: EXPANDED SOUL

Not all souls are created equally. Tier 1 Enchanters are bound to the lowest value of captured souls. Purchasing this Talent allows for Enchanters to squeeze extra soul stuff from soul stones. This has the potential to greatly increase the amount of Soul Points each soul provides.

Captured souls will now provide a range of Soul Points.

Soul Rank	Original Soul Points	Expanded Soul Points
Poor	1	1-3
Weak	3	3-6
Basic	6	6-10
Common	10	10-17
Luminous	17	17-35
Brilliant	45	45-70
Special	100	100-225
Resplendent	300	300-1,000

*No further upgrades for this Talent

---

*You have: **285 Talent Points** remaining*

It was even more amazing than he'd thought. The Talent did not disappoint at all. In fact, just by itself, it made a clear demarcation between Tier 1 and Tier 2 Enchanters. Now he could get more soul stuff from the spirits of trapped monsters. The range meant that a lower-ranked soul could give as much as the lower limit of the next rank up. At least that was true until *Brilliant* rank was reached. Considering the fact that those souls came from the equivalent of lower-ranked angels and demons, it wasn't something he really needed to worry about. It was true that he was deadly, but he was still outclassed when it came to those kinds of enemies. Even in the Battle of Wills, he'd basically just been able to fight Xuetrix to a draw, and still had some suspicions about that.

This time only one new Talent was revealed.

Checking if prerequisite Tier 1 Talent has been obtained: **Increase Enchantment Success...**

Congratulations! You have revealed 1 new Tier 2, Orbit 2 Talent!

For the second time, the key to unlocking the second orbit of the second tier was the first orbit of the first tier. He was starting to see a pattern. The first revealed Talent was called *Vital Enchanting*.

VITAL ENCHANTING
Normally, the amount of extra health, mana and stamina that a creature can receive from enchantments is limited to 25% of their base total. With this Talent, items that you enchant can increase the total boost to Health, Mana and Stamina to 50%.
Requires +1 extra measure of Powdered Crystal per item
Cost: 100 Talent Points

The prompt answered a question that had been in the back of Richter's mind for a long time. He'd always wondered if there was an upper limit to the stat boosts rings and bracelets could provide. If there wasn't, then theoretically, if a level five nobody had the right enchanted gear, they could have higher numbers than a level twenty Professed Warrior. In a game that would be considered a cheat.

Of course, if there was one thing Richter knew, it was that The Land was not a game. Finding high level enchanted gear just laying around was like finding an unlocked Lexus, keys in the ignition and a Rolex on the dash. Even the weakest of magic rings that gave +5 to Health would cost more than half a year's wages for a basic worker in Yves. The powerful rings that Richter wore, giving +70 and +80 to his stats, would take decades for that same worker to even consider buying.

That didn't even take availability into account. Forging rings of the caliber that Richter was wearing took high level materials and even higher-level expertise and skills. There just weren't that many high-level Crafters around. One needed to be blessed with a high enough affinity for the requisite skills, be lucky and tough enough to survive leveling up, be able to gain the points needed to buy useful Talents, and have access to rare and expensive materials ... all to have even have a chance of making such high-class items.

Luckily, Richter had his own village, perfect affinity for every skill thanks to his Limitless ability, and lands rich in materials. If he was lucky enough to survive what The Land threw at him, he could still learn enough to make super high-level gear. Rings, bracelets and armor that were enchanted to such a high level that he could crush anyone that dared go against him.

What this new Talent was showing him though, was that while it was still technically possible to enchant yourself into a total beast, there were serious checks and balances. Just like the fact that it was going to take five times as much XP to reach his next level, his plans to become an enchanting god were similarly hindered.

Richter suddenly realized something. For a while, he'd been enjoying the power and superiority that his advanced level gave him over most enemies. The Attribute Points you gained through leveling didn't make you a swordmaster, but having a Strength over fifty made it really unlikely that someone would get back up when you hit them in the head. Now he'd hit a wall though, and he'd have to earn five times as much XP to get another level.

Since he now knew everyone reached a Threshold sooner or later, that meant everyone who hit that wall should have roughly comparable stats and numbers. Seeing as how he didn't have a combat Profession, it was highly likely that any Warriors, Mages or Rogues would have the edge over him in a stand-up battle as well.

That didn't take certain things into account, of course. The fact that he gained 50% more points per level made him an outlier, but he was sure he wasn't the only person out there who had secrets. Reaching a Threshold was no mean feat. That meant other people who did were probably the nastiest and baddest sumbitches the enemy's mama had ever squirted out.

It was like what his uncle had once said. The man had grown up in one of the toughest ghettos in old America. He'd started training in Aikido from the time he was three. Growing up, he'd fought every tough kid within a five-block radius. When he could beat all of them, he'd fought the guys in the surrounding neighborhoods. The average punks in his neighborhood were easy to beat, but he'd swallowed his own blood a couple times before he beat the toughest dudes.

By the age of thirteen, he'd started competing on a national level, and five days after his seventeenth birthday, he grabbed the title. His uncle said the most important thing that came out of that was when he'd been invited to train with a true Aikido master. His uncle had told him how excited he'd been. He'd expected to learn some next-level ninja moves. Instead, the master had started teaching him the same opening katas that he'd been taught as a child.

His uncle said that his disappointment must have been easy to read because the master had stopped the lesson and invited his uncle to attack. "Show me everything you know," had been the simple instruction. Richter had never known his uncle to be a humble man. Apparently, that arrogance had been a hundred times worse right after winning a national tournament with his fists. The way his uncle had described it was that the younger version of him had been a "six-foot cock, full of blood and ready to rock."

That was why he'd attacked the master as soon as the invitation was made. What happened next still made his uncle wince involuntarily thirty years later. Apparently, the master had let him go all-out without making a single offensive move of his own for a solid ten minutes. His uncle hadn't landed a single hit.

What was worse, the master had only used the beginner katas to defend himself. After ten minutes had passed, the master had used another beginner move that any Aikido student would recognize to strike back. The difference was, he used it with a grace, power and control that even the new "tournament champion" had never been able to accomplish.

His uncle said he just remembered getting hit, blacking out, and waking up. Three cracked ribs had resulted from a single hit from a man whose head was full of white hair. His uncle had never objected to one of his master's lessons again.

When his uncle had finished the story, he'd told Richter, "Just remember, kid, there is always someone more badass than you. Don't ever stop training, or the one guy that beats you might stick you in the hospital for a month." Then he'd told Richter, "If you find one of those guys though, there's no shame in crying or running away so they don't kick your ass. Later, you can always hit them with a brick while they're sleeping." His uncle had been a complicated guy.

Point was, even though he was a badass, being able to increase his stats past the 25% barrier might help when he ran into a bigger badass. Having a higher health, mana and stamina than others expected would be a great proverbial "brick."

Vital Enchanting would make his enchantments valuable as well. It might even increase their price more than *Supplemental Enchantments*. Having another two rings was nice after all, but having an extra two rings that could raise your health, mana or stamina by 50% could increase the battle power of a fighter or caster by two or even three times.

Great as the Talent was though, his own stats were already pretty high up. Health was what was getting the biggest boost from his rings and he still wasn't near 25%. Even if he was, down here he had no way to enchant items strong enough to take him past the threshold. At one hundred TPs, the Talent was going to go unbought for now, and the Talents that stemmed off it would have to stay hidden.

He turned his attention back to the next first orbit Talent. *Supplemental Enchantments* could be useful down the road, but he wasn't tempted right now. It would be great to have an extra magic ring to wear, but he only knew how to make low level health rings. Getting another +10 health wouldn't change much, not enough to justify the TP expense. He also didn't have the materials. He moved on to the next one.

Shared Enchantments would be useful at a later date, but wasn't right now. He needed another Enchanter to make it work. *Activatable Enchantments* offered great versatility. With the high-level enemies down here, it would be great to be able to *Freeze, Burn,* or *Shatter* enemies at will rather than just having to wait for his luck to trigger the enchantment. It was a shame that he didn't have an enchanted weapon, only the club and the ichorpede pincer.

He'd never tried to enchant random items that he'd just found. He knew for a fact that he could destroy items by putting more soul energy into them than they could handle. A failed attempt could also badly injure him. Even if he was able to find a way to add enchantments to his makeshift weapons, he couldn't risk destroying his only offensive items, not until he found something better to replace them with. That was why, as much as he'd like to buy the Talent, he had to pass on it for now.

The next first orbit Talent was one that he just had to buy though. *Soul Flavor* cost fifty-eight Talent Points.

> **You have Purchased: SOUL FLAVOR**
>
> No longer will a soul be judged only by its rank.
>
> There is a chance that when you use a captured soul, it will bring with it a
>
> characteristic of the monster it was captured from. The specific
>
> characteristics of captured souls you use in your enchanting may now be used
>
> to augment enchantments and add extra abilities and powers to enchanted
>
> items.
>
> *No further upgrades for this Talent

*You have: **227 Talent Points** remaining*
*Checking if prerequisite Tier 1 Talent has been obtained: **Golem***
Enchanting...

Stop! You have not met the requirements to unlock these Tier 2 Talents! You
are not qualified to glean this knowledge.

The chaos lord blinked. For the first time, he'd come across a set
of Talents he wasn't "qualified" to have uncovered. Now, the rational
part of his mind knew that he just hadn't bought the requisite Tier 1
Talent. It also knew that the prompt was essentially an inanimate
object. A larger part of himself wanted to say, "Who the hell you
think you're talking to?"

Richter calmed himself down and forced a smile onto his face. It's
no big deal, he thought. Yeah. His head started nodding and his chin
jutted out. Yeah. He was fine. Of course, the rapid speed he was
blinking at told a different story.

He decided not to buy any other Tier 2 Talents for the moment. It
had always been his plan to convert some of his spells into enchantments and buy more Tier 1's as well. The fact that he'd just been
rejected by the second tier had nothing to do with it. He was fine.

The chaos lord focused on one of the red spheres. His Essence

Specialty let him convert his spells into enchantments if he could pay the TP cost. With more than eighty spells at his fingertips, he had a lot of options. What he really needed was a way to protect himself though. He spent 10 TPs to unlock the enchantment for one of his spells.

You have chosen to unlock the enchantment for: **Weak Static Earth Shield.** *This enchantment can be applied to two mediums:* **Armor and Items.** *You must choose which medium you wish to unlock. Unlocking further mediums will require purchase with Talent Points.*

Richter chose "Items."
You have: **217 Talent Points** *remaining*

> You have now unlocked the (Item) enchantment: **Earth Boundary**
>
> **Enchantment Size:** Unknown
>
> **Enchantment School:** Earth
>
> You are currently at 0/10,880 of the mana cost to learn this enchantment.
>
> **Effects:** Unknown

Richter never knew exactly what the effect of the enchantment would be until he finished paying the mana cost, but he was hoping it would let him make a force field around himself. Otherwise, when he inevitably slept again, he'd be exposed. The chaos lord began investing his excess mana into the enchantment. At his current rate of regen, it should take five to six hours to learn it, provided he didn't have to cast too many spells in the meantime.

The chaos lord started smiling. He still had more than two hundred Talent Points at his disposal, and he'd already uncovered some awesome new facets of his Profession. He could even make his own powdered crystal! All he needed was some rocks that he could turn into the resource, and a few more he could turn into soul stones. After that, the only resource he would be missing was a captured soul. If his experience so far was any indication, he shouldn't have a hard time finding a monster to kill.

Richter started looking around the tunnel with a broad grin on his face, searching for a couple of fist-sized stones to convert into crystal. He might as well get started on that while he decided which Tier 1 Talents to purchase. His smile started to slip as he looked back the way he'd come and didn't see anything. It slipped a bit more as he realized the only loose rock he'd seen so far were pebbles the size of tic tacs. He looked the other way, and saw more of the same clean bare rock. The smile disappeared completely.

"Well, shit," he cursed sourly.

CHAPTER 26

DAY 151 – JUREN 2, 0 AOC

*F*rustrated, Richter placed his hand on the stone wall of the tunnel, hoping against hope, and tried to use *Crystal Touch*. The Universe slapped him down immediately.

The rock you are trying to use is too large... Do better.

"Goddamn it," Richter muttered under his breath. The jerky tone of the notifications was not helping his mood. The fact that the prompts were only dickish because they were a reflection of his own personality didn't factor into the calculation for him.

He hadn't really thought it was going to work anyway, so he wasn't too disappointed. If his Talent had worked that way, Enchanters would be more effective than any siege weapon. Also, when was anything ever easy? Richter was about to look at the available Tier 1 Talents when he had the strangest feeling.

It was like a not-quite-unpleasant itching feeling. He furrowed his brow, examining the sensation. It wasn't localized to any one part of his body. After a while, he noticed there was direction to it, like every cell in his body was leaning the same way. It was really weird following directions from every point in his body. He'd never really experienced anything like it. It was almost like his body was quietly shouting, "Look over there, dummy!"

Richter finally understood the impulse enough to realize it was leading him to the remains of the nesting stone slime. He'd already given the lump a cursory examination, but no prompt had been triggered. It wasn't classified as an herb so his Herb Lore skill hadn't helped, and it wasn't an item so his identification Talent couldn't come into play.

Now, however, a prompt filled his vision. It was a mix of green and purple. Looking at it, the window honestly looked sinister to Richter. Reading it, he quickly understood why.

> A set of remains has triggered your Epic Vile Bloodline: **Petrifying Ghost Harvest**.
>
> The base cost to *Harvest* the remains of a *common* soul creature is **10 Bloodline Points**.
>
> Know This! Harvesting a set of remains will severely degrade the targeted body.
>
> Attempting to use *Harvest* on *degraded, aged and/or altered* remains decreases the chances of obtaining a component by a substantial amount.
>
> Do you wish to harvest the *Nesting Stone Slime*? Yes or No?

Richter's eyebrows shot up. With everything that had been going on, he hadn't even thought about the *Harvest* function of his bloodline. He still wasn't super excited about the "vile" appellation, but he was definitely curious about what his new power could do. Maybe it would turn the remains into something he could use.

Also, as bad as his situation was, he still had a gamer's love of discovering new lore. He checked his interface and found that he had nineteen Bloodline Points. That was when something occurred to him. During the battle, he'd zero'd out his BP pool. He regen'd 7.4 BP/hr and he'd had 15 BPs when he'd woken up, which meant he must have been passed out for about two hours after the fight with the slime. He realized again how lucky he was that nothing had eaten him while he'd been helpless. He also had a makeshift way to tell time now.

Shrugging to himself, Richter decided to spend the points. Before he did though, he figured it was worth examining the slime's body again before his bloodline "severely degraded" it. His resources were painfully finite underground, and he couldn't waste anything. His skull-crushing fingers reached into the thick gelatin of the slime's dead body. This time, he didn't just examine the outside, he poked and prodded it.

After only a minute, he felt a hard lump. It took several more minutes to work it free from the slime's dead body. The skin of the gooey sac resisted him, but his thick sausage digits ripped it apart after a while. He brushed the last few bits of remains off the hard nodule and held it up to his ball of *Simple Light*. It was then that Richter was reminded that what he didn't know about The Land could just about be squeezed into the Grand Canyon. He was holding an emerald!

You have found:	Gem Class: Unusual
	Gem Clarity: ???
Slime Core of Nesting Stone Slime	Carats: ???
	Durability: 94/94
	Weight: 0.8 kg
	Traits: This is the core of a slime. Cores are ubiquitous in slimes, but the high amount of Earth magic in the Nesting Stone Slime has transformed it into a magically active gem.

So not an emerald exactly, but it sure looked like one. Looking closer, Richter realized he could see a faint light in its center. It was the "magically active" part of the description that caught his eye. This might be something he could use. He wasn't sure how, but he wouldn't throw away any potential tool. He'd use anything if it could buy him another day of life. The core went into the ragged pouch he'd made from his shirt.

Once secured, he let the power of his bloodline flow into the slime's remains.

Sadly, he got a red warning prompt.

*The set of remains you are attempting to Harvest has been **disturbed**. This decreases the chance of a successful Harvest. Do you wish to continue?*

Looked like he couldn't cheat his new bloodline by butchering an enemy himself and then trying to use *Harvest*. Richter wasn't too upset, thinking that the slime core was a good find, but it was important to remember for the future. He still decided to give his new *Harvest* ability a shot.

Startling him, a purple-and-green light shot from his hand into the monster's remains. It danced over the grey lump of dead slime while a line of text traced in front of the chaos lord's eyes.

*Attempting to Harvest... **Success!** Yield reduced by 37% due to remains having been disturbed.*

It was a mixed bag, but it was still a win. He watched the magic take hold and sink into the body. Next, the surface of the dead slime started to bubble and dissolve away. To Richter's surprise, a cylinder of grey stone appeared out of the remains and floated up into the air. He fingers grabbed it easily, and he noted how cool and heavy it was in his grasp. A prompt appeared in Richter's vision even before the light faded.

You have found:

You have found: **Earth Stone**	**Item Class:** Uncommon **Durability:** 114/114 **Weight:** 3.4 kg **Traits:** Earth stone is rock that has absorbed enough ambient Earth energy to enhance enchantments that use Earth magic. Mana level of 2 (base 3 – 37%).

The outside was rough like concrete, but as Richter's vile bloodline worked upon it the grey surface smoothed and threads of green crystal appeared. A feeling of grave cold had filled him when the process started. As it continued, he felt absolutely frigid, but the feeling didn't last long.

> Know This! Your Petrifying Ghost Harvest Bloodline has obtained an *uncommon* drop
> from the remains of the Nesting Stone Slime: **Earth Stone**

Richter thought that was the end of it, but to his surprise, a wisp of jet black energy shot from his fingers into the cylinder of stone. The ebon power played across the surface before sinking in. A second later, green light started to glow through some cracks in the stone. At the same time, a prompt appeared that made him grin ear-to-ear.

*Your Dark Mastery ability, **Hidden Treasures**, has triggered, increasing the yield of your find by 30%!*

In addition to the prompt about his new bloodline, a new window showed the change to the Earth Stone.

You have found:

You have found:	**Item Class:** Unusual
Elemental Earth Stone	**Durability:** 154/154
	Weight: 5.9 kg
	Traits: This stone has been created from an Earth Stone with a mana level of 2; it has been refined to create an Elemental Earth Stone. Elemental Earth Stone is known for striations of emerald which make it an ideal crafting and enchanting material for Earth-magic related goals. It also possesses partial affinities for Life and Light magic.
	Mana level of 3

Richter couldn't get rid of the doofy look on his face. Who is the master! Sho-nuff! His new Mastery of Dark magic was already paying off. He didn't understand the importance of a higher mana level, but based on the prompt, his harvest had evolved into a more useful form. It also now had some affinity for Life and Light magic. That particular detail made sense to the chaos lord. The Basic Elements balanced each other out and could be represented as an eight-figure mandala. Life and Light stood on either side of Earth in the diagram.

What was important was that he had a crafting material now. If only he had tools to work the coke can-sized piece of stone, he might be able to make a wand or something else helpful. His eyes traced over the lines of green light that now glowed along the stone's surface. Looking at it, he couldn't help but think that the green tracings looked a lot like blood vessels. In fact, the light was pulsing slowly, almost like a heartbeat.

An idea struck like a lightning bolt. What he really needed down here was someone to watch his back. He needed an ally. His old shale adder, for instance, would have come in really handy right about now. Of course, the problem with that was he wasn't skilled enough in Blood Magic to reliably tame any of the high-level monsters down here. If he was able to luck upon a reptile then that might change, but looking at the dry stone around him, he didn't think that was too likely.

Even if he did tame something, he'd have to keep casting the spell to keep it under his control. *Tame* had a two-day duration, but a one-day cooldown. That meant he only had two chances to keep something under his control. With the high-level monsters down here, his chances of success were way under 50%. It just wasn't a reliable option right now.

His summoned creatures helped, but they only lasted for minutes and the spells had hours-long cooldowns. He needed something to permanently be on his side. Necromancers could reanimate creatures for long periods of time, sometimes even indefinitely. A robot would be really great right now, he thought to himself jokingly, but since the tech of The Land was medieval, that probably wasn't going to happen anytime soon. If only, he thought eyeing the cylinder of glowing stone, there was a fantasy equivalent.

Richter hurriedly reopened his Talent page. This time, he focused on the Tier 1 blue spheres. His target was a branch of his Profession he'd almost completely ignored, macroenchanting. It was one of the six main branches of the first tier. The enchantments let him enchant buildings to be stronger, create siege engines that spit fire and enspell ships that would glide through the air like a plane. The branch that he was interested in was *Golem Enchantments.*

Maybe the core could serve as a power source for a golem! And if he happened to qualify and prove that he *was* good enough for that branch of Tier 2 Talents, then who was it hurting? Not that that mattered at all.

He pulled up the prompt.

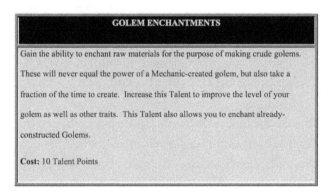

GOLEM ENCHANTMENTS

Gain the ability to enchant raw materials for the purpose of making crude golems. These will never equal the power of a Mechanic-created golem, but also take a fraction of the time to create. Increase this Talent to improve the level of your golem as well as other traits. This Talent also allows you to enchant already-constructed Golems.

Cost: 10 Talent Points

Feeling like he'd just cracked the code, Richter excitedly spent the points, the cost minimal compared to the cost of Tier 2 enchantments. The prompt that appeared was much longer and more involved than most Talent prompts he'd seen.

You HAVE: **207 *Talent Points** remaining*

The prompt cleared up a lot of questions Richter had. First, it specifically quantified why his Talent prompts had continually implied that an enchanted golem would be weaker than a constructed golem. Back on Earth when he'd thought The Land was only a game, there had been an artificer that had spent about a hundred thousand in real-world dollars to buy a large quantity of mithril in-game.

That man had then spent more than a year making a constructed golem that was formed completely of the dense metal. Richter hadn't understood everything that went into its construction, in-depth engineering had never really been his thing, but he did remember the international waves the golem had made when finally unveiled. It had absolutely wrecked entire armies.

Both its speed and attack value were pretty high due to whatever power source the artificer had used, but what was most insane was the defense. One thing that had remained true between the game and the real life of The Land was how damage was calculated. To overcome the defense of a +5 piece of armor, a weapon needed at least a +5 attack.

Of course, real life wasn't as cut-and-dried as that. Even if a hammer blow was blocked by a shield, the shield might be fine, but the muscles propping up the shield might be shredded, or bones shattered, if the force was strong enough. Similarly, while a breastplate might turn aside a sword stroke, a thrust at the right angle into the armor's weak spot would factor in other modifiers.

Removing all other variables though, attack and defense values gave a pretty reliable indication of the strength of your gear. Having weapons and armor made of better materials could make you an absolute nightmare to your enemies. Just ask the many goblins that had had stupid shocked looks on their faces when his elementum short sword cleaved through their lesser-quality, inferior-material weapons. Of course, you couldn't do that. That was because right after he carved through their gear, they had come down with a fatal case of there's-a-sharp-piece-of- metal-sticking-out-of-me-itis.

In the game though, the artificer's golem had been unstoppable because even high-level weapons had barely scratched the mithril monster. The man that created it had named it Dreadnaught. While Richter fully understood that The Land wasn't a game, many of the same principles applied. If his enchanted golem was made out of just dirt and roots, there was no way it could stand up against a constructed golem made out of orichalum or high steel.

It also looked like golems would be reliant on having their base element nearby them at all times. That reminded Richter of an old myth from his past life. Hercules had destroyed an Earth golem by lifting it off the ground. Without a connection to the ground, the golem had died. It was another example of how a constructed golem, reliant on engineering rather than magic, was superior to an enchanted golem.

That meant he wouldn't be making a Light golem down here in these tunnels. The surrounding darkness would snuff it out and probably inhibit its powers. On the other hand, an Earth golem would be perfect down here. The elemental earth cylinder that was going to serve as its magical focus was also compatible with Life magic, but Earth was almost certainly a better option in a fight.

On the plus side, the prompt made it clear that enchanted golems were substantially easier to make than their constructed cousins. Outside of the fact that he had neither the tools, nor the knowledge, nor the materials to build a golem, it probably took weeks to months. Just the cost of the materials alone might bankrupt his whole village.

The main reason Richter remembered the story of the artificer from his past life was what had happened in real life afterwards. There had been a follow-up story about how the man had bankrupted his family just to purchase the in-game mithril. As the chaos lord recalled, the man's wife had tazed him in the nuts after hearing he had spent their nest egg.

To make an enchanted golem, on the other hand, all he needed was the cylinder in his hand and a good amount of a common material. Glancing around at the stone tunnel he was standing in, that didn't look to be a problem. It also kept his goolies safe, something he was always in favor of.

The *Golem Enchantments* prompt also gave him other needed info. Namely, how many golems he could make. The Land was a place of great power, but it always had a price. An Enchanter who could make an army of golems would be seriously overpowered. Seeing as how he hadn't heard about any enchanter warlords yet, barring his own fine self, of course, it had been a safe bet that the power of golems was limited somehow. The answer was that his Enchanting skill would determine the number he could create.

He also found out that the golem's level was dependent on his skill level in Enchanting. That meant he could make a level twelve golem. That was when Richter remembered that he had another 75% of Enchanting percentages to distribute. It was the work of a second to increase his Enchanting once again.

Congratulations! You have reached skill level 51 in **Enchanting.** *All enchantments are now +51% more effective and you have an increased chance of enchantments taking hold.*

Advancing *Enchanting* wouldn't increase his golem's level, but that was only because the Talent was still only rank one. If he increased it to level two, it should increase the golem's level from twelve to thirteen. Which was something he was going to do right now.

You have: ***187 Talent Points*** *remaining*

He read the prompt that appeared, and just like he'd thought, if he upgraded it one more time, the base level of the golem would increase again. This upgrade cost 40 TPs, which made him hesitate, but he went for it anyway. He didn't enjoy investing so many points in one area, but if he was miserly, and his golem was under leveled for the dangers they would face, then those points would be a cold comfort in death.

He bought the next upgrade and read the prompt.

You have: 147 Talent Points remaining

He really hoped he wouldn't regret spending so many points on a single Talent later. Only time would tell. For now, he focused on the two Talents that had been revealed when he bought *Golem Enchanting*. Unnoticed by Richter, the fog had also pulled back on the second Tier.

Congratulations! You have revealed 2 new Tier 1, Orbit 3 Talents!

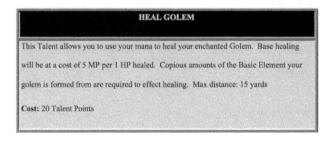

This one was definitely a gimme. If he didn't grab it, any damage his golem suffered would be permanent. It looked like his healing spells wouldn't work. Reading the next option though, he realized why it was smart not to make purchases before shopping around. You never knew when there was going to be something awesome around the corner.

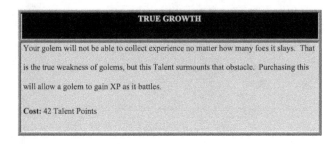

This one was absolutely essential. It would let his golem get stronger over time. He hoped his bloodline would provide more magically active materials, but he couldn't bank on that. If this golem died, then that was all she wrote.

Richter decided to buy *Heal Golem* and *True Growth*.

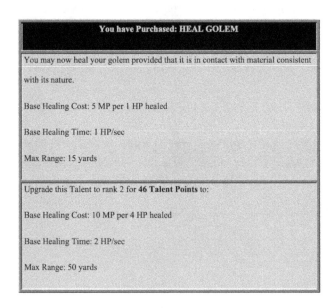

The upgrade doubled the cost of healing but quadrupled the effect. It also increased the speed of healing and really upped the range that it could work. If Richter had googobs of points, he'd have purchased the second rank. Seeing as how he didn't though, he moved on.

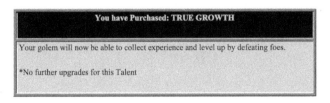

You have Purchased: TRUE GROWTH
Your golem will now be able to collect experience and level up by defeating foes.
*No further upgrades for this Talent

You have: **85** *Talent Points remaining*

And like that, he was back in double digits. There weren't any other prompts coming off those two. That was fine by him. He had everything he needed to start making his golem. As soon as he was done, he could start moving again. This time his construct would take point and hopefully trigger any monster attacks that might come along. He wouldn't know its capabilities until it was created, but no matter what, it would be a good idea to have a tank to soak up some damage. A much better idea than his own unarmored body getting pummeled, especially until he got rid of these damned debuffs.

That thought brought his desiccated throat to mind and he swallowed hard. There was pain and it felt like he was feeling a small tearing. Part of him wanted to see if his parched tissues were actually bleeding, but no good would come of that. He just worked his mouth for a few seconds until his body reluctantly made enough spit to swallow. He ignored the faint coppery tang. It was time to make a golem.

CHAPTER 27

DAY 151 – JUREN 2, 0 AOC

*R*ichter had seen some amazing things since coming to The
Land. One of the most magical was the fact that knowledge could just be downloaded into his mind. Purchasing the *Golem
Enchantments* Talent had been like that. The basic process of how to
make a golem had been conveyed to him. It was only the broadest of
instructions, but it was enough to get him started. He'd have to figure
out the rest as he moved forward.

He placed the cylinder of elemental stone on the rocky ground
and held his hand about a foot above it. Then he reached inside of
himself and triggered his new power. Pale blue light sprung into
being around his outstretched arm. The glow grew brighter. After a
few seconds, the blue light began to drip off his hand like water. It fell
upon the cylinder, making the green lines of the stone grow brighter
with each drop. A prompt appeared.

*The power of your Enchanter Profession has come into contact with a
magically active substance. Do you wish to create a golem? Yes or No?*

Richter chose "Yes" and another window opened up.

*Know This! The characteristics of a magically active substance will determine the type of golem that can be created. The Elemental Earth Stone has a Mana level of 3 and is **perfectly** attuned to Earth and **minorly** attuned to Life and Light.*

A multicolored table appeared, reflecting the colors of three of the Basic Elements: green for Earth, gold for Life and white for Light.

Based upon the magical focus you have provided, you may choose to create 1 of 3 golems. The greater the attunement, the stronger the golem that can be created.

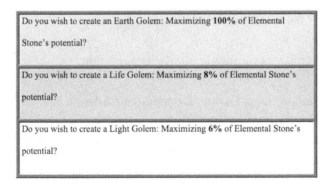

Do you wish to create an Earth Golem: Maximizing **100%** of Elemental Stone's potential?

Do you wish to create a Life Golem: Maximizing **8%** of Elemental Stone's potential?

Do you wish to create a Light Golem: Maximizing **6%** of Elemental Stone's potential?

It wasn't a hard choice. He chose to make an Earth Golem.

The color of the energy around his hand shifted from blue to the rich green of Earth mana. The drips of energy decreased in frequency until they stopped, but the cylinder glowed brighter. The light pulsed slowly, waiting for Richter to trigger the next step.

Another prompt appeared.

*Know This! The power of an Enchanted Golem is determined not only by its level. While golems possessing a higher level will be stronger, increasing their rank can increase their power by an order of magnitude. The ranks of enchanted golems are as follows: **Inferior, Lesser, Minor, Intermediate, Advanced, Major, Greater, Grand,** and **Supreme**. Each Rank is substan-*

tially more powerful than the one before, and the gap widens as Ranks progress.

The maximum rank your golem can achieve will be determined by the magical focus and the expertise of the Enchanter. By feeding your mana into a golem, it will reach the lowest rank of Inferior. At that time, you may claim your golem or attempt to increase its rank.

Be warned! If you fail to reach the next rank, there may be consequences, including but not limited to: creation of a lower-ranked golem, destruction of the golem, explosion of the spell matrix, perversion of the arcane energy, mana feedback into the enchanter, and/or disruption of the Enchanter's Profession. Choose well and beware the lure of power.

Well that's not ominous at all, Richter thought.

*Your magically active substance, **Elemental Earth Stone**, has reached Mana Level 3. It can create Earth Golems of the first three ranks, **Inferior**, **Lesser** and **Minor**. Each rank also requires a greater amount of mana.*

Golem Rank	Inferior	Lesser	Minor
Mana Required	1,000	2,500	5,000

A sharp stabbing pain came from Richter's abdomen. At the same time, his stomach growled loudly. The chaos lord closed his eyes and breathed through the discomfort. This was starting to happen more often. The happy mood he'd had after defeating the slime was also starting to slip. He could feel the hangry coming back.

It didn't help that swallowing felt like two razor blades rubbing together in his throat. Struggling to control his emotions, he realized that even the elated feeling that was now fading was probably due to his debuff making him emotionally unstable. He was trapped underground in monster-infested tunnels. It wasn't exactly a happy place!

Richter reigned in his mood. Several breaths later, he was in control again. He blew out a slow breath and tried to focus. He had to make this golem, then he could get the hell out of here. He'd find food and water and everything would be all right, but first things first.

Richter mentally reviewed everything he'd learned about golem creation. Higher-ranked golems were more powerful. The downside was that each rank required a greater investment of mana. Higher ranks were also more difficult to create. Finally, there were consequences if he failed. Which meant he had a decision to make.

Of course, he wanted the highest-ranked golem the elemental earth stone could make. A higher rank meant a stronger helper. A rank three, *minor* golem might have seriously increased combat abilities compared to a rank two, *lesser* or rank one, *inferior* golem.

The problem with that was Richter had long ago learned the dangers of overextending yourself with magic. He'd caused an explosion more than once while enchanting. It almost always happened because he was using more energy than he could control. When he'd blown up the spiked mace, he'd ended up with a several-inches-long shard of metal sticking out of his chest.

He'd been lucky enough to be wearing armor when it happened. If he hadn't, the spike would have blown a hole straight through him. He'd also lost access to his Enchanting powers for a time. When it had happened, it'd been an inconvenience. Down here, if he made a mistake it might be his last.

The prompt had even warned him of the danger of making a higher-ranked golem. In his experience, The Land didn't care about anyone. When it gave a warning, it was because so many people had died that the warning was necessary for the common good. Richter took such cautions seriously.

It had even listed some of the consequences of failure. Explosions didn't seem to be the worst of it. "Perversion of the arcane energy" had stuck out to him. Not because he knew what it meant, but because it sounded fucking horrible. Richter knew one thing for sure. He didn't want to pour a bunch of magic into this golem and have it turn on him.

He'd narrowly escaped from the ichorpede nest. His summoned creatures, even after he'd evolved them, had barely slowed the monsters down. The spider had been torn apart in seconds. His evolved saproling had basically just been a toothpick the centipedes could pick their creepy, venomous teeth with. He needed an ally, and he needed it to be as strong as possible. Otherwise, summoning this golem might just be a waste of time and resources. If it couldn't go toe-to-toe with something like an ichorpede or nesting stone slime, then what was the point?

Richter thought it over a few more times before arriving at the decision he'd already known he was going to make. Difficult or not, he needed to make the strongest golem. That decision made, he forced his hunger- and thirst-addled mind to focus on the task at hand.

When he had bought the Talent *Golem Enchanting,* the basic knowledge of how to make one had come with it. In a strange way, it felt more like unlocking information, rather than learning something new. It felt like remembering the words of a forgotten song once someone sang the first few words. It was only the most rudimentary of understandings, however.

Reading the prompts had filled in some of the gaps, but the truth was, making this golem was going to involve some trial and error. When starting a new project, Richter had always been a big fan of measure twice, cut once. That was why he was looking at the facet of golem creation most likely to trip him up, the mana required.

Anyone that had tried to do math while hungover or hungry would sympathize with him. Richter lost his train of thought several times before he was able to run the numbers. He currently had a magic pool of seven hundred and eighty. The *inferior* golem was pretty much paid for by just his initial pool. With his high Intelligence, making the lowest rank was easy. The third rank was a different story.

The *minor* golem needed a whopping five thousand mana to create. If his Wisdom wasn't so high, this would have been an impossible task. With a Wisdom of fifty, his base mana regen was thirty.

Thankfully, his magic rings hadn't been destroyed along with his armor, and he still had the Ring of Flowing Thought. The *rare* ring increased his regen by 20%, up to a very respectable 36 MP/min. It was way better than the six per minute he'd had when first born into The Land.

With an irritated harrumph, Richter realized his mind was starting to wander again. He made himself focus on the numbers. He'd just started to calculate how long it would take to make a *minor* golem based on his regen rate when something occurred to him. If his eighth-grade math teacher knew how much he was relying on algebra, he'd probably be laughing in his grave.

At least Richter hoped the man was dead. The guy had been a serious asshole. He'd also somehow become the coach of the girl's swim team. Years later, a scandal made the local news. The man had been shtupping the students. Why it had taken so long to figure out, Richter had never understood. The man drove a van for god's sake. It there was ever a warning sign...

No! No! Focus! Richter thought to himself angrily. Even after getting some sleep, these debuffs were seriously messing with him. He slapped both of his cheeks, stiff and hard, to get his mind back on the subject at hand. After a couple of deep breaths, he started to talk his way through it. "Subtracting my existing mana pool, I'll need to supply the rest with my regen. That means...

Irritation surged in Richter again. Why in the world was he having to do math of all things when he was dying of thirst and hunger? "Gah!" he shouted, standing up. He kicked at the air and swung his fists around wildly. If Sion was there, he'd have thought his best friend was fighting an invisible enemy... and was losing. Anyone that had sat through a four-hour Baptist church service though would recognize the telltale signs of irrational hangriness.

It took the chaos lord several more minutes to master himself again. The anger wasn't gone, but it was like a banked fire. There were still glowing embers that might spring up again at any moment, but at least there weren't any active anger flames. That was how hangry operated. She was a sadistic bitch that said you were done arguing, but you knew, you *knew*, it was just a matter of time if you didn't feed her.

Praying for a better result this time, he tried to focus once again. The total mana he needed to make a *minor* golem was five thousand. Subtracting his starting mana, he'd need forty-two hundred more. With his regen rate, that would take about two hours. Richter rubbed his eyes. That was easier said than done.

This was hours of attention and control he needed to commit to. Manipulating magic wasn't just a question of focus. The very act itself eroded mental control. That wasn't usually a problem when casting a spell. The few seconds it took to throw a fireball were barely noticeable by Richter, especially with his mental boost from Alma's Psi Bond. Right now though, he was anything but at his peak.

Using magic was a lot like using muscles in some ways. There was a strain that prolonged use would put on his mind. It grew harder to concentrate, headaches bloomed into migraines, and if you weren't careful, you could do serious damage to yourself channeling power that you couldn't control. Richter's mental strength was nothing to scoff at, but he'd never done something like this before. The longest he'd ever channeled mana without a break before was about thirty minutes when he made dual enchantments. Doing it for two hours straight was going to be a serious test.

Richter cracked his knuckles. He wasn't someone to hem and haw when there was work to be done. He never had been, and his will had only grown stronger since surviving the trials of The Land. The chaos lord gingerly settled into a relatively comfortable seated position. He held his hands out over the glowing cylinder of stone and prepared to begin.

Enchanting a golem required three components: an object of concentrated elemental power, copious amounts of material consistent with that element, and an Enchanter with the prerequisite mana and Talent. He triggered his will and a tether of blue mana connected him to the stone.

For the first minute, nothing seemed to happen. His mana poured out of his hands in two thick streams. It splashed upon the cylinder like water pouring on rock. Some of the mana fell off the sides, but the rest was absorbed by the stone. The green light in the soda can-sized rock grew brighter. Then, with no warning, the rock in the floor started to flow over it.

The liquid grey rock gathered around the cylinder. Richter kept his mana flowing into the elemental earth stone, and the rock started to flow faster. He kept pouring his mana into it at a measured rate. Over the next several minutes, a rough humanoid figure began to appear, lying on the ground. It had two arms, two legs and a feature-less head. As opposed to just being made of stone, it was constructed of a collection of packed earth, roots and rock. He was a bit under-whelmed by the fact that it was only about two feet long.

A prompt appeared.

Inferior Golem being constructed. 5% completed. Enchantment Efficiency: 47%

Reading the prompt gave Richter pause. It was good news that the golem was being made, but for the first time he could see how effi-cient he was being. Rather, he could see his lack of efficiency. This was only because he was now a Tier 2 Enchanter. He remembered what the prompt had said when his ascended Talents had been unlocked.

*You now understand the flow of soul stuff and the binding of magic to items at a much deeper level. Whereas before, an enchantment's outcome was determined by absolute success or failure, now, your enchantments may increase in power due to your **Enchantment Efficiency**.*

When he'd first read this, he'd thought that knowing his effi-ciency meant if he did well, then his enchantments would get stronger. He'd never thought it was a barometer to show how badly he was messing up. He supposed that was a bit of arrogance, assuming he was already doing great. According to that 47%, he was effectively failing.

With a frown on his face, he checked his mana, making sure not to stop the mana flow. If he did that, even for a moment, his creation would fail. Looking at the MPs he'd already spent, his suspicions were confirmed. There was a problem.

It was good news that the golem was being made. It was crap news that his efficiency was so low. He'd wondered if the fact that he saw his mana spilling to the side when it struck the golem was just a visual effect, but it clearly wasn't. Even without the Tier 1 bonus to his Profession which told him about his Enchantment Efficiency, he'd have known there was a problem.

To make a rank one, *inferior* golem, it cost one thousand mana. Simple math meant that 5% progress should have cost 50 MP. The problem was that he'd already expended 77 MP. At this rate he'd still be able to make a rank one golem, but making a rank three would be a pipe dream. Seeing some of the mana he was investing spilling to the sides of the growing earth, he now knew he was seeing physical proof of the magic he was wasting.

Richter didn't lose heart. The good thing about being crap at something was that there was a lot of room for improvement. He decided to try different things. He sped up the mana flow and then slowed it down. He moved his hands over other parts of the golem. At one point he put them close together, and another further apart. Then he moved the magic tether to different parts of the golem's body.

While he experimented, his Enchantment Efficiency did indeed go up sometimes. It happened randomly, however, not in direct connection with anything he was doing. It would just as suddenly go down again. The overall number remained between 48-55. He just couldn't figure out what helped and what hurt. The two tethers of blue mana coming from his hands just kept splashing onto the golem, wasting nearly half of his efforts.

He groaned in frustration. He just couldn't see what the problem was. That was when it hit him. He couldn't *see* what the problem was. The construct was slowly getting bigger while it absorbed more rock, but his mana was still draining faster than it should have for the progress he was making. Thankfully, he might finally have the solution for that. He just hadn't been using all the tools at his disposal.

With a mental flexion, he channeled his mana not just in the two tethers, but in a third direction as well. It was a mental exercise that would have stymied a normal man. Thanks to Alma, it was no more difficult than rubbing his belly and patting his head.

Magic flowed through the Monocle of Niclewis. It took a full minute to activate, but when it did, he was able to see the tracings of power that were forming the golem's power matrix. Seeing the glowing green lines that had previously been hidden from view, the problem became absolutely clear. He couldn't help but let out a soft and surprised, "Oh."

What had once been just lifeless grey stone came alive in his eyes. Just like Neo finally seeing the beauty of the machine city, Richter was able to see the delicate, glowing lines of power that were bringing the golem to life. He actually looked around in wonder, curious if he could see any hidden power in his surroundings. The rock walls remained dormant, but the emerald core from the nesting stone slime lit up like an intricate galaxy of green energy. Richter got lost in it for a few seconds, before the falling bar of his mana meter brought him back to the task at hand. He reduced the flow of mana going into the golem as much as possible, and the blue bar began to slowly refill.

Now that he could see the energy hidden within the golem, he knew exactly why his enchantment efficiency was so low. The construct wasn't just an automaton made of dirt, roots and stone. What could be seen with the naked eye was actually the least important part in some ways. What Richter could now see was a rudimentary nervous system comprised entirely of green Earth magic. As soon as the blue mana coming from him touched the golem, it was absorbed and converted into energy that the golem could use.

The hidden network of light looked like a stick figure. Richter could also now see that the canister of elemental earth stone was in the center close to where a heart would be. Radiating out like a starfish, there were five lines extending to the head, arms and legs. At the end of each line was a glowing cluster of energy. Pulses of light flowed up and down each pathway.

He could now see that the reason he'd been wasting mana was that some parts of the golem were more brightly lit than others. The pulses of light were also irregular in some areas, making the lines of light shake. It was obvious now that the mana he was supplying wasn't being distributed equally. Because his mana had to be both converted and redistributed when it entered the golem, it was causing some of his energy to be lost to the ether.

After a bit of experimentation, Richter found that while the lines connecting the clusters of energy to the elemental earth stone could absorb his mana, it was a much better idea to channel his power into the main nodes. Now that he could actually see where his power was going, the mistakes he'd been making were so obvious!

Richter slowed the mana transfer even further and let both of his hands hover over the cluster of energy in the lower leg. This section of the golem was the darkest. After only a few seconds, it started to glow brighter. The pulses of light flowing between the energy cluster and the elemental earth stone also steadied. He checked his progress, and let out a very satisfied sigh.

Inferior Golem being constructed. 14% completed. Enchantment Efficiency: 68%

Just that one change increased his efficiency by 20%. Excited, Richter poured more mana into the left leg, but quickly slowed back down. When he'd increased the flow, the pulses of light had grown more chaotic. That was when he realized that it wasn't just where he was placing the energy, but at what rate. The pulses evened out again, and Richter saw that the node in the right arm was beginning to darken compared to the rest. He held one mana tether over the arm's cluster and, again, the pulses of light started to flow more regularly. Not only in the extremities, but through the entire golem.

Inferior Golem being constructed. 15% completed. Enchantment Efficiency: 73%

Richter kept experimenting, sometimes keeping both hands in the same place and other times keeping them separate. Once or twice he stopped the mana flow altogether when he saw the lines of light growing unstable, the matrix needing time to assimilate the energy he had provided. As soon as he saw conduits begin to darken or the pulses of light begin to slow, he would start the mana flow again. It was clear now that the process of golem creation was as much art as science. If he didn't have the monocle, this would have just been a process of blind experimentation and blinder luck, but with it, he was able to achieve something great. The prompts he received confirmed it.

Inferior Golem being constructed. 97% completed. Enchantment Efficiency: 90%

His efficiency had catapulted. Richter kept trying new things, looking for that solid three-digit one hundred, but once his efficiency hit ninety, almost nothing he did seemed to get it any higher. Since he'd done so much better than before, he wasn't complaining. A minute later, he got an even better notification.

*Congratulations! You have created a **Rank 1, Inferior Earth Golem** with a 90% Enchantment Efficiency. At this point, you can finish and claim your golem, or you can invest more mana to increase its rank. It should be known that by achieving a 90% efficiency, your current golem will be awarded a bonus. If you attempt to increase its rank further, only the final Enchantment Efficiency will be considered.*

What is your wish, Enchanter?
1) Cease transferring mana
2) Continue transferring mana to increase your golem's rank

You have 1 minute to decide. During this time, you can cease the mana flow with no decay of the golem's body or matrix. 60, 59, 58, 57...

Richter took the break gratefully. Not only would it let him replenish a bit of his MPs, but he could also examine his creation.

During its growth, it had just looked like a loose collection of dirt, pebbles and roots, albeit in roughly humanoid form.

Now that its first rank was achieved, its surface grew pebbly. The spaces between its constituent parts grew smaller, and it looked more cohesive. It was four feet long and he could see the faint aspect of a face on its head. It lacked any distinct sensory organs, but had a knob for a nose and faint slit for a mouth.

While the exterior was unimpressive, the glowing matrix underneath was beautiful to him. All five nodes and the cylinder core were glowing in sync. Packets of energy flowed up and down the five lines of its frame. They all met in its center, glowing in perfect harmony. Richter couldn't help but feel a swell of pride as he looked at his creation. Any craftsman would understand.

As much as he liked it though, he was hungry for more. The chaos lord chose the second option. He watched, mesmerized, as the golem's matrix evolved. New clusters of energy appeared on the stick figure, five in all. Four of them were positioned where elbows and knees would be. The fifth formed a groin. Whereas the *inferior* golem looked like a star, the magical framework of the *lesser* golem looked much more like a man.

The energy that had been flowing languidly in the *inferior* golem grew chaotic as the new nodes fought to siphon energy from the whole. Thanks to the monocle, this situation did not last long. Richter started pouring his mana into the new nodes a bit at a time. He had to move his hands frequently to balance out the energy, but soon the power inside of the golem had evened out once again.

After that, it was only a matter of continuing to supply the mana it needed to reach its 2,500 MP threshold. There was only one real problem. To create the *inferior* golem, he'd been able to limit his mana output to only 5 MP/minute. Once he'd learned about the hidden framework, that had been all that was required to keep the matrix stable. He'd found that he could safely increase the flow rate to 15 MP/minute before the structure began to degrade.

That would have been no problem, but using the monocle required 1 MP per second. He'd had to turn the *epic* device on and off to keep his mana expenditure lower than his regen. The strain of doing so had worn at him though, and the problem only got worse now that the golem he was trying to craft was of the second rank.

The *lesser* golem required a minimum of 10 MP to be invested per minute. He also found the new framework could take a flow of 20 MP/min. That was good and bad. Good because every second he spent doing this was eroding his concentration. It had taken almost an hour and a half to reach the *inferior* rank. A headache had started to form thirty minutes in, and it was a steady throbbing by the time he'd finished. Being able to invest mana faster meant he could be done faster.

The downside was that using more mana increased the strain on his mental reserves. It would get harder to focus, and his headache would worsen into true pain. Still, he proceeded as quickly as possible. It wasn't just the strain of prolonged magic use he had to worry about. He needed to find food and water. Right now, his hunger and thirst were making him angry and causing him pain. If he ignored them, the debuffs would kill him.

Another hour-and-a-half later, his enchantment efficiency had dropped by several points. His headache had evolved into a full-blown migraine. He could hear a faint ringing in his ears, and his arms were aching. Feeling within himself, he saw that his own mana channels were getting "sore" for lack of a better word.

He'd never kept a sustained flow of magic up for this long before. It was like asking an MMA fighter to hold up a five-pound weight. At first it would be laughable. After several hours, it would be painful. If you forced it long enough, tendons could snap.

Thankfully, all his hard work wasn't without reward.

*Congratulations! You have created a **Rank 2, Lesser Earth Golem** with an 87% Enchantment Efficiency...*

The rest of the prompt was the same as before, including his one-minute grace period to decide what to do next. His efficiency had dipped a bit, thanks to the new structure being harder to keep the energy flows balanced in, but he'd still done a good job in his estimation. The final matrix was just as stable as when he'd completed the *inferior* golem. In contrast, the exterior of the construct had changed a good deal.

The "skin" of the golem had progressed from just being a loose collection of rocks to looking like it was composed of grey mortar. It had also grown a foot in height. All told, it was a little over five feet in length. The facial features were more pronounced and three stubby digits now tipped each appendage. If the chaos lord had to guess, it must weigh at least another hundred pounds compared to its previous rank.

Richter didn't hesitate long before making his decision. He'd spent nearly 3,000 MP to make this golem, taking the waste into account. His mana pool was still full, but the mental strain was taking a serious toll on him. He'd almost lost his concentration twice. Both times, the framework had started to vibrate violently, but he'd regained control. The threat of failure was much more real now that he knew he was looking at something that contained thousands of points of mana. It only cost thirty mana to throw a lightning bolt or eighty to summon a fireball. He didn't want to be sitting next to the golem if the thousands of MPs went wild all at once.

In spite of all of that, Richter felt he could still handle the next rank. It would have been impossible without the Monocle of Niclewis, but with it, he was in control. Besides, when his back was against the wall, that was when he shined. It had definitely been harder to stabilize the flows for the second rank, but Richter knew he could do more. Even down in the depths of The Land, forgotten and outgunned, he was still a goddamn boss!

Richter chose to advance his creation to the third rank. As soon as he made his decision, the matrix evolved to a higher level of complexity. It had the same basic stick figure structure, but more nodes were added. Four went to where someone's shoulders and hips would be. The largest change, however, was the number of lines connecting the nodes. Now there were two lines between each cluster of light. One line had pulses travelling away from the elemental cylinder, and the other had pulses travelling toward it.

With these changes, the matrix immediately grew unstable again, and Richter had to scramble to stabilize it. It quickly became apparent that this was more difficult by an order of magnitude. For the lower ranks, all he'd needed to do was pour energy into the nodes, and the packets of energy flowing between them would equalize. With two distinct links between each cluster, one might flow faster than the other. That made one node too strong, triggering instability, and the other two weak, darkening that part of the matrix. He swiftly found that in addition to putting mana into the junctions, he had to delicately add energy to the linkages themselves. With so many new nodes, there were more than a dozen energy tethers.

One final detail made it even worse. The bare minimum mana flow the matrix could accept was 25 MP/minute. With needing to use the monocle as well, his regen rate was pushed to the limit. It took all of Richter's focus just to keep up with the framework's demands. He felt like a man bailing water out of a sinking ship. Nearly every move he made to correct an imbalance caused another part of the matrix to become unstable. His enchantment efficiency fell.

Again and again, Richter had to dip into his mana pool to shore up a weak part of the golem's structure. Sweat ran down his face. The monocle protected his right eye, but he was forced to close his left. He couldn't even wipe the sweat free for fear the golem would destabilize. Both of his hands played over the construct's body like a pianist playing Flight of the Bumblebee. An hour passed, then another. Richter's attention began to seriously wander.

After months of using magic, channeling his mana wasn't difficult. Richter thought of it like driving a car. When you were learning to drive it seemed impossible to keep track of all the other cars, but in time it became like second nature. Just like being on the road though, a certain amount of mental focus was required. If you didn't pay attention, you could still wind up in a ditch. Given enough time, your brain power got exhausted and the chances for mistakes increased exponentially.

The problem was, using magic had a cumulative negative effect on one's concentration. The longer you used it, the more of a toll it took. Richter had heard from the new village magicians that they had to rest between spell castings, even if they had enough mana for a spell. They just couldn't focus enough to ensure they wouldn't miscast. That was one of the first times he'd really understood how powerful the mental focus boon of Alma's Psi Bond could be.

Richter had never really had a problem with the mental drain of casting. Between his training with Alma, his Psi Bond ability, and the fact that his spells were all low level, he rarely had a spell miscast, and almost never had a spell feedback, the true bane of casters. If that happened, a mage was rendered helpless, unable to move, let alone use magic.

Even when Richter cast several spells in quick succession, each time he channeled mana lasted only for a few seconds. The cumulative time was never more than a few minutes between his depleting his mana pool and his spells' cooldown times. Creating the golem was different. The same way the monotonous road could make your mind drift, so did investing his mana in a gradual way over a period of hours.

The situation was actually even worse than that. It was not only because the increased mana flow required by higher-ranked golems was harder to control, but also because his mana pool was getting ever closer to being depleted. There was a physical effect to bottoming out your MPs. While a drop in stamina would make you feel exhausted, a decrease in mana caused headaches, decreased concentration and even loss of consciousness. Put another way, while the demands on Richter's concentration were growing, his mind was growing more fatigued from overuse and his mental energy was draining.

He still didn't quit. The main thing keeping him going was his Psi Bond ability having advanced to level seven. The actual description of the bonus to his mental abilities was "Tasks that once required great mental discipline are now laughably easy. Massively reduced risk of spell miscast." He certainly wasn't laughing, but despite his

Dehydrated and *Ravenous* debuffs Richter forced his mind to stay focused. Failure was not an option.

More time passed. Ultimately, more than two hours had elapsed in the tunnel and his Light spells had long since faded away. The only light now came from the flow of mana into the golem. Richter wouldn't have noticed even if there was no light at all. All of his focus was on the golem's glowing matrix. Almost in a fugue, the chaos lord forcefully ignored the pain in his head and body. He was as helpless now as when he'd passed out, but there was no other choice. He had to finish the golem's framework. If he faltered for even an instant, all the magic it contained could go rushing back into him.

Sweat beading his brow, the chaos lord poured his very essence into his creation. He lost his concentration several times. Near the end, he poured too much mana into a node. It had flashed wildly, shooting power through the entire system. Energy leaked out of the construct, lost to the ether.

The elemental cylinder had started flashing dangerously and, in his heart, Richter knew he was only seconds away from complete failure. It was only with quick, nearly intuitive, actions that he'd managed to stabilize the energy matrix. His breath came in wild huffs and his heart thudded in his chest. The golem creation counter dropped by 5%, but moving deliberately and with great care, Richter regained the lost ground.

After more than four hours, it was finally done.

CHAPTER 28

DAY 151 – JUREN 2, 0 AOC

*R*ichter fell back on the ground, pulling in deep, shaking breaths. His sides heaved liked he'd just finished a mile-long sprint. There was such relief that he didn't need to focus anymore that tears fell from his eyes. When he wiped them away, the sweat finally found its way in and stung him terribly. A prompt awaited his perusal, but the chaos lord ignored it. The next few minutes were for him. He lay there, celebrating that he hadn't blown himself up, and just breathed.

If any other enchanter knew that Richter was able to successfully make a third rank golem with no support, or potions to replenish his mana, they'd faint from shock. That feat would make him desirable in any kingdom's court. The fact that he had done it on the first try would make them look at him like he was a monster.

Golem creation was a demanding and exacting art that ended in failure as often as not. Even finding an elemental resource with a respectable mana level was difficult. The chaos lord didn't know it, but the cylinder he'd just used could be sold for several hundred gold. Most Enchanters wouldn't be able to obtain one even if they had the money. People did not often sell these kinds of precious resources.

Even if someone managed to procure such an item, having it and being able to unlock its potential were two completely different things. Richter's augmented psyche, the use of the monocle, his bloodline and his Limitless ability made possible something that should have been beyond the capabilities of a new Enchanter. If any one of those had been lacking, he would have failed, most likely with tragic results.

After long minutes, he finally composed himself enough to see the fruits of his labor.

*Congratulations! You have created a **Rank 3, Minor Earth Golem** with an 81% Enchantment Efficiency. You have reached the maximum rank of the base resource provided. An efficiency rating of 70% was required to successfully create a Minor golem. For exceeding this limit, you shall be rewarded accordingly!*

There was more to the prompt, but Richter stopped reading in shock. What was all this about a minimum required efficiency? Did that mean if he hadn't improved his performance, then he still would have failed even after putting in all that work? Would the damn thing have exploded anyway? He gritted his teeth in consternation. Damned hidden knowledge! Once again, he'd nearly been killed, not by a monster but by his own ignorance. It was enough to drive a man mad!

Eyes wide, Richter also realized that this was perhaps another secret benefit of having progressed his Profession to Tier 2. He hadn't even known about the concept of enchantment efficiency before he'd ascended. If he'd have tried this while he was still Tier 1, would it have failed without even an explanation as to why? If that was the case, it was no wonder that most attempts to make a golem ended in failure!

Richter heaved out a heavy breath. He decided to be thankful that he was lucky enough to have had things fall into place. There was no denying that it was his own effort and hard work that had let him fit the various pieces together to obtain a positive result. There was also no doubt, however, that without a series of fortuitous events, he wouldn't have even had the pieces he needed. Was this his aura? Was it his high Luck? He guessed he'd never know, which made him no different than everyone else.

He read the rest of the prompt, still wondering at the inanity of it all.

For exceeding the required Enchantment Efficiency, your golem will be augmented.

Its original level was determined by your 51 skill levels in Enchanting and was determined to be: 17

Its final level will be 19 due to your high Efficiency!

At least he got a bonus. Looking at the construct's relatively high level, he felt much better about raising *Golem Enchanting* all the way to the third rank. If he hadn't upgraded it, the golem's base level would have only been twelve.

The glow slowly faded from around the golem, leaving the chaos lord in darkness. Richter cast *Simple Light,* and then observed his creation in all of its Earth-magic glory. It was made from the same colored stone as the tunnel Richter was squatting in.

At the *inferior* rank, it had looked like a jumble of dirt, small stones and roots stuck together in a humanoid shape. The *lesser* golem had looked much like the first, but bigger and coated with a layer of a concrete-like material. The *minor golem* was made of solid rock. Looking at it, he felt like it shouldn't be able to move. It lacked any joints. But when he placed his hand on its chin, it turned the solid stone of its neck as easily as he could move his own. He looked at its face and saw that it had a distinct nose without nostrils and a slit for a mouth. Two medium lips framed the opening. Dark stones sat high in its face where its eyes would go.

Through the monocle, Richter could see that it was almost burning with green Earth energy. After hours of work, the golem had solidified into a truly massive creature. Looking at Richter, it gave him a shock. Without moving its mouth, it spoke in a voice like gravel scraping across rock, "Maaasssteeerr."

Its voice was accompanied by a prompt.

*Congratulations! You have created a Level 19, Rank 3, **Minor** Earth Golem! Earth golems are the slowest of Basic Element golems, but also have the highest defense and health. Creating a higher-ranked Earth golem has greatly increased its capabilities.*

The ranks of the Earth golems you created have the following stats per level:

Golem Rank	Base Attack Inc per Lvl	Base Defense Inc per Lvl	Base H/M/S Inc per Lvl	Base Speed Inc per Level
Inferio r	5 +0.1	7 +1	50/0/50 10/3/10	10 ft/min +0.5 ft/min
Lesser	7 +0.25	10 +1.5	75/10/75 15/5/15	12 ft/min +1 ft/min
Minor	10 +0.5	14 +2	100/25/100 25/8/25	15 ft/min +1.5 ft/min

Yeah! Richter thought. Even though he was wiped out, he couldn't help but grin. His *minor* golem had twice as much attack, defense, health and stamina as the first rank. Its speed was nothing special, but it was literally a walking tank. Looking at the second line in each box, he saw that the difference in potential was even more impressive. Each level increased his *minor* golem's attack four times as much as the lower rank. The increase in defense was twice as fast, and stat growth was massively higher. Basically, his higher-ranked golem was born more badass, but also would gain more power faster than the lower ranks. He was even happier that he'd upgraded *Golem Enchanting* on his Profession page.

Not only had increasing the rank of his golem increased its stats, but each rank also unlocked a new special attack. The total stats for his golem were summarized in the next table. As he read it, he knew the golem had been worth every ounce of pain and effort.

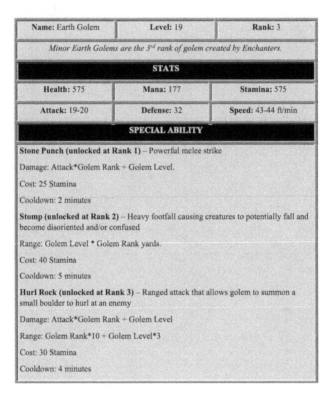

Name: Earth Golem	Level: 19	Rank: 3
Minor Earth Golems are the 3rd rank of golem created by Enchanters.		
STATS		
Health: 575	Mana: 177	Stamina: 575
Attack: 19-20	Defense: 32	Speed: 43-44 ft/min
SPECIAL ABILITY		
Stone Punch (unlocked at Rank 1) – Powerful melee strike		
Damage: Attack*Golem Rank + Golem Level.		
Cost: 25 Stamina		
Cooldown: 2 minutes		
Stomp (unlocked at Rank 2) – Heavy footfall causing creatures to potentially fall and become disoriented and/or confused		
Range: Golem Level * Golem Rank yards.		
Cost: 40 Stamina		
Cooldown: 5 minutes		
Hurl Rock (unlocked at Rank 3) – Ranged attack that allows golem to summon a small boulder to hurl at an enemy		
Damage: Attack*Golem Rank + Golem Level		
Range: Golem Rank*10 + Golem Level*3		
Cost: 30 Stamina		
Cooldown: 4 minutes		

Its stats were better than he could have ever hoped for. While the base values had been okay, the high potential of a *minor* golem was shining through. At level nineteen, all its numbers had received an insane boost. Its health was as high as a Professional Warrior, with an attack value greater than moonstone weaponry. Its defense was even higher, and should be able to weather sword strikes with ease. Considering the fact that it was solid stone and lacked vital organs, maybe it was even more resilient than he thought. He doubted even his elementum short sword would have been able to shear through it. Now, Black Ice, on the other hand... but then, that was too sad to think about.

Its speed was also not too bad. It could run faster than the average man, if only just. For being the slowest type of enchanted golem, it was certainly not too bad. What truly shined, and made him ecstatic that he'd increased its level as much as possible, were its special attacks.

The first ability, *Stone Punch,* magnified its initial attack dramatically. Considering its rank and level, it would be bringing almost eighty points of pain with its several-ton body following behind. That was enough to turn a man into pink mist. He had to think the same would hold true for monsters.

The second ability, *Stomp*, was an AoE ability. Even better, it was crowd control. Richter was pretty confident in his combat abilities, even without his gear, but no matter how tough you were, an enemy with superior numbers could wear you down. *Stomp* could help him even the odds. At the very least, it might let him run away.

The third attack, *Hurl Rock,* even gave him a ranged option. It also had an attack of eighty, with an impressive range as well. He didn't know how accurate the golem would be, but it could throw a boulder the length of a football field. That was something to be feared.

Down in the dark, Richter was missing a lot of items that he'd started to take for granted. What he wished for more than almost anything else though was his bow. It wouldn't do much in tight tunnels, but there were plenty of open spaces down here in the depths. When he'd finally escaped from the ichorpedes, for instance, the pain he'd been able to deliver had been limited by the distance between them. His spells had gotten the job done, but they were mid-range options at best. *Weak Fireball* and *Magic Missile* were his longest ranged spells, and they only covered a hundred feet. They also had minutes-long cooldowns like the rest of his magic. Spells were powerful, but a trained archer with a good bow was a killing machine you could never even get close to.

Richter's head was throbbing and his throat felt like a sand snake's bung hole, but he was so happy that he'd taken the hours to make the golem. He was even happier that he'd chosen to buy the *True Growth* Talent. Over time, his golem's stats and attacks would grow stronger. Looking at how strong it was now, he had no doubt it would destroy his enemies. It was only a matter of time before it leveled again.

Curious, Richter pulled up just how much XP it would need to reach level 20. A second later he chuckled ruefully, thinking: and there's the balance.

*XP for the Earth Golem to reach Level 20: **3,275,000/3,825,000***

It would take 550,000 XP to get the golem to the next level. In that moment Richter did not know it, but he learned why golem enchanters normally invested all of their TPs in leveling up *Golem Enchanting*. This was also why most thought that purchasing *True Growth* was something only a sucker would do. The amount of XP required to increase a construct's level was far higher than it was for a living person. It was generally considered smart to just accept that whatever level a golem was born at would be the same level it would one day die at.

Richter was starting to suspect that he'd made a bad move in his strategy. When he thought about how he could have bought the next rank in Golem Enchanting rather than *True Growth,* he'd pretty much decided that yes, he had been a bit of a gyoti. Seeing as how no one else would ever know though, he didn't stress it too much.

Richter was almost ready to go. There were just a few things left before he and his giant new ally could go find some dinner. He stared into the black stones that served as its eyes and tried to make a mental connection. Forming the psychic bond felt decidedly weird. It didn't have the warmth or life he was used to feeling. Even forming a bond with an undead had a... wobbling frequency to it, something to let him know there was activity on the other end.

The bond with the golem was just still and static. The connection felt lifeless, like a piece of wire. Richter experimented and found that despite the strangeness of it, he could send the golem instructions and even take direct control of its body if he really focused. When he tried this though, he immediately pulled his mind back. Its consciousness felt completely alien. Suppressing a shiver, he decided he wouldn't do that again unless the situation was dire. Even after connecting to it, Richter wasn't sure it was truly intelligent. It could speak, but he didn't know if it had any desires.

Maybe he'd figure that out in the future, but what mattered now was that he'd succeeded. There had been a few near misses, and it had cost him time, but he had won! He had turned the near-tragedy of the slime's attack into victory, and no matter what happened next, no one could take that away from him!

With well-deserved joy in his heart, he told his golem to stand for the very first time. The golem rose to its feet, several tons of loyal servant. He watched his construct pick itself up off the ground like a god watching their creation rise from the primordial ooze. With what he imagined was the same mixture of love and pride, he witnessed it stand to its full seven feet of earthly glory... and slam its head into the top of the tunnel.

It certainly wasn't the triumphant ending that Richter had imagined, but no big deal. It was still a massive creature that... a frown creased the chaos lord's face... a massive creature that... He paused again, looking at his giant of an ally from a slightly different terministic screen.

He'd made a very large rock creature that had broad, inflexible shoulders, more than seven feet of height and a thick barrel-shaped torso; the kind of creature that would inspire fear in the hearts of his enemies... if it could ever make it out of these tunnels. Tunnels, Richter thought with a Titanic-sized sinking feeling, that were often tight and winding, and in which even he had lost skin in places while trying to squeeze through them...

Richter looked at the golem that was too big to maneuver around in the tunnels, threw both hands above his head in absolute fury, and screamed, "Goddamn monkey-scrotumed mother fuckeeeerrrrrrr!"

CHAPTER 29

*R*ichter might have started crying. Straight up, hangry, frustrated man-tears. He had no way to make the golem smaller. There weren't even any other Talents dealing with golems. Was he really going to have to leave this thing behind? After all that work? And he was so hungry. It wasn't fair!

Few know this, but there is no greater suffering than a large man who hasn't eaten. It was superseded only by a grown man with a cold. He was two seconds shy of balling up a fist and stomping his foot when something occurred to him. He stood there, blinking *way* too hard, with a seven-foot-tall Earth golem standing over his shoulder, as he thought about it.

Desperate hope kindled in him and he pulled up an old notification.

*Checking if prerequisite Tier 1 Talent has been obtained: **Golem Enchanting**...*

Stop! You have not met the requirements to unlock these Tier 2 Talents! You are not qualified to glean this knowledge.

That was no longer true though, was it? At the time Richter hadn't met the prerequisites which had triggered this overly rude red prompt ... which didn't bother him at all. But now! Now he did "qualify" and to hell with anyone who thought differently!

Richter pulled up his Tier 2 Talent tree and looked at the spheres branching off *Soul Flavor*.

Congratulations! You are qualified to reveal 2 new Tier 2, Orbit 2 Talents!

Damn straight, he couldn't help but think before examining the first Talent. Reading the Talent, he realized there must be a god in The Land, and the dude liked him.

AUGMENT GOLEM

Golems of the Basic Elements do not have the broad utility of constructed golems. They are much more specialized based upon the element they are constructed from and the magically charged materials used in their formation.

Purchasing this Talent allows you to augment the powers and nature of your golem with another magically charged item or material. This item must be compatible with the nature of your golem.

If it successfully bonds, your golem can develop new powers and characteristics. Be warned, however; augmenting your golem with the wrong materials can weaken it, destroy it or cause a loss of the Enchanter's control.

Cost: 48 Talent Points

Richter smiled. He'd just found a use for the emerald slime core.

You have Purchased: AUGMENT GOLEM

You may now add 1 magically active item or material to augment the powers and qualities of your golem.

Be warned, however; augmenting your golem with the wrong materials can weaken it, destroy it or cause a loss of the Enchanter's control.

Upgrade this Talent to rank 2 for **52 Talent Points** to be able to add a second material or item and further augment your golem

---

You have: **37 Talent Points** *remaining*

The warning was right there, but for once, Richter completely ignored it. If he didn't do something, sooner or later his golem would be left behind. He had no idea if the slime core could help, but he really had nothing left to lose. No matter what happened, he needed to get going again, though his life expectancy would be much higher if he could bring the construct with him.

Taking the slime core out of his makeshift pouch, he looked at the tall, silent stone figure. I've got a gift for you, baby boy. Just as the Talent *Golem Enchantments* had provided the knowledge to create a construct, *Augment Golem* gave the same type of general knowledge. Thankfully, it was much simpler than what he had gone through to create his automaton. Richter placed the slime core on the golem's head.

*You have brought a magically active and compatible substance, **Core of a Nesting Stone Slime,***

Richter could have cheered, but he kept reading.

in contact with your Rank 3, Minor Earth Golem. Be aware that not all augmentations are beneficial. Do you wish to augment your golem? Yes or No?

Richter took a deep breath and then chose "Yes." He prayed this would work out, but the truth was, he had no idea what would happen. He was hoping that because the core was from the same slime as the golem's magical focus, there wouldn't be any problems. He was also hoping that since the core had come from a creature as malleable as the slime, it would fix the problem of the golem's large size and its inability to navigate the tunnels. It was only a hope though.

An invisible force lightly plucked the slime core from Richter's hand. It sank into the golem's head. Before it disappeared, he could see that the clear emerald rock had come alive with virescent light. Using the monocle, he saw that the core continued to flash after entering the golem's stone body. Soon the pulses of light flowing along the construct's matrix synced with the core's pattern. The flashes grew brighter and faster, until the energy of the core exploded. Adrenalin shot through Richter, and he wondered if he'd made a horrible mistake, but the power was absorbed into the matrix without a trace. The only change he could see was that the golem's green framework now matched the bright emerald green of the slime core rather than the deep forest green of Earth magic.

For a few seconds nothing else happened, then the surface of the golem rippled. Before Richter's eyes, the skin of the golem grew a bit more translucent, likely heavily clouded quartz. He heaved a sigh of relief when its body grew slimmer and shorter. A faint green glow the same size as the slime core appeared in the center of its chest. The golem shrunk by about eight inches, and its overall volume decreased by 30%. Richter's Luck seemed to be holding so far, but he did feel a bit nervous when a new prompt appeared in his vision.

*Congratulations! You have successfully augmented your golem! The **Core of the Nesting Stone Slime** is highly compatible with your golem! It has evolved your Minor Earth Golem into a Minor Flowing Rock Golem!*

Your golem has gained markedly increased Agility!

Your golem has gained new special abilities:

Your golem has had a small decrease in defense.

Your golem gains a +20% damage reduction to Blunt attacks.

Your golem suffers a +10% damage increase to Slashing and Piercing attacks.

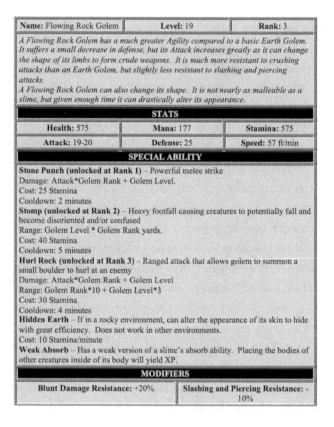

Name: Flowing Rock Golem	Level: 19	Rank: 3

A Flowing Rock Golem has a much greater Agility compared to a basic Earth Golem. It suffers a small decrease in defense, but its Attack increases greatly as it can change the shape of its limbs to form crude weapons. It is much more resistant to crushing attacks than an Earth Golem, but slightly less resistant to slashing and piercing attacks.
A Flowing Rock Golem can also change its shape. It is not nearly as malleable as a slime, but given enough time it can drastically alter its appearance.

STATS		
Health: 575	Mana: 177	Stamina: 575
Attack: 19-20	Defense: 25	Speed: 57 ft/min

SPECIAL ABILITY

Stone Punch (unlocked at Rank 1) – Powerful melee strike
Damage: Attack*Golem Rank + Golem Level.
Cost: 25 Stamina
Cooldown: 2 minutes
Stomp (unlocked at Rank 2) – Heavy footfall causing creatures to potentially fall and become disoriented and/or confused
Range: Golem Level * Golem Rank yards.
Cost: 40 Stamina
Cooldown: 5 minutes
Hurl Rock (unlocked at Rank 3) – Ranged attack that allows golem to summon a small boulder to hurl at an enemy
Damage: Attack*Golem Rank + Golem Level
Range: Golem Rank*10 + Golem Level*3
Cost: 30 Stamina
Cooldown: 4 minutes
Hidden Earth – If in a rocky environment, can alter the appearance of its skin to hide with great efficiency. Does not work in other environments.
Cost: 10 Stamina/minute
Weak Absorb – Has a weak version of a slime's absorb ability. Placing the bodies of other creatures inside of its body will yield XP.

MODIFIERS

Blunt Damage Resistance: +20%	Slashing and Piercing Resistance: -10%

Richter blew out a sigh of relief. The augmentation had been a success. And what a success! Its skin had a slightly wet and fluid appearance now. The grey stone color had also disappeared. Instead, it was faintly transparent, like an extremely occluded quartz. Just like he'd hoped, it was also smaller now as well. He ordered it to move around and was delighted to see how fluid its movements were. When it had stood up before the augmentation, it had made a racket like rocks grinding together. Now the only sounds were its heavy footfalls.

What he was most excited about was its ability to change shape. At his mental commands, its hand turned into a mallet and then into a crude spear. The tip wasn't sharp, but with enough force behind it the weapon could pierce an enemy's body. It didn't flow like the slime had, and it definitely would not be able to squeeze into small cracks, but it would easily be able to move through any tunnels that would accommodate Richter.

He was also pleased with the change in its stats. The slight decrease in armor didn't concern him, especially with the substantial bump in its attack. The health, mana and stamina stayed the same. It had also gained a stealth ability and another way to gain XP. Maybe *True Growth* wasn't such a waste after all.

All in all, he'd gotten himself an amazing tank. With the golem finally complete, he couldn't distract himself from his aching belly or nagging thirst any longer. It was time to move out. Richter extinguished his floating light and cast *Far Light* instead. The globe of white light stuck to the chest of the golem. It would be as good as a signal flare down in the dark. With any luck though, he'd lure something that was potentially edible to attack his golem.

He needed food, and if he didn't find water, blood would do to slake his thirst in the meantime. A nagging voice told him that the salt content in the blood would make his thirst even worse, but he was being pushed to the edge. Logic was becoming less important under the steady demands of survival.

Richter looked at the silent golem. There was just one more thing to do. After having spent so much time making it, his boy needed a name. Gazing at the pinkish quartz face, he felt like he noticed a resemblance. He reached his hands up and pushed on one side of its head until it was misshapen. He pulled on the left cheek until that eye sat lower. Then he gave it a mental command to open its mouth wide.

With a manic smile, he now knew where he'd seen this face before. All the golem needed was an "S" on its chest and some red suspenders. The resemblance even fit the construct's personality, not too smart, but intensely loyal. Richter certainly wasn't going to be called Chunk, but he'd found his "Sloth!"

With his golem named, Richter sent a mental order. His golem started down the tunnel. He took stock of his own status, letting a bit of a lead develop between him and his construct. His missing health was still gone thanks to his dehydration debuff. He was alive though, and once he ate and drank, he'd be ready to cause a ruckus. Richter grabbed his bone club and followed the faint light into the dark.

CHAPTER 30

DAY 151 – JUREN 2, 0 AOC

*E*very couple hundred yards, Richter cast *Weak Find Water.* Each time, he was left disappointed. Every fifteen minutes, he also cast *Call Weak Small Creature.* It would bring a small animal to him if there was one within range of the spell. It wouldn't call anything powerful, or even as big as a rat necessarily, but a small mouse or vole might come. Part of Richter felt a bit bad at using Life magic to lure a helpless creature, but right now, Mickey sounded like a great breakfast.

Richter climbed through tunnels that ranged from only a few feet across to as large as a subway tunnel. A few times there were multiple branching pathways, and he always chose the option that led toward the blinking red light from Xuetrix's quest. More than once he came to a dead end and had to backtrack. The tunnels wended left, right, up and down. He also came across several caverns ranging from the size of a kitchen to the size of a stadium.

The only thing that broke up the monotony was when he found rocks along the way. He'd always stop long enough to cast *Create Soul Stone (Luminous).* Richter saved a few to turn into powdered crystal later, but he wasn't willing to wait the ten minutes it would take, not with the debuffs hanging over his head.

The entire time, his hunger and thirst were getting worse. He also had to answer both ends of a call to nature. A part of him considered drinking his urine, but he wasn't that desperate... yet. As he saw the stream sinking into the scattered dirt of the tunnel floor, however, he wondered if he would regret wasting it.

Richter kept walking, refreshing the light on the golem as needed, until something miraculous happened. They had just entered a medium-sized cavern. The ceiling was only about fifteen feet high, but the cave stretched out, the far end hidden in darkness. He was looking about, scanning for any hostile creatures, and casting his spells almost as an afterthought. Right after, his heart started pounding in excitement. His spell had found water!

In front and to the right of him, his magic had highlighted a trickle of water coming through a crack in the wall. Without his spell, he would have easily missed it. The trickle was no wider than a finger and was only exposed for two scant inches before disappearing back into the rock. To Richter, it was a blessing from the banished gods! Collapsing to his knees like an addict grasping for a fix, he shoved his face against the wall. His lips bruised and the dry skin split, but he suckled the wall greedily.

The water was gritty and had the heavy tang of metal. Minutes went by, but he barely managed to get a cup's worth into his body. Despite the horrible taste, Richter was gazing expectantly at his interface, hoping for the *Dehydrated* debuff to disappear. Tragically, he received a different window.

*You have been **Poisoned** by ingesting water polluted with a toxic metal! - 2 HP/min for the next 60 minutes. **Random Vomiting**, **Severe Headaches** and **Debilitating Stomach Pain** will also occur during this time frame.*

Richter's eyes opened wide in shock. Could nothing go right?

He frantically cast *Weak Cure Poison*. The gold magic sank into his body, but did nothing.

*Your spell cannot cure **toxic metal** poisoning!*

Then he tried filling his hand with some water and casting *Weak Purify Water* with the other. Another red prompt greeted him.

Your spell cannot purify the metals from this water!

Gah! These *novice*-ranked spells were useless! He took stock. The loss of HP wasn't fast, but it was prolonged. He was already down several hundred thanks to not being able to replenish his lost health. Now he was going to slowly lose one hundred and twenty more. The chaos lord knew over twenty Life spells, but none of them could deal with this.

He'd spat the water out of his mouth as soon as he got the prompt, but the damage was done. Richter had even started to stick his finger down his throat, but the debuff beat him to it. A thin stream of yellow bile squirted out of his mouth. It was a lot less than should have come out in light of the powerful spasms wracking his body. It was just that there wasn't much in his system to bring up. Even the poisoned water he had consumed over the past minute had been greedily absorbed by his parched tissues. Another wave of pain hit him, like someone had reached into his body and made a fist.

It was in that perfect moment of weakness when the next monster attacked.

Thankfully the strike went toward his golem, not Richter himself. If the chaos lord had been the target, he might have died without even knowing what hit him. Instead, Richter had fallen to his knees and was retching when he heard a sound like metal striking stone. He looked up in surprise, the sudden move overcoming his control. A fresh stream of yellow, flecked with blood this time, splattered against the rocky ground. Unable to help it, he doubled over in pain. The next thing he heard was something making a hissing noise, and his golem hit the ground with a loud thud.

Richter looked up wildly, his mouth still filled with sick. What was attacking them? Had some humanoid swung a sword at his golem? Was there a snake that was making that hissing noise? How big was the attacker? It couldn't be small if it had knocked down his nearly six-foot-tall construct.

When he finally saw the attacker, he saw that it wasn't a person or a snake. Sadly, it was quite big. Richter was looking at a scorpion the size of a small car. Its pincers were the size of his torso and its barbed tail was poised seven feet in the air. As Richter watched, it scuttled onto the golem's chest. The tail, tipped with what looked like a matte-black short sword, quivered as it prepared to stab down on Richter's construct.

Richter randomly remembered that Indiana Jones had said that with scorpions, the bigger the better. Well the chaos lord was calling bullshit! With bile coating his mouth, he sent an urgent mental command, *Stone Punch!*

From its back, Sloth's right arm flared with green elemental light. Its left pushed against the scorpion's body, giving it space to obey Richter's command. With room to throw the punch, the golem triggered its special attack.

The arachnid shot its bladed stinger down at the same time that the golem punched up. The tail was faster, sinking into the golem's chest just above its heart. In a flesh-and-blood opponent, that would have been the end of the fight. Even Richter, with his advanced attributes, would not have been able to survive its downward strike. The golem barely noticed.

A split second after the stinger pierced its chest, the golem's fist hit the scorpion in the side of its face. A heavy *dong* shot through the air, quickly followed by the bug's body. It sailed twenty feet before landing heavily on the ground. A garbled cry came from its half-ruined mouth. The scorpion got back up on its legs, or at least it tried to. It fell twice in the time it took the golem to get off its back and begin stomping toward its enemy. A grim chuckle came from Richter's mouth at seeing how effective his construct was. Then he threw up on himself again. The flecks of blood had turned into streaks.

"I don't have time for this," Richter grumbled, wiping his mouth.

The sounds of battle continued. Stone hitting metal. Metal hitting stone. Richter picked up his bone club and stalked toward the battle. As he did, he checked the status of his golem and used *Analyze* on the scorpion.

Name: Ironspine Scorpion		Disposition: Angered	
Level: 41		Tier: 1	
Ironspine Scorpions can form an exoskeleton of elemental iron. This metal is much harder than the more common raw iron used in the forging of weapons. The scorpion also possesses a powerful corrosive poison in its stinger.			
STATS			
Health: 1,371/1,618	Mana: 76/76		Stamina: 725/794
ATTRIBUTES			
Strength: 38	Agility: 47		Dexterity: 41
Constitution: 162	Endurance: 79		Intelligence: 8
Wisdom: 9	Charisma: 6		Luck: 19
SPECIAL ABILITY			
Poison Spray – Can launch a spray of acid from its stinger			
Flurry of Claws – Can make its claws move in a series of quick and deadly strikes			

The information flowed into Richter's head in an instant. What concerned him the most was the part about the stinger's poison being corrosive. He was pretty sure he knew what that hiss had been now. He didn't think he needed to worry about the golem being poisoned since it didn't have a circulatory system, but stone could definitely melt.

*Your Golem is **Melting**: Losing 4 Health/second for the next 22 seconds*

The fact that Sloth could fight a powerful monster that was double its own level spoke to the power of having a higher-ranked creature, but it was still punching above its weight class. The hole the scorpion's tail had punched into its crystalline body was bubbling. The edges kept melting, giving the golem an ongoing damage effect similar to *Bleeding*.

The initial hit hadn't dropped the construct's health too much, but the acid-like poison would consume almost a hundred HPs before the debuff faded away. Richter had initially planned to personally attack the scorpion, but seeing how dangerous it was, he couldn't even imagine what would happen if that poison landed on his unarmored body. He might not die immediately, but he might lose a limb. Instead, he pushed the pain in his abdomen to the back of his mind and buffed the hell out of the golem.

First, he used his Talent, *Heal Golem*. He had to move within fifteen yards of the battle. Luckily, the scorpion was completely distracted by the golem. The two of them were rolling on the ground, each looking for the upper hand. The scorpion was definitely faster, but the golem's greater weight let it keep the upper hand. As Richter moved closer, he also saw how the Minor Flowing Golem's body shifted in size and shape to never let the scorpion stay on top of it. The chaos lord was careful to keep his distance. He didn't want the arachnid to trigger any special attacks with him as the target.

Richter used 100 MP to buy the golem 20 Health Points. It wasn't a lot, but it was something. He was definitely glad that he'd bought the Talent. The healing didn't have a cooldown, which was great. The downside was Richter could only afford to use it a few times. The mana cost was just too large.

While the two creatures fought, rock flowed up from the ground and over the golem's body. The hole in its chest started to close. After that, Richter started casting spells. *Weak Haste* increased the golem's movement and attack speed. The base increase was 10%, but with his high Intelligence and Air Mastery, the effect of the spell more than doubled.

Next, blue light surrounded his fingers and he cast *Weak Slow* on the ironspine scorpion. The increase from his Intelligence paired with his Water Mastery. The baseline 10% decrease in speed would have more than doubled, but the monster's magic resistance decreased it to 14%. Resistance or not, the spells made a noticeable difference.

They were both back on their feet and legs respectively, and the two were circling one another. The scorpion clacked its pincers angrily, looking for the right moment to strike. A second set of jaws jutted in and out of its mouth, showing needlelike teeth. The golem circled as well, looking for an opening to attack. The construct did not actually have any guile and would have just kept attacking, but Richter had ordered it to place a small amount of distance between it and its opponent. Now that that had happened, he ordered it to use its second special attack, *Stomp!*

Green light surged in the golem's right leg a moment before it raised and slammed its foot onto the tunnel ground. Impossibly, ripples appeared like the stone had turned to water. It radiated out in all directions, quick as can be. Richter had hoped it would make the scorpion fall to the ground, but he learned two unpleasant lessons about his golem's power.

The first was that against opponents with multiple legs, the golem's crowd-control ability left a lot to be desired. The scorpion wobbled a bit, but soon stabilized and retaliated with its special attack, *Flurry of Claws.* A series of lightning-fast blows rained down on the lower-level golem, each chipping away at both the stone of its body and its health.

The second lesson was that he needed to pay more attention to his own battle awareness. *Stomp* was indiscriminate against friend or foe. Richter was caught with the AoE and fell to the ground. His already horrible nausea flared again and he vomited while flat on his back. For the briefest of moments, he looked like the world's worst fountain, before that stream of yellow sick rained back down onto his face.

"Gah!" he spat. Blearily, he wiped his face and eyes clean, before staring at the scorpion in pure hatred. One thought went through his mind. Alright! This chick is toast!

He'd only lost a few points of health in his fall, so his red bar was full. He hadn't used much stamina either, but his mana was falling fast. Between healing, buffs and debuffs, his MP had fallen by one hundred and five. His Water Mastery ability, *Tranquil Soul,* helped preserve his mana dramatically, but he wasn't a combat wizard. He couldn't sling spells indiscriminately. He had six hundred and seventy-five points left, not including his mana regen. It never crossed his mind to hoard them. Months of battle had taught him that fights to the death did not last long.

Richter mentally ordered Sloth to start whaling on the scorpion again, and he started his own experiments to see if it had any weaknesses. *Weak Magic Missile* summoned two balls of white light that flew unerringly toward the scorpion. They impacted with two bright flares against its hide. He might as well have been throwing spitballs. A few points of health were shaved off, but otherwise there was no effect.

The same was true for *Weak Ice Dagger* and *Weak Life Bolts.* Compared to the scorpion's more than one thousand points of health, it was like chopping down a tree with a pocket knife. He decided to stop playing around and uses his most powerful attack spell, *Minor Sunbeam.* That finally got him some attention.

After the four-second cast time, a bar of incandescent white light shot from his hands onto the scorpion's face. It hissed like a tea kettle too long on the stove and triggered its own special attack in retaliation. Its barbed tailed quivered before shooting out a stream of corrosive black acid. Thankfully, the *Blind* debuff from Richter's attack took over. The chaos lord dove to the side, and it couldn't track his movement. When he landed, his own poisoned debuff made him vomit again, but he looked back up grinning, with yellow coating his teeth.

The corrosive poison spewed across the cavern in a wild arc as the scorpion scuttled backward to protect itself. Being blinded could cow even this mighty monster.

But while Richter had avoided the attack, the golem wasn't so lucky. The corrosive spray landed on its right arm and chest. The *Melting* status it had acquired before stacked and refreshed.

*Golem is **Melting**: Losing 9 Health/second for the next 36 seconds*

This was getting serious. The golem had already lost 10% of its health and it was about to lose three hundred more. If he couldn't heal it, his construct might be useless even if they won the battle. Richter's own attack had carved away about fifty points of the monster's health, but it just wasn't much compared to the total. The sunbeam's damage would have been even less, but he'd struck it in a sensitive area. The scorpion's metal skin gave it too great of a defense. The spell had also cost one hundred and twenty-five MPs. Richter realized if things continued this way, he was going to lose the battle.

His spell had accomplished two things. It had pushed the scorpion off-balance, and it had blinded the monster for a few precious seconds. That let the golem attack with impunity. Richter checked, and then watched with joy as a counter reached zero. While the flowing rock golem closed with the panicked monster, he gave another mental command. *Stone Punch!*

Green light highlighted the golem's arm for a second time. Unlike the first, it was now in perfect pugilist position and the strength of its attack wasn't hindered by it laying on its back. Its arm flew so fast it left a green afterimage behind it. A stone fist the size of a bowling ball hit the scorpion's injured mouth. Its face crumpled like a tin can. The metal carapace fractured and the monster's blood sprayed over the Earth creature. The golem's special move had nearly quadrupled the golem's base attack. The insect was sent flying once again. One of its arms had been struck as well. The limb hung limp, pulped and useless.

Before it even landed, Richter gave another order. This time, he didn't bother with a mental command, too bound up in bloodlust, "Hurl rock!"

The golem stopped moving forward and soundlessly raised one hand. The stone of its body rippled and flowed upward, coalescing into a boulder in less than a second. Then it threw the rock at its enemy with crushing force. With a whistling noise, the stone struck the scorpion's middle leg on the right side. The segmented appendage was crushed in an instant.

The scorpion made a noise for the first time, squealing in pain. The sound echoed off the walls of the cavern. It had good reason to cry out. The thrown stone hadn't just bounced off its body. After destroying the leg, the boulder sank into the iron carapace like a bullet. It pulverized whatever soft tissue structures lay beneath. The remaining two legs on that side shook and spasmed arrhythmically, making Richter think that something vital had been damaged.

He didn't give it any time to recover. Richter ordered the golem to straddle its fallen foe and start raining blows upon it. The scorpion, still blinded, was struggling to get back up when the Earth creature arrived. With no hesitation, Sloth fell on top of the scorpion and started punching. With its speed magically augmented by Richter's spell, the hammer blows fell at a fast tempo. It also showed its slime nature. The ends of its arms formed mallets, adding force to each blow. The insect hissed and screamed, but it couldn't move. One side of its legs was ruined, and the other set just wasn't built to lift several tons of rock.

The scorpion's last good pincer tried to grab Sloth, but the angle made the attack weak. The claw could reach its back, but not with enough force to damage the living boulder sitting on top of it. If it wasn't for its tail, the fight might have been over, but that bladed appendage was still deadly.

The monster managed two punishing stabs that would have meant the end of any flesh-and-blood creature. It was even an attack that Sloth was susceptible to, suffering an extra 5% damage. The construct felt no pain, however, and though its health fell with each blow, it had no vital organs. It did, on the other hand, have Richter.

At its master's command, the golem's hands formed fingers and grabbed the tail after the second stab. The scorpion cried out in frustration, but it could not pull itself free. Sloth remained on top of the arachnid. The two of them wound up in a strange stalemate. They were both two high-defense creatures who could no longer harm each other. Looking at it, it was both sad and comical. Kind of like two turtles with their shells glued together. Richter's mind wandered for a second. That had been a fucked-up night.

In a one-on-one battle, the scorpion might very well have prevailed, given time. Its corrosive poison had already consumed more than half of the golem's health. If it managed to get its tail free, it could deliver damage faster than the golem. Too bad for the monster that so far as Richter was concerned, one-on-one was for suckers.

There was only one truth in battle: sprinkles are for winners.

CHAPTER 31

DAY 151 – JUREN 2, 0 AOC

*R*ichter watched the two titans struggle for a few seconds longer while he decided on a strategy. What he landed on was bashing the hell of it. It might not have been nuanced, but it could work. Also, Richter had a bad case of metal poisoning, a bachelor party-sized headache, and, oh yeah, *sixty-seven* points of friggin' Strength! His teeth bared in a crazy grin. This was going to be better than therapy.

Pretty or not, his plan did have merit. When he'd been born into The Land, he'd only had ten points of Strength. That had been nothing to sneeze at. It meant that he had a max carrying capacity of one hundred kilos, two hundred and twenty pounds.

Every point of Strength he gained added ten kilos to that value. That meant that now he could carry almost fifteen hundred pounds. That was enough power to pick up a fridge and throw it. It was enough for him to crush a human skull in his bare hands. It was enough to go into a biker bar and order a glass of milk! It had to be enough to beat this damn scorpion into submission.

In an ideal world, he'd have already absorbed the knowledge of his expertise book. There was no time to worry about that now though. Besides, he was strong as hell. Whacking it really, really hard would have to do. Richter approached the scorpion from the side, staying well clear of its claws. With a barbarian's bellow, he rained down blow after blow on the scorpion's body, legs and tail. Pent-up frustration and anger over being trapped underground let loose all at once, and the bone club beat a steady tattoo against the arachnid. In that dark, deep place, the fury of a chaos lord was unleashed.

It accomplished exactly dick. On the plus side, he did vomit on the scorpion twice. So even though he wasn't really hurting it, he counted that as a moral victory. A bit of spew got on his golem as well but, eggs and omelets.

After a few minutes of whaling on the scorpion's body, he realized it had barely lost a few points of health. At this rate, his debuffs just might kill him before he could kill it. As he stood there panting, he realized what the problem was. It was almost like the scorpion was a high-level monster coated in metal, and he was hitting it with a damn leg bone!

Irritated was a mild description of his mood. That's okay, he thought, nodding angrily. We'll do it the other way.

Richter walked toward the front of the scorpion, keeping at least ten feet between him and it. The monster hissed with renewed anger when it saw him in front of it. Another gout of corrosive venom shot from its tail. Thankfully, the golem still had the stinger pointed in the other direction. The stream of acid splattered harmlessly against the ground. The chaos lord paid it no notice. He was busy casting a spell.

Black-and-gold light surrounded his arms. There was a time that dual casting Deeper Magic would have taxed his mental capabilities. Even a *novice*-ranked Spirit spell might have been beyond him. With his boon from Alma, the words fell easily from his lips. The ten-second cast time was nine seconds longer than most of his other spells, but the result was worth it.

As he harnessed his magic, the scorpion started to struggle like mad. It might have been a dumb beast, but it was high leveled. That meant its senses were developed far beyond that of a common animal. It could feel that it was in danger.

While Richter cast *Weak Aura Lance*, ribbons of black power tinged with gold radiated from his body. Two foci of energy grew, one between his hands and the other in his chest. The interaction between these two points of Spirit magic interacted, growing strong as they mixed. A small seed of magical energy appeared, quickly growing larger. The last time he'd cast this spell, the sphere had grown to the size of a kid's basketball. This time it grew noticeably larger thanks to his Intelligence having nearly doubled.

The black sphere was darker than night and gold lightning danced across its surface. Words of Power fell from his lips, each growing thicker than the last. With his *Exhausted* debuff gone though, they were no impediment to his iron will. The last words left his lips and the ball shot toward the iron scorpion. It transitioned from a sphere into a spear the moment before it struck. The power disappeared into the arachnid's body. Someone watching might have thought the spell had failed. Richter knew better. At such a short distance, there was no possibility of the spell missing.

The scorpion's iron skin immediately fractured, web-like cracks covering its entire body. Millimeter-thin pieces peeled away from the scorpion's body over the next few seconds. They floated up and dissipated like dust in the wind. When the process was done, the creature looked exactly the same as if the spell had had no effect. The prompt in Richter's vision told another story.

*Richter has struck the **Ironspine Scorpion** with dual cast **Weak Aura Lance**. Basic Element spell-type resistances decreased by 13.7%. Any resistance dropping below 0% will cause a resultant susceptibility to that spell type.*

The chaos lord was more than satisfied, but he noticed something for the first time. Looking at the resistance reduction more closely, the prompt showed that the initial 5% reduction had been increased by 156% thanks to his dual casting. His Intelligence had only increased the effect by 11.7% though. With Intelligence at an astounding seventy-eight, the effect should have been greater. Each point of the Attribute usually increased the effect of his spells by 0.5%. This time, it looked like he'd only gotten half that.

Richter blinked. Now was really not the time to worry about math. Not with Sloth sitting on a truly pissed-off giant scorpion only five yards away. Shaking his head, he realized that back-in-the-day he would never have started considering such things in the middle of a battle; it was insane. Now, it was just another day. A part of him wondered if that meant that *he* was insane, but meh, why worry about it either way. A few seconds later, he realized that the Attribute Point boost was probably reduced because he was casting a Deeper Magic now instead of a Basic Element spell. Mystery at least partially solved, he cast a Blood spell.

Dark red light surrounded his hands while he cast *Tame*. Using Spirit and Blood magic in quick succession was a risk, but his mental defenses kept him safe. He walked around to the back of the scorpion and placed his hand on it. If this worked, he could heal it and he'd have a pretty amazing new pet.

You have failed to **Tame** *the* **Ironspine Scorpion***!*

That wasn't a surprise. Its level was far higher than his skill in *Beast Bonding*. He'd hoped lowering its spell resistances might make a difference, but he wasn't sure *Weak Aura Lance* affected Deeper Magics. Either way, there was only one option left now.

Richter walked back to the front of the scorpion, looking into its last good eye. It squealed at him as if it knew he'd just tried to steal its will. He just stared back impassively before saying, "You're going to wish that had worked." Then he started to bring the pain.

The scorpion had shrugged off his magic before, but no longer. His mana had taken a serious hit from the dual casting, dropping six hundred and twenty-five points. In another setting, he couldn't have afforded nearly bottoming out his mana. The spell's duration was a full hour though, and his MP regen rate was respectable. Over the next thirty minutes, Richter started casting attack spells with short pauses in between to regen his mana. People watching him might call him a sadist and a sicko, torturing a helpless creature. He considered it an interesting exercise and therapeutic stress relief. The scorpion considered it hell.

It might have shrugged off his *Weak Flame* before, but now, the magical fire burned through the arachnid's iron carapace, leaving black scorch marks. *Weak Lightning Bolt* was even more effective. Richter's aura lance must have lowered its resistance into the weakness range. One crackling bolt stunned it and made it collapse. It only came back to itself about ten seconds later, much longer than the normal *Stun* effect of the spell.

Richter kept casting, going through his long list of spells. Few magi could do what he was doing, using magic from all eight Basic Elements. His Limitless ability gave him perfect affinity for all magic skills. That was why the scorpion wasn't so much an enemy as a whetstone for his skill.

At first, the monster tried to grab him with its claw. After it found that futile, it just tried to protect its ruined face, using the pincer as a shield. Others might have taken pity, seeing a living creature being slowly burned alive. That was no longer in Richter. Monsters did not have pity. Neither would he.

He just kept chaining his spells indiscriminately. After twenty minutes, both of its arms were a smoking husk, one laying just as limp as the other. He would have done it faster, but he had to wait for his mana to recharge.

Whenever Richter's blue bar started falling too far, he would just wait. Time and again, the scorpion tried to struggle free of the golem's grip and weight, but it only got weaker as time went on. The chaos lord chuckled a bit, realizing that he was beating a high-level monster using grade-school techniques. It was basically like sitting on a smaller kid while your friend shot spit wads. Kids were gross.

After the third round of rest, Richter just decided to sit down. He crossed his legs and closed his eyes, adopting a position he'd seen Yoshi use plenty of times. Seeing its tormentor relaxing while it lay there suffering made the ironspine scorpion hiss like a tea kettle. Its thrashing still accomplished nothing. Without even opening his eyes, Richter flapped his hand at it in the universal asshole sign for, "Just wait a sec. I'll be back with you soon."

This pattern continued. Rest and attack. Rest and attack. While he was recovering, he tried to focus on the current moment and push his concerns aside. Mostly he tried to ignore his horrible thirst and hunger. If anyone were watching, seeing him in this zen pose would really have cemented the whole serial killer vibe.

Each time he rested, he tried to regulate his breathing and ignore his thirst. He wanted nothing more than to go find food and water, but he had to take care of the scorpion first. Leaving it alive, even heavily injured, would just be foolish. He didn't believe in hurting something a little bit.

On the sixth session of being in the lotus position, Richter received a surprise. He'd gained a new skill.

Congratulations! You have learned the skill: **Meditation.** *By practicing mindfulness in the face of suffering, you have achieved a clarity of thought. This has allowed the mana flow of your body to stabilize. While in a meditative state, your mana regeneration and ability to perform mental tasks will improve. True masters of this skill can walk through hellfire without losing their resolve.* **+2% Mana Regen rate while meditating. +1% Concentration permanently.**

The bonuses from the skill weren't bad. He wouldn't be able to use the improved mana regen in battle, but it could really help him when he was training his magic. *Meditation* also increased one of his Secondary Attributes. That didn't happen too often. The *Exhausted* debuff had illustrated just how important Concentration was. It was the difference between successfully casting a spell or getting an axe to the face because your spell failed. His base Concentration was already much higher than the average person thanks to Alma. The modifier from *Meditation* could really add up over time.

It took several more rounds, but the scorpion finally gave up the ghost. While he'd been slowly reducing its health, Richter had experimented with a few things. He'd used the monocle of Niclewis to see if he could trace the magical energy of the monster, but all he saw was a diffuse glow. Using *Harvest* had been similarly useless. The bloodline power wouldn't trigger on a living creature.

Neither of his new capabilities could be used in battle. That was okay. His old spells worked just fine. It had stopped moving several minutes ago. Richter made sure to cast *Soul Trap* before the end. With a final gout of flame to its scorched face, rainbow light swirled through the air. The ribbon of spirit disappeared into his makeshift satchel, filling one of the empty soul stones. Its tail went limp and Sloth let it collapse lifelessly to the ground.

Notification windows appeared in his vision.

*You have slain a **Level 41 Ironspine Scorpion**. You have gained 1,283 XP.*

XP deficit remaining: -3,842,559

Richter looked ruefully at that line. The high-level scorpion had given him more than a thousand experience, but it barely made a dent. He valued Alma for many reasons, but her *Brain Drain* attack was one of the biggest. Having to rely on battle to progress was a slog.

The experience he'd gained from the fight would have been enough to launch him up an entire level when he first came to The Land, but now his high level was working against him. Also, as his level was higher than the scorpion's, the XP he'd gained had been reduced. He examined his combat log and saw that there was a second reduction due to the scorpion being a tier lower than him.

He realized it was just another one of The Land's checks and balances against rampant power. His high level made him formidable, but it also slowed his growth to a crawl unless he killed higher level enemies.

On the plus side, Richter checked and saw that his golem had gained the same amount of experience. It wasn't great news, seeing as how it needed more than half a million XP to level up, but it was something. The next prompt was a lot more satisfying.

You have captured:

You have captured:	Durability: 20/20
Soul of an Ironspine Scorpion	Item Class: Common
	Stone Level: Common
	Soul Level: Common
	Status: Filled
	Weight: 0.3 kg
	Soul Flavor: This soul contains notes of metal and corrosion

Most of the prompt was the same as any other notification of a captured soul, but there was something new. The last line reflected his new Talent, *Soul Flavor*. From what he could see, it hinted at extra effects that might appear if he used it to fuel an enchantment. Only time would tell if it was actually useful.

He was just happy it was a *common*-ranked soul, not stronger or weaker. A weaker soul wouldn't be too useful, and he didn't have a soul stone that could capture a stronger one. Not only couldn't he cast that level of magic, but to create a *luminous*-ranked soul stone, you needed precious jewels.

There was another benefit to his continued use of magic. Two of his skills leveled up.

*Congratulations! You have reached skill level 9 in **Dark Magic**. New spells are now available.*

*Congratulations! You have reached skill level 2 in **Spirit Magic**. New spells are now available.*

Before continuing on, Richter used *Harvest*. Walking for the past couple hours had let him regen another sixteen BPs. Ten of them went into the scorpion's body. The beam of purple-and-green energy shot toward the dead monster and played over its body. The blood-line power struggled to sink into the remains and serve its function.

*Attempting to Harvest... **Failure!***

Well crap, Richter thought. Then he threw up again.

CHAPTER 32

DAY 151 – JUREN 2, 0 AOC

*T*he good news was that the debuff from the poisoned water elapsed not long after. The bad news was that he'd lost another one hundred and twenty points of health. Not from the horrifying giant scorpion. Nope. It was because he suckled at a poisoned stream like it was a tit filled with Hennessey. He glared at the trickle of liquid angrily.

It had occurred to him that although it was poison to him, toxic metals might have been downright tasty to a scorpion covered in metal. The fact that he'd been attacked right when he found the water wasn't an accident. Any location with reliable access to resources had to be prime real estate down here. If he was going to get what he needed, he should expect to fight for it.

He had fought though, and he'd won. As the saying went, to the victor goes the spoils. After all, there had been one other amazing benefit from killing the scorpion. Meat! While he'd been attacking it with spells, the smell of roasting flesh had filled the air. If he wasn't so dehydrated, then his mouth would have filled up with water.

Now that it was dead, he wasted no time ordering his golem to rip apart its metal carapace. Starting at the hole in its side, Sloth cracked it like a lobster. The racket of having a stone golem tearing metal was something Richter hadn't been prepared for, but his eyes remained glued on the body. As soon as the hole was widened, the chaos lord reached in and pulled out a mix of blood, guts and muscle.

Staring at the messy glop, Richter wasn't disgusted. He was as excited as a kid on Christmas morning. He dropped his feast on the ground and cast *Weak Flame*. Moving the fire this way and that, he started to cook it. After a couple minutes it looked less runny, and he flipped it over. Doing that burned his fingers, but he didn't care. He just started bathing that side in flame as well. The dirt and small particulates were seared into the meat. If Richter had noticed, he would have just shrugged. Who didn't like extra flavor?

A few minutes after that, Richter greedily shoved the "cooked" mess into his mouth. Any other time it would have tasted burnt and disgusting, but in that moment, he couldn't care less. All he wanted was to fill the needs of his newly ascended body. The fact that it was only partially cooked in some places and charred in others didn't bother him at all. It was so good! While he scarfed it down, he realized that Red Lobster had nothing on his own brand of BBQ claws with *Ravenous*-debuff sauce. His eyes closed and an involuntary croon slid into the air. He wanted more!

Richter reached his thick fingers into the scorpion's body three more times. Each time, he used *Weak Flame* to kill as many microorganisms as possible. The truth was, he would have eaten it raw if he'd had to. After his second helping, his *Ravenous* debuff improved.

*You are **Hungry**! Stamina regeneration decreased by 15%. Emotional control decreased by 10%.*

After the fourth, the debuff disappeared altogether. Richter felt his mind clear and his shoulders loosen. A satisfied belch echoed lightly in the cavern. "Lord baby Jesus god, that was nasty." He said it with a smile on his face though. After the third helping, his hunger had faded enough for him to experience the actual flavor. He consoled himself with the fact that it still wasn't the nastiest thing he'd ever put in his mouth. Besides, all that really mattered was that at long last the hangry demon had been banished.

While he'd been eating, he'd thought, "I really hope this isn't poisonous." That thought hadn't slown him down at all, but thinking about it had answered a question he'd had since childhood. Richter had always wondered how people originally figured out if something was good or bad to eat. Apples were red after all, and red was usually a danger sign in nature. How could they have known that if you squeezed those red fruits you could make a golden juice that was akin to the nectar of the gods? Answer: they couldn't have known. There had probably just been a hungry dumbass like him eating whatever he came across like a sad man at a nude beach.

Now that he was fed, Richter looked at the large carcass. In an ideal world, he'd be able to take it with him. Such a large creature could feed him for days. Unfortunately, it was already starting to stink. One thing any Georgia hunter knew was that raw meat didn't last long without salt or cold. He didn't want it to just go to waste, but even carrying some of it with him would mark him with the scent of a fresh kill. He'd bring every monster within miles running to him.

Without another option, Richter used *Harvest.* The past couple hours had let him regen twenty-two Bloodline Points. Ten of them went into the scorpion's body. The beam of purple-and-green energy shot toward the dead monster and played over its carcass. The bloodline power struggled to sink into the remains and serve its function.

Attempting to Harvest... Failure!

Richter grimaced slightly. His attempt had failed. It had also turned the scorpion's body into a foul-smelling pile of runny slag. He tried to use *Harvest* again, but a prompt told him the remains were too degraded. Not seeing the harm now, he tried to get Sloth to use its *Weak Absorb* ability. Another red prompt showed that all relevant energy had already been expended. The chaos lord shrugged. It looked like harvested remains couldn't then be absorbed. At least his hunger was gone now. He felt a faint burble in his stomach, but it quickly passed.

He sat down and meditated again, restoring his mana. He also had to heal the golem, which slowed him down further. It was great that he could heal it, but the 5MP/1HP conversion was garbage. Sloth had suffered several hundred points of damage. Just fixing it put him back another hour.

The whole time, he never lost sight of the fact that there was a hidden clock counting down the seconds until his remaining debuff worsened. He didn't know when the count would reach zero, but when it did, it would mean his death. Richter was relieved that his hunger had been sated, but there was no doubt that thirst was a deadlier enemy. That was why he was so eager to hurry on. Even pressured, however, he didn't lose himself to panic. Without Sloth, the scorpion would probably have killed him. He couldn't travel again until his golem was back in fighting shape.

When they were both finally ready, Richter tried to decide on his next path. There were several exits from the cavern he was in. He was about to pick the one that seemed to go roughly in the direction of Xuetrix's marker, but then his *Tracking* skill triggered. Small points of light appeared in his vision, showing the steps the scorpion had taken. It led down another tunnel, a bit to the right of the one he had originally chosen.

Richter looked at the large monster. It made sense that it had been drawn to this water source, but would that trickle have been enough for this gargantuan creature? Looking around, the cavern didn't have any signs of being its lair. If his theory of monsters congregating near natural resources was right, then if he followed these tracks, he might find its nest. If he found that, there might be water!

His reasoning was thin, and he knew it. Truthfully, it was downright anorexic, but it was better than nothing. Even if he didn't find water, at least following the tracks might lead him to his next meal.

The only problem was that he couldn't just let the golem take point. Its heavy footfalls could destroy the tracks. Instead, Richter adopted *Stealth* and cast *Darkvision*. He and the golem started walking again, this time with Richter in front. Following the faintly glowing trail, the duo moved through the darkness of the earth.

CHAPTER 33

DAY 151 – JUREN 2, 0 AOC

*Warning! Your **Dehydrated** status will progress to **Severely Dehydrated** in
3 hours! At that time, you will continually lose 10 HP/sec! Any lost health
cannot be restored.*

*W*ell that's not good, Richter thought grimly. He'd been
following the scorpion's trail for an hour when the
prompt appeared. That had been an hour ago. He only had two left.
While he walked, a mantra had been on loop in his mind. All living
things need water. All living things need water. All living things need
water. He had to hope that wherever the scorpion had chosen to nest
would have access to the precious resource. He continued to walk and
crawl through the dark tunnels, his golem trailing behind.

Less than half an hour later, Richter's prayers were finally
answered. He started seeing more tracks like the scorpion's. They
crossed to and fro, and after examination, he could tell that many
were older. That meant one thing. He was getting closer to its lair. He
refreshed *Darkvision*. Five minutes after that, he found the nest.

He was in a tunnel that was only two paces across. In front and to
the right was a black hole that had countless scorpion tracks in front
of it. Richter stalked forward while still stealthed. His MP was full

and he had eight BPs. His stamina was down by about seventy thanks to his intermittent use of *Stealth*. There was still plenty left.

In an ideal world, he'd buff himself, but the magical flash of light would give away his position. Instead, he crept forward and looked inside. What am I going to find, he wondered? A massive cavern filled with monster scorpions? Nope, he discovered with a smile. Just a bunch of scorpion babies.

Of course, "babies" was a bit of a misnomer. Every one of the scorpions was the size of a full-grown Doberman. They were scuttling around, sleeping or pulling pieces of rotting meat into their maws with the creepy small mouths that shot in and out of the bigger ones. There were about twenty-one in all.

Richter also found out why they were called ironspines. It looked like only an adult scorpion would get a full metal covering. The back of each of the scorpions was plated in dark iron like their slain parent, but the rest of their bodies were just covered in a pink exoskeleton. The chitin probably still offered some defense, but not nearly as much as the metal skin of the adult. Lower defense meant this had just gotten a whole lot easier. It'd also be easier to eat that meat!

While still in stealth mode, Richter sent a mental command to his golem. It activated its Hidden Earth ability and walked closer. He thanked the gods of luck that he'd upgraded Sloth with the slime core. The original construct would have made enough noise to wake the dead. As a flowing rock golem, it made much less noise, and the scorpion babies remained completely unaware. He watched for another couple minutes, but didn't see any more monsters. Richter didn't know if this species was all about the one-parent household or if other adults would be coming back soon. He wasn't planning to wait.

The chaos lord ducked out of sight and dismissed *Darkvision*. Blackness blanketed him, the only sounds the air moving through his lips and the squabbling scorpions. Richter breathed out two firm breaths as he prepared for battle. *Whoooo. Whoooo.* His mind was calm. He was ready to eat. Right before he formed a spell he thought, sorry kids, but your mama tried to eat me. Now she's dead and you're dinner... it's hakuna matata.

Purple-black light formed around his fingers. That light alarmed the scorpions in a way that the golem's footfalls hadn't. They all started hissing and turned toward the cave opening with stingers raised. They couldn't see what was causing the light yet, but the juvenile scorpions were prepared to defend themselves. Of course, Richter had known his spell would alert them. It just made what came next even easier.

A disc of death magic appeared on the ground and five level-six bile rats rose into existence. Richter made eye contact with all of them at once, forming a mental bond. Then he sent two into the cave, running in opposite directions for all they were worth. The scorpions' hissing filled the cavern as they attacked en masse. He listened to the panicked squeaks of the rats and heard the sizzle of acid hitting rock.

The acid was what Richter feared most. The small scorpions' defense was almost definitely lower than their parent's, but that didn't mean their corrosive venom was any less deadly. Riddick and Indiana both agreed the small ones were the worst. That meant he wasn't about to put his life, or his golem's body, at risk. At least not without drawing fire first.

The rats' squeaks turned into piteous death cries. First one, then the other, were slain. A couple seconds after the first two rats died, Richter sent in a third. Once again, it was a rat tragedy and more acid hit the ground. The fourth went in and a minute later the fifth. With the last one, he heard barely any sizzle. He hoped that meant their guns had run dry. As soon as the last rat died, Richter cast another spell, this time of Light.

A white glow surrounded his fingers before three balls of light flew into the cave, providing faint illumination. Another Light spell summoned a mirror. The reflective surface appeared floating in front of the cave. It hovered at a forty-five-degree angle in front of the entrance. The mirror was insubstantial, only a trick of the light, but it served the chaos lord's purposes.

First, it let the scorpions see him.

In response to his mocking grin and cocky wave, the dog-sized arachnids hissed like tea kettles. One or two shot acid from their stingers, but it was little more than a dribble. That was the second reason for the mirror, so that Richter could assess the situation and make sure they'd run dry. All fourteen rushed toward his image, clacking their pincers together. And lastly, he thought with satisfaction, they were now bunched together.

The cavern the scorpions called home was about the size of a Waffle House. Too big to fully cover with any of his AoE spells. If he somehow managed to get them bunched together though, well that was a different story.

As soon as Richter saw they were out of venom, he began his third casting. The spells so far had all been low level and he'd only spent forty MP. That, coupled with his wide array of low-cost spells, was great news for him. Not so much for the monsterlings.

A ten-by-ten-foot area of the ground was soon covered in brown sludge. A few of the running monsters wiped out, but most kept their feet. *Grease* was a great spell for crowd control, but it wasn't so effective if the target had more than two legs. That wasn't why he'd cast it though. While the spell was still manifesting, Richter began another incantation. A gout of orange flame shot from his hand and the entire patch caught ablaze. The scorpions' hisses turned to screams.

Sixteen of the twenty-one scorpions were caught in the AoE. They ran around in a panic, crashing into each other. The other five reared back in fear. An intelligent opponent might have just skirted the fire to press their attack, but these monsters lived in darkness. The sudden heat was like hell coming to earth. Richter didn't pause for a second. Once more, red light surrounded both hands and he dual cast *Weak Fireball.*

A marble of flame appeared between his hands and shot forward two seconds later. After leaving his hands, it grew in size. The spell exploded on the ground, several feet to the left of the raging inferno. Four of the unharmed scorpions were caught in the blast, along with five that were already in the inferno. That only left one completely unharmed. It ran toward the cave entrance, squealing in anger. Richter wasn't worried. This was literally what Sloth was born for.

A mental order brought the Earth construct running into the cave. After that, it was just cleanup. Richter kept spamming his spells to attack from afar. A few scorpions made it out of the fire, but every one of them was afflicted with *Burn* status. Even leaving the patch of blazing grease didn't save them, as their very bodies were ablaze now. The DoT would fade eventually, but the juvenile beasts wouldn't live long enough to see it.

The few that made it toward the entrance of the cave were crushed under his golem's feet. The others died either electrocuted, fried or riddled with holes from Dark magic. The BBQ actually smelled pretty good in Richter's opinion. His stomach gurgled, something that had been happening since he ate their mom. Clearly, he still had room for more.

He made sure to cast *Soul Trap* copiously as well. Every death was heralded by a swirl of rainbow light. After he saw the last scorpion stop moving, he dismissed his *Grease* spell. Without that, the sea of flames went out. The only light was from two monsters that were still burning like creepy candles.

He banished the darkness completely with a few seconds of casting. Ten balls of *Far Light* shot around the chamber. Individually the balls weren't too much stronger than a candle, but together they were enough to let him see. He observed the cavern for a full minute, and made sure to check behind him as well. The last thing he wanted was for another monster to take a bite out of his butt. There was no movement. Carefully, he sent the golem ahead of him and walked behind it. Gold light surrounded his fingers and he cast *Weak Detect Hostile Intent*.

The spell let him know about any creatures within a ten-yard radius that had active, hostile intent toward him. The short range didn't make it practical to have it on while traveling. It also didn't register all threats. If there was a sleeping monster, for instance, there would be no intent to make the spell ping. Similarly, there were predators that didn't mean you ill, but would attack if you got too close. A well-fed lion wouldn't trigger the spell, but would most certainly maul you if you got too close.

The Life spell definitely had its limitations, but for checking a small space after a battle, it was perfect. The chance that there was something still living in the monster lair that didn't want to hurt him was small-to-none.

Richter walked along, pulses of gold light radiating out from him in a slow throb. To his relief, nothing turned red. As he walked, he cast *Far Light* several more times. The spell only cost 4 MP thanks to Tranquil Soul, and more light was definitely a good thing in Richter's book. Most definitely a good thing. While he cleared the room, he also cleared out the notifications that were waiting for him.

*You have slain **Ironspine Scorpions (juvenile)** x 21. You have gained 651 XP. XP deficit remaining: -3,841,198*

The piss-poor amount of experience made Richter curse. He'd just killed nearly two dozen monsters, some of which had had a higher level than the average level of his villagers, and he'd only gotten a measly six hundred and fifty-one experience? Seriously?

The chaos lord had never really paid too much attention to battle XP before. With Alma being able to *Brain Drain* it had never been that important. Now that he had a several million XP deficit though, sure as shit was shiny it mattered now!

He focused on the experience he got from a level ten scorpion and saw that the base experience the monster offered at its level was 407 XP. From a half-remembered conversation with Terrod, he recalled that for every ten levels he was higher than his enemy, the XP gained would be halved. So if he'd been level twenty, then he'd have gotten 203 XP. At level forty-five, that had shrunk down to only 68.

To add some truffle butter to the crap sandwich, his new tier further decreased any experience gained from lower-tiered creatures by an additional 20%. That meant the grand total he got from each monster was about 30. Thirty points for a Doberman-sized scorpion that shot acid out of its ass. How the hell was a guy supposed to make a living?

He was seriously disheartened by the experience decay. He'd need to kill a hundred and twenty-five thousand more of the bamas to pay back his XP deficit. If he managed to do that, then boom, Bob's your uncle. Of course, then he'd have to kill another thirty thousand to make it to level forty-six. At that moment, Richter's view of monsters shifted in a fundamental way. They stopped being fearsome entities and started looking like sacks of XP. "I need to find some higher-level things to kill," he muttered.

His mood lifted a bit when he stepped over a particularly well-cooked scorpion. Unlike some of the others, it wasn't blackened, and the chitin on one of its claws had split open. He could see orange-pink flesh beneath. Some steam was rising out of the hole, and it looked better than a crab boil. His stomach gurgled loud enough to rouse the dead. With a smile on his face, he thought, don't mind if I do.

Richter reached down and tore pieces of the shell away. The chitin was flexible and tough, but his super strength made quick work of it. His fingers got burned slightly, but he didn't notice that any more than he noticed the meat searing his taste buds a second later. He munched on two of the claws while he looked a bit frantically around the cavern. The fight had gone well, but it had taken about fifteen minutes. He had less than an hour left before his debuff killed him. He had to find water.

As he searched, he realized that the cave was not as simple as he'd first thought. There were a few short tunnels and smaller caves, in addition to the main cavern. Seeing that, he made the golem explore them first, but there weren't any other monsters. Most were just filled with trash. There were bits of rotting flesh, gnawed bones scored with sharp teeth, and everywhere he looked, smears of a crusty white substance.

The entire cave was like that, just a trash heap of the scorpions' daily lives. To his mounting concern, there wasn't a drop of water to be seen. His spell didn't find any either. Richter was starting to think that he'd have to rush blindly back out into the tunnels. The danger in that was obvious, but what else was he going to do?

He'd just finished checking the last side tunnel when, despair gripping him, his Tracking skill saved his life. He noticed the faintly glowing trail of an adult scorpion's footprints leading to what he'd thought was bare rock. Curious and desperate, he walked over and looked behind an upraised lip of stone. There he discovered a small tunnel that had been hidden from view. Without his *Tracking* skill, he never would have found the scorpion's trail. The entrance was only about three feet across and two feet high. With the weak light from his spells, it would have been easy to miss. It led downward at a steep angle.

One thing gave Richter hope. Unlike the rest of the monster nest, only a few prints led down the passageway. The rest of the den looked like Grand Central Station, but it seemed the juvenile scorpions rarely traveled down this one shaft. It might have been the home of the adult. Maybe, just maybe, he'd find something worthwhile down there.

He still wasn't just going to shove himself down a hole with no room to wiggle around. This wasn't college. Death magic wreathed his fingers as he summoned rats again. They ran down the hole and spread around. When he didn't hear any dying squeaks, he figured it was safe enough. Magical light illuminated his way as he squeezed his muscular body into the hole. He began cursing as he lost skin on the rock walls. He'd never been a big fan of tight spaces, but he comforted himself that if the scorpion had managed to climb through the tunnel, he could too. Richter did his best to ignore the voice in his head pointing out that bugs could compress their bodies in ways that he couldn't.

After what felt like an hour but was actually only minutes, he emerged into a small cave. It would have been just big enough to fit two bunk beds side-by-side with no space left over. There was no other exit, but that didn't matter to Richter. The only thing that mattered was that his nose had picked up the scent of water!

Richter cast *Weak Find Water* once again. Immediately, the spell located a small stream flowing along the back of the cave. If his body had had enough water he would have cried. As thirsty as he was, he didn't forget the toxic metals he'd drunk just hours ago. Cupping a hand in the stream that was no more than a foot across, he brought it up to his nose. Sniffing, he couldn't smell anything off. It took major willpower, but he cast *Weak Purify Drink.*

No major impurities detected.

With an audible cheer, he slurped it down.

While the meat from the scorpions' claws had made him croon in pleasure, the water nearly made him swoon. He literally felt it flowing into his tissues. He dipped his hand into the stream several times, before setting aside all shame. He got down on all fours and placed his lips on the surface of the water flow. "Umm. Ummmm. Um!" were the only sounds he made while he finally gave his poor body what it needed. It was sweeter than any wine he'd ever had, and after several swallows, he read something even sweeter.

*You are no longer **Dehydrated.***

A surge of relief shot through him. Richter cast *Weak Slow Heal* and *Minor Slow Heal* in succession. At long last, he could restore his health. While his red bar refilled, the low level of constant pain that plagued him faded away. It was possible that this was the happiest moment of his new life. He fell onto his back and laughed in giddy exuberance.

He was alive. He had fed and his thirst was quenched. The chaos lord lay on the rough stone and realized that the cold stone, in that moment, was more comfortable than any bed. He gave a mental order for Sloth to guard the entrance of the side tunnel, then just gave in. His consciousness sank into the still surface of the bottomless Sea of Dreams, with one thought echoing across the mirror of smooth water.

I'm alive. I'm alive. I'm alive.

CHAPTER 34

DAY 152 – JUREN 3, 0 AOC

*R*ichter woke up feeling like a new man. His light had gone out while he was lying down so he opened his eyes to darkness. For a moment he was disoriented, but not worried. It was the kind of confusion that only comes from sleeping so deeply that you suffer from temporary memory loss. Despite that lack of knowledge, he was so relaxed he just didn't care. A prompt flashed in the corner of his vision. He checked it with the absentmindedness of scanning for emails when you just woke up.

Congratulations! You have learned the enchantment **Earth Boundary, Level 1**		
Enchantment Type: Item		
Enchantment Size: 5		
Enchantment School: Earth		
Effect: Create a stationary shield comprised of Earth magic.		
Base Defense: +2	**Base Health:** +50	**Radius:** 10 yards

Richter blinked away the cobwebs. This was great! Now had a way to make a shield to protect him while he slept. The defense and health weren't much. Even a low-level monster could probably get through it in a couple seconds. It wasn't meant to really keep anything out. It was an alarm system. If he got even one moment of warning, it could save his life.

Sadly, there was more to the prompt.

> To create a shield enchantment, an object with a **Mana level of 1 or higher** is required.

"Hmph." Just like that, his dreams of a force shield faded away. He'd only recently become aware of the importance of mana levels when he'd killed the slime. Unless he found something magically active, he wouldn't have a shield any time soon. It wasn't all bad news though. This wasn't something he could use down here, but what if he leveled it up after returning to the village? It was something worth thinking about.

After redirecting his excess mana to unlocking the third level of *Sonic Damage,* Richter turned his mind back to the here and now. Checking his Bloodline Points, he saw that the purple-green bar was full, so he'd been out for about eight to nine hours. The chaos lord sat up and worked his tongue around his teeth. A slight exertion of will and a few muttered words of power later, balls of light attached themselves to the walls of his small cave. Except for a vague unsettled feeling in the pit of his stomach, he felt great.

For the first time, he closely examined his surroundings. The three balls of light were more than enough to illuminate the cavern he'd slept in. Absentmindedly, he ran his fingers through his long black curls, then stopped when he felt something crunchy. With a suspicious look on his face, he pulled it out and looked at it. Yep. That was not dandruff. It was doodoo. The small cavern was covered in scorpion excrement, just like the rest of the nest.

Seeing as how he probably smelled like week-old medical waste in Nevada, having slept in dried monster shit was the least of his problems. Other than some old gnawed bones, there wasn't much else in the cave. Still, he kept looking around, trying to find an explanation for the uneasy pit in his stomach. After another minute, he thought, maybe I'm just stressed. Not like I have any reason to be, he thought with a chuckle. Who wouldn't love to be trapped miles underground in monster central? Richter smiled. It was amazing how much a meal, a drink and a nap could improve your mood. Pushing the hint of worry out of his mind, he crawled over to get some more water.

The stream ran out of a hole at the back of the small cave. It continued along the wall for several feet before disappearing back into the wall. It couldn't have been more than a foot across and six inches deep, but to Richter, it was a treasure. Cupping his hands, he drank several mouthfuls. The luxury of being able to drink clean water made him feel like a king. It wasn't much, but compared to fighting monsters in near-total darkness with debuffs threatening certain death, it was everything.

After he drank his fill, he turned his head to the side, and saw that his first perusal of the cave had actually missed something. There was indeed another living thing here. It was a weed-like plant that wasn't much to look at it. It was stringy, only a couple feet tall, and had been partially hidden by an outcropping of stone. That coupled with the fact that it was gunmetal grey and blended into the rock made it easy to see why he hadn't seen it immediately. Actually, it was the white pods hanging off it that had finally caught his eye.

Thinking the plant might be edible, he activated his Herb Lore skill. Since acquiring the skill, useful plants could glow in his sight. It didn't always work. He was only a third-ranked *apprentice* in the skill after all. Higher-ranked plants might be beyond his ability to identify. Most useful herbs would light up though and he'd gain valuable information about them. The aura around useful herbs normally didn't vary much, but this time was different. The glow around the white pods of the withered tree was brighter than the luminescence of any common root or vine.

A prompt appeared. To Richter's surprise, the notification had the red color of a *rare* item!

You have found:	Herb Class: Rare
White Iron	**Herb Quality:** Vibrant
Beanpod	**Uses:**
	Novice: None
	Initiate: None
	Apprentice: Consuming the seeds of this beanpod offers a chance to strengthen the body.

Richter had never seen an herb description like this before. Not only was it *rare*, but it didn't have any *novice* or *initiate* uses. That meant that if his Herb Lore skill was just a few levels lower, he probably wouldn't have been able to identify the plant at all. Every skill had benchmarks. Reaching a certain level in the skill would advance you to a higher rank, progressing from *novice* to *initiate* to *apprentice,* and then to *journeyman, adept* and *master.*

There were always perks to advancing ranks. One of the bonuses for *Herb Lore* was that every rank he achieved could potentially reveal another use of a plant. Typically, the higher-ranked the use, the more powerful the effect. It wasn't always true. Richter had definitely found plants that did not have effects for every rank. Some only had uses up to the *initiate* rank or even just the *novice rank.* Before today, however, he'd always assumed any useful herb would have a *novice* use. This white iron beanpod was the first plant he'd come across that skipped the first two ranks. He started getting excited, wondering if this might mean that the *apprentice* effect was more profound than the simple description suggested.

The plant was about three feet tall and had several thin branches. Looking closer at the ground around it, Richter could see that there were a few empty husks lying at the base. The beans were missing. Had the scorpions been eating the peas? Ironspine scorpion and white iron beanpod sounded too much alike to be a coincidence. Maybe the beans strengthened their carapace and imbued it with metal.

He accessed his Tracking skill. Faint trails in the dust lit up in his vision. From what he could see, there were tracks from juvenile scorpions around the plant, but not nearly as many as in the other parts of the cave system. It made sense to him that the adult had monopolized this herb, rationing both it and the water out to the rest of the nest.

As fascinating as the social dynamics of slain monsters were, the question now was what to do with the plant. Everything pointed to the fact that it was powerful. That didn't mean it was safe to eat. One of the first lessons his granddad had taught him was not to just put things in his mouth, even on a dare. He still remembered the old man correcting himself. Especially not on a dare!

There were four pods left hanging on the plant. Two were small and immature, but the others were large and full. He could see the contours of three beans inside of each of the mature pods. The *apprentice* effect of "strengthening his body" sounded great, but who knew if a human body could process the beans. The toxic metal had drawn the scorpions, but had poisoned him. The same thing might happen here.

Richter thought about it for a minute before regretfully shaking his head. Stuck underground without any help, access to medicine, or any other information, it was too big of a risk to eat these. This was especially true with the curse still hanging over his head. He didn't even have any shoes.

That had nothing to do with eating the beans, but it was just sad and annoying.

He wasn't going to eat the beans, but that didn't mean he was just going to leave a potentially useful resource behind. Richter reached out and picked one. It separated from the branch with a small *snap*. The pod was heavier than he'd expected. He was about to harvest the rest when a new notification window appeared.

> Quest Update: **Chaotic Flux**
>
> You have discovered a powerful resource that can help nourish your **Tier 2** body!
>
> Would you like to absorb the power of the **White Iron Beanpod**?
>
> Yes or No?

His eyebrows rose in surprise. He certainly hadn't expected to find something that could nourish his body so quickly. It also looked like he could just absorb energy from the beans directly. That meant he could use the *rare* herb without having to roll the dice by eating it. Not seeing any downside, he chose "Yes."

The window disappeared and black-and-gold light surrounded his hand. It flowed into the beanpod before being absorbed back into him. On its way back, it had a small bit of white light attached. As he watched the pod shriveled, and felt energy flow into him.

It tickled a bit.

> Quest Update: **Chaotic Flux**
>
> **Tier 2 Points absorbed:** 2/100.
>
> **2%** chance of skeletal system being iron-strengthened when flux period is over.
>
> **98%** chance of Quest Failure
>
> **25 days** until flux period ends.
>
> Absorbing a total of **100 Tier 2 Body Points** will trigger an automatic change to your body.

He smiled, not only because he'd found a way to advance the Quest, but also because he understood it better now. Before now, he'd had no idea what the "relevant energy" in the original quest prompt had been talking about. Apparently, it meant substances powerful enough to be considered ascended.

Just one little beanpod had gotten him 2% of the way to a bonus to his body. If he was reading this right, it meant that the plant could infuse his bones with metal. After his initial excitement died down, he realized he actually wasn't sure how he felt about that. While it would be great to not have to worry about a monster biting through his leg, would it also make him heavier? Would it interfere with his mobility or his archery skills? There were too many unknowns for him to absorb any other pods. At least right now.

Richter plucked the other three bean pods, including the immature ones. He wouldn't consume any more right now, but even if he didn't eat them there were other potential uses. His thoughts were of the future. This plant had already been beneficial and who knew what other hidden uses it might have.

Both Elora and the Hearth Mother were high level herbalists. They would be able to see if the *rare* plant had other uses. At the very least, the beans inside of the last pod might serve as seeds when he got back to the village. He stopped a moment and reflected that after filling his belly and getting some rest, a safe return to his village seemed way more likely.

Touching the plant itself didn't let him absorb any energy, unfortunately. After the pods had been picked, *Herb Lore* didn't register anything else useful about it. He tried to uproot it. Who knew if there were any hidden roots he could use? He might as well have been trying to pull down a mountain. Even with his sixty-four points of Strength, he couldn't snap off a branch. It didn't seem possible, not looking at its stringy appearance, but then again, it was magic, right?

He was still giddy from just having food and water, so it didn't really bother him. Finding the plant also made him think. He'd already come to the conclusion that monsters might build their lairs near water and food sources. What if they also gathered around useful herbs and resources? It made sense. It was even how animals acted back on earth. Deer would often congregate near a salt lick.

If he raided other lairs, he might find more herbs that could nourish his Tier 2 body. He needed XP anyway. If he got strong enough, there was even a chance that he could go back and pay his ichorpede friends another visit, he thought with a savage smile.

Fucking dicks.

With a broad smile on his face, he looked around one last time. There wasn't really anything else in the chamber. It seemed his gut feeling had just been nerves. On a whim, he scooped some water onto the plant, one good turn deserving another, then made his way back up. He lost a bit more skin, wiggling his broad shoulders up the narrow tunnel, but a quick Life spell fixed that. The flash of golden light showed that Sloth silently awaited him, looking like a stalagmite in the dark.

From where the golem was situated, it hid the already difficult-to-find tunnel entrance. There was no way a large monster would have been able to enter his sleeping cavern without passing by it. He realized he'd just found a pretty great home base. He even had food in the form of the slain scorpion babies. Richter sent the golem to stand guard at the cave mouth and cast *Far Light* and *Simple Light*. In the candle-weak white glow, his sight fixed on the dead scorpions.

He approached the first body. As crazy as it sounded, he was already a bit hungry again. The increased metabolic needs of his ascended body were no joke. He couldn't wait for the adjustment period to be over. This first carcass wasn't for eating though. It was time to use his new bloodline.

Richter searched inside of himself and found his new power. He marveled at how easy it was to use it. Even though it had only been a day, triggering his bloodline was easy. It was just like when he learned a new spell. The calculations to cast even a *weak* spell could fill a dictionary-sized book, but after the knowledge flowed into him, using it was as simple as walking.

When you thought about it, walking should be difficult. Two hundred muscles were required to take a single step. If anyone tried to control each individual muscle, they'd slam their face into the ground. Instead, you just "walked." Using the bloodline was the same. The power flowed through him. He wasn't sure if it was creating new pathways in him or just awakening never-before-used conduits.

His veins glowed purple-green, lighting his mahogany skin and making him look like a fell creature. His gaze flicked to his interface, the new purple status bar in the upper right corner of his vision. It was full, containing seventy-two Bloodline Points. He already knew that the scorpions were *common*-souled creatures. That meant usage of his bloodline should expend ten BPs. He'd be able to use *Harvest* seven times before his points ran out.

He hoped his bloodline ability wouldn't fail because he was using it on a younger monster. One of the great things about collecting souls was that it didn't matter if a creature was young or mature. You still got the same yield. That was why he was now the proud owner of fifteen *common* souls. Now he just needed something to enchant.

The energy finished building in him and a beam of purple-green energy shot into the carcass. The power flowed into it, lighting the body up from within. The body began to soften like melting wax. Fell purple energy continued to leak through the cracks, growing brighter as the energy looked for a foothold. All of a sudden, the magic winked out.

Attempting to Harvest... **Failure!**

Crap. All that was left in place of the body was a small heap of burnt black matter. A faint curl of foul-smelling grey steam rose off of it. Shrugging, Richter turned his attention to the next.

Attempting to Harvest... **Failure!**

Richter's cheek twitched a bit. He tried it again.

Attempting to Harvest... **Failure!**

And again.

Attempting to Harvest... **Failure!**

It wasn't until the fifth try that he finally succeeded.

Attempting to Harvest... **Success!**

Each attempt had turned the dead scorpions into piles of black goo. This time, the remains turned into a black crap pyramid, just like the rest, but something else happened as well. An item floated up from the scorpion's remains. It was a square of grey metal about six inches across and a quarter-inch thick. It hovered several feet off the ground, waiting for him to grab it.

Richter plucked it from the air. To his surprise, it even had the feel of metal, but was as flexible as cloth.

You have found: Malleable Iron	**Item Class:** Scarce **Durability:** 9/9* **Weight:** 0.25 kg **Traits:** This is a *scarce* drop from an ironspine scorpion. It can seamlessly meld with other pieces of malleable iron and contour to nearly any shape. This material is highly prized by crafters and seamstresses as its durability will increase by a factor of ten when treated with magic. Despite this great increase in defense it will remain flexible, and will provide far better defense than simple mined iron. **Latent Power:** 22 *Increases to 90/90 when subjected to magic

There was no denying that this stuff was cool. At first, he'd been disappointed. This was his new bloodline power after all, and all he'd gotten was a sheet of metal. He now knew better. It was absolutely perfect for light armor. Not only was it easy to manipulate due to its low durability, but once it was in the right shape, it could become far harder than forged iron. In fact, its final durability would be harder than moonstone. Unlike that creamy white metal, malleable iron was impossibly light. He had to have more!

Richter also noticed that there was a new line item in the description, one he'd never seen before. This was thanks to his new Enchanter Talent, *Latent Power*. He could pour more soul stuff into this material because of the Talent. With a value of twenty-two, it meant anything he created using the malleable iron would be able to hold a very strong enchantment.

If he used the harvest drop to make a *superb* quality armor, for instance, the malleable iron would more than double the item's base enchantment potential. Richter was actually rather relieved the value was so high. That was because it had "iron" in the name. Raw iron was notorious for having a low enchantment potential. Iron weapons and iron were just as likely to explode as to hold an enchantment. Thankfully, this material only shared the name.

Hoping his Luck would finally kick in, Richter used *Harvest* again. His prayers must have been answered, because his next two attempts were successes. Two more six-by-six squares floated up. Unfortunately, that left him with only three Bloodline Points. Unlike his mana, his bloodline pool did not fill quickly. Thankfully, there were no negative consequences from bottoming out the purple status bar. That wasn't the case for health, mana or stamina.

Having a low health caused a diffuse pain that could become excruciating. A low mana made it hard to think and focus. It was one of the main reasons wizards couldn't just spam spells, even if they had replenishment potions. A low stamina caused dizziness and disorientation, and risked loss of consciousness. It was great that he didn't need to worry about anything similar with his bloodline.

He dragged the rest of the scorpion carcasses to one of the side caves. The rock room would serve as his larder. Once he was done, he turned his attention back to the harvest. This new material gave him an idea.

Once he was situated and had summoned more magic light, he took out the ichorpede pincer. The tip and inside edge were both wickedly sharp. He'd cut himself more than once struggling through narrow tunnels. Now though, he was glad he'd kept it. Using the point, he carefully scratched at the malleable iron. Without too much effort, he was able to cut it. With a smile on his face, he carefully carved off a long thin strip.

"This is going to work," he said in delight.

CHAPTER 35

DAY 152 – JUREN 3, 0 AOC

*R*ichter accessed his Profession tree and prepared to spend the majority of his remaining Talent Points. This time, he didn't meander. He just went straight to the Talent he needed.

You have Purchased: SPATIAL FOLDING

This Talent allows you to create enchantments that fold space. At the lowest rank, you can create Bags of Holding and Expansive Quivers. The size of objects that can enter the dimensional space will be limited to a ratio of 1:5, when compared to the external size of the bag.

At Rank 1 of this Talent:

Bags of Holding can have 1x1 to 5x5 slots. Each slot requires 1 Soul Point at the time of creation. Bags can range in size from a small pouch to a satchel.

Expansive Quivers start with 10 slots.

Upgrade this Talent to rank 2 for **61 Talent Points,** to create larger dimensional spaces and attach them to smaller physical objects.

And like that, he was Talent Point-poor once again.

You have: **7 *Talent Points*** *remaining*

Richter wished he could have held onto more of his TPs, but he had to bow to practicality. He'd been using a torn piece of shirt to hold his meager belongings. His soul stones had fallen out more than once. If that had happened over a crevasse, or while he was running, those resources would be lost. Down here in the depths, that could mean death. He needed a way to keep his belongings safe.

Also, the ichorpede pincer was being held in a tear of his already ragged pants. It had drawn blood from him several times already. The cuts hadn't been life threatening, but they had been insanely irritating. Richter just consoled himself that *Spatial Folding* was a Tier 1 Talent, otherwise he would never have been able to afford it. Also, that nagging feeling in his stomach didn't flare up, so he felt like it was the right choice.

Congratulations! You have revealed 3 new Tier 1, Orbit 4 Talents!

The fog that surrounded his blue Profession Talent Tree pulled back and three new Talents were revealed. They all focused on making better Bags of Holding. They could reduce weight, make more slots and increase the size of objects that could be placed in the bags. All of them were attractive, but no matter what they did, he couldn't afford another Talent.

On the plus side, purchasing *Spatial Folding had* answered a question that had bugged him for a while. He'd always been curious why it mattered if a Bag of Holding was a belt pouch or a bookbag. A smaller container had always seemed like the better choice. It'd be easier to move around with, more innocuous. Now he knew better. An externally small dimensional pouch wouldn't be able to store large weapons and armor, not without the Enchanter buying upgrades.

It also showed how his previous bag was a bit of a Cadillac compared to the Pinto he was about to create. His old one had one hundred slots, four times as many as the basic version he could now make. Just that difference meant it would take 100 Soul Points to create a comparable bag. That meant he'd have to use *brilliant*-ranked souls. Those only came from monsters on par with the dark aberration that had nearly tentacle-raped him.

The memory of that battle was horrific, but thinking about using a *brilliant* soul just to make a pouch was terrifying as well. *Brilliant* souls cost hundreds of gold each. Just the monetary cost of the captured spirits would be the equivalent of hundreds of thousands of dollars, not to mention the cost of the other materials and the skilled labor.

His old bag had also reduced the weight of whatever was put in it by 90%. Coupled with the fact that it was soul bound, he could understand why he had needed to pay thousands of gold for it. Of course, the price had also been inflated because he'd unknowingly been dealing with a Professional Trader, but best not to focus on that.

Knowledge had flooded into him when he bought the Talent. He now knew everything he needed to make a Bag of Holding. He had the Talent and he had the souls. All he needed to begin was the pouch and powdered crystal. Thankfully, the malleable iron filled in the first missing piece.

Richter laid two sheets of malleable iron next to each other. What happened next astonished him. Even though he'd read about it in the prompt, seeing the two pieces join together seamlessly was miraculous. A moment after putting them side-by-side, he had a six-by-twelve-inch piece of flexible metal.

With the ichorpede pincer, he cut pieces away from the sheet. Between his Strength and its sharp edge, it was an easy process. Soon, two flask-shaped mirror images appeared, each six inches long. He folded the metal cloth so that the mirror images lay atop one another. Once again, the malleable iron fused so flawlessly that you couldn't tell it hadn't always looked like that. It was obvious why the material was highly sought after by craftsmen. Now all he needed was a way to cinch it tight. In a pinch he could have used his own hair for thread, but that would have been super weird.

Using the ichorpede pincer again, he made several small cuts at the top of the pouch. For the last step, he threaded the small strip he'd cut from the remaining piece of malleable iron. With that done he cinched it closed, and he had made his very first pouch. To his surprise, it earned him a prompt.

Congratulations! You have crafted an:

Congratulations! You have crafted an: Ironscorpion Pouch	**Item Class:** Uncommon **Quality:** Exceptional **Durability:** 17/17* **Weight:** 0.7 kg **Latent Power:** 22 **Traits:** This pouch has been created from Malleable Iron, a *scarce* drop from an Ironspine Scorpion. It has the possibility of greatly increasing its durability if exposed to mana. **Bonus Trait:** The powerful materials used will have a particular effect on any stored poisons, adding a corrosive quality over time.

Not bad for my first try, he thought with a grin. Not bad at all. Richter was an *apprentice* in Crafting, and he barely qualified for that status. That meant the quality of items he could make almost always fell within four ranks: *Above Average, Well-Crafted, Exceptional,* and *Superb.* It was much more likely that any item he created would fall into one of the lower ranks than the higher.

Making something *exceptional* was a great outcome. It not only increased the durability of the pouch; it also increased the strength of enchantment the pouch could hold. That was a bit of a relief. Even though Richter knew exactly how many enchantment points various quality arms and armor could take, he was much less familiar with the enchantment potential of crafted items.

All he knew about crafted items was that they could generally hold more soul stuff than forged items, like swords and shields. That was why rings and necklaces, though physically more delicate than an armored helm, could hold more powerful enchantments. Even if he didn't know the exact numbers, having a higher quality pouch could only help. Between the *exceptional* quality and his Talent *Latent Power,* he just had to hope the small pouch could hold enough power to contain a dimensional space.

Richter was feeling very impressed with himself. At least until he read the accompanying prompt.

Using a high-quality material has increased the quality of your crafted item by +1 rank.

It meant he'd actually only made a *Well-Crafted* item. He didn't let it steal his thunder. He'd still done a good job, and the result was what mattered after all. This thing was awesome! The pouch even had a weird trait of strengthening poisons. He didn't actually have any poison so it wasn't too useful right now, but that was okay. It was kind of like finding Marilyn Monroe's sex tape on a Betamax. Useless, but still undeniably cool!

That bonus trait had nothing to do with his own efforts, but that was okay. Extra effects were why some artisans considered Crafting the strongest method of creating items; it was both a science and an art. Depending on the materials used, you could get weird and interesting effects.

There were generally held to be two approaches to Crafting. An example of the first was the Ring of Health he could create. Richter could only make that because of a Template. A Template was like a blueprint; anyone that followed its set instructions could make a magic ring. With a reasonable failure rate of course, depending on how skilled they were.

That was the "science" approach. The "art" path could create items with unique properties, but it could be prohibitively expensive. More than anything else, it required powerful base materials. It was much less reliable than following a Template, but it could make more powerful and unusual items. Also, having a Template was no small thing. They were as valued and coveted as high-tech blueprints were back on Earth. Not only were they expensive, but groups jealously guarded them, not wanting to have to compete with other crafters.

Of course, none of that really mattered at the current moment. The only thing on Richter's mind was what came next. Namely, turning his pouch into a Bag of Holding. To do that, the malleable iron would need to be able to withstand the magical tension of creating a dimensional space.

Not just any material could be turned into a dimensional storage space after all. They defied the very laws of physics. How could a common material like leather contain forces like that? While the Enchantment Potential of an item told you how many Soul Points it could hold, it didn't mean that the material would survive the process of accepting soul stuff. It was like pouring water into a container. A jar made of iron and one made of tissue paper might theoretically hold the same volume of liquid, but you wouldn't want to try and drink out of the second one. He had to hope the malleable iron was up to the task.

With that in mind, he decided to expose the pouch to magic before using his Talent. It couldn't hurt to trigger the malleable iron's special property of boosted durability. With his wide range of magical skills, he had his pick, but he decided not to cast a spell of the Basic Elements. Most of his magic that could target the pouch was destructive. He had healing spells, but they wouldn't lock on to inanimate objects. Deeper Magic had serious consequences and he wouldn't use it lightly. Higher Energy magic was also out. The only one he knew was Chaos magic. The results of that couldn't be predicted. It was in the name, right?

Instead, he employed a skill he'd barely used before: Mana Manipulation. When Hisako had aligned the mana channels in his body, it had hurt like grabbing a live wire with his butt cheeks. As fun as that sounded, he wouldn't repeat the experience if he had a choice. Despite the pain, he had learned the spell *Manifest Mana*.

The spell and his skill would supposedly grow together, but he hadn't had the time to invest in practicing it before now. This seemed like the perfect opportunity. At worst, the spell would cause one point of damage to the pouch. Even with the item's current low durability, such paltry harm shouldn't be a problem.

Before casting the spell, he made one last change to the pouch. Using the pincer as a stylus, he wrote three short lines of text. Grinning to himself at the result, he finally summoned his magic. A moment later, his hands glowed with blue light. Even before the spell connected, he could see wisps of power being absorbed by the pouch. At skill level one, each mana manifestation cost him 100 MP, but with his large mana pool that wasn't a problem. He summoned the magic four more times in all, and was finally rewarded with a prompt.

*The malleable iron of the **Ironscorpion Pouch** has increased in durability!*

Checking, he could see that its durability had skyrocketed to 170/170. That was a higher durability than high steel armor. Now all that was left was what he did second best: enchanting. Richter placed three *common* stones onto the ground in front of him. Thanks to his new Tier 2 Talent, *Expanded Soul, common* souls were no longer limited to a base yield of 10 Soul Points. Each could yield between 10-17 points of soul stuff. Richter examined each in turn to see what he was dealing with.

The first two souls came from the juvenile scorpions. His Profession let him see that they both yielded 12 SPs. The last soul was from the adult scorpion he'd killed first. It provided 33% more for a grand total of 16. Without *Expanded Soul,* he would only have been able to get 30 Soul Points from the three souls. Now he had 40!

Richter checked the rest of the souls he'd captured. He quickly noticed that the points the juvenile scorpion souls offered were all at the lower end of the *common* soul spectrum. Several only provided ten SPs, and the best yield from the younger monsters were the two twelves he'd already laid out. In contrast, the adult was at the higher end of the *common* soul spectrum. He didn't know if that was just a coincidence, or if it might poke a hole in his earlier assumption that a monster's age didn't affect the strength of its soul.

Total, he now had 40 Soul Points to work with. To max out the slots in his bag he needed fifty SPs. It might have been a problem, but thanks to his Tier 1 Talent, *Increase Soul Stone Yield,* that base number was increased by 25%. That gave him exactly what he needed. There was just one more task he needed to complete before he would be able to make his Bag of Holding.

While he'd been traveling through the tunnels, he'd been able to make empty soul stones with his Light magic. He'd either found rocks on the ground or he'd had the golem break off pieces protruding from the walls. It was easy to do that on the move. Making powdered crystal, on the other hand, was different. The Tier 2 Talent, *Crystal Touch* let him make the valuable substance, but it cost two hundred and fifty mana per attempt. Each try also took at least ten minutes. That was why he'd saved some of the rocks he'd gathered.

He couldn't be sure that he'd succeed right out of the gate either. As always, when he'd bought the Talent he'd been provided with the knowledge, but only at a rudimentary level. In his experience, there was always something left out. He'd learned something since coming to The Land: knowing a thing and being able to make proper use of that knowledge are two very different things. Put another way, there is a difference between knowing the path and walking the path.

Richter settled into a comfortable lotus position and slowed his breathing. He tried to fall into the light trance state that let his mana refill faster. Before long, his mana pool was full once more. It hadn't advanced his *Meditation* skill, but he figured practice couldn't hurt. With that done, he placed a few simple rocks before him.

He decided to activate the Monocle of Niclewis. He was curious what the monocle would show him while he was making powdered crystal. Picking up a rock, he focused and accessed the power within.

Purchasing the *Crystal Touch* Talent had taught him that powdered crystal was a substance with highly concentrated mana. Everything in The Land, including the rock in his hands, possessed mana to a lesser or greater degree. To turn the stone into powdered crystal, he had to compress the mana inside the rock into as small a space as possible. Once the power was focused, his Talent would take over and transmute the rock into powdered crystal. Only with the crystal serving as both a bridge and spark could he enchant an item. It was his desire to understand the process in greater depth that had prompted him to equip the monocle.

For several minutes, nothing happened. It was only after focusing for a time that Richter began to think he could feel something, like a faint static charge. On a deep level, he knew he was feeling the rock's ambient mana. The sensation was so faint that if he hadn't been focusing, he might never have noticed it. In fact, at first, he'd thought it was only his imagination.

It took several more minutes of staring through the monocle before he saw anything. One of the reasons it took so long was that his mind was battling his own false preconceptions. When he'd thought about the stone containing mana, he'd been envisioning distinct pockets of magic. In truth, the energy was faint and diffuse, like sand in churned water. What he was looking at was so small and spread out as to be nearly indistinguishable from the rest of the rock. After realizing that, he switched tack. In cases where you couldn't see your way forward, you just had to go by feel.

Richter had learned his lesson about trying to force his will on unknown magics and enchantments. Instead, he regulated his breathing. After another ten minutes, his consciousness was finally able to interact with the scant magic in the stone. Trying not to lose the connection, he started pulling the disparate motes of mana closer together. The stone grew warmer. His eyes widened with happy anticipation. It was starting to work!

Nope. It wasn't.

With a sharp *crack*, the rock split in half. A second later, the two pieces grew softer. Two seconds after that, grey sand was falling between his fingers. His first attempt to make powdered crystal was a failure.

At least I didn't wind up with a spike in my chest this time, he thought. Richter reached for another rock. This time his mind knew what it was looking for and the process of feeling the faint ambient mana went faster. He tried again to coalesce the stone's energy, but slower this time. This time was a success, of sorts. It took a whole four seconds before the rock turned to sand.

For the next hour he tried various methods to make powdered crystal. He tried going slower or faster, exerting his will more forcefully or delicately, using bigger or smaller rocks. Each time, it resulted in failure. Richter didn't give up though, and through it all he focused on the hazy mana in the stone. His trial and error helped him come to three conclusions.

One, if he was going to succeed, he needed to move the entire mana field of the rock all at once. Those were the only attempts that had shown any reasonable improvement. Moving only part of a stone's mana particles caused an immediate imbalance and destroyed it.

Two, his power only worked on rocks smaller than a bowling ball. He'd initially had the thought that this might be a way he could tunnel through the walls, but trying to siphon mana from the stone around him had instantly created a major imbalance. Rather than disintegrate the rock, the power had fed back into him. The resulting headache had been awful. He wasn't sure but he thought he might even have gone partially blind for a bit. Worse still, his Enchanting power had been blocked for an hour.

Mother Nature apparently didn't like it when you fucked with her. Needless to say, he decided not to do that again. It was a shame, because it made logical sense to him that the larger the rock, the more mana particles he could draw on. That led to his last conclusion. If bigger rocks wouldn't work, then he needed... better rocks. After that thought, he almost called *himself* a gyoti.

That was when his eyes fell on his golem. It was made of magical rock, wasn't it? And wasn't that exactly what he needed? Better rocks? Having made that mental leap, Richter was filled with excitement. He quickly ordered the golem to form a thin protrusion, and then snap it off. The quartz construct followed Richter's instruction without reservation. It handed the broken piece to Richter.

The chaos lord looked at it excitedly, until two seconds later when the clouded-quartz appearance faded and it turned back into the same dull grey rock as the caverns. Richter stared at it ruefully, but thought he understood. When Sloth was made, the common material that formed its body had been transformed into clouded quartz by the golem's energy matrix. Once cut off from that power source, any part that broke free would just turn back into the same, magicless common material. Sloth wasn't the answer.

Sadly, trying to use soul stones just shattered the amber gems. Richter even resorted to trying with a filled gem. This time, the gem shattered and rainbow energy dissipated into the air. The waste hurt, but worse was that he didn't know what else to do. After another hour of trying with various stones, Richter finally lost it. "Gah!" he spat in frustration. He was so close! All he needed was this damn powdered crystal. Why was this so hard? All he wanted to do was harness the fundamental powers of the universe so that he could fold time and space into a pocket dimension for his own personal needs. Was that so much to ask? Really!

He might have made more progress, but each attempt drained his MP by two hundred and fifty points. Even his high Wisdom needed seven minutes to recover that amount. That meant he could only make eight attempts an hour. Adding in his mishap of trying to convert an entire wall into powdered crystal, time passed far too quickly. While he tried to figure it out, he periodically felt that strange sense of unease in the pit of his stomach. No matter how hard he looked, he couldn't find a reason for it.

It would come and go, sometimes almost feeling like physical pain. Even casting *Weak Detect Hostile Intent* didn't show anything, so he turned his mind back to the problem at hand. There had to be way to make powdered crystal.

He came up with nada, also known as bupkis. Richter struggled to think of another idea. He needed to clear his head. Seeing as he didn't have a baseball bat to hold, he decided to take a lap instead. While he walked around the lair, he kept his monocle trained on the surrounding walls. The description of the glass device said that he could increase its sight abilities with practice.

The drain of 1 MP/min was negligible compared to his mana regen, and such a small amount of mana barely registered as mental strain. A higher mana cost would actually be good news at this point. If his capabilities with the *epic* item improved, the mana drain would increase as well. Sadly, it stayed at the bare minimum. Disappointingly, the monocle also showed that there was hardly any power in the surrounding stone.

Richter walked into several galleries off the main cave, but the result was the same. He even scanned over the remains of the scorpions' previous victims. He wasn't expecting to be able to use them to make powdered crystal, but had hoped that there would be something he could use. All he found was tattered skin and rotting meat. There was really only more thing in the lair. Sighing over his soon-to-be-lost skin, he went back down the hole to where he'd found the beanpods.

As soon as he got down to the bottom, he had to renew his magical light. Having to re-up his spell every couple of minutes had irritated him at first, until he realized how truly fortunate he was. His rare skills and magics had saved his life down here more than once. Without his Light or Dark magic, he wouldn't even be able to see. Those spells had kept him from falling to his death. There was also no doubt that he wouldn't have survived his first monster attack if he hadn't been able to see.

Without Life magic, he would have succumbed to his wounds long ago. Ichorpede acid would have eaten away at his body, and without his bloodline he would most likely have bled to death fighting the nesting stone slime. Without his Enchanting Profession he'd never have been able to create the golem or defeat the adult scorpion. Without his Cloud Running skill he wouldn't have been able to navigate the crevasse to escape the ichorpede lair he'd first fallen into.

Each of his rare and precious powers had contributed to his survival. How many other people had such a large constellation of capabilities, even in The Land? In a way, it was almost like he'd been bred to survive in conditions like these. Richter shook his head with a faint smile on his face. His irritation was replaced by appreciation, and he cast his spell.

After summoning the white light, his gaze was immediately drawn to the white iron beanpod tree. Looking at it through the monocle for the first time, he was astonished at just how much energy it contained. Compared to the faint and diffuse energy flow of the rocks, the plant was lit up like a Christmas tree. On the outside, it looked withered and nondescript. On the inside, it had well-defined pathways of mana.

They traced along the small branches, continuously cycling between the wooden tips and the small trunk, flowing up to the top and then back down to the base. His gaze followed the light trail to where the plant grew out of the ground. Some of the roots of the iron plant had pierced up through the rocky ground. That meant there were small rocks that had been forced up during its growth. To Richter's delight, they held a noticeably stronger glow of mana than the ones in the rest of the cave. The rocks' energy was definitely lower than the plant's, but it was still something!

He guessed that the plant had so much mana that some had leached into the surrounding stone. It was just a guess, but it made him wonder. Is this what ambient mana does? There was no way to know, and it really wasn't important right now. What mattered was that he might actually have a chance to make powdered crystal!

It had become abundantly clear that though his Tier 2 Talent, *Crystal Touch* was amazing, it required something to work with. It didn't let him convert something worthless into a valuable resource. He still needed something of value as a base material. In this case, stone that had a higher level of mana. Once again, The Land proved it possessed checks and balances.

Excited, Richter gathered up every rock that had a higher mana density. From stones the size of golf balls to tiny pebbles, he collected everything that seemed magically active. After that, he made his way back up the tunnel. He healed his bleeding shoulders and sat down to try again. This time, the process flowed much more smoothly.

Not only was it easier to gather the mana, but it coalesced in a way that he hadn't seen before. Richter's heart thudded in excitement. He had to force himself not to rush. About twenty minutes later, the rock crumbled. At first his heart dropped, but then he saw that it hadn't turned into grey sand. This time, the stone transformed into a pile of shining dust!

CHAPTER 36

DAY 152 – JUREN 3, 0 AOC

Congratulations! You have made 0.35 measures of powdered crystal!

*I*t wasn't a full measure, but it was a success! If he did that two more times, he'd be able to enchant his pouch. That amount had come from one of the golf ball-sized rocks. He had eighteen more of those and what he guessed was the equivalent of about ten more measures-worth of pebbles. Richter got back to work.

The next attempt was a failure, leaving only grey dust, but the one after that was a success. When he had finally exhausted his supply of rocks, his proficiency in creating powdered crystal had clearly increased. The first couple of times he'd only had a 25% success rate, but over time he was able to make the mana coalesce every other attempt. After four hours, he was the proud owner of five measures of powdered crystal.

Richter was finally ready to make his Bag of Holding. After focusing for so long, he was hungry and mentally tired, but his excitement kept him sharp. Also, the odd feeling of disquiet had come back several times and seemed to be suppressing his appetite for some reason. He put it out of his mind. Instead, he focused on the enchantment he'd been building up to for an entire day.

First, he sprinkled a measure of crystal onto the pouch. Then, holding the three *common* soul stones in his hand, he accessed the power within them. The first amber jewel shattered into small pieces and a ribbon of rainbow light flowed into the metal pouch. In his mind, a mental image of the pouch formed, showing a single grid square. He focused and the grid split, and split again, making a 2x2 square. More energy flowed into the pouch to accommodate the matrix. One after another, the amber jewels shattered, leaving dull shards behind. With each influx of soul stuff, the grid grew. Ultimately, three ribbons of energy flowed into the pouch, and he was rewarded for all his hard work.

*Congratulations! You have enchanted the **Ironscorpion Pouch** and created a **Bag of Holding!***

Richter grinned like an idiot. He was about to examine the pouch when he received a pleasant surprise.

*Your Enchanting Skill coupled with your **Personal Touch** Talent has increased the grid space from 5x5 to 6x6. Well done, Enchanter!*

The *Personal Touch* Talent both increased the chance of his enchantments to take hold and increased their strength by 25%, as long as he was using powdered crystal that he'd made himself. There was no denying that his Tier 2 Talents had increased the power of his Profession drastically. Just now it had increased the grid squares of his Bag of Holding by about 40%. *Personal Touch* was also not the only new Talent that had been triggered.

*Congratulations! You have used the souls of Ironspine Scorpions to enchant an item. These souls contained elements of metal and corrosion. Your **Soul Flavor** Talent has added a bonus to your item: **Ironscorpion Bag of Holding.***

Bonus: A vial of **Weak Ironspine Scorpion Corrosive Venom** *will be produced by your Bag of Holding every 7 days.*

That was shocking enough, but there were even more prompts waiting to be read.

Know This! The souls of the Ironspine Scorpions had a high affinity with the material used to craft your Ironscorpion Bag of Holding: **Malleable Iron.**

The bonus from **Soul Flavor** *has been increased.*

New Bonus: A vial of **Enhanced Ironspine Scorpion Corrosive Venom** *will be produced every 7 days.*

Richter's eyes widened in shock. Not only had the bonus provided him with another weapon that might just keep him alive, but he'd also learned something new about his Profession. The *Soul Flavor* Talent let his items gain extra bonuses based on the soul that was used to enchant them. It seemed that using materials and souls from the same type monster could increase those bonuses even further. Richter was finally starting to see the true power of Crafting.

To his delight, the final product had the red coloring of a *rare* item.

You have Enchanted the Ironscorpion Pouch as a Bag of Holding	Item Class: Rare Quality: Exceptional Durability: 170/170 Weight: 0.7 kg + total weight of items Traits: Can hold a large number of items in a 6x6 grid. Thinking of a desired object will retrieve it from the bag. Any stored poisons will gain a corrosive effect over time **Bonus Trait:** 1 bottle of Enhanced Ironspine Scorpion Corrosive Venom will be produced every 7 days.

His Bag of Holding had turned out better than he could have dreamed. It was all thanks to the *Harvest* power of his new Bloodline and his Tier 2 Talents. The Enchanter still wasn't done. Richter pulled out three more captured souls. Using them would leave him only eight more, but it was well worth the expense.

*It appears you wish to Soul Bind an item. For a Level 1 soul bond, you must spend Soul Points equal to the maximum base enchantment potential of the item's quality. This will impose serious penalties on anyone other than yourself who tries to use this item. Only you will have access to the item's magical properties. To soul bind the **Ironscorpion Bag of Holding,** you must spend 30 Soul Points. Do you wish to do so? Yes or No?*

Richter smiled even as he chose "Yes." He hadn't been sure how many SPs it would take, but it looked like crafted *exceptional* quality items had an enchantment potential of thirty. It was twice the cost of an *exceptional* sword or piece of chainmail, but it was nothing he couldn't handle. In fact, thanks to his *Increase Soul Stone Yield* Talent, he only needed two soul stones to meet the quota, leaving him with nine to spare.

He accessed his power once again. More rainbow-colored soul stuff flowed into the pouch. Finally, he was done.

*You have Soul Bound: **Ironscorpion Bag of Holding.** This can only be transferred with an open heart.*

An icon appeared in the corner of his vision. It looked like a miniature version of his new pouch. Accessing it, a grid popped up in his vision. He'd expected it to be empty, but to his surprise, one of the tiles was filled.

You have found:

You have	Item Class: Unusual
found:	Durability: 5/5
Vial of	Weight: 0.1 kg.
Ironspine	Quality: Enhanced
Scorpion	Traits: Causes 25 points of damage for 8 seconds. This poison has
Corrosive	a corrosive effect and will melt through anything it touches. Double
Venom	damage to non-living materials.

Richter whistled softly. This poison was serious. It wasn't just the two hundred points of cumulative damage, it was the corrosive effect. If this got on a suit of armor, it could eat through it in seconds before falling on an enemy's flesh. Deep gouges in the cavern floor showed just how effective the scorpion's acid was.

As great as it was to have a new weapon, it was the 6x6 squares that brought an unexpected relief. Having an inventory again felt like he'd rejoined civilization. It was like he'd been stranded in the wilderness and had found an essential piece of technology. Actually, it was exactly like that, he thought with a grin.

Before falling into the abyss, he hadn't known how much comfort his items brought him. Richter immediately started storing his meager possessions in the pouch. His nine filled stones went in first. They each glowed with the light of a captured *common* soul. Another slot was taken up by thirty empty amber jewels.

His ichorpede pincer went in next. Everything disappeared easily, and the outside contours of the metal pouch didn't change at all. The bean pods went in after that. Surprisingly, they took up two slots, one for the mature and two for the immature pods. He ever-so-carefully put in the vial of chaotic noxious scent as well. Twenty-eight slots remained empty. He didn't own anything else that needed to be stored.

His rings, bracelet, necklace, the rags he was wearing, and the monocle stayed on. Those few things, along with his makeshift club, comprised all of his worldly possessions. It really put things into perspective. He, Lord Mist, Master of a Place of Power, slayer of thousands, didn't even have a clean pair of underwear. It didn't bother him at all.

He was alive, he was fed, and he was stronger than ever. The things that lived down here were going to regret letting him live this long. They should have gotten him while he was weak, because now he was coming for them!

With grim anticipation, he examined the leg bone. It was scored with numerous bite marks, but none of them went too deep. It was solid in his grasp. Even banging it against the adult scorpion hadn't cracked it. It just lacked any real stopping power. Which drew Richter's gaze back to the remaining ironspine scorpion bodies. He needed more materials.

Richter had one more piece of malleable iron and fourteen carcasses left. He'd considered saving all of them for food, but he'd already pushed the envelope on their freshness. Anything he killed from here on out could go in his pouch. These had already sat out for a day. The decay was already well and truly begun. He'd save a few for his next meal, but then he'd need to hunt again.

Dimensional spaces had an anti-entropic effect that was as good as a fridge, but if something was already spoiling, it wouldn't reverse that fact. In regard to these bodies, he'd be much better served by obtaining *Harvest* drops. The seven hours he'd spent making powdered crystal and enchanting his bag of holding had let him regen thirty-nine Bloodline Points, bringing his total up to fifty-two. It was just enough.

He channeled his bloodline; as he did so his veins stood out once more, purple-black energy stark against his skin. He was really looking forward to freaking Sion out when he saw his friend again. The only current observer, the golem, just stood impassively at the cave entrance and continued to scan for enemies with its magical senses.

*Attempting to Harvest... **Failure!***

*Attempting to Harvest... **Success!***

*Attempting to Harvest... **Failure!***

*Attempting to Harvest... **Failure!***

*Attempting to Harvest... **Failure!***

*Attempting to Harvest... **Success!***

*Attempting to Harvest... **Failure!***

*Attempting to Harvest... **Failure!***

He'd failed more than three-quarters of the time, but it should be enough. One of his successes yielded the same six-by-six piece of metal that he'd gotten before. The other provided a smaller piece. That had come from the scorpion he'd already eaten the claws off of. The harvest was enough for his purposes. He fused them end-to-end, then started shaving strips off with the ichorpede pincer. He was struck again by how miraculous the material was. He considered harvesting the last bodies, but set them aside. They would be useful in the future.

More sure of himself this time, he easily shaped the malleable iron. He cut slashes into one end with the ichorpede pincer. One cut got away from him, but pushing the grey metal together again erased the mistake. Once the slits were just right, he laid it over his left hand and covered his palm with more metal. After that, he just pinched the strips around his fingers. The edges fused together, creating a glove. The remaining material he wrapped around his arm like a bandage. Each spiral melded with the ones before, making a sleeve that covered almost his entire forearm. To finish the project, he etched two lines of text into the glove where the flat side of his fist would rest. His luck stayed with him, and the quality was *exceptional*.

You have created an **Ironspine Forearm Glove**	**Item Class:** Uncommon **Quality:** Exceptional **Durability:** 174/174 **Defense:** +8 **Weight:** 0.9 kg

He saved the final pieces to augment his weapons. The first was cut into strips that were then fused into a single long strip of the material. Wrapping it around the base of the ichorpede pincer finally let him wield his improvised dagger without fear of cutting himself. He then used the remaining pieces to wrap around the head of the bone club. Both minor acts of crafting earned him prompts.

You have created an **Ichorpede Dagger**	**Item Class:** Common **Quality:** Well-Crafted **Durability:** 20/22 **Attack:** +6 **Weight:** 0.6 kg **Traits:** Made from the torn-off pincer of an ichorpede and bound with malleable iron, this makeshift weapon has a serrated cutting edge, blunt back side and sharp point.

Binding the ichorpede pincer with malleable iron didn't seem to do anything, yielding only a *common* crafting. Not surprising, as an iron dagger would have the same attack whether you bound the hilt in deer hide or dragon skin. On the other hand, wrapping the head of the large bone in iron like a duct-taped baseball bat made it register as a +8 weapon. When he applied mana to the iron to harden it, not only did the durability and attack shoot up, but the prompt shifted from the white of a *common* item to the green of *uncommon.*

You have created a **Malleable Iron-bound Bone Club**	**Item Class:** Uncommon **Quality:** Well-Crafted **Durability:** 92/92 **Attack:** +12 **Weight:** 1.1 kg **Traits:** This club has been made from the large leg bone of an unknown beast and malleable iron.

He finally had proper weapons and that could only be good news. Not only that, but his DIY mace had a damage that could rival a forged steel sword.

He looked at his glove and decided to enchant it. He still wasn't willing to risk the bone club or the ichorpede pincer. Not because they were more valuable than the glove, but because he didn't think they could bear the flow of soul stuff. The high durability on the prompts didn't mean they were a safe bet. He'd learned that when he'd made the mistake of enchanting a spear once. The high steel head had been fine, but the spear's wooden shaft had burst into splinters. After that, Richter had only enchanted spear heads before they were mounted.

The glove was different. It was completely made out of malleable iron. The defensive enchantments he knew weren't high rank, but they were better than nothing. He sprinkled powdered crystal on the metal glove and accessed his enchantments. To his great surprise, both the attack and defense enchantments were available. He'd expected the attacks to be greyed out. He didn't know if it was because the piece of armor was crafted rather forged, but he didn't care. Richter was about to make an attack gauntlet!

He chose to use his strongest enchantments, *Freeze* and *Sonic Damage*. The first was a level one, rank five water enspellment and the second was level two, rank four. Thanks to one of his new Tier 2 Talents, *Latent Power,* the glove could hold more soul stuff than almost anything else he'd ever augmented.

Malleable iron could take twenty-two points of soul stuff. The glove's quality added another thirty, his Talents and *Crafting* skill increased that to forty-eight. His status as a *journeyman* Enchanter added another fifteen. Altogether, the glove had a grand total of eighty-five enchantment slots! It was more than enough for him to maximize his enchantments.

Sadly, he just didn't have that much soul stuff to wield. He could only use three soul stones at a time. His strongest scorpion souls had eleven points each. With his 25% Talent modifier, that meant the most he could harness was forty-one points. His Tier 2 Talents were powerful, but again, they demanded a high cost to truly use them.

With only *common* souls to work with, he could bring *Sonic Damage* to rank four and *Freeze* to rank three. All three amber jewels shattered and rainbow energy sank into the glove. He felt some resistance before the enchantment took hold, but then a prompt told him about his attack gauntlet's powerful stats!

You have created:

You have created:		
Ironspine Gauntlet of Shattering Ice		
Item Class: Scarce		**Quality:** Exceptional
Item Class: Uncommon	**Quality:** Exceptional	**Charges:** 257/257
Durability: 174/174	**Defense:** +8	**Weight:** 0.9 kg
Traits		
+15 Earth Damage		+5-6 Water Damage
10% chance to *Disarm*	4-5% chance to *Shatter*	3-4% Chance to *Freeze*

He might be surrounded by danger, but his powers had grown to match. While it might be true that he couldn't go toe-to-toe with a Warrior in a stand-up fight, with his enchantments and magic he could kill his fair share. The gauntlet would add twenty points of magical damage with every hit. That wasn't even counting its special traits. They wouldn't happen every time, but when they did trigger, they could end a fight all at once. He couldn't wait to use it!

Richter's life expectancy had just gone up. The only weakness of the gauntlet was that it relied on charges. Every hit he landed would drain it. Once it was depleted, all the enchantment effects would be gone. That was another reason he wasn't interested in making more enchantments; he'd need his captured souls to recharge it. It would refill over time, but that could take days.

The charges were a minor negative. He had armor now! The original grey color of the glove now had a slight sheen of green and blue. The defense rivaled the base protection of a chainmail gauntlet, yet it was light and flexible. The thing fit like a second skin. It didn't even register as armor, which meant magic users could wear it with no penalty to their casting abilities. If he could find more scorpions to harvest, he could outfit every mage in the village with armor comparable to his fighters!

That was why he'd saved the last scorpion carcasses. His plan had required that he successfully make a bag of holding, but now that that was done, he could store the body with minimal degradation. If... when, he corrected himself yet again... he made it back to the village, he'd put it down the Well of Offering. Maybe he could hunt more of the creatures in the future. Again, he turned danger into power.

Nearly an entire day had passed, but it had been productive. He had a dimensional pouch and some armor. The gauntlet was deadlier than most weapons he'd seen. He'd even managed to make the pincer and bone club into proper weapons. Now that they both registered as a dagger and club respectively, his *Small Blades* and *Mace Wielding* skills would give him damage bonuses in a fight.

It dawned on Richter that he hadn't eaten for nearly an entire day. Between being distracted and the vague sense of uneasiness in the pit of his stomach, he just hadn't gotten around to it. As he thought about it, he got concerned. The increased metabolic demands of his new body were real. He knew that. So why wasn't he hungry? He decided that, appetite or not, he needed to try to eat.

Richter walked toward the small side cave where he'd stored the last five scorpion babies. It was nearly at the back of the cavern system. When he got closer, he caught a whiff of the larder. A day of sitting unrefrigerated hadn't been great for the aroma, but it was the only food he had.

He stepped into the cave and the scent grew stronger. It wasn't horrible, but it had an unintended effect. The nagging feeling of unease in him flared up in him again. This time was different though. This time, he knew what it meant. With nothing less than pure dread, he recognized what it was. It was something he'd been well familiar with in the past, but his high attributes had kept it at bay for so long that he'd forgotten. When the attack came, it was fast and without mercy. Richter knew in his heart that he had finally met an enemy that could not be beaten, only endured.

CHAPTER 37

DAY 152 – JUREN 3, 0 AOC

"*B*egone, demons!" Richter cried at the top of his lungs.

The chaos lord's large muscles strained and beads of sweat cascaded off his body. A vein throbbed in the middle of his forehead, standing up like a snake's trail through sand. His eyes were unfocused and bloodshot. They pierced the veil into oblivion.

Victory was a hopeless dream. All he could do was survive. While he battled his foe, he called upon gods that he knew would not answer. He called nonetheless. In times like this, you did not live your life by reason. You lived it by hope and faith. Richter felt as much as saw a fresh attack coming and he named his impossible foe.

"Diarrheaaaaaaa!"

You never knew how it would begin. The attack could be almost spiritual. A flash of pain that would twist your body into knots, but when you looked down, there was nothing there. It was only natural to ask yourself in those moments, how could so much agony have been endured with no yield? Without even a glimpse of a promise that the torture would one day end? That was the insidious cruelty of "Ghost" poopie.

Another feared beginning was the threat of structural damage. There was always the dread that as the evil left your body, it would leave utter devastation in its wake. Your body would have fought the good fight. It would have struggled and given all that it could. For a few hope-filled minutes, you might think that you would be able to stop the umber flow. You would cling to the gossamer hope that the danger had passed. That even though carnage and mayhem were all around you, the basic mechanics of your body would have survived the hurricane.

That was when it happened. That was when you knew. The storm had not passed, you were simply in the eye, and that eye was coming for your own nether oculus. Nature, after all, can never be overcome. Ultimately, the ceasefire just made the final loss so much worse. Like a levee being overwhelmed, the eventual flood that finally came would destroy towns, cities and bungholes. This was the false promise of the "Broken Dam" poopie.

In the twenty-sided dice roll of how these things were wont to begin, there was only one hope of salvation. One out of every million souls condemned to this hell-come-to-life was given a reprieve. Gods, who were both benign and loving, bade evil pass through you in one painful, but short, log ride of agony. And even when you wiped afterward, there was barely anything to clean up! This was the ever-sought-after and elusive "Clean" poopie.

Whatever primal forces were looking down upon Richter, however, he knew two things.

They were not benign.

They were not loving.

For the chaos lord, it began with a Gatling gun of sharp-edged diamonds leaving his body. In his mind, they made sharp *pings* as they encountered the rock behind him. Richter did not look, but he was sure the cavern must now be riddled with holes. While the sound effects might have been imaginary, there was nothing fake about the red-hot barrel inside his colon.

After that came the waterfalls. He'd barely had a minute to recover and wipe the drool from his mouth. Streams of brown, yellow and hate geysered from his body like a firehose from hell. The pain nearly made him pass out.

"Oh god! It feels like shitting a knife!"

Several times his eyes rolled back into his head, showing only the whites, before he wrestled his consciousness back under his control. Each demonic spray started with a fiery pain at the exit point. He wondered briefly if invisible spirits of vengeance were rubbing Carolina Reapers on his anus. That, of course, was ridiculous, as even ghosts would have been washed away by the raging rapids eroding the stone of the cave system.

Despite the pain, if this were all that had happened Richter would have been fine. Indeed, he would have counted himself lucky. He had endured worse. He was a warrior, a skilled mage, a leader of men. Mere pain could not undo him. As the last gallons of the waterfall phase trickled away however, he knew the true bill for his sins had come due. He had entered phase three.

The pain of this phase was worse than the first two. That was due to a fact that any true torturer would recognize. As wonderful as the sight of tears and splashed blood could be, breaking someone's body was never as sweet as breaking their spirit. That was why phase three saw the entrance of the most humbling of poopies, a "Dangler."

Long did Richter fight to force this brick through the tangled garden hose within him. Small flashes of red showed the HP he was losing. The true tragedy was that the lost health wasn't enough to kill him. Merely 1 HP here, another HP there. The scant amount of damage waged a form of psychological warfare as he fought to push a lump of glued glass shards out of his battered body.

After hours of struggle, promises to gods and demons alike, and body contortions that stretched the limits of his superhuman attributes, at long last he was rewarded with a relief that only the thrice-damned would ever know. Of course, in hell there is no true victory. That was when the psychological warfare and the insidious nature of the "Dangler" was revealed.

Richter had just been thinking he was going to need to poop knife this latest loaf of evil, when he realized phase three was not over. His envisioned salvation had been only a cruel ruse. For the "Dangler's" true power lay in the fact that the last bit remained attached. Some scientists had though this curse was due to the poopie having a hook at the end, or perhaps a right angle. Some had even surmised that during its slow passage the poopie fused to the nervous system, gaining awareness and a cruel will. A precious few said if you waited long enough, it might even crawl back in. None could say for sure. It was acknowledged that if the last theory were true, it was likely the afflicted never lived to tell the tale, so the supposition was placed in "Unknown Unknowables" right along with One-Eyed Willie.

None of that mattered to Richter, however, as he squatted, hands braced on the stone of the cavern entrance, hunched over in both pain and shame. His fists ground into the rough rock floor, hard enough to make a bloody slurry in the dust. As he thrust his hips this way and that, trying to dislodge nature's most hideous tail, he wondered if this was all because of Nexus.

Maybe he had never actually escaped the Auditor's realm and everything he had experienced had been nothing more than an illusion. Was he being tortured by the black-and-gold giant? If so, could he apologize and be released from this endless cycle of lament? Alas, not even the Auditor, with his demigod-like powers, would have had the stomach for this form of torment. Richter remained trapped in reality and could only endure the atrocity that had befallen him.

Richter's butt waggled like an epileptic dog at a rave, but it was not his actions that finally removed the "Dangler." It was the coming of the fourth and final stage. He felt it building while he was trying to shake himself free. What came next felt like the orgy love child of the Stay Puft Marshmallow Man and a sack of half-melted sugar-free gummy bears.

With the coming of the last phase, his legs locked into a worse paralysis than tetanus could ever cause. Like an animal spotted by a predator, his hindbrain drove him to immobility. His animal mind held onto the same vain hope as a velociraptor's prey. Maybe if he didn't move, it would cause the impending doom to pass over him and attack someone else.

Sadly, that only worked with a T. Rex.

It didn't work on raptors.

It didn't work on poopie.

Hope had abandoned him.

Somehow Richter knew on a deep level that what was coming was one of the most feared forms of poopie. Sometimes known as "Satan's Curse," "The reason for brown pants," or simply "The Finger of God," what was coming had served to end so many dates on Earth that it was actually the most effective, if unrecognized, form of birth control that existed.

"Wait. Please wait," he begged.

His pleas faded unheard. A pressure built in Richter, like a volcanic bubble in a lava flow. With the destructive promise of Goku's spirit bomb, phase four grew in power. Richter placed both hands on his stomach, pressing as hard as his sixty-seven points of Strength would allow. He tried to keep the demon fetus within him. With his prodigious musculature he could shatter skulls, rend flesh and even crush rock. No one, however, could stop fate. With a final whimper, he felt the bubble inside of him shift, ever-so-delicately downward, before this most horrible form of poopie announced its birth loudly to the world. A tear leaked from his eye as he stared into infinity, and his soul whispered, "The Twister."

"Oh my god!" he cried out in panic. "Oh my god, it's coming. Am I dying? I think I'm dying! Get out of me, poison! It's happeninggggg!"

A vortex of pressurized hatred shot from his raw beef sphincter. With a complete disregard for physics, the chunky brown slurry formed an ever-widening cone behind him. Ceiling, walls, floor, nothing was spared from this demonic whirlwind. Richter's cheeks flushed with shame as he felt the foul rain strike his thighs and calves with a hurricane rain's steady tattoo.

Monsters that had been prowling the area around the scorpions' nest raised their noses in the air, sampling a new scent. Without fail, even the most powerful creatures turned and fled. While they did not fear battle, deeply ingrained instincts told them that whatever had created the foul miasma permeating the bowels of The Land had contracted a terrible disease which must be avoided at all costs.

For another hour, Richter hunched upon shaky legs. Each time he thought the torture was over, a fresh round of damnation found him. His stamina dropped nearly to zero and only pure will kept him from collapsing into the lumpy pool behind him. Through all of this torment, Richter had to stare at the debuff *Food Poisoning* that had appeared during the first phase. The scorpions had found a way to enact revenge from beyond the grave!

When the monsters' retribution had finally passed, the chaos lord stood upright on weak legs. A corner of the cave wall was fractured and bloody from the death grip he'd kept on it throughout his lamentations. The only saving grace was that he had managed to shed himself of his scant rags and items before the tragic scene had played itself out. They lay in a pile not far from where he tottered.

Richter listed from side to side, exhausted and in pain, but also with a relieved smile on his face. He had survived. His gaze fell back on his only possessions and the nearly ruined clothes. He had even saved his only protection from the elements and the rough stone that continually scraped his skin free. At last the nightmare was over.

That was when a horrible thought occurred to him. His eyes went from his clothes to his hand and back to his clothes again.

How was he going to wipe?

CHAPTER 38

DAY 152 – JUREN 3, 0 AOC

*R*ichter leaned his face into the small stream. The cool water felt both good and painful sliding down his throat. It was a bit undignified drinking with duck lips, but he just couldn't bring himself to swallow anything from out of his hands. All he'd had strength for after his "episode" was to bathe his makeshift bathroom with his *Weak Flame* spell. The stench had ratcheted up while it had burned, but at least it *had* burned. Even though magical flames had bathed his hands, he still couldn't stand the idea of them touching his lips.

Not yet.

His golem was sitting at the tunnel entrance again, doing its best impression of a boulder. Not only would it attack any enemies that came near, but it would also hide the entrance of the narrow tunnel. Of course, that didn't mean much to monsters that lived in perpetual darkness, but it made Richter feel better.

The scorpion lair had been a godsend. If it wasn't for the fact that his bum had just birthed a demon, it might have been a great place to wait out the curse. He couldn't trust his food stores anymore though. Between his body's accelerated needs and the fact that he'd just lost a quarter of his biomass, he needed to hunt ASAP.

For now, the worst of the food poisoning had passed. He was hydrated and in a safe place. All he really wanted to do was sleep until the last of the residual stomach tremors dissipated. And if he was going to be out of his head anyway, it seemed like the perfect time to absorb some knowledge. It was time to become a granite breaker.

Richter lay on the floor of the small cave and made himself as comfortable as possible. If he passed out, at least now he was already lying down. He even pointed his feet at the stream, making it less likely that he'd roll into it if he thrashed around while he was unconscious. Then, ready as he was going to be, he focused on his interface and a prompt appeared.

Do you wish to absorb the Novice *rank knowledge of the Expertise Book:* **Granite Breaker***? Yes or No?*

He chose "Yes."

His vision zoomed in on the word. The chaos lord had time to absently say, "Oh," before blackness overtook his vision.

Light slowly came back to his world. A woman called out to him in the rolling brogue of the mountain dwarves, "Ach, he be too young, Laird."

"He be my firstborn, Aielas. One day, he will lead the clan. If ye want him to command the loyalty of the Stone Wardens, he must learn to break granite."

"Do na be telling me what ay already know, Laird!" came the waspish reply. "The seed may have fallen from yer wandering cock, banished gods forgive me, but the bairn grew in my fertile soil! Ay'll not be having ye tell me what ma own needs. He be only four years of age. It be too early!"

Laird was about to argue again. He had known it was going to be a fight getting his son away from Aielas. It was that very fire that had attracted him to her five years before. Truth be told, when he was in his cups he still came knocking at her door. If she had ever met him with anything sweeter than a knock on his head with her skillet, they might have more than one child.

Before the dwarf could speak though, Richter felt himself stand. While the man and woman had been arguing, the body his consciousness was inhabiting had been quietly observing through a thin curtain. He walked into the outer room and spoke in a young, but determined voice, "Ay am ready to protect our people, mama." Richter's tiny fists clenched resolutely. It was only then that he realized how small his body was. Even accounting for the short stature of dwarves, the two adults looked like giants to him.

Richter marveled at the inner strength he was feeling. He had met several men and women of strong will since coming to The Land. To "feel" it in this small child, however, was humbling. The bairn looked up at his father, "Ay'm ready, da."

His mother turned her fierce gaze on him. To the child it probably looked like hell was about to descend, but Richter's adult view saw the fragility behind the fire. She waved her hand in defeat and turned away, the only acquiescence she would give. Laird led his son outside, a heavy, callused hand resting on the lad's shoulder. As they walked away, a single tear traced down Aielas's cheek. She had faith in her son, and in Laird, banished gods help her, but *Granite Breaker* training killed children every year. Even if all went well, she would not see her child again for several years.

After leaving the house, what Richter was seeing skipped ahead several times. First, he went to his father's house, a much larger dwelling. From the reactions of other dwarves, Laird was in a position of authority. The boy was outfitted with furs and led away with about a dozen other young boys and girls. He was the youngest by at least a couple of years. All the children were placed on war boars, with one of the clan's warriors guiding each beast. With no talking, they left the mountain village and the only world Richter's host had ever known.

The next scene was of a thunderstorm above a mountain pass. A sound like boulders grinding echoed through the ravine before a wall of dark water stampeded toward the group of warriors and children.

Hurriedly, but with no panic, the warriors took out their maces and formed a line. As one, the weapons were wreathed with a green glow. Seconds before the water hit, the warriors struck the ground with a shouted, "Huu'wah!"

In front of each of them, a span of stone rose from the ground. Each was eight feet high, three feet wide and several inches thick. The rock walls appeared together, and the dwarves' skill was so great that they fit together with barely any gaps. Indeed, if they hadn't made the walls appear at an angle to better channel the water away, there would most likely not have even been a crack between the various stone spans. Such was the power and training of the Stone Warden *Granite Breakers*.

The work was not done. After the initial wave hit, the water roared past and over them. The initial impact left them wet, but breathing. The water level continued to quickly rise. If not for his father, they would have all drowned. Laird was not only a warrior. He was a leader, a geomancer and a Master of a Place of Power. While his men had been creating the rock wall, he had been casting an *adept-rank* spell. Laird finished the incantation and green *Earth* magic flowed from both of his hands. A triple shield of *Earth* energy domed over the party, maintained by the clan chief's will. The barrier formed a solid seal between the ground and the cliffside behind them.

Richter felt the pride and amazement of the body he inhabited, staring at his father resisting nature himself. The chaos lord felt the already-remarkable resolve in the young boy grow stronger. He would prove that he was worthy of this power. He would be even greater than his father-chief!

As soon as the cooldown on the warriors' technique elapsed, they slammed their maces into the ground again. More stone rose from the ground, making the physical wall higher and thicker. The few cracks were sealed. His father held his magic firm until the warriors could strike the ground a third time, finally making the rock walls high enough to withstand the flow of water. During the long minutes it took, the first two Earth shields broke amid shards of disappearing green light. The final barrier was actively maintained, only the geomancer's will standing between everyone and a watery death. Regardless, the faces of each warrior remained impassive, fully confident in their leader's abilities.

When Laird finally released his energy, his arms dropped heavily. His mana was nearly depleted, and it had taken a serious toll on his mental state to hold back thousands of pounds of water. Despite all of that, he hadn't fallen, and he did not rest even when the task was done. Instead, he checked on his fighters and the children under his protection. Richter felt the body he was in search Laird's face for some type of connection, but the clan chief remained distant, valuing his life no more than the lives of the other children. Rather than hurt feelings, Richter felt the pride in the boy swell. With that emotion came another. It was determination to live up to his father's example.

At an order from the chief, they made camp. The only ventilation came from a small hole at the top of the stone dome, but it was enough. Two days later, the waters had receded. The warriors struck down the stone walls, giving proof to the name of their combat technique. Time leapt forward again.

Richter next saw them going into the earth, not through a tunnel or cave, but a large crack in the ground. Each warrior tied a rope to their waist and the other end to one of the children. Like that, they scaled down the cliff face. Nearly every child fell on the way down, their young muscles and frames not up to the task of descending a sheer rock wall. Each time, it was only the unyielding strength of the warriors they were bound to that kept them alive.

Every child fell except for Richter's host. Even years younger than the other dwarf children, his focus and refusal to fail kept him from being a burden. The child never saw it, but Richter's strange all-around sight caught the look of admiration in Laird's eyes. He also saw the jealousy bordering on hatred in the eyes of the other children.

The scene blurred.

Richter's host approached a cliff face far underground. The chaos lord knew that they had not seen the sun for the last several days of travel. The dwarf warriors had needed to fight off monsters more than once. No matter how large the attacker, however, the beasts had fallen to the powerful combat skills and magic of the group. Now they had finally arrived.

Set into the rock face was a carved stone doorway. Every inch of the gateway featured expertly created carvings of dwarves in battle. The history of an entire people was captured in the artwork. Richter could feel his host's fascination with the doorway. Even the chaos lord felt like the carvings were so lifelike that they almost moved.

The warriors did not give them time to stop and stare, however. They shuttled the children through the doorway quickly. On the other side was a chamber with a ceiling so high that the torchlight did not reach it. In the center was a seven-sided stone stele. Standing before the monolith was a dwarf so old his skin had more wrinkles than smooth spots. For the long-lived race that meant centuries of life. Richter didn't know exactly what the lifespan of mountain dwarves was, but he knew it was several times as long as an average human's.

They stopped in front of the old dwarf. Despite his skin being wrinkled, muscles still bulged beneath. He held a stone club that looked like a snapped-off stalactite. Without even looking at the children, he addressed Laird. His voice was mocking and had the high-pitched whistle that only the truly elderly could possess. When he opened his mouth, Richter could see that every one of his teeth was encased in varying precious metals.

"Ye brought them. Now ye can leave. Unless ye want to go through more training yerselves, caha-caha-caha!" A cackling laugh punctuated his statement. Richter host turned his head and the chaos lord was shocked by what he saw. These fearless dwarf warriors that had braved rushing rapids and giant monsters all shared a look of dread. Only Laird stared back without flinching.

The clan chief's response was simple, showing respect and acknowledgement.

"Maistir Olrich," he intoned, placing his middle three fingers over his heart. With a short command, the entire war party filed out of the cave.

The old dwarf waved his hand and muttered a word of power. The doorway they had all come through vanished, replaced by unbroken stone. The kids looked at him in apprehension.

"Yer all here ta learn how to fight, aren't ye?" When no one responded, he repeated with a bark this time, "Well, aren't ye?"

"Yes," the children mumbled quietly. A figure that could scare even the brave warriors of the clan was not someone they would take lightly. In the mountains, strength was everything.

"When ye address me, ye say 'Maistir Olrich'!" he snapped. The early levity was completely gone.

"Yes, Maistir Olrich!" all the children shouted. Every dwarf child present hailed from the more powerful families of the clan, and they knew what was expected of the warriors they were training to become.

"Good," he responded with his metal-toothed smile. "Ye canna fight if you haven't had a good meal. It be time for dinner." He clapped his hands and cast a spell. Stone clubs, sized to the children, dropped to the ground in a loud clatter. "Afore ye eat, ye will all learn the first lesson of Earth. It does not care about ye. Do ye understand?" he asked pointing at one of the older girls.

"Yes, Maistir Olrich!" she yelled, while doing the best a six-year-old could to stand at attention.

"Pony crap!" the old dwarf responded, not believing her. "What about yew?" he asked pointing to one of larger boys.

"Yes, Maistir Olrich," the boy responded, making sure he yelled louder than the girl.

"Goblin balls on yer tongue, boy!" Olrich responded with disdain.

While the first two children had been responding, and the other children were trying to avoid eye contact with the crazy coot they'd been left with, the body Richter was inhabiting had picked up a stone club in his small hands. It was almost too heavy for him to swing. He held it up nonetheless, and was scanning the dark recesses of the cave for enemies. Olrich noticed.

"What about yew, boy?" the old dwarf asked slowly.

Richter's body met the maistir's gaze for a short eye lock, before responding simply, and in a calm voice, "Yes, Maistir Olrich." Then he started scanning the darkness again.

"Hmm," Olrich looked at the boy consideringly. The child didn't look like anything special, but the old dwarf's sharp eyes had noticed Laird's gaze lingering on the youth for just a second before the warband had left. The maistir liked to play into his role as a crazy old man, but his intellect and mind were among the greatest in the River Peninsula. If the boy was related to Laird, as he thought, not only was the child sharper than the rest, but he came from one of the strongest families. "Mayhap yew do understand," the maistir said under his breath.

The rest of the children looked at him quizzically. Olrich slapped his craziest grin onto his face, "Like ay said, it be dinner time, but ye need to learn another lesson. That be, ye shouldna take things for granted. Ay didna say if ye were being fed or if ye were the meal!"

He waved a hand and a heavy thud boomed through the air around them. It sounded like a door made out of pure rock crashing to the ground. After that, dozens of stone crablings came scuttling toward the children. They were only two feet tall, but their bodies' carapaces were hardened into pure stone. Their pincers could cut through a grown dwarf's arms. They were a serious threat to the children.

Olrich showed no sign of helping them, so the dwarven youths just picked up their stone clubs and a battle began. Richter's host swung his stone club in a strong overhand blow. The rock weapon crashed into a crabling's carapace with a heavy *thud*. The crab collapsed, but the boy's arms were numb. Another crabling climbed over the dead body of his first enemy and launched itself at the helpless dwarf lad.

Time sped up again.

Richter could sense that nearly four years had passed. Each year, the children that survived grew in strength and combat techniques. They still had not reached even the *novice* rank of *Granite Breaker,* but every child that remained in the training program was a deadly killer. His host's body was currently leaning against a rock wall, barely visible. A stone club was clutched in his hands. It was several times heavier than the one he'd used his first day. His host handled the weight easily. He patiently waited for his quarry to appear, and silently repeated the mantra of every student of Maistir Olrich.

"This is my club. There are many like it, but this one is mine. My club is my best friend. It is my life. I must master it as I must master life. Without me, my club is useless. Without my club, ..."

The mantra was so ingrained that the young dwarves spoke it in their sleep. At least, until Olrich had learned they were violating one of his many "Laws of Earth," namely that "Earth silently sleeps." The cadets found that there were many of these laws. In fact, a new one seemed to appear whenever Olrich felt like it.

A week of "special" training had ensured that, in the future, no trainee made noise unless they consciously decided to do so. That very principle was why a goblin platoon had just walked by several of the silent dwarves without knowing an enemy watched them. It was only when Richter's host swung his club and made ichor fly that the green-skinned humanoids knew they had fallen into a trap. By then, it was too late.

Richter, and other students of Olrich, proceeded to beat their enemies to death, each swing of a stone club pulping flesh and breaking bones. Only the screams of the goblins broke the underground silence. In a single minute it was over, and the only remaining sound was the drip of black blood from stone clubs. Richter's host raised his hand and made a tactical hand signal. Every other dwarf nodded, following the order of their team leader. Today's training exercise wasn't over. The deadly children faded into the darkness to hunt their next group of green-skinned experience points.

Time sped by.

Three more years passed, and a final scene played out. The battle forms Richter's host had been practicing for years had finally reached a proficiency that had earned Maistir Olrich's recognition. In a giant amphitheater, hundreds of other trainees filled the stands. Paden stood bare-chested in the center on grey sand. At eleven years old, the trainee already had the body of a warrior. Muscles stood out in stark relief on both his chest and arms. A short-cropped black beard hugged his square jaw. A well-healed, vertical scar traced from his temple to his cheekbone, a memento from a battle lesson he would never forget.

He was the first of hundreds of trainees who had qualified to take this test. If he failed, the consequences would be dire. Richter knew the feelings of his host though. All the young man felt was excitement and anticipation.

Olrich stood on a raised platform in the stands. When he spoke, his voice boomed out, easily heard by all present. For once, mockery was absent from his tone, "Head trainee Paden has chosen to challenge his *novice* test. If he fails, the penalty be death. Why is that, trainees?"

"The Earth is unforgiving!" came the thundering reply. Hundreds of young dwarf killers shouted the answer at the top of their lungs.

"Ay," Olrich intoned gravely. He locked eyes with Paden, "Knowing this, do ye still wish to challenge the test?"

"Ay do, Maistir Olrich," Paden replied.

"So be it." The maistir held his stone club upside down, and slammed his weapon on the ground three times. The echoing sound cut through the air like a gavel. In response, a stone gate opened up. What stepped through was a higher-ranked version of the first monster Paden had fought in his training. Rather than a two-foot-tall crabling, however, it was a pincer lord. The monster was five feet at the top of its shell and had four claws. Its defense was higher than *adept*-forged high steel. To destroy the monster, not only a high combat skill would be required, but also a high proficiency in one of the five special techniques of *Granite Breaking*.

Murmurs broke out in the gallery. Every trainee was familiar with the strength of this monster. Only a blind and deaf fool would confuse it with a crabling. A pincer lord was several evolutions stronger. There was even a standing order for trainees to retreat if one of these monsters was encountered in the wild. This particular creature even had a high level. Did the maistir have a vendetta against the head trainee? How was Paden supposed to survive? A sharp, "Silence!" from the maister quieted the murmurs, but not the internal speculation.

Paden did not panic at seeing the monster. Richter could tell that rather than alarm, the young warrior was just reviewing everything he knew about the creature. Its strengths, weaknesses, and likely health, mana and stamina. It never entered his mind that this was an unfair test. To him, it was completely understandable. While other trainees might not understand the maistir, he had long ago grasped a simple point. Olrich did not value the lives of any one of them. Rather, the combat master would easily sacrifice the few to forge the many. If Paden's gory death could serve as a lesson to the other trainees, Olrich would consider it a price well paid. The young warrior had understood all of that before he had asked to be tested.

Unlike the other trainees, he wasn't nervous, he was ready. As the pincer lord rushed toward him, Paden settled his feet into a ready stance. He then summoned his power and raised his club into the proper position. Performing an action that he'd practiced to the point of muscle memory, he stepped forward, swinging his club downward.

In the last years of his training, he and the other trainees had learned that by combining physical action, mental constructs and spiritual focus, certain attacks could achieve special effects. The success of combining these three factors was called Proficiency. The better you adhered to the specific combination needed for a special attack, the greater the power it would evidence. When attacks could take less than a second, it was easier said than done. Anyone who had undergone combat training knew that even a simple punch required diligent training to perform effectively. That was why it took years of practice to even reach the first rank of a Combat Expertise.

When a technique's Proficiency reached a certain level, energy would surround a weapon. The same energy that had surrounded the warrior's maces when they had raised the stone wall to block the flash flood. The same energy that was surrounding Paden's club now. With a heavy fall, the stone club slammed into one of the pincer lord's claws and knocked it aside. The dwarf's blow continued forward, striking the hard armor of the monster's face. Its stone carapace was crushed inward and orange-red blood leaked from the cracks.

It keened, all four claws waving wildly in pain. A prompt appeared in Paden's vision. Richter easily read the notification as well.

*Special Attack, **Crush**, was successful! Proficiency of 52%. +2% effect. 0 Proficiency Points obtained.*

After living through Paden's memories, Richter knew the importance of improving Proficiency. 50% was the minimum required to even trigger an attack. Anything less would just be a normal swing of your weapon. Fifty might not sound like a lot, but many warriors never even achieved that benchmark. Every Proficiency percentage after that gave a 1% boost to the attack, up to 60%. 61-70% increased the boost to 2%. 71-80% improved it to 4%. After that, the boosts to attack power grew much stronger until a Proficiency of 99% magnified a special attack by an astounding 250%. There were also other bonuses that came with high Proficiency, depending on the special attack being used.

This was the moment that Richter finally understood the true power of possessing combat expertise. He'd thought it was as simple as just knowing how to fight. The difference between a trained swordsman and someone picking up a blade for the first time. It wasn't only that, however. It was the bonuses to damage that could come through special attacks.

The move Paden had used was called *Crush*. It increased base attack by +5, but more importantly, magnified the damage to armor. The initial +5 damage was doubled to +10 against armor. The 2% boost to attack power from his 52% Proficiency wasn't enough to move the needle, but at higher Proficiencies, that increase might be enough to cripple an enemy in heavy armor. Even the 52% was

398

enough to add ten points of damage to Paden's attack and crack the pincer lord's hard carapace.

Richter had also learned that a warrior with combat expertise had greater potential than a Professional Warrior who bought a special attack with Talent Points. While a swordsman with a combat expertise and a Professed Warrior could both learn *Thrust*, the Proficiency of the Professed Warrior's attack would be stagnant unless they spent more Talent Points to level up the attack. The chaos lord knew full well that Talent Points were precious. No serious Professional would invest all of their points in just one Talent.

The swordsman with a Combat Technique however, could practice their learned special attacks at will to advance them. Achieving a higher Proficiency could level up the special attack. Paden, for instance, had received 0 Proficiency Points. That made sense because there was only an infinitesimal chance to earn any points with a Proficiency of 52%. Even if he had been lucky to gain a point, he'd only have earned one.

One could easily say that combat expertise was superior to combat Professions. That was a bit of a misnomer. The other side of that argument was that it took time and knowledge to excel in a Combat Technique. Paden has started his training at the age of four and after years of hard work was only now reaching the lowest rank of *Granite Breaker*.

It was obviously easier to just buy an attack if you managed to become a Professed Warrior. Without a teacher and the innate Talent to make the tutelage useful, even spending years on a form of weapon expertise might not yield meaningful results. One unexpected piece of Lore he picked up was that there actually was a correlation between skill affinity and the expertise to use that skill.

One of the primary reasons Olrich had cut trainees from his program was that their innate affinity for *Mace Wielding* was too low. Until someone reached skill level fifteen, they could not reach the first rank of *Granite Breaker*. The fact that Paden was able to fulfill the requirements at such a young age showed what a prodigy he really was.

Having lived through these memories, Richter also finally understood why Yoshi was always practicing the same moves over and over. He'd thought it was just about muscle memory. That was definitely part of it, but the half-sprite was also trying to achieve higher Proficiencies and gain more points to level up his special attacks. It would have been super helpful if Yoshi would have just told him that, but even though the man was only half-human, he was definitely full asshole. Richter turned his focus back on the battle.

Paden's first attack had hurt the pincer lord, but hadn't killed it. With its armor compromised though, he was able to land normal blows that chipped away at its health. When the cooldown on his special attack had elapsed, he used *Crush* on the crab monster's head again. This time, it completely ruined its face. The four-armed beast collapsed to the ground, dead.

All the trainees in the amphitheater banged their clubs on the ground in praise. Over and over, the thudding sounds gave voice to their admiration. None spoke, but they all looked at Paden with admiration. This was what a clan chief should look like, they thought.

Olrich waved his hand after a few moments, stopping the noise. Looking at Paden, he asked, "Are you ready?"

The other trainees started murmuring to themselves again. There was more? Paden had already killed a pincer lord in single combat? Wasn't this too ridiculous?

Paden looked back his teacher and, wiping some blood off his face, gave the same answer his father had given all those years before, "Maistir Olrich," and placed three fingers over his heart.

The old dwarf nodded and gave another order. Another thud reverberated through the small coliseum and Paden's next opponent charged forward. Richter watched as the dwarf used another special attack to defeat this enemy, this one better suited to dealing with a monster that specialized in ranged attacks. The third monster similarly required a third kind of special attack to defeat. Olrich had chosen monsters that each required a different usage of *Granite Breaker* to overcome.

When Paden was finally done, one of his shoulders was dislocated, his body was covered in scrapes and bruises and his left eye was swollen shut. Despite all of that, he stood tall. The other trainees could not restrain themselves to just silent applause this time. Their shouts and cries of praise were deafening. For once, Olrich did not restrain them. Instead, he placed one hand on Paden's head and the other on his heart. Energy flowed from the old dwarf into his protégé. Paden's pupils widened, his breath sucked in, and he *knew!*

CHAPTER 39

DAY 153 – JUREN 3, 0 AOC

*R*ichter came back to himself and was greeted by the flashing of multiple notifications. The first were the red of warnings. It said something that he'd gotten so used to bad news that seeing them didn't even make his neck tight.

*You are **Thirsty**! Healing effects decreased by 25%.*

*You are **Hungry**! Stamina regeneration decreased by 10%.*

Richter groaned in annoyance. At least the debuffs weren't as bad as last time. They didn't put him in imminent danger. He started to get up. That was when pain shot through him so hard that he wheezed involuntarily.

That hurt! Why the hell had just moving hurt? Curious, he turned his attention to the next prompt.

*Congratulations! You have progressed in a Combat Art! The mountain dwarf-based fighting style **Granite Breaker**! This fighting style ...*

Richter minimized the details of his new battle technique. As interested as he was in it, he was more interested in why it felt like he'd been beaten by a sock full of oranges. The kind that let 'em know who was boss, but didn't leave any bruises. He cycled through the windows and found another red warning prompt.

Your body has been altered to encompass the muscle memory needed to reach novice rank in the Combat Art: **Granite Breaker**. *These alterations have triggered a debuff.*

You are **Muscle Fatigued**! *For the next 10 hours you will experience extreme pain while moving. Your coordination will also be impacted. -50% to fine motor control. Decreases by 5% per hour.*

That explained it! Why was there always another damn debuff? Richter had pushed himself pretty hard in the past, but he'd never earned this one before. He was profoundly thankful for that fact. For how he felt, the damn debuff might as well be called "Gangbang Sore." He wanted nothing more than to just lay still but, despite the pain, he needed to drink. With a heavy groan, he rolled over and got to his hands and feet. He cupped some water and brought it to his mouth. It was only after drinking that he remembered an important fact about his hands and the residue covering them. Ultimately, he just shrugged. Like his granddaddy used to say, the time to worry was *before* it was in your mouth.

With the *Thirsty* debuff gone, he started feeling a bit better. Moving around still sucked, but it was what it was. Richter started crawling up the tunnel. It took him longer than it should have, and he even slipped a time or two thanks to his *Muscle Fatigued* status. It was a serious p in the a. Halfway up the tunnel, he considered ordering the golem to pull him the rest of the way but reconsidered, realizing the thing probably didn't know how to be gentle. Instead, he sent it to guard the cave entrance again.

When he was back in the main cavern, he took stock. Apart from the horrible soreness and the chafed feeling on his backside, he was doing okay. He'd found a reasonably safe place to stay. He'd successfully absorbed a Combat Art, at least up to the *novice* rank. He also had access to fresh water, shelter, and a dumb yet capable helper. All he really needed to do now was feed himself.

The obvious problem with that the only food he had was scorpion meat. The same food that had led to the creation of the poop cave. Even though he couldn't rule out that he'd picked up some weird magical microbe crawling the tunnels, his money was on the scorpions being the cause of his recent tragedy.

The question was, where had he gone wrong? Assuming that the flesh wasn't just poisonous to him, that left two options. Had he undercooked the meat? He'd basically just flash-fried the adult scorpion with his *Weak Flame* spell. Not really the best way to ensure your food was fully cooked. In retrospect, maybe someone that had gone to med school should have known that, but then again... he'd been so hungry!

That was the better scenario. The other was that the meat had just spoiled faster than he'd thought. That was obviously the worst scenario because it was all he had left to eat. Either way, he had to feed himself and all he had left were day-old monster babies.

After he'd finished evacuating his bowels, he'd had the wherewithal to store the bodies in his pouch. He'd only saved them as a last resort. Richter had fully planned to go hunting for something fresh. Now that he had this damn *Muscle Fatigue* debuff, that was off the table. With the accelerated demands of his Tier 2 body, he couldn't just not eat. He'd accumulate more debuffs and might be too weak to hunt something new. If that happened, he'd literally starve to death.

He just had to hope that the food poisoning was because of his poor preparation, and not that the meat was toxic or spoiled. The only thing that gave him any comfort was that he remembered feeling that sense of unease after eating the adult scorpion. It raised the chances of the poop cave's creation being because of his improper handling of the meat rather than a problem with the food itself. At least that's what he hoped. Remembering the torment he'd suffered and the indignity of... the Dangler, he hoped harder than he'd ever hoped before.

He had several uncooked scorpions left. One of them was going to be dinner. Before that happened, he needed to make a proper cooking fire. The first step was gathering up some kindling. There was an obvious lack of wood down here. What he did have were the remains from the scorpions' previous kills. The rotting remains. He wasn't looking forward to this for obvious reasons, but he didn't shirk from the task. Walking through the various caverns, he gathered any piece that looked like it would burn. Fur and hair were especially useful to him. Once he had a pile gathered, he pulled out one of the scorpions and cut a claw free.

Weak Flame ignited the remains, creating an extremely foul smelling, smoky fire. It was better than nothing. It would have been great to have a skillet and a stove. What he had instead was a golem. The Earth construct held the dead monster between its large hands. The flames licked the stone it was made of, but the fire was too weak to seriously harm it.

Richter had Sloth turn the claw periodically. He made sure not to have the meat directly in the flame. Anyone who had ever cooked knew that medium heat was always the safest bet. After watching the golem like a hawk for several minutes, he was awarded his second skill in as many days!

Congratulations! You have learned the skill: **Cooking.** *By preparing your first dish, you have started upon a journey that many banished gods considered the highest art. "The flavors of a meal are like the notes of a song. Each are finite, but in their combination, you may find the infinite love of god or..." True masters of this skill can prepare a meal that, when consumed, gives the might of dragons!* **+2% flavor of prepared dishes. +2% yield from ingredients.**

As often happened when he gained a new artisan skill, he could now assess more items. This time, a prompt appeared when he looked at the scorpion claw turning in the golem's hands.

You found an ingredient: Ironscorpion Claw Meat	**Ingredient Class:** Uncommon **Ingredient Quality:** Spoiled **Uses:** *Novice:* Chance to increase Strength by 1-3 points for 30 minutes

Looking at the prompt, Richter learned several things at once. One, he confirmed that the only meat he had left was spoiled. That wasn't a surprise. After growing up hunting deer in Georgia, you learned real quick to put meat on ice ASAP. If it wasn't cold weather, a buck would start to spoil within hours. The fact that he'd killed the scorpion two days ago and that it was only *spoiled* was good news. He was pretty sure that was thanks to the slowed entropy in bags of holding.

Learning the skill also gave him some new information about the "class" and "quality" ranks for ingredients. *Uncommon* meant it was the second-lowest-ranked class. Put another way, the meat could be helpful, but wasn't anything special. *Spoiled* quality meant there was a chance that cooking with it might trigger a debuff to the final dish and anyone that consumed it. He also now knew that cooking spoiled meat could make it safe. That wasn't good news overall, but it was a hell of a lot better than guaranteed sure sickness. His new skill should also give him a hint if the food was safe to eat. Unable to help his curiosity, Richter went into a side cave where he'd discarded the piece of meat he'd taken from the adult scorpion. As he read the prompt, he was horrified.

You found a dish: **Flash Fried Ironscorpion Meat**	**Dish Class:** Common **Dish Quality:** Inedible **Traits:** This disgusting reflection of poor life choices was only partially prepared in a magic fire. Raw in places, charred in others, it was also contaminated by the ambient magic used to "cook" it. It was *inedible* from the beginning, but several days of decay have made it a major health hazard. Whatever happens to the fool who eats this is well deserved. Hopefully they die before procreating.

Good god! He knew that the prompts were just a reflection of his own subconscious, but why did his subconscious have to be such a dick? Shaking his head, he pushed past his annoyance. Evidently, he'd found the reason for his explosive decompression. He'd also learned that using magic to cook things was evidently not the greatest of ideas. At least he had hope for his upcoming meal.

Richter went back and kept his eyes on the claw the golem was turning until its prompt changed from an ingredient to food. He still didn't have the golem stop for the next couple of minutes due to the *spoiled* status of the food. When he finally had the construct put his meal down, the prompt didn't disappoint.

You found a dish: Slow-cooked Ironscorpion Claw	**Dish Class:** Common **Dish Quality:** Edible **Traits:** This monster claw was slowly cooked... and then overcooked. This precaution has neutralized the food's *spoiled* status, but it has also decreased the strength and chance of any positive effects by 25%. **+1 to Strength for 22 minutes.**

A feeling of vindication spread through him. Not able to wait, he ripped the shell off, and enjoyed the aroma coming off the pink meat. It probably didn't smell great, but to him, it was heaven. He definitely could have let it cool a bit before he dug in. He decided the burned tongue was worth it. His debuff disappeared and he was ready to conquer the world!

Basic needs met, Richter found a comfortable place to sit. He rested his back against the wall while he digested and went through his new prompts.

Congratulations! You have progressed in a Combat Art! You are now a ***Novice*** *in the Mountain Dwarf-based fighting style:* ***Granite Breaker!*** *This fighting style incorporates* ***Mace Wielding*** *skills.*

The following bonuses are given to Novices of this form:

+10% Attack Speed when using a Mace or Club

+10% Damage when using a Mace or Club

There was a small disclaimer after the first two perks of learning *Granite Breaker.*

Know This! Similar bonuses from different fighting styles do not stack.

It looked like the 10% boost to attack speed he got from wielding a dagger wouldn't double if he was holding a mace in the other hand. The next prompts discussed special attacks. Just like with the sprite fighting style, *Sutinn Sumotri,* he was given a choice of special moves to learn.

There are 5 Special Attacks for the Novice rank of this Combat Art. As a Novice, you may now choose 2!

CRUSH (Mace Attack)		
+5 Damage. Doubles total damage against an enemy's armor.		
Cost: 20 Stamina	Cooldown: 45 seconds	Expertise: 0/250

FLOWING ROCK (Mace Attack)		
A defensive move greatly increasing the speed of your weapon to knock projectiles out of the air.		
Cost: 30 Stamina	Cooldown: 45 seconds	Expertise: 0/250

POWER BLOW (Mace Attack)		
Focus all of your power to greatly magnify your attack +15 Attack		
Cost: 35 Stamina	Cooldown: 60 seconds	Expertise: 0/250

STONE MACE
(Mace Attack)
Hold your mace against a nearby rock source to coat your weapon in this stone, tripling its mass. The perceived weight is the same for the wielder, but your attacks will hit as if carrying the extra weight of stone. Lasts for 3 strikes. Requires 5 seconds of uninterrupted contact with a large quantity of stone.

Cost: 30 Stamina	Cooldown: 50 seconds	Expertise: 0/250

ACID STRIKE
(Mace Attack)
+5 Acid Attack
Corrosive Effect will continue for 3 seconds

Cost: 25 Stamina	Cooldown: 35 seconds	Expertise: 0/250

Seeing the special attacks, it was obvious that not all Combat Arts were the same. The wood sprite's combat form was focused on fast attacks and penetrating defenses. *Granite Breaker* was focused on powerful attacks and crushing your enemies. Which wasn't to say that the dwarven fighting style wasn't without grace.

Ever since he'd woken up, his conscious mind had been integrating with his new muscle memory and unconscious knowledge. Even the way he was moving around, albeit still nearly crippled by pain, was different. Several minutes had gone by before he realized that he was balancing more on the balls of his feet as he walked. When he turned, he lowered his knees slightly to keep his center of gravity in an optimal position for battle. He wouldn't fully know the extent of the alterations until he was in battle, but he felt the changes within himself.

Another boon of living through the memories of the expertise book was that he understood what these "Free" special moves actually were. It meant that achieving the rank of *novice* in a fighting form would guarantee him a 50% Proficiency in the techniques that he chose, as long as he focused appropriately when he performed them.

The other techniques were not beyond him, but he would have to struggle and practice in order to manifest them. For *Stinging Storm,* the sprite Combat Art, he unfortunately wouldn't be able to learn the special attacks he hadn't chosen, not without further instruction. After living through Paden's memories, however, he now knew everything he needed to obtain a strong Proficiency in each of the five. In time, he could know them all!

Richter turned his gaze back to his options. *Crush* was obviously useful. In his fight with the adult scorpion, it might have been able to get through its metal carapace. The option to crack an enemy's armor was tempting. *Power Blow* might have worked as well. While *Crush* was great for destroying armor, the damage it caused to an actual opponent was much less.

Flowing Rock would have been a great help in the Mausoleum battle. Being able to knock aside arrows and crossbow bolts was quite literally a life saver. He was seriously tempted to grab it immediately.

Stone Mace was also crazy. Even though he was living in a world of magic now, physics still existed. He hadn't seen anything to prove that F didn't still equal MA. Increasing the mass of his weapon by a factor of three would triple the force he could put behind his blows. In addition to increasing the effect of the attack, it could push through an enemy's defense. While *Power Attack* sounded very, well powerful, it still wouldn't do much if it were blocked or diverted.

Acid Strike could also be very useful. Adding an extra element of damage to a hit could make the difference between victory or death. On the other hand, he was a Professed Enchanter. He could imbue his weapons with acid damage given enough time and materials. The attack had the shortest cooldown of the five options, which was tempting, but truthfully, all of the attacks had a rather short cooldown. Between the instant activations, short cooldowns and powerful effects, it was obvious why Combat Arts could give an overwhelming advantage in battle.

Richter scanned over the options, and decided to go with *Crush* and *Stone Mace.* He was already strong and had his magic to do direct damage. One of the biggest dangers to him was an enemy with a high armor rating. As far as *Stone Mace*, its weakness was that it wasn't feasible for being used in the middle of a battle. If he had some warning though, having the extra mass could let him one-shot some enemies. Used in conjunction with *Crush,* it could be a game changer. He made his choice.

Congratulations! You have learned the Combat Techniques: **Crush** *and* **Stone Mace.**

Continued use of these techniques in battle will allow you to advance both to more refined states, including but not limited to increasing damage, decreasing cooldowns and adding new effects.

The icon in his interface that showed his Combat Arts had updated. He now had four battle techniques, two from the *Stinging Storm* and two from *Granite Breaker*. His body still ached, but he had a full stomach, a mace, a dagger, and two swinging nuts. What could hurt him now?

CHAPTER 40

DAY 154 – JUREN 4, 0 AOC

*R*ichter woke up to a high-pitched screeching. He sat up quickly, the ichorpede dagger clutched in his hand. He was down in the small cave with the stream, and it was completely black. His magic lights had long since burned out. Casting *Simple Light* conjured a small globe to float by his head. Nothing was immediately jumping out at him, but he still heard crashing noises from above. He crawled up the tunnel with his dagger in hand, wondering what fresh new hell The Land had brought him.

The golem was fighting what looked like a pink worm covered in bristly grey hair. The salient point was that the damn thing was fifteen feet long. Before that moment, Richter might have wondered what a worm could possibly do to a creature made out of pure stone, no matter how big it was. Turns out, the answer was whatever it damn well pleased.

The worm had wrapped itself around the golem like a python. The construct's arms, body and neck were encircled. Pound for pound, Sloth was probably stronger, but the monster was successfully restraining it. The golem kept struggling. Richter's helper wasn't completely suppressed, but the few blows it managed to land only momentarily compressed the monster's body. Only a few HP dropped after each hit from the golem.

The worm, on the other hand, was causing serious damage. As Richter finished crawling out of the tunnel, he saw curved black spikes flashing in and out of its body like switchblades. The claws, teeth, talons or whatever they were hit hard enough to knock golf ball-sized pieces of clouded quartz off the golem. As each piece fell, it turned into plain grey dust.

Richter knew how high his construct's defense was, so he was surprised the worm was able to decrease its health so quickly. Then he realized the fact that he'd converted it from a simple Earth Golem into a Flowing Rock Golem had increased its susceptibility to piercing attacks, but it was still a tank. Gritting his teeth, he used *Analyze* on this latest enemy.

Name: Ravager Wurm		Disposition: Vicious	
Level: 52		Tier: 2	
Ravager Wurms are the evolved form of a lesser creature, the Raider Worm. Ravager Wurms can heal from most wounds by folding their flesh in on itself. The monsters have no true head or tail, but can form a mouth at any point on their body. They also possess hardened spikes that can penetrate armor and stone and can be moved to any part of their form. These creatures are associated with Life magic and possess regenerative properties.			
STATS			
Health: 3,692/3,711	Mana: 410/410		Stamina: 784/796
ATTRIBUTES			
Strength: 35	Agility: 47		Dexterity: 51
Constitution: 370	Endurance: 79		Intelligence: 41
Wisdom: 33	Charisma: 14		Luck: 22
SPECIAL ABILITY			
Regeneration – Possesses weak health regeneration Malleable Flesh – Can contort its body to heal from wounds and form orifices as needed			

It was Tier 2. It was Tier 2! In addition to having a higher level than him, Richter was blown away by its crazy high stats. A health of nearly four thousand? It had the highest health of any creature he'd seen except for the mauler. His recently slain mortal enemy had been a boss of the Labyrinth. Richter had wrapped his head around the fact that it was so strong because it came from the Labyrinth. There had been comfort in knowing that he'd be safe from such extreme danger outside of that horrifying alternate universe.

That hope had just shriveled up. This monster not only had a high HP, it had regen capabilities. The only other creatures Richter had come across with that ability were trolls, and they were an absolute nightmare. Even as he watched, its health increased by a tick. Its *Regeneration* special ability was at play. The fight had only gone on for less than a minute and the golem's health had decreased by nearly 10%. Meanwhile, the wurm's HP bar was almost full. It was obvious who would win this battle if nothing changed. Can't have that, Richter thought.

His mind scanned his available options and he settled on an Earth spell. The golem should have a certain amount of resistance to its own Basic Element. Richter raised his hands and a green glow surrounded them. Seconds later, a swirling wind enclosed both his golem and the ravager worm. Inside the storm, talons, teeth and claws could be seen for a split second before disappearing. This was none other than his Earth spell, *Weak Rending Talons*.

Hold it still, Richter mentally commanded. The AoE of the spell was ten feet, and he'd made Sloth the center of it. To his satisfaction, the combat log showed the Earth magic was hurting the wurm, but his golem was indeed immune to the low-ranked Earth spell.

*Ravager Wurm takes **5 points** of Slashing damage*

*Ravager Wurm takes **4 points** of Slashing damage*

*Flowing Rock Golem takes **0 points** of Slashing damage (base damage 6 – 6 for Earth Resistance)*

*Ravager Wurm takes **6 points** of Slashing damage*

The damage from a single hit was minimal compared to the thousands of points of health the wurm had, but more than a dozen strikes landed every second. It lost a hundred points of health in the first two ticks of the spell. The wurm screeched in anger, but it had wrapped itself around the golem like a boa constrictor. That positioning had originally served to restrict Sloth, but now it worked against the Tier 2 monster. The construct had two strong grips on its body and wasn't letting go.

Richter started to smile. Maybe this would be easier than he'd thought. It might have high health, but it didn't have anywhere near the strength of the mauler. Still, he didn't let up. *Rending Talons* was doing serious damage, but it only lasted eight seconds. At most it would take down a tenth of the monster's HP. He wouldn't make the mistake of underestimating his enemy.

It would have been great to spam *Rending Talons* nine more times, but the cooldown and mana cost made that impossible. Also, through the storm of claws he could see the tears closing thanks to the wurm's regeneration. The two edges of each wound were smooshing together like playdoh. When they were done, the wound had disappeared. That was why the chaos seed chose to cast *Weak Acid Sphere*.

It was also a rank one Earth spell, but the damage type was completely different. Maybe the wurm wouldn't be able to deal with corrosive damage. Green light surrounded his hand again, and then a lime-green sphere shot from his fingers. The globe was translucent, and as it flew you could see a bubbling solution sloshing back and forth inside of it.

It struck the ravager worm close to what looked like its middle and splashed over the creature. The acid only caused 4-6 points of damage, but it was a DoT and would erode the wurm's body for the next ten seconds. Some acid splashed on the golem as well. This cost Sloth a slow drop in health, but only one point every few seconds. Richter could live with that. The main point was to compromise the body of the wurm.

It looked like it was working. This time, its flesh didn't seem to be able to mitigate the injury. The combat log showed that the damage was only 2-3 points per second, most likely due to some innate resistance the monster had, but he would take it. Richter had a full-on smile on his face now as he prepared his next spell. He was already imagining the great harvest material that might come from a Tier 2 creature. He decided to try Fire magic next.

This entire time, the monster had been struggling to escape. All of a sudden, it stilled. Instead of trying to break free, its body instead began to vibrate like a rattlesnake's tail. Richter frowned at it, but still raised his hand to cast his next spell. Before he could begin the incantation, a black blur flew out of the monster's body and shot right at him.

It was only Richter's Agility of 37 that saved him from losing his hand. With unerring accuracy, the ravager wurm had fired one of its moveable claws at him. It rotated through the air like a spinning saw blade. If the chaos lord's Agility hadn't been nearly four times that of a normal man, it would have cut right through his wrist. As it was, he only managed to avoid most of the attack, instead letting the blade slice through his palm. The cut extended from his pinky to the middle of his hand. Red blood splattered in an arc, and pain shot up his arm and into his brain. Richter fell back with an angry cry.

"Arrgggh!"

He clapped a hand over the wound, trying to staunch the blood.

*You have sustained **29 points** of damage!*

*You are **Bleeding**! You will lose **8 HP/sec** until the bleeding is stopped.*

Richter cursed himself for being cocky. The wurm shivered again, and he immediately dove to the side. Landing in a roll, he narrowly dodged not one but two spinning spines that scored deep into the rock behind him. Richter was under no illusions as to what would have happened if either had hit him center mass. Namely, pain, death, and his body ultimately being turned into worm shit while his soul was cursed to wander as a tortured shade for all eternity. He decided it'd be best to avoid that if at all possible.

The chaos lord moved so the golem was between him and the wurm it was holding. The monster immediately began attacking his construct again, and the rain of small pebbles continued from its body. Richter nodded rapidly in anger while blood dripped from his clenched hand. Okay. Okay. You want to play it soft, we play it soft. You want to play it hard... we play it hard.

He murmured a quick Life spell and his flesh began to reknit itself. The bleeding continued, but it decreased by the second. Richter waited only until he had full use of his fingers again before issuing another mental command to his golem.

Hold that bitch up!

The golem raised both arms up like it was shouting "Ya Ta" and gave Richter a clear shot at the acid-compromised section of the wurm. Its flesh was already repairing the edges of the chemical burn. That's enough of that, Richter thought.

Using both hands this time, he dual cast a spell of Light. Both hands moving in concert, and with blood still streaming down one, he cast *Minor Sunbeam*. It was one of the only rank 2 spells that he knew. Both ends of the ravager wurm thrashed about, but the section between the golem's hands remained taut. A bar of incandescent white energy shot into the acid-weakened portion of the wurm's body. At the same time, Richter gave a mental command. Pull!

Between the previous damage and the white-hot fire of his dual cast *Sunbeam*, the monster's body was almost burned completely through. With a hard pull, the golem finished the job and ripped it in half. The Sloth might not have been smart, and it couldn't really fight for shit, but it pulled monsters apart *real* good.

Richter blinked back the headache that came from such a massive expenditure of mana. The spell had cost him nearly five hundred mana, more than half of his maximum pool. It was worth it. The two ends of the monster fell limp in the golem's hands. He would have smiled despite his impending migraine, but something made him frown.

*Ravager Wurm takes **1244 points** of combined damage!*

The monster had taken a huge amount of damage, but it wasn't enough to kill it. Truth be told, Richter had been hoping that its HP would fall to zero when it was ripped apart. It still had more than half of its health left though. He took a worried step forward. If that was true then, why was it just hanging limp in the golem's-

Before the chaos lord could even finish his thought, the severed halves of the monster came back to life. The two ends shot toward each other and something horrific happened. What had been the "head" and "tail" of it fused together so that it was once again an unbroken length of pure horror. Even worse, it used one of its moveable claws to cut one end of itself free from the golem's grasp. That end fell to the floor, leaving a torn and bloody hunk of flesh in the Earth elemental's hand. The newly freed end had stopped bleeding before it even hit the ground. It flopped once before forming a new mouth, and then it shot at Richter as fast as a striking snake.

What happened next couldn't be described as a conscious thought. Seeing the attack coming at him, something in Richter took over. He collapsed backward and rolled feet over head. While he was mid-maneuver, he grabbed his iron-sheathed club from the ground behind him. He finished the roll on his feet and was already swinging his weapon. With perfect timing, the iron head connected with the attacking monster in a swing that would have put the great Bambino to shame. The entire maneuver took barely a second, and was definitely not something Richter could have managed two days ago. It was the training of his Combat Art.

Richter strikes the **Ravager Wurm** for **25 damage**!

The chaos lord didn't stop and wonder at his new battle prowess. His training, Paden's training, would not allow for such a pathetic mistake. Instead, he jumped forward and stuck the snake again. He mentally ordered the golem to wind the wurm up like a garden hose while he fought the other end. His ichorpede dagger found its way into his off hand and a deadly dance began.

If Richter hadn't absorbed the fighting techniques of the dwarves he would have died in that moment. If he didn't have superhuman attributes, he would have died. If he hadn't trained with Yoshi for months, despite the half-sprite being a sadistic bastard, he would have died. If the monster wasn't restrained on one end, he would have died. As all those things were true though, he beat the snot out of it.

Richter used his Combat Arts as the situation required, switching between *Stinging Storm* and *Granite Breaker* as needed. Using both led to him making mistakes, and more than once he bled because of it. As time went on though, he started trusting his Combat Arts more, and the damage to his enemy accumulated. The wurm didn't know it, but he was using it to train.

His golem had turned out to be useless in fully immobilizing the monster. Each time Sloth tried to get a better grip, the Tier 2 wurm would almost break free. Richter couldn't risk fighting the monster unencumbered, so he ordered the golem to just keep one end of it immobile. If it got completely free, it would kill him quickly. He continued fighting and slowly whittling down its health. Far too slowly.

After several minutes, he'd taken off another several hundred HPs, but it still had more than a thousand health. Every second, it regenerated more. In contrast, Richter had only 20% of his stamina left. He'd found the serious flaw in using special attacks. His stats were respectable, but widely spread out among the nine Primary Attributes. He just didn't have the stamina for a prolonged battle at this level.

In contrast, the monster's stamina bar was more than 80% full. Baring his teeth in frustration, the chaos lord recognized just how foolish his earlier cockiness had been. Fighting an ascended monster one-on-one was not a simple task. Even though he'd gotten a bump in his stats, it seemed like this Tier 2 monster had gotten a larger one. That, or its higher level, made a larger difference than he'd expected.

Richter had to use the *Harden* power of his Bloodline more than once. He'd saved himself several grievous wounds by instantly increasing his body's defense. Each time his skin only remained tougher for a minute, however, and his Bloodline Points were swiftly running out.

He wouldn't have dealt any damage at all if not for his crafting and enchantments. The malleable iron head of his club was able to directly clash with the wurm's sharp talons. The claws could cut into rock, but his weapon held up. Even where the metal was scored, he should be able to smooth out the gashes once the battle was done. Malleable iron was truly amazing. If he'd been fighting only with the original bone club, it definitely would have been cut to pieces when he parried the wurm's attacks.

His gauntlet was even more impressive. It covered his off hand and held the ichorpede pincer in a reverse grip. In a way, he was wielding three weapons at once. While stabbing the worm only caused a temporary gash, punching it with the powers of Earth and Water made it reel back in pain. Its body must have been somewhat resistant to crush-type damage, because it kept coming back for more. Still, his armament let him stay in the fight.

He hadn't made it through the exchange unscathed. More than once it had lunged at him and formed a mouth as it did. If Richter had ever had a problem with not having enough nightmares, that would no longer be the case. The wurm would form a vertical mouth down its length that was at least two feet long, and lining that maw were more of those impossibly hard black spines that it had shot at him. It was easy to understand how they would shred whatever they clamped onto.

Richter had been hurt several times during the fight and blood leaked from various wounds on his body. The worst injury came when his *Simple Light* spell elapsed. All of a sudden, the cavern was plunged into darkness. Focusing on the fight, he'd forgotten to cast another spell. There was no blackness in the world above that compared to the darkness of the earth.

That mistake nearly cost him his life. He swung his mace wildly, and managed to deflect one of the monster's attacks. The next hit him in the stomach like a sledgehammer. The force was so great that vomit flew out of his mouth and small tears leaked out of the corners of his eyes. If not for his Ring of Spell Storage, that would have been the end of his story. Richter blindly pointed his hand and released *Weak Sonic Wail.*

Rings of invisible force flowed out from the ring and rippled over the wurm's body. The rank one spell wasn't enough to cause it serious harm, but it still made the beast recoil, shrieking. Richter spat the rest of the sour sick from his mouth and cast *Darkvision.* Everything within fifty-odd yards of him snapped back into focus. With a snarl, he started attacking the wurm again.

The two continued to trade blows. He hit it again and again, but Richter knew he was losing. His attacks chipped away at the wurm's health, but between its massive HP pool and regeneration, there was no way he'd be able to outlast it. Every blow he landed was a pinprick. Every hit he took, however, shaved off a serious amount of his health.

The melee battle was decided in a split second. Richter landed a heavy blow, but almost died as the wurm lunged at him in return. This time, it formed two mouths. He avoided the first but was surprised by the second. Only shoving his club directly into the second maw kept him from having his arm bitten off. It cost him his weapon though, and all he had left was the ichorpede dagger and gauntlet.

The chaos lord rolled away and glared at the monster. Sweat ran down his marbleized muscles. His chest heaved like a lathered horse. In defiance of all his efforts, the monster still had over one thousand health. Even if he still had his club, he'd come to the end of his physical capabilities. The wurm had taken everything he had to give and could still take more.

That meant he had to try something else. Something that he'd avoided until now. He needed to use a new spell of Deeper magic.

Thought magic made him cold and unfeeling. Spirit magic made his personality spiral out of control. It was also addictive. Deeper magic had serious consequences. Only his mental training with Alma let him endure using its power without losing control. Even then, if he overdid it, Deeper magic would overwhelm him. The last time that had happened he'd nearly slaughtered his friends and allies, which was the reason that was also the last time he'd used the most insidious of Deeper Magics, the magic of Blood.

Richter hadn't even experimented with this spell before, but now he didn't have another option. The Tier 2 monster was just too strong. He needed to take risks. The chaos lord formed his mindscape and began to summon his mental defenses. Alma had been trying to train him to always have the psychic bulwark in place, but he just hadn't managed that level of mental control yet. When he entered his mindscape, real time slowed down compared to his perceptions. That was good, because Richter was in for a shock.

His mindscape had always appeared as a clearing in a forest. In the middle of it was the mental representation of his psychic defenses. It had been a single-story castle, more like a fort, truth be told. He'd also always been alone in his mindscape unless Alma was with him or he was engaged in a Thought battle. Neither of those things were true anymore.

His cube-like fort had turned into a proper castle. It was two stories tall, and more than four times its previous size. Even the wooden gate at the front was no longer simple wood but instead was stout oak banded with black iron. The stones were tightly fitted, and he doubted even a flood would let water seep through. Everything about the place shouted, "Keep Out!"

The larger shock was that he was no longer alone. Patrolling the ramparts were men-at-arms. They were dressed in leather armor and held spears. More than a dozen walked the top of the wall. Their eyes roamed his mindscape searching for threats. Richter walked up to the wooden door of his Thought castle. Without needing to touch it, the gate opened by itself. Two figures stood by the entrance. Richter took a closer look at one of the men-at-arms, and a prompt appeared.

Basic Thought Construct. Level 1. Capable of Defense and Surveillance. Attack +1. Defense + 1. Health +10. The most basic of thought constructs, they will protect your mindscape and monitor for hostile intrusions.

The constructs wouldn't talk to him, but they would follow simple commands. Richter remembered his Thought battle with the lich Singh, though "one-sided ass whooping" would probably have been a better description. The lich had not only possessed a mental bulwark several stories tall, but he'd also had a bunch of undead in his mindspace. They had followed the undead mage's commands and had attacked Richter. They must have been Singh's thought constructs. Somehow, he seriously doubted that Singh's constructs had been *basic*.

Snapping out of his introspection, Richter realized he'd been distracted by the changes in his mindscape. In a panic, he snapped his attention back to the ravager wurm, but the monster had barely moved. With a sigh of relief, Richter realized the time dilation had increased along with his mental defenses.

This had to be a result of his evolution. The prompt had said that his mind, body and soul would all evolve from Tier 1 to Tier 2. He hadn't known what that meant, but this must be part of it. Not only had his mental defenses improved, but he now had these constructs to help keep him safe. His mind flashed again to just how much stronger Singh's mindscape had been and he shuddered. Was Singh's mindspace a result of his eldritch magic? Did that mean the lich had ascended to Tier 2? Even higher? Based on what he was seeing now, the lich had definitely been a tier higher than him, maybe more than one. It was no wonder the undead creature had thought Richter's attack was laughable. The guy had been one tough sonofabitch. Either way, Richter had chopped his head off. In the end, that was probably all that really mattered.

The chaos lord shook that off. He needed to finish this fight, not dwell on the battles of the past. After situating himself on the top floor of his mind castle, he cast *Vitality Puppet*. In the outside world, blood-red power began to surround his fingers. In his mental landscape, an ocean of blood flowed in from all directions. It splashed against the walls of his mental defenses, thankfully lower than his boundaries. Richter knew from horrible past experiences that the more Blood magic he used, the higher the red ocean would rise. If it rose past the level of his walls, and reached his mental avatar, he would be lost to the Deeper magic.

He also learned in that moment that using stronger Blood Magic would place a greater toll on his mind. The blood-red ocean was way higher than when he used *Tame*. The "water level" was far lower than when he had used the blood crystal, but not by much. Using higher level Blood Magic was no joke. *Tame* was only level one and *Vitality Puppet* was level ten, so he'd expected there to be greater risk when casting it, but not this much! If even *initiate*-ranked Blood Magic was this much of a threat to his psyche, what would happen if he used anything stronger?

For now, with Richter's strengthened mental defenses the effect of the Blood Magic wasn't a threat. That was what was important. For now, his mind was protected, and he was safe.

That was not a claim the wurm could make.

CHAPTER 41

DAY 154 – JUREN 4, 0 AOC

*I*t would have to wait a few seconds for any more of his attention though. While Richter had been harnessing the Deeper Magic, his body had paid the price. To cast Blood magic, blood must be paid. Rents appeared in his skin like those made with a surgeon's scalpel. His blood rose into the air, draining from his body at a rate that was sickening to see. All the while, his own vital fluids fed the deep-red energy surrounding his hands.

By the end of the spell, his health had dropped two hundred points and his mana had fallen by one hundred and twenty-nine. The ravager wurm had continued to snap at him, only the golem's tight grasp keeping it at bay. Still, in the first seconds of the spell, it had remained safely several feet away.

The wurm wasn't smart enough to know what was about to happen, but it was a Tier 2 beast. It had a greater connection to the world and greater instincts than a lower-tiered monster. Even the scorpion adult had sensed the danger of Deeper magic; how could this ascended beast fail to do the same? It could feel the dangerous power that Richter was harnessing. With an instinctual drive, it knew it couldn't afford to wait any longer.

Using several of its razor talons like blender blades, it cut several feet of its body off, finally freeing itself from the golem's grasp. It was still ten feet in length, more than enough to be deadly. As soon as it freed itself, its body coiled like a snake; it was only a scant second from an attack that would kill the chaos lord.

That moment was enough to end its life. In a cosmic parlance, the monster got a shitty silver medal. Meanwhile, Richter finished his spell, earned himself a gold, and was about to be balls deep in the prom queen.

It was the first time the chaos lord had cast *Vitality Puppet* so he wasn't sure what to expect. As soon as he targeted the wurm though, he could "feel" it, the same way he could feel his own body. Looking at it about to spring at him, he now understood the strange makeup of its biology. The reason it could contort and reform its flesh was that its body was basically like a sausage, with a semi-firm casing surrounding a fluid core.

It had a few organs, but they could float to any part of its body at will. Naturally, that would make landing a killing blow nearly impossible. The only other things inside of it were the two dozen black talons that could extend and retract like switchblades. He even saw how it could compress the fluids inside of its body to shoot out a blade under high pressure.

Richter could feel it attempting to fight off the influence of his magic, but the monster failed and his spell locked in place. Both absorbing that new knowledge, and his spell taking hold, occurred in the space between seconds. Feeling that in the next second it was about to uncoil like a striking viper, he finally understood Neo.

He stared at it impassively and pronounced judgement, "No."

The Tier 2 monster's attack was frozen solid by the Deeper Magic of Blood. At the same time, the rents in Richter's flesh closed like they had never been there. The pain remained and his health was still damaged, but the external signs of casting *Vitality Puppet* were gone. Richter was physically and mentally exhausted. He still couldn't help but stare at the monster in fascination.

He'd always thought that *Vitality Puppet* would basically be a stronger version of *Charm*. The Life magic spell convinced someone you were their friend. They believed it so strongly, they would even attack their former comrades. *Charm* was one of his most powerful spells, but it definitely had its weaknesses. You couldn't convince someone to knowingly kill themselves. They also might resist orders that went against their core beliefs. A virtuous person wouldn't kill a child, for instance. In fact, giving orders that were anathema to the charmed person's nature was a surefire way to break the spell.

Vitality Puppet was not like that at all. Unlike *Charm,* the monster did not look on him affectionately. Even though he'd cast the spell, if he hadn't forced it to remain motionless, it would still have attacked him. Now that the spell was cast and the order was given though, keeping it in place required only a minimal bit of focus. Richter had complete control over the beast. He could still feel it trying to break free of the Blood magic, but it was well and truly fucked.

Richter absently dual cast *Slow Heal,* as he watched it quiver only a couple feet away. Then he exerted his will, and froze the creature in place completely. Even the tremor that had been reverberating through its body ceased. It might as well have been a statue. With it fully immobilized, he decided to test how far he could push the spell.

He discovered the wurm would follow nonverbal orders. Moving it around was like ordering his own arm to move, only requiring slightly greater focus. Having it move across the cavern was easy. He then had it move in more convoluted patterns. It quickly became clear that the more complicated the command, the more of a lag there was between his orders and when they were carried out. Simpler orders were clearly better.

He tried another tactic and told it to attack a wall, but without any specific direction as to how. It carried out the command without hesitation. Loud thuds sounded out as it threw its body and talons at the stone surface. The chaos lord nodded to himself. He wouldn't be able to micromanage how a blood puppet acted, but he could give general orders that would be followed. Richter ordered it to be still again.

He tried to make the wurm cease its regeneration, but that failed. *Vitality Puppet* couldn't stop an involuntary process. The wurm couldn't stop healing any more than Richter could stop his heart from beating.

With the monster now under his control, he commanded it to lie still a dozen yards away from him. He then had the golem stand between him and the ravager wurm. After that, he settled into a lotus pose and tried to meditate. It wasn't easy. His body was exhausted and his stamina was near zero. Still, he tried. He had a decision to make.

Richter had two options for what to do with the monster. The first was to *Tame* it. He didn't have a lot of hope that would work, in light of its high level. Even if it did, he knew almost nothing about Blood Magic. For all he knew, there might be a bad reaction between *Tame* and *Vitality Puppet*. If the ravager wurm slipped his control, he wanted to be in top shape. That was why he intended for all of his status bars to be full and to restore the golem's health before doing anything.

If *Tame* didn't work, option two would require him to push the control of *Vitality Puppet* to the max. That also risked the wurm regaining control. Richter sincerely hoped option one would work. Not only because it'd be nice to have another ally down here. It was because option two would be... decidedly messy.

For the next several minutes, Richter regenerated his mana and restored the golem to top condition. He also used his Combat Art, *Stone Mace*. It was a bit amazing to see rock flowing from the cavern floor to cover his weapon. Even more astonishing, his perception of the mace's weight didn't change at all. The entire time he was recovering, he still kept an eye on *Vitality Puppet*'s duration. There were only twenty minutes until the spell elapsed. When that happened, ten feet of Tier 2 monster would be up his ass again.

When five minutes were left on the spell, Richter was ready. He and the golem approached the monster and he started casting *Tame*. Blood red light surrounded his hand, and he laid his fingers on the ravager wurm's skin. A red prompt greeted him.

*You have failed to **Tame** the **Level 52 Ravager Wurm**!*

No huge surprise, but still disappointing. He'd only had a max 35% chance to tame it. That wasn't even taking into account the monster's innate magic resistance. He had to imagine that a Tier 2 beast would have a stronger defense to magic than a non-ascended creature. Whatever the reason, he'd failed. Now the spell was on cooldown for the next eight hours. With only minutes left before the wurm took back control, he knew it had to die. Richter cast *Soul Trap*. After that, he tried to do something simple and just thought, "Die."

It did jack squat. Richter hadn't thought it would work, but he was just trying to avoid the mess of what came next. With no other choice, he gave an order that no sane creature would ever follow. Insane or not, this time the monster followed his directions. Each and every one of the ravager wurm's claws stuck out of its body at once. The blades were in two lines, positioned one hundred and eighty degrees from each other. That was the first order Richter gave. The second was just as simple.

"Cut."

The blades moved forward and back in a sawing motion. The wurm's body was bisected in mere seconds. Red-orange sludge fell from the wounds and its health fell by hundreds of points. Its regenerative skin tried to keep up with the damage, but the dozen or so blades wreaked too much havoc. That was when Richter gave his third order, not to the wurm, but to his golem.

The rock construct grabbed the top half of the monster's skin and started to pull. In starts and stops, the Tier 2 monster's body opened like a peeled banana. Its internal fluids flew everywhere, and it screamed like a tea kettle. After connecting to its body, Richter now knew those sounds were created by microperforations that formed in its skin. Sloth kept pulling until it was half-flayed. The sheet of skin landed with a wet *squelch*.

Even with half of its body denuded, the wurm was still alive. The tenaciousness of a Tier 2 creature associated with the Life element was insane. Its health was lower than one hundred now, but the digit in the one's column kept flickering. Despite half of its body being torn away, and with all its vital organs exposed, the creature was still attempting to heal itself.

Looking at the inside of its body, Richter could now see its few internal organs. In particular, he could see the pulsing beat of its three hearts. This thing was truly nearly impossible to kill, seeing as how it could heal from most wounds and move its vital spots at will. Even if one heart was destroyed, it had two backups. It also lacked a distinct brain. Instead, there were neural clusters that could work together. If enough were still chained in a row, severed segments could independently operate. This thing was a nightmare.

Under his control however, all of its options were gone. His Blood control was so great that he could even force the organs to bunch up and present themselves. A masculine part of him felt like after such a hard-fought battle, the ending should be equally climactic. A feminine part lied and said the climax wasn't that important. Like any man, Richter chose to believe that. He started hitting the wurm's gooey bits with his mace really, really hard.

Splat. Splat! SPLAT!

After three heartfelt blows, rainbow light spiraled through the air. The wurm quivered a final time and then, at long last, lay still.

CHAPTER 42

DAY 154 – JUREN 4, 0 AOC

*You lack a soul receptacle that can contain a **Luminous** soul.*

That particular red prompt was a flick to the teabag. His Enchantments could do a lot with a *luminous* soul. Regrettable or not, he couldn't change the fact that he could only make up to *common*-ranked soul repositories. If his Light magic was up to skill level fifteen, he could have unlocked the stronger form of his *Create Soul Stones* spell, but even casting Light spells nonstop, his skill hadn't advanced. It was probably because *Simple Light* and *Far Light* were only level one magics. Sadly, all he could do was watch the rainbow light vanish into the ceiling.

What remained of the wurm stank something awful. Richter didn't mind at all. He was already thinking of the harvest he could collect. His mind was also on something else though, and that was the power of Blood magic. *Vitality Puppet* had let him remove the free will of a powerful creature. If he hadn't known the spell, he honestly didn't know if he would have survived against the ravager wurm.

The spell was only level ten, the weakest level for an *initiate* rank spell. Still, it was amazingly powerful. What was bothering him was what would happen if he ran up against someone more skilled than he was in the Deeper Magic. Richter was suddenly relieved that there weren't more Blood magi running around The Land. If even this low-level spell could incapacitate something like the ravager wurm, what could a cadre of sanguimancers do to an army? As long as he was the only one with access, it gave him an incredible advantage. Richter wasn't fool enough to believe that would always be the case, however.

Shaking his head, he checked his prompts. To his surprise, his experience deficit got a noteworthy decrease.

You have slain a Level 52 **Ravager Wurm (Tier 2)**. *You have gained 5,782 XP.*

XP deficit remaining: -3,836,426

Just killing that one Tier 2 monster had given more experience than all the scorpions put together. It was nothing compared to what he owed, but except for the mauler, it was way more than he'd ever gotten for killing a monster before. It couldn't be due to just its high level; it was probably also because it was a Tier 2 monster.

Not factoring in the Talent Points he'd bought with his experience, it took about a million XP to advance to the next level for him. Before this, he'd wondered how someone could ever accumulate that much. It looked like the answer was to hunt higher-tiered game. If he were able to kill more monsters like this, he'd only need two hundred to level up again. Richter started to understand that high-tiered monsters weren't threats so much as strategic resources.

They were also, he hoped, good eating! Richter greedily examined its flesh. He was starving!

You found a Cooking ingredient: **Ravager Wurm Flesh**	**Ingredient Class:** Unusual **Ingredient Quality:** Poison **Uses:** You lack the *Cooking* skill to prepare this ingredient

Aaaand it looked like he was going to stay hungry. The skin and blood registered as a poison to his *Cooking* skill as well. He stared regretfully at the more-than-a-dozen feet of monster laying in front of him. With his new dimensional space, it might have lasted until the curse ran out. If he was a highly skilled cook, it might have yielded something amazing. Any doubt he'd had about the importance of the *Cooking* skill vanished as he stared hungrily at meat he couldn't use. With resignation, he realized that even if he hunted something down here, he might not be able to eat it.

"This is it," he bemoaned. "The moment my mother always warned me about. When the fact that I can't cook might really let me starve to death." Even in another universe, her being right still grinded his gears.

When you couldn't eat it, there was there was usually only one other thing you could do with a dead body. Luckily for both of them, *Harvest* gave him a third option.

> The base cost to *Harvest* the remains of a *luminous* soul creature is **20 Bloodline Points.**
>
> The cost to *Harvest* a **Tier 2 creature** increases final BP cost by **25%.**
>
> Final Cost: **25 Bloodline Points.**
>
> Do you wish to harvest the *Ravager Wurm*? Yes or No?

Harvesting a *luminous* soul cost twice as much as a *common* soul. The fact that it was ascended also increased the price. Richter had enough points to spare. He just hoped it worked.

> Attempting to Harvest... Success!
>
> Petrifying Ghost Harvest Bloodline has obtained an **uncommon** drop: **Mimetic Flesh**

"Yes!" he shouted, shaking a fist in victory.

His purple-green stat bar dropped by twenty-five points. He read the description of what he'd harvested.

You have Harvested: **Mimetic Flesh**	**Item Class:** Uncommon **Weight:** 0.6 kg **Traits:** Mimetic Flesh will adopt the ideal configuration of any flesh it is placed upon. Placing this on your skin will heal most injuries. It will also neutralize most diseases and poisons if used quickly.

The harvest looked like a bandage made out of the wurm's wrinkled white skin. When Richter ran his fingers an inch over the surface, the flesh rippled in response. It was like it was trying to bond with him. Curious, he picked it up, and it contoured to his hand. Not finding any injuries, it formed back into a lump and sat in his palm.

The prompt said it could heal him. Not just wounds, but diseases and poisons. Some might wonder why a Life mage would need something like this. That person must never have been in battle. His magic could take care of most of those issues, but in a battle, the MP required to cast Life magic could be better put to use by killing his enemies. There were also times when his magic didn't work. One of the main reasons he'd avoided using the Shadow Realm, even when his life was in danger, was that the monsters there carried diseases resistant to Life magic. Now that he had another option to cure himself, it opened up the possibility of using his Ring of Shadow Shift again. His *Harvest* power was amazing.

Surprisingly, *Harvest* had only consumed about 10-15% of the ravager wurm's body. That was good news and bad news. It meant that on larger creatures he'd have to use his Bloodline multiple times to get all the available resources. On the other hand, maybe he'd get more than if a creature was consumed all at once. It also gave him the chance to try again if he failed the first time.

He'd burned too many Bloodline Points during the fight. He had to rest for several hours before using *Harvest* again.

Attempting to Harvest... Failure!

His second attempt only left some ooze behind, but the third one succeeded. Even better, it offered a much better drop!

Attempting to Harvest... Success!

Petrifying Ghost Harvest Bloodline has obtained a **scarce** drop: **Ravager Wurm Blood Essence**

A clear sphere appeared out of the degraded remains. It floated up to Richter like every other harvest. When he gingerly grabbed it, the skin of the globe felt slightly sticky and soft. He was pretty sure he could pop it if he squeezed hard enough. The globe was half-filled with a slightly glowing liquid the same orange color as the wurm's blood. He had no idea what he was supposed to do with it, but a prompt appeared.

You have Harvested: **Ravager Wurm Blood Essence**	**Item Class:** Scarce **Weight:** 0.1 kg **Traits:** Blood essence can be used as a spell component, Crafting material or Alchemy ingredient, in addition to a host of other purposes.

The prompt didn't offer too much information except for showing him the glowing orange liquid might have a bunch of different uses. To Richter's surprise thought, two more windows appeared right after.

Congratulations! You have discovered a substance that can improve your Bloodline: **Ravager Wurm Blood Essence**.

As this material is not consistent with the Death energy of your Bloodline, the original **10 points** of Bloodline Growth will be heavily penalized and reduced to **2 points**.

To evolve your Bloodline to the next rank, you must gain **100 Bloodline Growth Points**.

Do you wish to consume the energy of the **Ravager Wurm Blood Essence** to improve your Bloodline? Yes or No?

Before Richter could even be shocked by what he'd read, another window appeared.

Quest Update: **Chaotic Flux**

You have discovered a powerful resource that can help nourish your **Tier 2** body!

Would you like to absorb the power of the **Ravager Wurm Blood Essence**?

Yes or No?

Richter whistled softly. His bloodline was even more powerful than he'd thought. Not only did it make him deadlier, it also offered him paths to greater power. In addition to the immediate boost to his Attribute Points, Richter was starting to understand why higher-tiered beings were so strong. It wasn't only that they got more points per level. It wasn't even the evolution of their skills. It was because The Land itself offered them more power if they were strong, brave and foolish enough to seek it out. Power and danger really are close bedfellows, he thought. It hadn't occurred to him that using *Harvest* on Tier 2 creatures could help him take advantage of his Chaos body's flux period. It kindled an even greater desire to hunt the monsters down.

That was for later though. Right now, he had a decision to make. Looking at the two options, Richter had initially been tempted by the evolution of his Bloodline. It had already saved his ass a couple times, and making *Harvest* stronger was super tempting. The reduction in Bloodline Growth Points was discouraging though. Two points would barely make a dent in the one hundred he needed to evolve it.

Adding the essence to his Tier 2 body, on the other hand, increased the chances of him getting an awesome bonus when the quest was completed. He already had two points from the bean pods and could probably get another six to eight Tier 2 Evolution Points if he used the iron beans stored in his Pouch of Holding.

The only problem was, just like with the bean pods, he had no idea what the effect on his body would be. He had no desire to be turned into a wurm for instance, or for his organs to just be floating freely around his body... or for his mouth and sphincter to be inter-changeable. Still, he only had twenty-two days until the flux period was over, and the evolution prompt had promised the reward would be random, but powerful. He decided to use the blood essence on the quest.

Quest Update: **Chaotic Flux**

Tier 2 Points absorbed: **8/100**.

2% chance of skeletal system being iron-strengthened

6% chance of gaining passive health regeneration

92% chance of Quest Failure

22 days until flux period ends.

Absorbing a total of 100 Tier 2 Body Points will trigger an automatic change to your body.

The blood essence had gotten him another 6%! Not only that, but the bonus was awesome. He could get passive health regeneration. He had no idea how much his HP would regen, but anything could be a game changer. It might even help him fight off poison or disease, both of which had laid him low several times since coming to The Land. Eagerness kindled within him. He needed more points. He had to finish this Quest!

In addition to getting him more points, absorbing the *Harvest* drop did something else. It spurred Richter to action. He'd been thinking defensively, just wanting to wait out the curse. He'd even come to believe that death might be an acceptable, if not ideal, scenario after Singh's magic faded. Now though, an old and familiar desire kindled in his heart.

How could he just cower in this disgusting cave? Adventure and treasure were waiting for him out there! True, the monsters were out there too, but that just made it more fun. He was southern after all. It was time to roll the dice!

CHAPTER 43

DAY 154 – JUREN 4, 0 AOC

*E*ager or not, hungry or not, he wasn't about to leave the scorpion's cave until he was ready. Namely, until all of his stats, including his bloodline, were fully replenished. He also wanted to see what he could make out of those twenty-some-odd super-hard talons he'd taken out of the monster.

His magic light winked out, and for the first time, he didn't rush to cast another. In the darkness, a white smile grew against his black skin. His eyes were trained on a faintly glowing trail leading out of the caves. It was the trail of the ravager wurm. A trail that, sooner or later, would lead back to its nest and more sweet, sweet points. His grin grew even more shark-like, and anyone seeing it would have felt the fear of a monster's hunger. Don't worry, he thought to the creatures he'd be hunting. You'll be joining your mama soon.

It took the better part of a day, but he was able to *Harvest* the rest of the ravager wurm. Even with the points he'd invested in his Constitution, he only regen'd 7.4 Bloodline Points per hour. Sadly, he only had one more success, and it wasn't blood essence.

> Attempting to Harvest… Failure!
>
> Attempting to Harvest… Failure!
>
> Attempting to Harvest… Failure!
>
> Attempting to Harvest… Success!
>
> Petrifying Ghost Harvest Bloodline has obtained an **uncommon** drop: **Mimetic Flesh**
>
> Attempting to Harvest… Failure!

The lumpy white tissue went into his pouch along with the other one. During the time he'd been waiting for his Bloodline to replenish, he also restored the durability on his golem, bringing it up to fighting shape. It was almost time to hunt.

To help with that, he'd also used the sharp claws from the ravager wurm's body. He'd been able to harvest twenty-four in all. Most went into his pouch. He'd found they made good throwing weapons. Eight were used to augment his club.

After unwrapping the malleable iron, he examined the gouges it had suffered when fighting the ravager wurm. The amazing material "healed" itself as he pushed the edges together. Once the bone head was bare, he carefully hammered the talons through the club with a rock. The claws were so sharp they easily passed through. He positioned them so the spikes would protrude from every cardinal angle, and turned his club into a spiked mace.

You have created a Spiked Ironbound Bone Club	**Item Class:** Uncommon **Quality:** Well-Crafted **Durability:** 72/92 **Attack:** +19 **Weight:** 1.8 kg **Traits:** This club has been made from the large leg bone of an unknown beast and malleable iron. Though the iron head is strong, the bone has a fracture in it and risks being destroyed if too much pressure is applied. It has further been augmented with the talons of a Tier 2 Ravager Wurm. These ultra-sharp spikes aid greatly in penetrating armor. **Special Trait:** Ignores 5 points of Defense

The addition had increased the attacking power of the mace by more than 50%. Driving the spikes through the bone had decreased its overall durability, but it was worth it. The weapon had gained a new special trait! His Crafting skill had allowed the weapon to utilize the special properties of the ravager wurm's claws. In addition to its high attack, it had also gained an *Ignore Defense* ability. Richter couldn't wait to bring the pain.

While that was good news, the hours of waiting had earned him another debuff. He was so tired of these!

*You are **Hungry**! Stamina regeneration decreased by 15%. Emotional control decreased by 10%.*

He needed food. With the new needs of his Tier 2 body, he couldn't afford to just wait around. Especially with Singh's magic hanging over his head. There were still two to three more days before the *Curse of Eternal Servitude* dissipated. If he could just find some meat, he'd have everything he needed to outlast Singh's spell. Then he could start making his way toward the beacon again. He hefted his spiked mace. It was time to go meet the neighbors.

Richter went to the front of the cave. He could already feel the hunger gnawing at his belly. He hoped following the wurm's trail would yield something, but he didn't relish going into battle with his nerves frayed and his stamina regen hampered. That was why he decided to try something. Something he wished he didn't have to do. It just felt wrong somehow.

Desperate times.

Gold light surrounded his fingers and he cast *Call Weak Small Creature*. If there was a small animal anywhere close, it would come to him and follow simple commands. He'd cast it before but nothing had responded. This time, lucky or not, a ferret-like creature crawled out of a small crack. It had all-black fur and three eyes. It was about nine inches long. The creature looked up at him expectantly, waiting for orders.

Quick as a flash, Richter grabbed it. It didn't even struggle, not even when he put his hand on its neck. With a sharp twist, he broke the three-eyed ferret's neck. Even though he'd felt a certain kind of way about using his magic to lure an innocent creature, he couldn't argue that the method worked. Until the warning prompt appeared.

*Woe and Bad Tidings! You have violated the essence of your **Life magic!** Life spells are unavailable for the next 1 **hour!** Repeated instances of anathema will lead to severe consequences! This is your only warning!!!*

And like that, Richter lost his ability to cast Life spells. Blinking in disbelief, he tried to cast one anyway.

*You have suffered **Spell Backlash!** Mana regeneration is frozen for 10 minutes! Spell casting is blocked for 5 minutes!*

Pain exploded in his mind, intense enough to blur his vision. He staggered backward. That was *not* a good idea! While he squeezed his head with both hands, Richter remembered an old conversation with Hisako.

The chaos lord had asked about capturing the souls of summoned creatures. If it were possible, it'd be a great boon to his Enchanting Profession. Hisako had told him that summoned creatures would always disappear, along with their souls, except in certain special instances, like summoning a demon within a pentagram. Even then, there were serious consequences to attempting what he proposed. She hadn't elaborated more, but he had just found out about at least one of the consequences she'd warned him of. Richter wondered if his reticence to use his Life magic like this had been because, at an unconscious level, his magic had been warning him off.

Richter looked at the dead body. He'd dropped it when the pain from the spell backlash had triggered. He wondered if the greater sin would be eating it now, or leaving the carcass alone and possibly letting it go to waste. He searched his feelings, and even though his rational mind said the damage was already done, the chaos lord ultimately decided not to eat the three-eyed ferret.

He placed it in his pouch, thinking he'd find a way to dispose of the body respectfully at some point. Getting an even stronger punishment from his Life magic was something he keenly wanted to avoid. A part of his mind wondered if this was another check and balance of The Land. Would the power he garnered always come with strings attached? The Deeper Magics had an immediate price to pay when he used them, but maybe the Basic Elements had a cost as well. Maybe it was just more subtle. It was something to think about.

Now that he had the debuffs, he didn't dare leave the cavern yet. If he couldn't heal, that was a serious detriment in a fight. If he couldn't even cast spells or regenerate his mana, *that* was a death sentence. Instead, he waited for the spell backlash to elapse. Once that was done, and the pain in his head had faded, he started practicing his combat forms.

He started with *Granite Breaker.* Again, he was struck by how forceful the dwarven technique was. It was all about overpowering and overwhelming. Which wasn't to say it lacked nuance, that wasn't true. It didn't just use powerful swings. The hilt of the weapon came into play as well. Controlling the power of blows was just as important as the strength behind them.

He moved on to *Stinging Storm,* which was more graceful. It was about never-ending movement and body positions as much as sword swings. Richter worked not only on refining both Combat Arts, but melding them together.

The hour passed fairly quickly and his debuff disappeared. Lesson learned, Richter moved out using *Stealth.* The golem used its *Hidden Earth* special ability to reduce its presence. When it wasn't moving, it melded almost seamlessly with the rocky surroundings. The chaos lord started following the ravager wurm's trail.

With his *Tracking* skill activated, the monster's tracks lit up in his vision. Truth be told, he might have been able to follow it even without his skill, as it left a slimy residue behind. For the next hour, Richter followed the trail through the tunnels. The passage he was following got larger and larger, until it was the size of a subway. Small tributaries branched off it periodically.

After an hour, the trail finally deviated from the larger tunnel.

The main artery continued on, but the monster's trail turned to the left, through a large crack in the rock. The side passage was more than large enough to let him through. The entire time, Richter had been using *Stealth,* and he'd had to stop a couple times to regen his stamina. He'd also had to move a bit slowly, but that had let the golem keep up. Sloth had been able to go toe-to-toe with the Tier 2 creature, but there was no denying Richter could have moved faster without the golem.

Richter continued down this new tunnel; it got smaller and smaller until he was forced to crawl on his hands and knees. Like before, he was relying on *Darkvision,* so his line of sight was limited. He stopped and listened periodically. After another hour, he finally started hearing sounds. It wasn't the hissing steam noises he'd heard from the ravager wurm. What he heard were voices crying out and screams of pain. Specifically, "Help! Help! Banished gods, they're eating me! Help!"

There was more than one voice.

CHAPTER 44

DAY 155 – JUREN 5, 0 AOC

*S*ix months ago, Richter might have rushed forward. There
were people screaming for help after all. Countless life-
and-death experiences had cured him of his knight in shining armor
complex. He was a warlord now. A nice one, he'd like to think, but a
warlord and a killer nonetheless.

It wasn't his job to save everyone. Not everyone even deserved
saving. Before he inserted himself in this situation, he needed more
information. What was more, the words weren't being spoken in
Common tongue. They were a language he hadn't heard before, but
that his Gift of Tongues ability translated and named. The words
were in orcish.

He'd run into a great number of races since coming to The Land.
Some of them had had classic fantasy names, and had fit the stereo-
types they'd had on Earth. High elves, for instance, were pretty much
pompous dicks. Even in the village, they were aloof and looked down
on others.

The wood sprites, on the other hand, weren't small, fairy-sized
creatures. They were xenophobic samurais that loved killing anyone
else that wandered into their territory. And their character was
different from forest sprites or hill sprites. The point was, he didn't

know what to expect from orcs. Even if he'd met some before, he couldn't assume the entire race was all the same. That certainly wasn't true for humans, so why would he think it was true for anyone else? He needed more information. With screams echoing down the tunnels, he moved forward cautiously.

As he got closer, the sounds grew louder, and he finally heard the monsters themselves. He also started smelling blood. It had the coppery tang of blood, but also another more acrid scent mixed in. The chaos lord kept climbing through the tunnel until it ended in a cavern with swirling lines of brown crystal tracing through the grey stone walls. Unlike the scorpion cavern, it wasn't a warren of inter-connected smaller caves. It was one large amphitheater, with stalactites and stalagmites lining the ovoid space like monstrous teeth. In the center was what Richter could only call an orgy of blood and flesh.

Four humanoids with dusky green skin and sharp ears were facing off against a nest of monsters. *Analyze* showed him they were orcs, and were all levels twenty to twenty-five. The ones still on their feet were Professional Warriors. Five or six were lying on the ground, being eaten alive while they screamed. Twice that number were already dead and in pieces. Discarded torches lay on the ground, some already extinguished in puddles of blood, but enough were still lit to illuminate the scene. Richter dismissed *Darkvision* and saw the cave was bathed in orange flickering shadows. The firelight revealed a grim scene.

Worms were feasting on the bodies of fallen orcs. Some even crawled through ribcages of the fallen. Sounds of bestial pleasure filled the cavern as the worms in the lair gorged. The luckiest of the fallen orcs were already dead. The rest screamed in pure terror.

Richter looked at the beasts with a critical eye. Only a few were the size of the ravager wurm. Most of the others were smaller, measuring five to seven feet in length. *Analyze* showed that they were called raider worms, and they were Tier 1. He realized these must be what the ravager worms had evolved from.

The raider worms seemed content to consume the bodies of the fallen. One orc woman, an orcess, Richter supposed she would be called, was trying to crawl away. Unfortunately, her left leg was snapped at an unnatural angle and the horde of beasts were between her and the four Warriors. She continued to cry out to them for help, but they just looked back grimly. They might not have feared the Tier 1 raider worms, but no less than three Tier 2 ravager wurms were slowly approaching the fighters. The Warriors had been backing up, but now their backs were literally against the wall.

Richter took in the scene. There was another large exit from the cavern, almost one hundred and eight degrees from his position. It was much larger than the small tunnel he was in. Clearly, the other exit was the main egress. He was tempted to just leave the orcs to their fate. He almost started to do just that. As soon as he stepped inside the cavern, however, the most peculiar sensation overtook him. The mist lord had only felt it a few times before, but it was unmistakable. Somewhere in the cavern, among all the blood and pain, was a source of Chaos.

He had no idea what the Higher Power was emanating from. Richter only knew of a few things that possessed Chaos, and all of them were interesting. The first, and potentially most dangerous, option was that one of the orcs might be a chaos seed. Alternatively, there might be a chaotic particle, or even a chaotic shard, somewhere in the cavern. The ironspine scorpions had built their nest around the iron plant and the stream. He could definitely see other monsters making a lair around a source of Chaos.

Either option was enough for him to get involved. One would let him talk to someone else from home. He might even be able to use his new status as a chaos lord to gain more power. A source of raw Chaos would give him some much needed Chaos Points. He couldn't just walk away.

The question was, what to do now? He had to kill the monsters and save the orcs. Any of them could be from Earth. The ones on the ground were already a lost cause, but he could save the Warriors. Even if the chaos seed was one of the fallen, saving the fighters could still be helpful. He might gain some temporary allies that could lead him to civilization. That could lead to supplies, safety and maybe even a map that could lead him to Xuetrix's damn flashing dot. If the orcs didn't want to play nice after he saved them, well he had an answer for that too. His hand gripped the haft of his bone club tighter.

Richter used the *Ghost* function of his bloodline. Fourteen Bloodline Points tripled his Concealment for one minute. After adopting *Stealth,* he turned into a hazy shadow so far as anything else in the cavern was concerned. Once again, his Bloodline showed its power, but also that it had a high cost. He could only keep *Ghost* going for five minutes before his BPs were completely spent. It would take at least two to three minutes to get into position. There wasn't time to waste.

He told the golem to use *Hidden Earth.* It concealed itself and started easing forward. As Richter moved closer, he started to come up with a plan. There were about thirty Tier 1 raider worms. *Analyze* showed they ranged in level from single digits to the low thirties. No monster could be taken lightly, but thankfully, the worms lacked the regenerative properties of the Tier 2 ravagers wurms. With their smaller bodies and lower attributes, they might not even be able to pierce the defenses of his golem. The real threat were the wurms.

Each of the Tier 2 monsters had a status window similar to the one he'd fought. They ranged from level forty-two to fifty-three. The big kahuna was his target. The last fight had shown that he didn't have much in his arsenal that could take out a ravager wurm, much less three. That was especially true if the apex monsters could bring the entire lair of Tier 1 raider worms into the fight. He had to use the magic of Blood.

The two of them kept creeping into the cave. In a movie, there might have been ominous music slowly building, but in reality, his stealthy approach was only accompanied by the screams of the fallen orc woman and the slurping feeding noises of the worms. All the other fallen orcs had been killed. To him, that was good news. He could still feel the Chaos energy in the cavern.

Richter circled around to the left while the golem moved to the right. The three Tier two monsters continued to threaten the orcs, barely held at bay by raised shields. The orc woman was finally silenced when a worm clamped its mouth around her face. With a sharp jerk it tore her head off, and a gout of purple blood sprayed across the stone floor of the cavern.

The wurms finally made their move. The whistling sounds they'd been making the whole time rose to a fever pitch. All three shot forward, dagger-like talons extended from their bodies like horns. One of the orcs roared in response. He was the only one wearing plate armor and holding a tower shield. To Richter's surprise, blue energy extended from the shield in all directions. It made a wall that blocked the attacks of the three ravager wurms. The shield bearer was forced backwards with a grunt, and large cracks extended out across the blue barrier, but he stayed on his feet. More importantly, the attacks of all three monsters were stopped cold.

The wurms recoiled and prepared to attack again. The other orcs didn't remain idle, however. One swung a double-headed axe with a guttural shout and red light extended from his weapon. He triggered his Warrior Talent *Savage Blow*, and a blade made of angry ruby energy extended eight feet past the head of the weapon. At the same time, a third warrior swung his metal mace and the other sliced his sword through the air. Every strike was accompanied by the use of a Talent, and magical power shot toward their enemies.

Seeing all of this, the chaos lord stopped in spite of himself. This was his first time seeing a team of combat Professionals working together. The power they wielded put the fighters of the Mist Village to shame. Richter had no doubt that these four could carve through a platoon of his people. Even if they were taken down eventually, they would harvest a terrible number of lives. What was just as impressive though was the coordination between the four Warriors. The shield bearer dropped his force field at exactly the right time to not impede their attacks. All their blows also struck the same enemy in roughly the same spot.

The targeted wurm lost half of its health and flew back across the ground. The magical wounds carved deep into its body and its orange blood sprayed all around. The cumulative attack caused serious damage but, unfortunately, not enough to kill. The four Warriors attacked the other two wurms, praying they could kill them before the injured one rejoined the fray. Their original target writhed in pain, but was already regenerating. Richter could see its flesh was trying to push together to stop the blood flow. As impressive as the attack had been, it wasn't enough.

The Warriors had significant powers, but they couldn't contend with higher-tiered monsters. The strongest wurm shot three talons out in quick succession. The orcs were forced to abandon their attacks and defend themselves. Before the plate-wearing orc could position his shield, one of the whirling blades found its mark. Two were blocked, but the third cut deeply into the defender's side. It sank completely into the man's body and remained embedded. Purple blood flowed and the fighter wasn't able to keep in a pained cry. Both sides had loosed their opening salvos and claimed blood. The three orcs and two ravager wurms started trading blows, but the monsters' high health and regenerative properties showed what the outcome would ultimately be.

Richter was happy the monsters were occupied. It let him and the golem get closer. He hid behind a large stalactite that was within thirty yards of the ravager wurms, the maximum distance of *Vitality Puppet*. He'd made it into the fray without being detected, even though he'd had to spend another 14 Bloodline Points to keep his Concealment high. What he needed now was a distraction. A mental command to the golem was all it took to bring some chaos into the raider worms' orderly little massacre.

Sloth dropped its *Hidden Earth* ability and used *Hurl Rock*. A boulder materialized in its hand a moment before it threw like a pitcher on the mound. The powerful attack struck one of the Tier 1 worms and turned it into orange mist. The projectile hurtled through its first victim and wounded three more of the anaconda-sized worms. The rest of the monsters looked up from their bloody feast to see who would dare attack them in their own lair. The golem gave them an answer.

It ran into their midst and used *Stone Punch*. Its huge stone fist descended like the wrath of an angry god. It pushed through the body of another worm like it was made of jelly. The monster was pulped and an impact crater was left in the rocky ground. More than two dozen worms started whistling like tea kettles as they dove at the Earth creature. The raider worms weren't nearly as powerful as the Tier 2 ravagers, but they still had large talons. The construct kept fighting, but its health immediately started to fall.

It had served its purpose. The only light in the cave was coming from the sputtering torches. As powerful as Blood magic was, it still showed a telltale glow when Richter summoned it. For those five seconds of cast time, he was like a beacon in the dark. If he was attacked, not only would the spell be disrupted, but he was risking a feedback with Deeper Magic. He couldn't even imagine the consequences of that. At a minimum it would deprive him of his life, and with the curse still active, his soul as well. He needed to be able to finish the spell at all costs. Thankfully, the orcs did their part.

Richter was positioned behind the wurms, but in direct eyeline with the Warriors. They couldn't see him behind the stalagmite, but they did see the blood-red glow. The fighters didn't know what to make of it. The fact that a monster made out of clouded quartz was attacking the worms was even stranger. As insane as it sounded, help had come to them in the deep dark! They launched a ferocious attack on the wurms, thinking that salvation had somehow found them. They didn't trust Sloth, of course, but anything that relieved the pressure on them was a tool that could be used to win.

The chaos lord finished his spell and once again slashes appeared on his brown skin. Blood flowed from the rents on his body and his health dropped by two hundred points. His mana dropped by more than a hundred. The magic descended on the alpha ravager wurm. It struggled against the spell's power and Richter's own will, but it succumbed just like the last one had. Richter wasted no time ordering it to retreat.

To the orcs' surprise, and the surprise of the other wurm, the alpha pulled back. Richter could have ordered it to attack the monster next to it, but he didn't trust the orcs. They needed to stay occupied for a bit. So while the other wurm continued its battle against the Warriors, Richter ordered his blood slave to kill the one that was still healing.

Without hesitation, it dove at the wounded monster with all the speed of a Tier 2 predator. It struck the still-healing wound made by the orcs' attacks and literally ripped the other monster in two. This didn't destroy the wurm completely though. Both halves started attacking Richter's blood slave. His controlled monster fought back. Each of the wurms stabbed their talons into each other's bodies as fast as possible. In seconds, orange ichor was raining like a small storm. The sounds of tearing flesh filled the cavern. The chaos lord turned his attention back to the Tier 1 worms.

In just seconds, the golem's health had fallen by over a hundred points. If it wasn't for Sloth's high defense, it would have already been destroyed. Still, the innumerable attacks from the two dozen worms were wearing it down. The golem wouldn't last much longer. As far as Richter was concerned, it didn't need to.

The battle had been split into three sections. The four orc Warriors fighting their wurm, the blood-controlled alpha killing its former comrade, and the largest section, Richter and his golem against the Tier 1 monsters. The worms might have been a lower tier, but they still weighed more than a hundred pounds each and had a strength greater than an adult man.

Richter healed the golem. The Earth construct couldn't do anything more than stand there, weighed down by the sinuous bodies of the worms. It was basically a punching bag, but that was good enough for now. The chaos lord summoned reinforcements and evolved them.

*Know This! Your spell Akaton Evolution has evolved your **Saproling** into a **Whip Vine Elemental**, a rank 2, **Uncommon** Evolution. This is 1 of 4 possible evolutions. Max Tier of evolution for this creature is Tier 1. There are 3 other known evolutions: Thorn Saproling: (common rank), Hardwood*

Saproling: (common rank), White Arborast (unusual rank) Attack increased by +7. Defense increased by +5.

Special abilities:

Burrowing Tendrils *– Can sends attacks underground to attack from beneath*

Briar Patch *– Makes a defensive mesh of sharp thorns that surrounds the Whip Vine Elemental; the patch's thorns are coated with a stamina poison*

The saproling he'd summoned had originally looked like a large badger made out of vines and branches, but now its body looked like a Venus flytrap. It forced roots through the rocky ground, losing its ability to move around. At the same time, a circular wall of two-inch-long thorns sprung up around it. The tip of each was tipped in a blackish-green residue. Richter had finally unlocked the fourth evolution of his saproling. There was no doubt it was more powerful than the base creature.

His chokespore arachnid evolved into a new form as well. Just like with his saproling, his evolution into a chaos lord had unlocked a new evolution. Luck was with him and it changed into one of the strongest forms!

*Know This! Your spell Akaton Evolution has evolved your **Chokespore Arachnid** into a **Springdrill Spider**, a rank 2, **Uncommon** Evolution. This is 1 of 5 possible evolutions. Max Tier of evolution for this creature is Tier 1. There are 3 other known evolutions and 1 unknown evolution: **Solvent Spider Queen**: (common rank), **Mesmer Spider**: (common rank), **Cinder-spore Arachnid** (common rank), unknown (uncommon rank)*

The two-foot-tall spider doubled in size. Its forelegs now ended in spears with broadhead-like points. Its abdomen lost the fungal spore holes and turned thin and sleek. With a hard shake, a new set of legs popped out of its thorax. The entire thing shouted one word: "dangerous!"

Attack increased by +8. Defense increased by +3. Speed increased by +6.

Special abilities:

Armor penetration – +25% Attack vs armored targets

Lunging Jump – Double speed during jumps

Richter ordered both creatures to attack. Tendrils shot up through the ground, raking the worms' bodies with hardened thorns. Somehow, the whip vine elemental could even burrow through solid rock. The spider dove forward so fast it blurred. Two worms were raked with deep wounds before it even landed. It then set to attacking anything within reach.

The spider's hardened legs easily penetrated the monsters' bodies and more orange ichor stained the rocky ground. The summoning had only taken twenty seconds, but the golem's health had already dropped down to 60%, despite the healing. With the intervention of the summoned creatures, some of the worms were pulled away and the golem could get back on its feet.

Richter didn't stay out of the fray. After making sure the orcs and Tier 2 monsters were still occupied, he went in swinging. The spikes on his club easily cut through the worm's bodies. There was a kind of symmetry in using a ravager's talons to rip apart the monster's less evolved cousins. Most of the worms were level twenty. They would have torn him apart when he'd first come to The Land, but that Richter was only a pale shadow of his current power. Every blow was powered by his sixty-seven points of strength and hit like a hydraulic press, splattering his enemies. Each swing of the studded mace ripped through the worms' bodies like they were made of gelatin.

Even with that fighting prowess, his plan wasn't to kill the dozens of monsters by hand. Even with his newly summoned allies and golem, that was a risky proposition. He was just making room for the next phase. The raider worms were only the appetizer of this battle; he had to plan for the main course.

Richter's head was splitting from having depleted nearly all his mana. Almost any other fighter or mage would have had to rely on their mana regen. The chaos lord wasn't known for his patience.

As soon as he'd cleared the monsters within immediate reach, Richter called on the power of Earth. Green light surrounded his fingertips and a sphere of forest-shaded light sprung up around him. The mana expenditure nearly bottomed him out. If not for his high magic regen, he wouldn't have had enough MPs to enact the last phase of his plan.

With a migraine and the edges of his vision blurry, he cast one final spell. Ruby light surrounded his fingers and connected with the bloody remains of more than a dozen orcs that had been slaughtered by the monsters. The wood sprites had a saying, *"Tsini cha nu majresushi."* It translated into, "Always fear a Blood mage, and always kill him first." The worms were about to learn why.

Battle-drunk laughter spilled out of Richter's throat as streams of ruby light rose from the bloody ground. In his mindscape, more blood flowed toward his mental fortress, but his Tier 2 mind was more than safe behind its high defenses. His magic was siphoning mana from the life blood of the orcs. Each blood source could restore one mana per second for every skill level of Blood magic Richter possessed. At skill level twenty and with so many bodies, his mana bar filled as fast as pouring water into a glass. Not only did his MPs get replenished, but the max capacity of his mana pool increased at the same rate. For the next hour, he was able to harness more mana than he ever had before. He stared out at the worms assaulting his Earth shield with an almost sexual anticipation.

"Let's play."

Weak Rending Talons, Weak Sonic Wail, Weak Acid Sphere, Weak Thorns Underfoot!

Every offensive spell he had in Earth magic shot from his finger-tips. They might all be rank I spells, but that didn't reflect the damage they could wreak against opponents that couldn't fight back. The worms desperately tried to get through his defensive shield, but that would have taken long seconds they just didn't have. With every spell, the worms were injured further. His summoned creatures and golem literally tore them into pieces. Richter knew the pain and anguish of wanting to kill a mage that was just beyond reach. It was the most frustrating thing in the world to not be able to attack someone that was hurting you with abandon. Now that he was on the other side of the coin though, he realized this wasn't half-bad!

The last spell he cast was *Grease,* catching half a dozen of the worms in the AoE. After that, he stepped backward while casting. His back touched his shield, banishing it. Showing perfect timing, he finished the incantation for *Fireball* at the same time. A sphere of pure flame shot from his hands and detonated, burning three worms and killing one of them outright. The edge of the explosion set the grease alight and the monsters that had been trying to escape joined their brethren in the hell of being burned by a merciless god. Like the Chinese, Richter had a lot of hells.

The monsters that were still able to move whistled like tea kettles at seeing their quarry finally come out from behind his defensive wall. Richter was still moving backward though. One hand was casting another spell and the other presented his middle finger. A new spell shield sprung into existence around him. The ruby-red streams of Blood mana passed through the Basic Element walls like they were nothing, but the monsters were stopped cold again. It was true that *Weak Static Life Shield* had both lower HP and defense than *Weak Static Earth Shield,* but there were only a few raider worms left. Most importantly, he could now cast Life spells through his defense.

Healing magic flowed onto his summoned creatures, bringing them both back up to 100% health. The golem couldn't be healed that way, but with its high defense, it was fine for the moment. Over the next minute, his minions slaughtered most of the remaining worms. A few were left for their master who dropped his spell shield again and waded back into the melee. Again and again, he cast *Soul Trap* on monsters that were near death, netting him another seven *common* ranked souls.

Every last raider worm got that treatment, except for one. Richter chose the lowest ranked worm that was still alive, a level twenty. Blood-red magic surrounded his fingers. He cast *Tame.* A higher-level monster would obviously have been stronger, but it would also have been harder to control. To fully tame a monster required it to stay under the thrall of his Blood magic for four days for each level it had. That meant he had to successfully master its will over and over. Yeah, a higher-level monster would be stronger, but a lower level monster was easier to control. This was clearly an 'a boob in the hand is worth two in the bra' kind of situation.

This time, the prompt was a verdant shade of awesome.

*Congratulations! You have tamed the **Level 20 Raider Worm!***

A silent resonance pinged both of their souls and the magic brought the raider worm's spirit in sync with his own. For the next forty hours, its will was trapped behind a lattice of Blood magic. With his skill level of twenty-eight in Beast Bonding, the Tier 1 creature had an almost zero chance of breaking through before the barrier elapsed. Richter had just gained another ally!

The XP from the battle chimed pleasantly in his battle log.

*You have slain a Level 47 **Ravager Wurm (Tier 2).** You have gained 5,018 XP.*

You have slain 26 Level 18-35 Raider Worms (Tier 1). You have gained 4,611 XP.

XP deficit remaining: -3,826,797

He was less than excited to see how much he still owed on his XP debt, but he'd also gained almost ten thousand experience for half an hour's work. He really couldn't complain. Richter turned his head and took in the rest of the scene. The entire time he'd been killing the Tier I monsters he hadn't lost sight of the larger battle, so he knew everything was well in hand.

His puppet ravager wurm had finally slain the wounded one. Both monsters were built for resiliency, but between his controlled monster's higher level and the fact that the other one had already been grievously hurt, his puppet had won the day. More than half of its health was gone, but that fit in with Richter's plans perfectly.

The last part of the battlefield was about to quiet as well. Working together, the four orc Warriors had managed to chop the final ravager wurm into pieces. All of them were injured, one quite seriously. The green-skinned fighter had two wurm spikes sunk deep into his chest. From the red froth on his lips and his agonized breaths, Richter knew a lung had been punctured. Wounded or not, one of the orcs brought his axe down on the last segment of worm that was still quivering. He must have hit a vital organ because it stopped moving.

The chaos lord examined the four orc fighters. Their names were Ryuu, Darkensi, Kenae and Drafna. The highest leveled was Darkensi. The plate armored orc was Ryuu, who was hurriedly quaffing a health potion. The others were drinking potions as well, ready for whatever was about to come next.

The Warriors looked at Richter, not letting their guard down at all, not that he blamed them. As impressive as their musculature was, it had nothing on his hulk-like body. In fact, his overall appearance was something to give a grown man nightmares.

His body and hair were drenched in blood of different colors. The still-gleaming gauntlet on his arm made him look part-Terminator. His spiked mace was dripping gore, and they had all seen the streams of Blood magic flowing into him. That marked him as one of the most dangerous types of magic casters in The Land. They'd have to be fools to trust him. The still-burning bodies of monsters he'd just massacred served as a backlight, clothing him in dancing shadows.

The chaos lord stared at them, flanked by his puppet ravager wurm, tamed raider worm, evolved summoned creatures and golem.

The Warriors stared back, each of them bleeding, bruised and overall unhappy about the situation. The silence grew thick before he asked the four of them in perfect orcish, "Any of you fuckers know how Bond takes his martinis?"

Five sets of eyes stared back at him in anger, fear and curiosity.

~ The Story Continues ~

Thank You

This journey started four years ago. I never saw my life taking this turn, but I am so thankful you're sharing the path with me! There are many more stories to come and I hope you continue on the journey with me.

The fact that I can share this story with awesome people makes all the thousands of hours spent creating it worthwhile lol.

As always, Peace, Love, and the Perfect Margarita!

Aleron

INDEX and Epilogue

I will be continually updating the index this time so save this link: https://www.litrpg.com/book-summaries-for-book-8

There is also an Epilogue that you can only find by following the link! https://www.litrpg.com/8-index

I'm also starting a new series! Find the information and the first chapter of God's Eye: Awakening in the links above!

Gnomes Rule!

Good people of the Mist Village, **PLEASE** leave a review.
I am an independent author, and you are my greatest strength
Even leaving some stars would be enough.
Thank you so much again!
I am honored to share my world with you.

How to contact Aleron!

1) <u>AUTHOR PAGE</u>:

Join me for almost weekly FB lives convos, giveaways and lots of laughs https://www.facebook.com/LitRPGbooks/

2) <u>FACEBOOK GROUP</u>: Join THOUSANDS of other Mist Villagers to joke about The Land, harass Aleron about writing faster and to win great loot! Signed books, Free T-shirts, etc: https://www.facebook.com/groups/AleronKong/

3) <u>WEBSITE</u>: www.LitRPG.com

It has a list of ALL the LitRPG out there, awesome t-shirts and signed books, my blog and just all around awesomeness!

4) <u>PATREON</u>: For sneak previews of upcoming books and seeing new artwork first, please join my patreon account. I am an indie author which means no publishing house. Your support means the world to me! www.patreon.com/AleronKong

5) <u>INSTAGRAM</u>: @LitRPGBooks

6) <u>NEWSLETTER</u>: The best choice if you just want to know when the next book is coming out. I do a monthly newsletter with updates, uplifting stories and funny vids. You can sign up here. If you sign up, you get a free copy of The Land Comic lol! eepurl.com/cns1UH

7) <u>YOUTUBE</u>: Me and my friends make funny/stupid videos 😊 I also do video testimonials with occasional spoilers! FREE on Youtube (yes I know youtube is always free but hey... its FREE lol) http://www.youtube.com/c/LitRPG

The Mist Village Cares

Over the last 4 years, with the help of the Mist Village, Aleron has raised almost **$100,000** for various charities!

A few of the charities Aleron has donated to include:
The Water Project
Able Gamers
Texas Blue Armor Brotherhood
The Breast Cancer Research Fund
Red Cross

Thank you all for being part of the solution!!!

If you want more information on charitable efforts, feel free to follow Aleron at any of the methods above.

If you want to stay connected and know when my next work comes out, the BEST way is by <u>NEWSLETTER</u> and my <u>AUTHOR PAGE</u>.

Unfortunately, Amazon doesn't update you when new works come out some of the time, but if sign up for the newsletter or like my author page, you'll know immediately.

You also get a secret FREE Comic for The Land when you sign up! Shhh, don't tell anyone!

GUILD MEMBER HONORABLE MENTION

I would like to give a special thanks to everyone who supports me on my Patreon Page! Specifically, I would like to thank:

Vice Manager		
WizardZonder		
Assistant Deputies		
Michael Clack		
Luke Clack		
Patrick		
Officers		
Gabe Yohn		William Haviland
JQ Phillips		Keith H Anderson
Thomas Adams		Tyler Heino
Aryeh Winter		Spencer Lee
Sergeants		
Charles Eybs	Ryan Galle	Oscar Guerra
Erik Farnsworth	Mark Jackson	Johnny K
Ben Peacock	Mike Lyons	Alex
William B. Akin	Tristin Hermanson	Thomas Spencer
James Doulgeris	Kenny Ash	Richard Rochin
Ben Jensen	Daniel Sheehan	Andrew Trosper
Kyle J Smith	John Osborn	Brian Thompson
Cryos	Mark A French	Mark Chapman
Kentyiro Lopez	Martin Hansen	Alicia Fleming
Michel Noris	Aksel Westrum	Skyler Cooper

Thank you ALL for helping me make this dream a reality!!!

CPSIA information can be obtained
at www.ICGtesting.com
Printed in the USA
BVHW050740210223
658736BV00044B/1287/J

9 780578 830109